AUSSIE! AUSSIE! AUSSIE!

A GREAT BIG BOOK OF AUSSIE LEGENDS, ICONS AND ANIMALS

WRITTEN BY
LORETTA BARNARD
CHRISTOPHER CHENG
ANNE INGRAM
PEGGY O'DONNELL

ILLUSTRATIONS BY
GREGORY ROGERS

RANDOM HOUSE AUSTRALIA

A Random House book
Published by Random House Australia Pty Ltd
Level 3, 100 Pacific Highway, North Sydney NSW 2060
www.randomhouse.com.au

30 Australian Legends and Icons first published by Random House Australia in 2006
30 Amazing Australian Animals first published by Random House Australia in 2007
30 Australian Sports Legends first published by Random House Australia in 2008
This bindup edition first published by Random House Australia in 2009

30 Australian Legends and Icons text copyright © Anne Ingram and Peggy O'Donnell 2006
30 Amazing Australian Animals text copyright © Christopher Cheng 2007
30 Australian Sports Legends text copyright © Loretta Barnard 2008
Illustrations copyright © Gregory Rogers 2006–2008

The moral rights of the authors and illustrator have been asserted.

All rights reserved. No part of this book may be reproduced or transmitted by any person or entity, including internet search engines or retailers, in any form or by any means, electronic or mechanical, including photocopying (except under the statutory exceptions provisions of the Australian *Copyright Act 1968*), recording, scanning or by any information storage and retrieval system without the prior written permission of Random House Australia.

Addresses for companies within the Random House Group can be found at
www.randomhouse.com.au/offices.

A Cataloguing-in-Publication Entry is available from the National Library of Australia

ISBN 978 1 86471 975 8

Cover design by Leanne Beattie
30 Australian Legends and Icons internal design and layout by Donna Rawlins
30 Amazing Australian Animals internal design and layout by Donna Rawlins and Anna Warren
30 Australian Sports Legends internal design by Anna Warren,
developed from original concepts by Donna Rawlins

Printed and bound in Hong Kong by Sing Cheong Printing Co. Ltd

10 9 8 7 6 5 4 3 2 1

30 Australian Legends & Icons

Anne Ingram & Peggy O'Donnell

pictures by
Gregory Rogers

RANDOM HOUSE AUSTRALIA

Brumby photo (page 38) courtesy of Michelle Walter.

Portrait of Albert Namatjira at Hermannsburg Mission, Northern Territory; (page 87) Arthur Groom. Courtesy of the National Library of Australia.

Sydney Opera House statistics courtesy of 'Sydney Opera House', Australian Stories, Australian Government Culture and Recreation Portal
http://www.cultureandrecreation.gov.au/articles/sydneyoperahouse/

For our support team extraordinaire – our families and our West Street friends, who have opened doors for us and made life fun. Our thanks to all.
A.I. and P.O.

For Harry and Pudding – the legends on the Avenue.
G.R.

Contents

Introduction – The DNA of Legends • 1

1 • Our History in Song • 3

2 • The Fat Tree and Friend • 7

3 • Our Ghostly Past • 11

4 • Bushrangers • 16

5 • The Overlanders • 20

6 • The First Public Transport • 26

7 • Cobb & Co – In for the Long Haul • 29

8 • Simpson – The Man with the Donkey • 33

9 • The Tradition of ANZAC • 36

10 • Busby's Bore – Water for Sydney Town • 41

11 • Working Marvels • 44

12 • Help for the Bush • 51

13 • The Ghan – From Camels to Trains • 56

14 • Lighthouses – Beacons on the Shore • 59

15 • Surf Lifesavers – Safe in the Surf • 64

16 • The Great Barrier Reef – The World's Largest Living Ecosystem • 68

17 • Flight – Balloons and Kites • 72

18 • Isobel Bennett – Seashore Expert • 75

19 • Nancy Bird Walton – 'My God! It's a woman' • 78

20 • Sir Hubert Opperman – The Man of Incredible Feats • 82

21 • Albert Namatjira – Aboriginal Painter of World Renown • 86

22 • Melbourne Cup and Phar Lap – Horses at Their Best • 89

23 • Cricket – The Ashes and Bradman's Bats • 93

24 • Ladies First – Our Dawn and the Golden Girl • 96

25 • Flavours of Australia • 100

26 • The Big Ones • 107

27 • The Principality of Hutt – A 'Nation' within a Nation • 111

28 • Flags – Rallying Symbols • 114

29 • The Sydney Opera House – The Glory of the Harbour • 119

30 • The Black Cat – Phantom of the Mountains • 123

The DNA of LEGENDS

Australia's first inhabitants have legends going back to the Dreamtime. They were passed on by word of mouth, drawings and dance, some going back many thousands of years.

Our country's written history is very young, and it started in a scrappy way when Europeans began searching for the Great South Land. The stories of well-known people, places, things and happenings that began after this are the nearest we have to becoming legends.

As many of our early settlers could not read or write, our first stories spread as yarns and songs that were shared around the campfire by drifters and workers as they travelled the vast distances between settlements looking for food and jobs.

These stories grabbed our imagination as we tried to picture ourselves being in the unique situations that faced so many of our icons. We were overcome with admiration for the physical endurance, the innovative minds and the sheer determination of men and women to adapt and to 'make do' when faced with a challenge.

We became engrossed in the research, the insight into their minds – the thrill of early flight, the excitement the jockey must have felt when he rode Phar Lap to win the Melbourne Cup, or what Our Don felt as his first Test century went up on the scoreboard.

We have many great stockmen, pastoralists, miners, business people, sportspeople, academics, writers and artists. The list is endless.

This is a selection of people, places, things and events that we think are exciting and help make Australia great. They are only a cross-section of our country's stories. There are many more – explore!

one
Our History in Song

'Waltzing Matilda'

Once a jolly swagman camped by a billabong
Under the shade of a coolibah tree
And he sang as he watched and waited till his billy boiled
Who'll come a-waltzing Matilda with me?

Waltzing Matilda, waltzing Matilda, who'll come a-waltzing Matilda with me?
And he sang as he watched and waited till his billy boiled,
Who'll come a-waltzing Matilda with me?

Gumleaf music was played by early settlers, who learnt the art of playing from Aboriginal people who used gumleaf music to supplement the notes they created with the didgeridoo and clapping sticks. When you blow at the edge of one leaf, or two held together, you can make 'music'. The strength of your blow and the position of your lips has a lot to do with the sounds you can make. But be patient, it takes lots of practice to make recognisable songs.

The city of Maryborough in Victoria regularly held a Golden Gumleaf Competition as part of their Wattle Festival where old favourites, including 'Waltzing Matilda', were played on gumleaves. There are still experts in gumleaf music today.

'Waltzing Matilda' is still our most popular, legendary outback song, loved by all and often spontaneously sung by large crowds at sporting events.

This bush ballad was written by bush balladeer and poet 'Banjo' Paterson with music adapted from a Scottish folk song. It was first sung in public at the Winton Hotel in Queensland on 6 April 1895. In bush slang, a swagman was an itinerant worker and matilda was his swag – his sleeping bag. It is thought that the word 'matilda' came from the German word for a soldier's rolled up blanket – mathilde.

'The Wild Colonial Boy'

There was a Wild Colonial Boy,
Jack Doolan was his name,
Of poor but honest parents,
He was born in Castlemaine.
He was his father's only hope,
His mother's pride and joy,
And dearly did his parents love
The Wild Colonial Boy.

So come away me hearties
We'll roam the mountains high,
Together we will plunder
And together we will die.
We'll scour along the valleys
And we'll gallop o'er the plains,
And scorn to live in slavery,
Bound down by iron chains.

There are many versions of this song, all telling the colourful and romanticised exploits of our bushrangers. In those painful years of the 1820s, when floggings and starvation were often the fate of convicts, they sang this defiant song to annoy their guards and to lessen the pain of the men being lashed.

It is still sung regularly in Australia, particularly at country concerts.

'The Dying Stockman'

A strapping young stockman lay dying,
A saddle supporting his head.
And his comrades around him were crying,
As he leant on his elbow and said.

'Wrap me up in my stockwhip and blanket,
And bury me deep down below,
Where the dingoes and crows will not find me
In the place where the coolibahs grow.'

This song was first sung in 1892 around the campfire as a lament to the many young stationhands who died on the job. The lyrics tell of the life of the stockmen and drovers who usually owned their own horses, often starting with an unbroken colt. They had their own saddles and used whips of plaited hide.

They carried food for themselves and their horses in saddlebags and tied a rolled up swag to lugs on the pommel of the saddle. They cooked beef and damper over the fire before bedding down under the stars for the night. Many days were spent away from the station, riding the boundaries and checking the fences. Culling and branding the stock were everyday parts of the job. But the job also involved many dangers, like drought and venomous snakes.

two
The Fat Tree and Friend

THE FAT TREE

The legendary fat trees of north-west Australia are boab trees, also known as bottle trees, dead rat trees or prison trees. They have even been used as burial places.

Boabs and giant anthills make a spectacular sight, dotted through the Kimberley landscape. The trunk of the fat tree is like an enormous, swollen bottle; it can be up to 24 metres in circumference and is crowned by spreading branches that lose their leaves in the dry season.

The large white flowers are usually 10 centimetres across, and they have prominent stamens and a sugary juice. The flowers open at night, attracting nectar-eating bats that help in pollination. The grey, furry fruit look like rats and have a mealy pulp that is supposed to taste like sherbet. The seeds taste like hazelnuts or almonds and can be eaten raw or ground up. The white sap looks and tastes like spaghetti. Besides all these goodies, the bark can be soaked in water to make a pleasant drink.

The Boab is a supermarket of bush tucker and in times of drought is cut up as stock fodder. This generous tree can be both a home and a food source for many of the shy, small creatures of the Kimberley area.

Boab trees have a place in most accounts of seamen touching the north-west coast. On the shore of Careening Bay, in the Prince Regent Nature Reserve, a large, old boab tree still grows. It has a deep niche cut in one side of its trunk and the word 'Mermaid' carved in the other.

People speculate that, somewhere around 1700, adventurous Macassan sailors, collecting bêche-de-mer, cut the deep niche in this large boab to hold an Islamic prayer icon so they could pray there when they came ashore looking for water.

Bêche-de-mer is also known as a trepang or sea cucumber. It is a fat sea slug that can extrude its stomach when disturbed and then, when danger is past, suck it back inside again!

In 1820 Phillip Parker King was commissioned to finish the work that Matthew Flinders had not completed on his expedition around Australia. King had command of the ship *Mermaid* to explore and chart the coast of north-west Australia.

When the *Mermaid* sprang a leak and put into Careening Bay for repairs, the sailors found the boab with the deep niche and carved the ship's name into the other side of the tree.

When King returned some time later in the *Bathurst*, he was disappointed to find no fresh water in the creek but wrote in his diary that 'the large gouty-stemmed tree on which the *Mermaid*'s name had been carved in deep indented characters remained without any alteration and seemed likely to bear the marks of our visit longer than any other memento we had left.'

The 'Mermaid Boab' is now an important feature of this beautiful part of Australia's long coastline.

There is another very big boab near Derby in Western Australia called 'The Prison Tree'. It is about 1500 years old and measures 14.7 metres around its middle. The early white settlers used this tree as a temporary detention place for Aboriginal prisoners. There is another well-known prison tree near Wyndham that has a very large hollow trunk.

THE TOOTH TREE

Flindersia maculosa, the leopardwood tree, does not grow much higher than 7 metres and is only found on the red soil of the low rainfall areas of north-western New South Wales and the western slopes of Queensland.

The 'spotted' leopard tree starts life as a small, very prickly shrub. After taking several years to establish roots, a single stem

The Australian Boab is very limited in its territory as it likes the sandy plains and stony ridges of the Kimberley region, rarely growing more than 200 kilometres from the coast.

appears and grows up its middle, staying within the circle of prickles. Gradually, as it grows, this becomes a trunk, sending out branches to make a canopy of leaves. The tree is still protected by the prickles at its base.

The tree sheds its bark in oval pieces, leaving small depressions that are coloured white, pink or pale yellow. Seen through the scrub, it looks like a leopard and is very striking in the dry, arid, stony country. Its flowers are creamy white, forming fruit that are brown, woody and make spiky, 30- millimetre-long containers for its seeds, which have wings to help distribution.

Gum from the leaves and bark is used by the Aboriginal people as an item of food and as an important medicine that helps cure toothache and prevent tooth decay. It also makes good glue when dissolved in water. The leaves and limbs are useful as stock food.

At dusk, this ghostly tree has given many bushwalkers a fright when they sight what looks like an escaped 'leopard' in the scrub!

three
Our Ghostly Past

FISHER'S GHOST

This story of our most famous ghost, Frederick Fisher, is the result of reading every possible story already told about Fisher and from all sources, factual as well as fictitious. It must be remembered that this is a true story and that a man was hanged for a murder that he committed, although the body was only discovered because of this ghost. It is interesting to note that throughout the trial not one mention is made of this helpful apparition.

Frederick Fisher, a convict who had been granted his freedom, shared a small farm in the Campbelltown district with a friend, also an ex-convict, George Worrall. They managed to eke out a small living, but the farm was not large enough to support the two of them in any degree of comfort.

One day, early in 1826, George Worrall walked into the local inn at Campbelltown where he and Fisher were frequent guests and told everyone that his friend had suddenly decided to return to England and had left the district for good. Worrall also told all the locals that Fisher had transferred his share in

their farm to him and left him all his possessions because he intended to start a new life in the old country. This story was accepted without question and life continued on a smooth course for Worrall, who was now far better off with no Fisher to share the returns from the farm with.

Then on the night of 17 June 1826 John Farley, also a resident of the Campbelltown district, came bursting into the Plough Inn, white and shaking. He stated that he had just seen a ghost, a phantom figure, sitting on the rail of the bridge across the creek on the road to his farm. This story was greeted with laughter and many interjections, but Farley would not change his story, stating that not only had he seen a ghost but that he had recognised it as Fred Fisher.

The story now gained serious attention and the details of the sighting were given by Farley. It appears that as he was driving home from a day at the Sydney market, he came to the bridge over the creek that ran at the foot of Fisher's farm. He was surprised to see a figure sitting on the rail of the bridge because it was quite late at night, but as he drew closer he realised that he could actually see right through the figure to the rail it was resting upon. At that moment Farley suddenly recognised the apparition as Fred Fisher. Farley began to back away, but the apparition kept beckoning him to come and see something in the creek. Farley was too scared to move and as he watched, the figure slowly began to melt away.

By the following morning the local police sergeant had heard the story of the sighting of Fisher's ghost. Because he had already started investigations into the sudden disappearance of Fisher, he decided to look into this strange story.

With a trooper and two Aboriginal trackers, the police sergeant set off to take a closer look at the bridge. As soon as they arrived one of the trackers, Gilbert, pointed out marks on the railings of the bridge that he said were traces of dried blood. Gilbert then climbed down to the creek, which was really just a chain of water-holes because of a long dry spell that had gripped the district. He examined particles floating on the top of the waterhole and declared that they were 'white man fat'. The waterhole was then thoroughly examined and the decaying body of Fisher was found.

After a long and exhaustive investigation, the police finally arrested Fisher's old friend Worrall and charged him with the murder. Though he protested his innocence throughout the long trial, Worrall was found guilty of the crime and

Some ghost hunters believe that spirits leave behind a light, oozing substance called ectoplasm that helps the ghosts become visible and play tricks.

sentenced to be hanged. On the morning of his execution he confessed that he had committed the crime and deserved to die.

There is an interesting sequel to this story. Although no mention was made of the ghost throughout the trial, people never forgot Farley's story and many years later, when Farley was dying, a close friend asked him if his story about the ghost was really true or whether he had made it up because he was suspicious that something might have happened to Fisher. Farley raised himself on his elbow and, looking straight at his friend, said: 'I saw that ghost as plainly as I see you now.'

THE PHANTOM OF THE OPERA

Every country has its collection of theatre ghosts and Australia is no exception. There was one at the old Tivoli in Sydney for many years, but this story from the Princess Theatre, Melbourne, in the 1880s is better authenticated.

There was a packed audience that night at the Princess Theatre. They had come to hear the famous Italian basso, Frederici, sing the role of Mephistopheles in *Faust*. This was a wicked character, so Frederici was dressed and made up for the part in red tights and pointed cap, with lots of sulphurous smoke about.

During one scene Mephistopheles has to disappear through a trapdoor in the stage floor as if he is descending into Hell. This is a high point in the opera for the audience. On this particular night, however, a greater drama was being acted *beneath* the stage.

As Frederici climbed down the steps from the trapdoor, he slipped, fell and lay still. His colleagues crowded around him trying to help but were unable to do anything. They carried Frederici to his dressing room and gently lowered him to a couch, but Frederici was dying and no-one could save him.

Some time after Frederici's death, when the theatre was running a season of *Macbeth*, a stagehand was wandering through the empty auditorium one evening after a performance. He looked towards the dress circle, and there was a sight that made the poor man turn cold and rush back to his mates who were working backstage.

A man was standing in the dress circle, in top hat and black evening coat. When the stage hand returned with several of his mates for support, the figure was still there, motionless, waiting, watching.

With moral support from his friends, the stagehand found enough courage to call out to this 'person'. There was no answer, only the echo of his voice came back to him. Suddenly the figure in the dress circle just melted into the air as the stage hands stood watching.

One thing they all agree on was that the phantom that they had seen was the late Italian singer, Frederici, as there was no mistaking his imposing build.

This story was passed around. Other people working late at the theatre would meet the ghostly figure of Frederici, standing or sitting quietly in the dress circle, his gaze riveted on the stage.

There were times when Frederici would also appear during a performance. He would join with the chorus during an opera, or stand quietly at the side of the stage during a play. He would be in full view of the audience who were unaware that this extra member of the cast was really a ghost returning to the scene of its sudden death.

four

Bushrangers

JOHN CAESAR – THE FIRST BUSHRANGER

The first bushrangers were mostly escaped convicts who were fleeing from the lash and the hard life of the early settlement in Sydney Cove. The first bushranger of note was John Caesar, a 'First Fleeter'. He is reported to have been a good worker with an enormous appetite and could eat two days' rations in one sitting. So, to stop hunger pains, he turned to stealing food. This was a flogging offence, particularly as the early colony was always short of food.

'Black' Caesar made two attempts to get away from this 'hellhole' but was captured each time and flogged again and again. On his third attempt he stole a musket and ammunition and went bush, stealing food and supplies from settlers around Sydney.

Over several months eight fellow escapees joined him, forming the first gang of bushrangers, but Black Caesar's luck ran out when, in 1796, Governor Hunter posted a reward of five gallons of rum for him, dead or alive.

Wimlow, a free settler, used his skills to track Caesar through the bush and finally caught up with him and shot him dead. He became a wealthy man with his five gallons of rum!

MATTHEW BRADY – THE GENTLEMAN BUSHRANGER

The gold rush in Victoria in the 1850s was a great opportunity for bushrangers to bail up diggers who struck it rich. The outlaws' special knowledge of the bush allowed them to get away fast and stay hidden.

'Gentleman Matt', an ex-butler for gentlemen in Manchester, England, was famous for his 'genteel ways'. He was transported to Van Diemen's Land (an original name for Tasmania) for forgery.

During the early nineteenth century, conditions were so harsh that escape became the best choice; it was a hanging offence but many felt it was worth the risk to get away from the penal settlement. They chose to escape even though any recaptured escapees were hanged, starved or shot. It is believed that some prisoners were killed and eaten by their hungry fellow convicts.

During an official's visit to the jail, Brady and his gang managed to overpower their guards and steal a whaleboat, sailing up the Hobart estuary with bullets whistling around their ears. Foolishly, they attempted to rob a military officer, and six of them were recaptured and hanged. Brady and a few others survived to escape again.

The next escape found the Brady gang making their way north, collecting more desperados on the way, robbing homes, burning places and killing anyone who opposed them.

At the township of Sorrell they broke into the newly built jail and freed all the inmates, who then joined the gang, and on they went, looting, burning and robbing.

The acute shortage of coins in the early period of settlement meant that settlers would exchange things between each other – the barter system. Rum, an alcoholic drink, helped ease the hardship of life in the colony and became very valuable.

They were so dangerous that Lieutenant-Governor Arthur formed a civil defence force and offered £25 reward for every member captured. John Batman, a young settler, brought in Aboriginal trackers from New South Wales, who helped corner Matt in Launceston. By then his 'crime sheet' listed 350 crimes.

When his trial was held in 1826, the ladies of Hobart, who loved this 'gentlemen's gentleman', showered him with fruit and flowers, and after he was hanged the ladies and their men abused those who did the deed.

John Batman later went on to stand on the banks of the Yarra River in Victoria and say 'this is the place for a village' – the village became the city of Melbourne.

CAPTAIN THUNDERBOLT

Fredrick Wordsworth Ward, born in or about 1836 in Windsor, New South Wales, was a highly regarded stockman, but he fell to temptation and stole a horse. He was caught and sent to Cockatoo Island in Sydney Harbour to serve his time. Cockatoo, like all the island prisons, had men chained to the rocks with very little shelter and was considered escape-proof, but Ward and his friend, Fred Britten, escaped with the help of 'Black Mary', Ward's girlfriend. She swam over to the island in a heavy fog and passed Ward a file so he and Britten were able cut off their leg irons. They stole some clothes and made their way to the Hawkesbury River.

Captain Thunderbolt, as Ward became known, robbed the wealthy, holding up the travellers on the roads from Newcastle to Queensland for almost six years. Black Mary was his constant companion; some say she was the brains of the gang. When she fell ill in 1867, Captain Thunderbolt lovingly nursed her until she died. He was heartbroken and continued rampaging through the New England district for three more years. Despite his criminal ways, he was credited with giving help to the poor.

One of his 'victims' was Wirth's Circus. Mr Wirth and his two sons, plus their German band, were playing in the Tamworth district when Thunderbolt appeared and robbed them of their takings of £20, even making the band play a tune for him.

Thunderbolt then bargained with Mr Wirth, saying he would return the £20 if the Circus band played loudly enough to cover the noise of his gang stealing the winner's purse from the Tamworth race meeting. The gang took the money and Mr Wirth found the £20 from Captain Thunderbolt at the next town's post office.

On 25 May, near Uralla and Glen Innes, Thunderbolt held up a salesman, who tricked the bushranger into thinking that he was letting his horse free to graze. Instead, the salesman raced to the police and two constables set out to capture Thunderbolt, but when one policeman fired his gun, his horse immediately bolted in the wrong direction. The second policeman, now alone, shot Thunderbolt's horse and cornered him in a muddy lagoon. After a struggle, the policeman won the battle and brought Thunderbolt down with a bullet.

five

The Overlanders

KIDMAN – THE CATTLE KING

In the 1860s there were vast areas of Australia's north that had not been explored, let alone settled. It was during these early years that the young Sidney Kidman saw opportunity beckoning and dreamed of owning a cattle station, growing meat for the young nation, even of sending beef to England.

Sid left his hometown of Adelaide in 1870 at the age of 13. He acquired a cheap, broken-down, one-eyed horse and headed north. He worked at many odd jobs on various stations around the track that led to the copper deposits, fast learning to be an expert bushman. He talked to everyone and listened to the drovers, the men looking for work and the hopeful miners, keeping all the knowledge he gained in his memory bank. The thread running through the talk he heard was 'feed and water' – the essentials for raising cattle in the driest country in the world.

He became known as 'the kid who knew his way about' and rode hundreds of miles helping new settlers. At one point he joined up with an Aboriginal boy, Billy. They shared the work around the rough camps and talked of their different cultures; the bond of friendship was very strong and Kidman learnt and remembered all that Billy taught him. Although there was little that Kidman could teach Billy, except bits about his short time at school and city life in Adelaide, they shared a lot of laughter and fun together. Kidman never lost his knowledge, love and respect for the Aboriginal people.

After the Darling River flooded in 1864, a land scramble for leaseholdings took place in Queensland. The area was lush with feed and great numbers of squatters moved into the western Darling country. When the young Kidman headed there, the Mount Gipps Station was the biggest, covering 2250 square kilometres in the Barrier Ranges. The Kidman brothers all got jobs there, with Sid earning ten shillings a week as a rouseabout. His brothers, George and Sackville, were paid more because they were older.

The station was like a small town and, although the work was hard, Sid found it exciting and kept learning. The knowledge of how a big spread was run and what was needed to make it work stood him in good stead in later years. He was a great question 'asker', and they called him 'The Kidman Kid'.

It was in these years that he saw the bad effects of swearing and boozing and, we are told, he never did swear, drink or smoke. He avoided the louts and found great interest in talking to the men who were part of the push west of the Darling towards the Cooper and the Diamantina rivers in the arid corner of Queensland. He realised the money he could make if he was part of this growth and started the business of guiding the 'new chums'. With his earnings he bought a bullock team, transporting supplies to the area.

On hearing that copper had been found at Cobar, Kidman upped sticks and moved there, where he opened his bough-shed butcher shop, built by himself from small trees the night before. After making a considerable sum of money, he moved on to Menindee, where he ran into his elder brothers who were droving a mob to Adelaide. An extra hand was needed, paying 25 shillings a week, and young Sid made sure he got the job. At Kapunda he met and fancied Isabel Wright, a schoolteacher. He promised to return the next time he was in that area.

Sidney Kidman helped develop the idea of freezing beef for export overseas. His company, S. Kidman & Co Ltd, founded in 1899, now runs a 200,000 strong beef cattle herd.

When the mob reached Adelaide and was sold, Kidman used his wages to buy horses and spent several years travelling through the outback, trading in horses and seizing the opportunity to learn about this harsh country. He observed how the creek beds were shaped, reasoning that low banks meant floods, which in turn meant flood plains. Isabel Wright had talked of this and had maps of the rivers for him on his next visit to Kapunda.

Water was, and still is, everything in the bush. It was water that led Sid to plan a series of properties leading from the vast outback to the flood plain areas, always getting closer to the markets of South Australia and then the world. When he returned to Kapunda, Isabel told him about the geography of the outback rivers, and so was born the concept of a whole series of Kidman properties.

The planned 'chain of supply' was to follow the watercourses all the way from breeding stations to markets. The North-South chain ran from the Gulf country down the three rivers to a holding depot in Mundowdna, South Australia. The Central Australian chain ran from the Western Australian and Northern Territory holding to Mundowdna. From there the cattle were to be trucked to market.

Sid's grandfather had left him £400 for when he turned 21. He'd forgotten about the

legacy until his brother Sackville gave him a letter advising him of the inheritance. He decided to talk to Sack about his grand scheme and they went into partnership, buying their first acreage. When Sack died soon after this, Sid continued with his plan to acquire water-safe properties.

Sidney Kidman slowly became the big man in cattle farming, running the largest pastoral holding in history and owning over 100 stations, covering three per cent of the area of Australia.

In his lifetime Sir Sidney had built his dream: cattle stations running from the north to south of Australia with water and feed all the way from the three rivers – Cooper, Diamantina and Georgina – the 'chain of supply'.

In 1921 he was knighted for his services to Australia. S. Kidman & Co Ltd is still family-owned and run, occupying a massive area of Australia's cattle country. It is estimated that the Kidman holding is the equivalent of 400 million house blocks.

The people in the north-west area of New South Wales still talk of Sid's achievements. A remark made on our visit to Broken Hill in 2005 was, 'No-one could ever hope to repeat what he did. All the stock walked and what he created was a line from go to whoa in his own country.'

THE LEGENDARY DURACKS

The Durack family made the Kimberley region known throughout the world, not just by their large cattle holdings, but also through the books and paintings by Mary and Elizabeth, grand-daughters of Patrick Durack.

The family arrived in Australia around 1849 and settled near Goulburn, New South Wales. The younger son, Patrick, wanted his own land, so at 18 he set off for the Victorian goldfields, expecting to make his fortune – and he did! He left the goldfields with a sum of £1000, a fortune in those days, and immediately bought land near the family holding.

The talk around the campfires was of the opportunities of the land near Cooper Creek, so Patrick set off in the company of his brother-in-law, with 100 horses and 400 cattle. They settled near Quilpie in Queensland where, despite droughts and other misfortunes, the family's fortune continued to grow and they began looking for more opportunities.

At this time the Western Australian Government had sent Alexander Forrest to explore and report on the land in the north of the state. Patrick heard about this and went to Perth to talk to Forrest. As a result of these talks, the Duracks selected one and a half million acres along the Ord River. This land was released by the authorities on a 'leasehold' arrangement at a rental of ten shillings a thousand acres.

In the 1970s the inundation of Lake Argyle in Western Australia, formed by the damming of the Ord River, was to flood the Durack homestead. The house was taken apart and stored for reconstruction at a new site. A grandson of Patrick Durack, Kim, helped plan and construct an irrigation project, creating the largest man-made lake in Australia. Cotton was expected to grow in this area but failed; the magpie geese ate the seeds and insect pests loved what little grew. The area now grows tropical crops. The homestead has been re-erected as a museum overlooking Lake Argyle, since the family is now scattered throughout northern Australia.

six

The First Public Transport

BULLOCKS – THE MEAN TEAMS

In the 1820s early settlers soon found that the bullocks that had arrived from South Africa could do as much work as a horse on half as much food and were able to pull their drays (carts) through mud up to their knees in the wet, as well as coping with the dust and discomfort of the hot, dry season.

They were quicker than horses to get going each morning as they were yoked in pairs, while horses were individually harnessed. Horses moved faster than bullocks but were unable to work as well up steep hills and over rough ground. A good bullock cost much less than a horse to buy and to feed.

Two-wheeled or four-wheeled drays were used – the smaller ones could not carry such big loads but were more manoeuvrable. Most of the drays used for rough work were 'pole drays', having a centre pole. The bigger ones were double-shafted with a moveable front axle to allow the longer dray to turn.

The bullock drivers were a tough lot, skilled in the use of the greenhide whip made of untanned leather. It had a handle at least

2.5 metres long, with a great length of greenhide fastened to it that would 'sing' through the air in the hands of an experienced stockman. A good driver could flick a fly from the ear of his leading animal.

CAMELS – THE SPITTERS

The first camels in Australia were a pair brought to Hobart in December 1840 from the Canary Islands. The following year they were taken to Melbourne and exhibited and then overlanded to Sydney where a calf was born. Mother, father and calf were put on display in the Domain to the amusement of Sydneysiders. After this pioneering trio, the next significant group of camels worth mentioning were the 24 imported from India by the Victorian Government for the disastrous Burke and Wills expedition in 1860.

In 1865 Sir Thomas Elder imported another 120, mainly females, from India for riding, carrying packs and breeding. Drivers from Afghanistan, known as 'Afghans', came too. They understood how to look after their animals and how best to load them without causing saddle sores on their humps. The

Camels spit bile – a nasty, smelly, greenish liquid. When they are angry or fighting, they can vomit it up from their liver/gall bladder. Keep away from their front end, but the back end is not so good either!

camels could go for a considerable time without water and feed, and they did not appear to need as much rest as horses or bullocks.

Without camels the outback would have stayed just that – out of reach – and the Overland Telegraph would not have been built for many years. Their ability to carry heavy loads over long distances and very difficult terrain with little water or food made the construction of things like the telegraph and the opening of the north possible in the nineteenth century.

The advent of the motor vehicle made camel and bullock carting unprofitable, and most of the camels were turned loose in the 1920s. There are still many camels living wild in the desert areas, becoming pests, particularly in drought times when they eat native plants and trample vegetation. In recent years Australia has been exporting camels back to their homeland in the Middle East!

seven
Cobb & Co
In for the Long Haul

Freeman Cobb, a young American who ran a coaching service during the Californian gold rush, came to Victoria in 1853 to investigate the possibility of starting a coach service to the new gold rush areas in Australia. He saw an opening and shipped out a Concord Coach from the United States, a better suited vehicle for our conditions than the heavy British ones that had no springs or, at best, steel ones.

The steel springs did not stand up to the rough Australian tracks and were always breaking. The Concord Coach's body was slung, like a hammock, on leather straps called 'throughbraces' that were fastened to brackets fixed to the underbody of the coach.

Together with the coaches, Cobb imported some 'Yankee whips' – experienced coach drivers who had learnt their skills in the American Wild West. They were accompanied by some strong, well-trained horses. He had already joined up with three

In January 1854 the first Cobb & Co coach left the Criterion Hotel in Melbourne bound for Forest Creek, Victoria, near Bendigo.

Americans and together they started a coach service from Melbourne to Port Melbourne and then to the goldfields of Bendigo, Ballarat and Castlemaine.

The company grew and changed owners several times over the next few years but the new owners always retained the name Cobb & Co. In 1858 James Rutherford, with several others, took over the business and opened up a new era in transport that lasted 70 years.

Soon there were four coaches leaving Melbourne daily, the 162-kilometre trip taking 13 hours and costing £3. With each coach carrying 15 passengers, it didn't take long for Cobb & Co to make heaps of money.

They split the routes into stages and an inn was established at each stage, supplying refreshments for the passengers and a change of horses. The fresh horses could travel at increased speeds, and gradually the travel time shortened and routes were extended to other areas.

Rutherford secured the Royal Mail contract worth £10,000 a year and added the Royal Coat of Arms to the door of the coaches. He further strengthened his reputation by treating his horses well and having drivers who had learnt quickly from the Yankee whips.

Cobb & Co had a great reputation for speed and safety. Its drivers became legends in their time as they kept to timetables despite dust storms, floods and fires. Carrying gold from the diggings, they suffered very few hold-ups;

the drivers carried rifles and were prepared to use them. Only four drivers were reported to have died from accidents.

As the gold ran out some of the men settled in the nearby towns, while others went further afield taking up '40 acre selections'. The squatters went further and further west as the good land was claimed, followed by Cobb & Co.

When the railway made its way to the mining centres in Victoria, the use of coaches fell away, so Cobb & Co moved to New South Wales and established its headquarters in Bathurst for another 50 years.

Rutherford started a coach building enterprise there but, as the railways were extended, the coach routes had to move further to the west and the heat caused the coaches' bodywork to dry out, crack and split. The wheels began to warp, too. These big problems led to the coach building factory moving to Charleville in Queensland where the climate was so hot and dry that the timbers could cure (dry) before being made into coaches.

Besides Cobb & Co, there were many other companies servicing the remote parts of the country. The mail service covered the operators' basic costs, but to make money they had to carry passengers and goods. As the railways were extended, the coach companies went further and further afield, helping to open up the far distant areas.

Cobb & Co had built a reputation that none could equal. Their name stands for resourcefulness and reliability. Their drivers were able to solve any problem, and their coaches were more comfortable than others. The company is regarded by historians as a pioneer of transport in Australia.

eight
Simpson The Man with the Donkey

One of Australia's most loved legends from WWI and the battlefield of Gallipoli is the story of Simpson and his donkey.

Private John Simpson Kirkpatrick, simply known as Simpson, was a member of the 3rd Field Ambulance in the Australian Army Medical Corps at the bloody landing of troops on Anzac Cove in 1915. When donkeys were landed, mainly to be water carriers, Simpson was given one to help him rescue the injured, and he called him Duffy.

Simpson gave the wounded first aid and, with Duffy's help, carried our men non-stop, day and night, to the first aid stations. During Duffy's rest and feeding time, he used another donkey, but Duffy was his mainstay. Together, they saved many lives, going up and down from the fierce fighting in Monash Valley to the beach, where the wounded were treated and taken to the waiting ships.

When Colonel Alfred Sutton of the 3rd Field Ambulance saw the gallant efforts of this pair, he wanted Duffy to be 'a proper member of the Unit'. The Colonel quickly removed his own Red Cross armband and tied it around Duffy's head, and the donkey officially belonged to the Field Ambulance.

Simpson and his donkey became a symbol of endurance for the men fighting in terrible conditions. Simpson was killed on 19 May 1915 while leading Duffy, who was carrying two wounded soldiers, out of the line of fire and down to the first aid station. Simpson was buried on the beach at Hell Spit.

Simpson was posthumously Mentioned in Dispatches for outstanding service during the Gallipoli landing. Dispatches are written messages to the units of the regiment, and to be mentioned in these certificates is a great honour. The headstone on Simpson's grave reads, 'He gave his life that others may live.'

There are two old letters from soldiers on record. One says, 'Simmie the Donkey man was killed by a sniper on Dead Man's Ridge, he had a wounded man on his donk.' The other says, in part, 'There was an old chap, a stretcher-bearer with a donkey, which had a Red Cross band around its neck. He used the donkey for carrying wounded soldiers to the beach when snipers got him and the donkey one day.'

Not much is known of Duffy's fate.

Donkeys are sure-footed, slow and patient and have extra-long ears. They are used as beasts of burden as they are strong, obedient and live longer than other members of the horse family.

nine

The Tradition of ANZAC

The name ANZAC was first used in World War I (1914 to 1918) by the clerks in the Cairo headquarters (HQ) of the army. The area outside the clerks' room was filled with boxes that had to be marked 'Australian and New Zealand Army Corps'. This long title was soon abbreviated to A & NZ AC. The clerks then found an even quicker way of marking the boxes; these initials were small enough to fit on a rubber stamp! This was then called the ANZAC stamp, so Major Wagstaff, a staff officer at HQ, suggested the use of ANZAC as the code name for the Corps. It seems to have come into general use in January 1915.

The Rising Sun badge worn by our Army personnel is an image of a half circle of swords and bayonets radiating from a crown. It was first worn by the Commonwealth Horse contingent in the South African Boer War (1899 to 1902). General Bridges, the officer in charge of the Australian Imperial Force in WWI, decided it would be worn as the identification of his forces.

The slouch hat, still worn by the Australian army, dates from the Sudan War of the 1880s. Legend has it that Colonel Tom

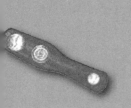

Two-up is a gambling game involving two coins that are tossed or 'spun' using a flat piece of wood called a 'kip'. Developed by the fossickers during the Australian gold rush in the 1850s, Anzac diggers frequently played the game in the trenches during World War I. Two-up games have become a part of the Anzac Day tradition and draw large crowds.

Price of the Victorian Mounted Rifles turned up the left side of the troops' hats instead of the right, which was the accepted way. This was logical as the mounted troops carried their guns on the left shoulder.

THE WALERS

Australian bred horses were shipped to South Africa for service in the Boer War and used by the British Army in India. They were specially bred in northern New South Wales as remounts from 1890 to 1940. Hence the name 'Walers'.

When the Australian Light Horse arrived in Mesopotamia during World War I, their mounts were so used to the rocky, sandy ground that they could travel faster and further than other horses. Each man's horse was his own responsibility to look after, and the relationship between man and horse became very strong, with soldiers often sleeping beside their best 'mates'.

The Walers were considered the best cavalry mounts in the world as they could carry an average of 133 kilograms all day for at least 17 days with only half the normal food and water of other horses and were very sure-footed.

The Light Horsemen mounted on their Walers took part in one of the world's last great cavalry charges during the battle at Beersheba in 1917. It was a fight against the Turkish

Army and the Australian Light Horse won an unexpected victory, entering the history books as an Australian battlefield legend.

When peace was declared and the Australians were coming home, their horses were not allowed back into Australia due to the quarantine rules. General Bridges's horse, Sandy, was able to return, but the others were shot, mostly by their distressed riders, particularly as they knew the hides were turned into leather. When Sandy died he was stuffed and now stands in the War Memorial in Canberra as a symbol of the bond between man and horse.

The descendants of the Walers' parents are still roaming free in northern New South Wales. Their blood lines have been strengthened by the inclusion of some mares bred from Arabian stallions, and an association has been formed to look after what are now called the Brumbies of Guy Fawkes National Park.

THE WAR ON HOME GROUND – DARWIN BOMBED!

It was 9.50 a.m., 19 February 1942, almost ten weeks to the day after the Japanese had attacked Pearl Harbor, when Japanese bombs fell on Darwin – the war on home ground had started. The event marked the first time ever that our territory had been attacked by a foreign power. They struck again two hours later when 128 planes formed an attack force commanded by Mitsuo Fuchida – the same number of aircraft and the same officer that devastated Pearl Harbor.

Darwin seemed to have had no warning, though it is thought that authorities should have expected the attack. Singapore had already fallen and Japanese aircraft were seen over Bathurst Island Mission, within easy reach of Darwin.

Darwin Harbour was full of ships; 21 were sunk including the USS *Peary*, which lost 91 seamen. Bombs hit Government House, the post office and the Berrimah Hospital. Two hundred and forty-three total casualties were recorded, and many were wounded.

This attack united Australia in a way not experienced before, and the war effort began to have a real purpose. Australians were no longer always fighting on foreign ground.

SYDNEY ATTACKED!

Since 1788 Sydneysiders had been fearful of foreign invasion and had spent many man-hours and much money building fortifications, mostly around the harbour foreshores.

The first foreign attack on Sydney was on 31 May 1942, when three Japanese midget submarines managed to get through the Sydney Harbour boom that protected the port's entrance. They headed for the city and Garden Island, where US ships and the Australian fleet were moored.

The first submarine, number 14, became entangled in the boom net protecting the harbour entrance and its crew blew themselves and the sub up. The second sub, number 21, hit the bottom of the harbour near the depot ship HMAS *Kuttabul*, which was moored near Garden Island. It still managed to fire a torpedo and hit the

Midget submarines – 24 metres long and 46 tonnes – were released from the decks of larger, 'mother' submarines. The midget subs only had room for two men and could fire two torpedoes.

former ferry, which sank with the loss of 19 sailors. Australian ships managed to locate the sub and fire depth charges. They sank that sub, but the third disappeared, never to be found.

On the night of 7 June, Sydney and Newcastle were shelled by Japanese submarines patrolling off the coast of New South Wales. They did no damage, just frightened a lot of citizens!

These attacks prompted many owners of harbourside homes to sell their houses for a song and prices for country houses to boom as people moved away from the coast and the perceived threat of invasion.

ten
Busby's Bore Water for Sydney Town

In 1823 Sydney's water was in short supply, much like it is today. Sydney's early water came from the Tank Stream, a spring near Hyde Park that flowed into Circular Quay, following a line that would be nearly George Street today. It had been polluted by the settlement's sewage and rubbish and the settlers urgently needed to find another source of water.

John Bigge, a judge and King's Commissioner, was appointed to advise Governor Macquarie on conditions in New South Wales. He commissioned John Busby, a civil engineer and expert in mining, to supervise coal mining in Newcastle and to ensure that Sydney had an adequate water system installed.

Busby first suggested pumping water from the Lachlan Swamp, now the duck pond in Centennial Park, by a tunnel or bore to a reservoir at the Racecourse, now Hyde Park. Busby, as a mining engineer, called a 'tunnel' a 'mine'; after all, they are both just holes in the ground.

His next plan involved, in his words, 'driving a mine the whole way' to take the water to a high enough level to make use of gravity

The convicts who built Busby's Bore were unskilled and there were great difficulties with the strata of rock they had to drill through, so the tunnel took ten years to finish.

to supply a standpipe (a long pipe standing upright so a tank could be filled under it) and run a water wheel. The water wheel would drive the water past the standpipe and so service more people.

This plan was approved and the tunnel was started in 1827. The convicts who built it were unskilled and there were great difficulties with the strata of rock they had to drill through, so the tunnel took ten years to finish. The water wheel was never built but the bore (tunnel) continued to be Sydney's only water supply until 1858. It collected water from springs and seepage along the way as well as from Lachlan's Swamp before it reached the standpipe in Hyde Park.

The diameter of the delivery pipe was very small and could only release a little water at a time. During the 1838 drought a charge of threepence a bucket was made. This was very expensive. Eventually, after more pipes had been laid from the bore to various parts of the town, selected houses were connected at a cost of five shillings a room.

The Botany Swamps Water Supply Scheme was installed in 1858 and this led to the eventual disuse of Busby's Bore.

The pump at Barrack Hill in Oxford Street, Paddington, is a relic of how the residents collected their water in buckets. Parts of the Tank Stream and Busby's Bore can be visited today through arrangements with the local authorities.

In 1872 the tunnel had its first clean-out and

1,475 drayloads of sand and debris were removed. The tunnel's measurements were recorded at the same time. Its height varies from one to three metres, in some places forming a big cavern. Its 'measured' length is 3.3 kilometres with up to six dead ends, but the surface distance, as the crow flies, is only 1.8 kilometres.

eleven

Working Marvels

BEAUT UTES

Motor cars rapidly became popular in the bush when Henry Ford introduced mass production lines that reduced their cost to within everyone's reach. Farmers used their car to carry all sorts of 'junk' – from pigs to ploughs – making a mess of the inside, so they resorted to cutting the back end off and fitting a tray behind the front seat. This worked, but was not very safe for the goods on the tray and dangerous when carrying livestock.

In 1933 an enterprising farmer wrote to the Australian branch of the Ford Company, telling them that, like most farmers, he was unable to afford both a car and a lorry. He was fed up with cutting his hands and his farming goods on the rough edges of the tray fitted to his makeshift car/lorry. And his wife continually complained about riding to church in her Sunday best in a smelly vehicle.

He asked Ford to design a purpose-built vehicle: one that he could use to take his pigs to market, pick up stock feed during the week and drive to church in comfort on Sundays.

When Henry Ford saw one of the first utes from the Geelong factory in 1935, he called it a 'kangaroo chaser' and built his own American version.

Lewis Brandt, a 22-year-old engineer working at Ford, set to work and designed the Australian Utility that came off the production line as:

'The Ford Coupe Utility – This new utility model has a smart Coupe body similar to a passenger car type with fine interior fittings. Rear compartment has ample loading space.'

This was one of the first advertisements to appear for this newfangled vehicle, the world's first successfully mass produced one-piece coupe utility body, that went on to sell in its millions throughout the world.

THE VICTA MOWER

The mower that revolutionised lawn mowing, the first Victa mower, was made in 1952 from bits and pieces lying around Merv Richardson's backyard. He used billy-cart wheels, an old peach tin and some pipe. A small petrol engine powered the blades.

In the beginning, Merv sold them from his front yard after placing a small advertisement in the local paper. He was soon overwhelmed with orders and realised he had invented a winner.

His 'backyard mower' had blades that spun around horizontally whereas existing mowers went round vertically, pulling the grass into the cutting edge. The Victa had four cutting blades, spinning in a circle parallel with the grass, cutting everything in its path, right

up to garden beds and paths – no trimming of edges – and it could cut weeds.

Not only did the early Victa cut everything in its path but occasionally toes as well. It became known as the 'toe-cutter' and sturdy shoes were a safety requirement. The body of the Victa is now shaped like a half moon, making a canopy, and nearly reaches to the ground so toes are less vulnerable.

More than 7,000,000 mowers are now keeping the lawns of Australia tidy, and it is a fair bet that a Victa mower has cut most lawns in Australia at some time. 'Turn grass into lawn', Victa's famous slogan, has become part of our gardeners' language.

THE BLACK BOX

The black box isn't really black, it's orange. The colour 'orange' is not a natural colour in bush or sea, so it's easily seen by searchers. The prototype was made from any black metal that came to hand, so even with all its technological advances, it is still known as the black box!

After the crash of several Comet airliners in 1953, investigators could not come up with any evidence of what caused the accidents. There were no survivors; all that was left was a big mess of metal.

In Melbourne, Dr David Warren, a chemist specialising in aircraft fuels, listened to the investigators wondering about the possible causes, and he began to think of how to record the crews' conversation and protect the recorder from destruction. He thought that, while it was hard to trace the causes of a crash, the crew might have known what the emergency was and talked to each other about how to fix it.

David first designed a small instrument that was fully automatic, with a memory of four hours, that could record the pilot's voice and the aircraft's instrument readings at a rate of eight per second. If the plane crashed, the black box stopped recording.

Five years on and the British were still the only ones in the aeronautical industry enthusiastic enough to encourage David to improve his original design. He increased the reading rates of the aircraft's instruments and made it easier to install and use – a 'fit and forget' operation. After a BBC television and radio news story, airway operators began to see the tremendous advantages of David Warren's instrument. The new 'black box' flight recorder was to be gradually installed in British aircraft.

Australia was slow to make use of this box, perhaps because there had not been any major air accidents for many years.

After an unexplained crash of a Fokker aircraft in Queensland, the judge heading the inquiry recommended fitting a crash recorder in all airliners. A magnetic tape was first used as it carried multiple recording tracks, but this was harder to make fireproof (a big danger in all crashes was the flammable fuel). The special steel wire that David Warren had used in his original black box had a single channel with different frequency bands for speech and data. All of these problems were overcome when the black box was computerised.

In 1967 Australia became the first country to make flight data and cockpit voice recording compulsory. It is now being recommended for use in ships, trains and other forms of transport.

David Warren and his black box have done much to improve the design of aircraft. After a crash, the investigators can follow the steps that led to the accident, helping the designers of aircraft make flying safer.

HILLS HOIST

Mrs Hill hated washing day. She was fed up with the old clothesline running between two posts in the backyard. The prop was always falling down or breaking and the clean washing would land in the dirt. She asked her husband, Lance, to do something about it, quickly.

Rotary lines had been around for years but they had to be set at one height and pity help you if you were too short to reach it!

Lance was a motor mechanic, so after realising this drawback in rotary lines, he thought of using a gearbox to transfer power from a winding handle to send the line up or down as needed – bring it

down to hang out the clothes then raise it to catch any wind to dry the clothes and keep them off the ground.

The rotary clothesline was a great success with his friends and neighbours, but he had many problems raising enough capital to buy materials and tools, all of which were in short supply so close to the end of the war. Lance enlisted the help of his brother-in-law and with a small amount of money from his father, the rotary clothesline became a goer.

The Hills Rotary Clothes Hoist was on the market by 1948.

COOLGARDIE SAFE

Cooling by evaporation has been around since man realised that a breeze blowing on sweat cooled the body. We know the Egyptians adapted this principle by hanging mats soaked in water across the open entrances of their homes, creating the first air conditioners.

The diggers of the 1890 gold rush in Coolgardie, Western Australia, used the principle of refrigeration by evaporation to stop their food spoiling as temperatures soared. They stretched canvas or hessian over an open frame with the ends of the fabric sitting in a tray of water. By keeping the sides of the safe continually wet, the evaporating moisture drew off the heat. Any breeze blew cold air through the frame, cooling the contents as it went. This is why so many Coolgardie safes sat on verandas of rural homes well into the twentieth century.

They also stood the legs of the safe in used Cocky's Joy syrup tins full of water, making sure the frame did not touch the sides of the tin. This created a barrier of water between ants and the food.

The canvas water bag was the precursor of the Coolgardie safe and is still occasionally seen today. Most oldies will remember the canvas water bag hanging in front of the car, cooling the water as the miles rolled by. For centuries the Aboriginal people carried their water in kangaroo skins, which the explorer Sir Thomas Mitchell saw and adapted. He found using canvas was an easier method of carrying water than the wooden kegs he had been using on his journeys, giving his party the added bonus of cool water.

twelve

Help for the Bush

THE PEDAL WIRELESS

Between 1924 and 1926 efforts were made by many people to develop a lightweight radio transmitter. All that was available at the time was a radio that could only transmit Morse code signals over a distance of 480 kilometres. Although it was simple and worked on batteries, there was a need for the same compact sort of wireless that could transmit and receive signals over the long distances that separated the settlements in the Far West.

Alfred Traeger, an Adelaide electrical engineer, set to work and invented the pedal wireless. The operator just pedalled madly, as though he was riding a bicycle up hill. The bike powered a generator and, though it still sent Morse code's dots and dashes, messages could travel the long distance of 1500 kilometres. Traeger was still not satisfied; he continued to improve his wireless and by about 1930 had developed a transmitter that could both send and receive the human voice.

CORRESPONDENCE SCHOOL

Correspondence school was developed in Australia to provide isolated country children with an education. Arthur Biddle, the school's first appointee, planned a workable program to use the post to send lessons directly to the children, who would complete and return them for correction and comment. This became known as 'The School in the Mailbox'. Some of the early and very remote pupils received their work by camel train. But they had to wait quite a while for mail, as these 'trains' were the only regular contact that isolated properties had with the outside world.

When many small bush schools were closed during World War I, lots of bush children turned to correspondence lessons. This sudden increase in students meant more teachers, and the school needed bigger accommodation. It moved to the former Teachers College at Blackfriars in Sydney. By 1924 it had 2335 pupils and 47 teachers and followed a system of lessons divided into subjects set by the Department of Education. These lessons were graded according to the ability of the student, always by the same teacher.

Today, teachers and pupils continue to write letters to each other, exchanging jokes and stories, and excitement reigns when lesson books come back from the teacher with a gold star for work well done. This communication helps make each student feel that they are an individual and can relate to their teacher, helping to defeat the feeling of isolation. The school encourages personal visits to Blackfriars whenever possible, and this is a big event.

With the advent of Alfred Traeger's pedal wireless radio, the teachers could see the advantages of using the Flying Doctors' network to give bush children a chance to instantly talk to their teachers and other children. The Royal Flying Doctor Service, the Correspondence School and the School of the Air joined forces and have worked together since 1951 to help educate and care for our children of the bush. Special lessons are available for students living overseas.

The United Nations Educational, Scientific and Cultural Organisation (UNESCO) made a film called *School in the Mailbox* that has been shown at international conferences on education. Blackfriars, as it is always known, became the model for worldwide correspondence school systems.

THE ROYAL FLYING DOCTOR SERVICE

Powered flight had already proved to be a reliable form of connecting people thousands of miles apart. The Reverend John Flynn, the first Superintendent of the Australian Inland Mission, had floated the idea of an aerial medical service as early as 1917. With the development of Traeger's pedal wireless, Flynn could see that by joining plane and wireless communication together, he could create a 'mantle of safety' over the isolated inland of Australia.

John Flynn was continually raising funds for his mission, so he set to work gathering enough donations to buy an aeroplane. He enlisted the help of Sir Hudson Fysh, a director of the Queensland and Northern Territory Aerial Services Ltd that would later become Qantas Empire Airways Ltd in 1934. The company, now known simply as Qantas, is one of the country's leading airlines.

Together, after years of dreaming, they raised enough money to have the world's first airborne medical team – the Aerial Medical Service – with its doctor and aeroplane always at the ready.

Sir Robert Gordon Menzies, Australia's longest serving prime minister, called the Royal Flying Doctor Service the 'greatest single contribution to the effective settlement of the far distant back country that we have witnessed in our time...'

The inaugural flight took off from Cloncurry, Queensland, in May 1928 with a Qantas pilot and the first flying doctor, Kenyon St Vincent Welch.

The prefix 'Royal' was authorised by Queen Elizabeth II who visited the base and spoke on the radio during her first trip to Australia in 1954.

John Flynn and Alfred Traeger were the inspiration for the establishment of many services in the outback, including the School of the Air that gave children the means of communication with teachers and other children and opened up the world to our isolated families.

The Royal Flying Doctor Service is still saving lives, thanks to John Flynn's vision of a 'mantle of safety' over the people of the outback.

thirteen

The Ghan

From Camels to Trains

The Ghan, running from Adelaide to Darwin, is our newest luxury train. Its forerunners were the Afghan camel drivers. In 1840, both the drivers and their animals were introduced to transport goods – even pianos and furniture – to the sparse settlements of the inland. They were brought into the country from Afghanistan because their home country's climate was as hot and dry as Australia's inland. We shortened the name of the camel drivers' nationality to 'Ghan' and the route has been called that ever since.

In 1860, 24 camels were imported for the Burke and Wills expedition that was endeavouring to cross Australia from Melbourne to the Gulf of Carpentaria. They reached the fringe of the Gulf of Carpentaria in February 1861. Burke and Wills died on the way back south on the banks of Cooper Creek, just by the tree that has the word 'dig' carved in its trunk. Provisions had been buried there for the explorers, who failed to dig in the right place and died of malnutrition. This tree is now known as the Dig Tree and you can still read the inscription.

The Ghan is now a modern, fast passenger and freight train going all the way to Darwin. The section of the line from Alice Springs

The Ghan wasn't always fast and luxurious. The original line, closed in 1980, earned the nickname 'the train you can walk faster than'.

to Darwin has only recently opened and is proving to be a great tourist attraction. One day it may be classed as one of the great train trips in the world along with the Indian Pacific that snakes its way from Sydney to Perth across the Nullarbor Plain, travelling a distance of 4352 kilometres.

The station at the beginning of the Ghan train line going from ocean to ocean north across the middle of Australia is in Adelaide, the capital city of South Australia named after Queen Adelaide, wife of England's King William IV.

An important station on the route is Alice Springs, known as The Alice. It was named after Lady Alice Todd, the wife of Sir Charles Todd who was in charge of the building of the Overland Telegraph Line.

The station at the other end of the line is Darwin, named by the Captain of HMS *Beagle* in honour of Charles Darwin who was the naturalist on an early trip by the *Beagle* in 1839. Darwin was looking at the origin and evolution of life on Earth.

fourteen
Lighthouses
Beacons on the Shore

The Australian coast is very rugged and very long – 19,500 kilometres when last measured. This fact accounted for the many shipwrecks along our coastline and meant that lighthouses were needed.

In the early years of settlement there were no long-distance warning signals for sailing ships that would give them the space they needed to turn about when danger loomed – they had no brakes! The first known wreck was in 1622 with many more on record. Even today there are shipwrecks in our waters, because sometimes the warning lights are not noticed by the lookouts.

In 1793 a lighted beacon was built on the south entrance to Sydney Harbour. Governor Macquarie soon realised the need for a permanent guide to the new settlement of Sydney and appointed Francis Greenway to design one.

The first Macquarie lighthouse was built on the heights of South Head in 1816. It was made of local stone and had oil-burning lamps controlled by a clockwork mechanism. Its light was visible 35 kilometres out to sea, flashing once a minute. In 1883 a new, bigger lighthouse was built by James Barnet on the same site. It had larger

The first lighthouse in the world was built in 290 BC in Alexandria, Egypt, at the mouth of the Nile. It was 117 metres tall, the tallest building in the world at the time after the Great Pyramid, and its mirror reflected firelight and sunlight that could be seen 50 kilometres offshore.

It is considered one of the Seven Wonders of the Ancient World.

lights that could be seen 72 kilometres out from the Heads.

Hornby Light, built in 1857 after two shipwrecks, stands on the inner South Head and marks the entrance to Sydney Harbour and the South Reef. It was made of curved, dressed sandstone and had two cottages for keepers. Its light shines out 22 kilometres.

As settlement spread, ships needed lights to guide them into the new harbours. The early ones were located at Port Phillip in Victoria, Moreton Bay in Queensland, Gulf St Vincent in South Australia and at the mouth of the Swan River in Western Australia.

There were three lighthouses built by convicts in Tasmania from 1832 to 1838, who sometimes even manned them. One was situated at the mouth of the Derwent River as a temporary building and was replaced the next year by a stone tower.

Along the north-eastern coastline of Australia lies the Great Barrier Reef, a World Heritage site. Ships travelling through these dangerous waters have a difficult course to navigate. They must thread their way through sunken reefs and coral cays and the passage of each ship is strictly controlled.

To guide the ships, lighthouses on the reef are spaced about 24 kilometres apart, forming 'lead-lights' through the narrow passages as well as warning of sunken coral reefs. Winds blow up very quickly

and can reach 210 kilometres per hour, making steering a ship difficult. Weather warnings are issued constantly.

In contrast, the Great Australian Bight on the southern coast has no lighthouse for 1100 kilometres, although it is hit by the fury of the south-westerly gales blowing in from the Antarctic. The Bight's shipping track is planned well out to sea.

As lighthouse keepers had to attend to the lights day and night, houses were built for them and their families close to the lighthouses. Usually their families helped with this never-ending job. The more remote lighthouses had supplies brought in every few weeks and the isolated children went to boarding school or had correspondence lessons.

All lighthouses are gradually being converted from man-operated to automatic with solar power. This means that the profession of lighthouse keeper is dying out and their homes along Australia's coastline are being converted to guesthouses where you can stay, right on the edge of the sea.

LIGHTSHIPS

Double-ended, steel-hulled lightships were anchored on coasts where permanent structures could not be built. These vessels were the greatest gift to the seabirds, they had somewhere to sit and sleep – and poo!

Four of these lightships were commissioned in Australia, two to work and two to be refitted after their turn of a year anchored on the edge of the dangerous shoal waters, mostly on the Queensland coast. These four 'boats' had a 'mother ship' that did the maintenance checks and the towing. Its crew had to position the replacement lightship, attach the towline to the relieved ship and make sure all was shipshape for the tow.

The seamen crewing the mother ship had a tough job towing one in and one out. The big rise and fall of the tides in the north meant the lightship had to be anchored by heavy chain with a huge steel swivel. This became a haven for marine growth and had to be covered in thick grease – a messy job. On top of this, the seabirds, using this wonderful perch, spent their nights pooing, which mixed with the grease and caused the entire slop to harden in the hot sun, creating a 'skating surface'. The crew slipped and slid all over the deck!

As the chain and anchor were raised with the capstan, the marine growth mixed with the poo, called guano, splashed all over the men. Before the job was finished, they were covered from head to foot in a slippery, smelly mixture. When they returned to their mother ship, they shed their clothes, sometimes throwing them overboard, hosed each other down with the ship's hose and raced to their cabin for a hot shower.

At the end of the tow back to port, the lightship was greeted by the town's gardeners, all pushing wheelbarrows to help clean the upper decks of the lightship. Guano is great for gardens and this fertiliser was free to anyone who offered their labour.

The lightship *Carpentaria* is now moored and on display at the Sydney Maritime Museum.

fifteen

Surf Lifesavers
Safe in the Surf

Surfing only really began in Australia in 1902. This late start was due to the 'wowser' law, forbidding people to swim between the hours of 6 a.m. and 8 p.m. When the editor of a Manly newspaper defied the authorities, saying that he would swim whenever he wished, Manly Council was prompted to rescind its 'no bathing' rule. It still kept the beaches roped off with signs saying, 'Men to the right – Women to the left'. Daylight surfing was beginning in earnest and segregation of sexes didn't last, as it proved impossible to enforce.

The world's first surf life saving club was formed in Australia – was it in 1906 or 1907? Was it Bondi or Bronte? This is a matter for argument. The records show that the formation of the Bondi Surf Bathers Life Saving Club was quickly followed by others around the world.

The first recorded rescue was at Bondi Beach on 3 January 1907 when a young Charlie Smith was pulled from the ocean with a cork lifebuoy attached to heavy rope tied to the club house. The same Charlie, who in 1915 enlisted in the AIF, transferred to the Royal Flying Corps in 1917, navigating the very basic planes of

The biggest wave ever surfed rolled in on 16 April 2004 – part of the legendary break off the North Shore of Maui. Pete Cabrinha broke the world record by tackling a 22-metre-high wave.

the time during WWI in France. He went on to set flying records all around the world.

This boy from the Bondi club was to become our world-famous aviator – Sir Charles Kingsford Smith or 'Smithy'. The sea claimed him back in 1935. He was lost in his plane, the *Lady Southern Cross*, somewhere in the Indian Ocean while flying from England to Australia.

In 1906 Lyster Ormsby, the captain of the Bondi Surf Bathers Life Saving Club, was experimenting with ideas to make surf rescue safer. He made a small model of a more effective reel using hairpins and a cotton reel, which was the forerunner of the reels used today.

Another Bondi member, Walter Biddle, designed the 'Surf King' – the first boat ever made especially for use in the surf. It was a catamaran type vessel with two kapok-filled, torpedo-shaped tubes built of wood, tin and canvas. It must have looked a bit like a modern Zodiac!

In 1908, to encourage public interest in the lifesaving service, the first properly organised surf carnival was held at Manly. The voluminous costumes caused much laughter among the crowd and the event was a great success.

Black Sunday is remembered as one of the most frightening days on Australian beaches. It was a perfect Sydney day in February 1938 and 35,000 people were enjoying Bondi Beach. Suddenly, with tremendous force, three gigantic waves hit the beach, one after the other. As the waves ebbed to re-form, they made a deep

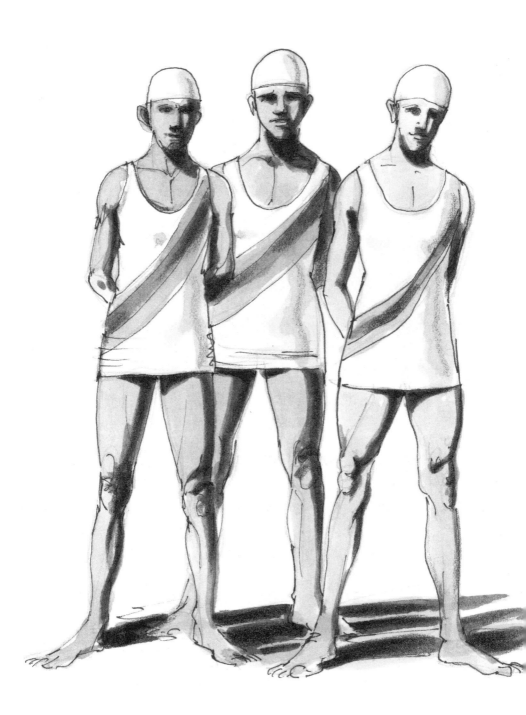

channel that pulled the swimmers in and carried them out to sea. There was mass panic and hysteria as men, women and children fought for their lives. Many were not strong swimmers.

Lifesavers reacted immediately, some grabbing what floating aids they could find and others manning the reels. As the rescued were bought to shore, the police and medical teams arrived. It took over 30 minutes for everyone to be brought to the beach – 250 needed serious medical attention, 35 were unconscious and five died. Those who were rescued have never forgotten the horror of that February day. The coroner who investigated the tragedy said of the lifesavers, 'Their work is voluntary and it is wonderful work they do.'

Surf lifesaving has spread around the world. Even the Changi prisoner-of-war camp in Singapore during World War II had a small club formed by Sir Adrian Curlewis, who was president of the Surf Life Saving Association from 1933 to 1975.

The association was formed as a voluntary service and still operates that way. By the year 2000 over 440,000 rescues had been recorded in Australia.

Today there are unpaid surf lifesavers patrolling over 300 beaches around Australia. They are supported by Life Saving Support Services, including Westpac helicopters, jet rescue boats and a communications centre, all combining to save up to 11,000 lives every year in Australia.

The International Life Saving Federation was started in 1993 with the Surf Life Saving Clubs of Australia playing a major part in its formation as part of its humanitarian efforts to save lives on beaches around the world.

sixteen

The Great Barrier Reef
The World's Largest Living Ecosystem

A world of sparkling seas, vivid colours and clear water – a wonderland to explore – the Great Barrier Reef, lying along the north-east coast of Australia, stretches 2,300 kilometres. The depth of the water varies from tidal flats to the deep water of the Coral Sea. It is alive with life and colour, constantly moving.

Coral is a living organism that feeds on micro-bacteria and builds layer after layer of calcium carbonate (basically lime) on itself, making a home for creatures you just can't imagine.

Scattered through the reef are 'bombers', little mountains formed by the coral, that are home to some of the most beautiful sea anemones, known as the flowers of the sea, firmly attached by basal discs. Their bodies can extrude or retract stinging tentacles that wave in the currents of the sea and are used for defence and to collect of food. Clown fish live amongst these tentacles, having developed an immunity to the stings of the anemones. Sponges, which live near them, are called the vacuum cleaners, because they filter the water for bacteria and debris, and some even build 'chimneys' to increase their catchment area.

Sea stars are shaped just like stars; they have many arms radiating from a central body, with suckers along the arms for collecting food – micro-organisms – and bringing it to their mouths. Sea stars are coloured and patterned in many different designs and textures; most have bumps. Like many other reef creatures, they have extraordinary bright colours.

The crown-of-thorns sea star can have up to 20 arms, covered in long toxin-coated spines. It feeds on living coral, turning its stomach inside-out over the coral and sucking the tissue off the skeleton. This leaves the coral dead and bleached white. It is a prolific breeder and has destroyed large sections of the Great Barrier Reef. The Reef Authority is working on this problem.

The fish defy description, from minute schools flashing with colour to the large potato cod, the giant amongst the bony fish. When it opens its mouth at you when you are snorkelling, all you can see is a big black cavern – quite scary. The moorish idol has a long thin fin floating above, and it can darken the large white centre strip across its body at night, making it all black and invisible.

Tiny cleaner wrasse have 'cleaning stations', usually near a bomber, that could also be called dinner plates: they eat the foreign bodies attached to the fish. Big and little fish come to these stations to have the parasites invading their gills and skin removed. Large queues of fish wait for their turn to be cleaned. The

The long line of the Great Barrier Reef is as noticeable from space as the line of the Great Wall of China.

wrasse even clean inside mouths, no toothbrushes needed!

Reef sharks feed mainly on fishes smaller than 30 centimetres. They rarely attack humans and then only if you are feeding them and they mistake your hand for food. It is heart-stopping when you are snorkelling and suddenly come face-to-face with this streamlined creature built for speed.

Rays come in large and small sizes. The larger manta and eagle rays slowly cruise the ocean, looking for their dinner; small fish and squid are the main food. They have a hard mouth with no teeth, which crushes any food they collect. The smaller stingrays and horny rays are bottom huggers, sifting through the sea floor for crustaceans and molluscs. They are usually harmless, though if you tread on one, it can flip its tail and drive a venomous barb into you. This can be painful!

The crustaceans are lobsters, prawns, crabs and the like; their name simply means 'a hard crust'. Molluscs are what we call shellfish. They both have suits of armour that protect them from most predators and are a favourite food of humans who have tools to defeat their armour!

There is as much life at night as during the day. Some fish have developed neon lights; others can hunt by feel or even get their dinner by waving long feelers with the tidal action of the water.

This World Heritage part of Australia is unique. It is the largest coral reef in the world, nearly the size of Texas, USA. It has up to 400 species of coral, 2000 species of fish and 4000 species of molluscs and is the breeding ground for a large part of the world's marine life and seabirds.

seventeen

Flight — Balloons and Kites

Many of Australia's early fliers are legends. The distance and isolation encouraged experiments in building heavier-than-air flying machines.

One dreamer was Dr William Bland, a convict who was transported from England for killing a sailor in a duel. He was quickly pardoned as the colony had few doctors. He gained credit as a scientist, particularly for research into fire, looking at the spontaneous combustion of the bales of wool ready for shipment and coal seams in mines. They would burst into flames for no apparent reason.

In 1851 he had a vision of a steam-powered balloon, flying to London in four or five days, carrying people and cargo. His balloon, called the Atmotic Ship, was planned as an elongated balloon capable of being steered. The envelope was filled with hydrogen gas in a series of compartments. It was to be powered by two steam engines, one at each end of the suspended cabin.

Models were exhibited in London and Paris, but the Atmotic Ship was never built, though it is now considered the forerunner of the modern airship or dirigible.

It wasn't until 1858 that the first balloon rose into Australian skies. The *Australasian*, piloted by William Dean, made the first ascent from Melbourne's Cremorne Gardens on the banks of the Yarra River. The balloon was made from more than 450 metres of French material and took about 877 cubic metres of gas to inflate.

The crowd paid five shillings (50 cents) to watch the historic event, and as Dean's balloon slowly left the ground, only just missing the garden gates, he threw bags of sand ballast overboard to enable him to rise higher. Suddenly, up he went, reaching about 3 kilometres high and travelling 11 kilometres. He landed on the Sydney road with a jolt. He was only slightly bruised. Many cabs had followed his flight and, on landing, he was picked up by one of them and driven to the waiting, cheering crowd in the Gardens.

In 1883 Lawrence Hargraves, a young astronomer, began experimenting with models of heaver-than-air flying machines. He studied the flight of birds, the movements of fish, worms and even jellyfish, taking measurements and noting how they moved and changed directions. He made many models of cane, paper and lightweight tubing, some with flapping wings, others propelled by

The largest kite festival in Australia is held every September at Bondi Beach. The Festival of the Winds features hundreds of traditional kites and strange flying creations in the shapes of dragons, helicopters, trains and birds.

wound-up rubber bands. In 1893 he developed the box kite – a wing form used by the designers of the early aeroplanes. Flying his kites from Stanwell Park beach in New South Wales, his four kites, joined as one, lifted him about five metres high from the sand!

Hargraves continued his experiments, designing the curved wing that the Wright brothers may have adapted and used in the construction of their 1903 aeroplane, the *Wright Flyer*. He built a series of extremely light engines, the most remarkable one a radial rotary engine. This engine became the basis of most European aero-engines for the next 20 years and led to the development of World War II fighter planes.

He did not patent any of his inventions, believing they should be free to anyone. He offered his models and plans to museums in Australia, Europe and the US, but only the Deutsches Museum in Munich displayed them. Many of his models were destroyed when the Allies bombed Germany in World War II. After the war the Deutsches Museum gave Sydney 12 of his models that survived.

The challenge of man flying is never-ending. One day in the future we might even be able to book holidays in space.

eighteen

Isobel Bennett
Seashore Expert

Marine biologist Isobel Bennett is one of the top authorities on the world's marine life and its seashores. After joining the staff of the University of Sydney as Professor W. J. Dakin's assistant in the Zoology Department in 1933, she became a research assistant, lecturing on and researching the marine life around our shores.

Isobel and the professor collected and identified many of the known plankton species – the microscopic water organism that is food for many sea creatures – and the marine life that lives on the rock platforms around the coast. Their scientific work on this ecology led to the publication of *Australian Seashores*, the first authoritative book on Australian shores, which is still available.

There are many scientific papers and books to her credit. She has travelled and studied most of the oceans of the world and is internationally recognised for her knowledge of intertidal animals and coral reef biology.

Isobel was one of the first women researchers to visit Macquarie Island in the Southern Ocean; she well remembers the

Isobel Bennett's research in marine life has been so important that one genus of marine worms, a coral reef and five species of marine animals have been named after her.

wonderful sight of thousands and thousands of penguins, standing around in their black-and-white suits as though they were waiting for a party.

Another fascinating journey was aboard the Danish naval ship *Galathea* researching the South Australian Deep in Bass Strait. A later trip was on the American university Stanford's research ship, *Te Vega*, a 42-metre, two-masted schooner that served as a floating laboratory for twelve students and three staff from Stanford with a crew of fifteen. This expedition lasted for four months and sailed across the South Pacific and East Asia.

It was Isobel's photo of *Sagamimopteron ormatium*, an almost shell-less, highly coloured mollusc, that led to Emperor Hirohito of Japan, in 1966, telling his Grand Chamberlain to request Isobel Bennett visit him to discuss the animal that he had collected in the Sagami Bay of Japan near Tokyo. This was just one of many visits to marine and oceanographic laboratories around the world.

In her many books she has vividly described the rich vegetation, fish and bird life around the seashores and discussed the future of our reefs, particularly warning of the increase of the crown-of-thorns starfish that devours and bleaches the reef. Oil drilling and spillage from shipping, plus the effects of coastal development, add to her worries of the continuing welfare of our wonderful Great Barrier Reef.

In 1962 the University of Sydney conferred on Isobel Bennett the first honorary degree of Master of Science they had ever presented. In 1984 Isobel received the award of Officer of Australia (AO) for her services to marine biology. Then, in 1995, the University of New South Wales conferred on Isobel an honorary Doctor of Science. She continues to be active in the Great Barrier Reef Marine Park Authority.

nineteen

Nancy Bird Walton
'My God! It's a woman'

'My God! It's a woman.' These words greeted Nancy Bird Walton, one of Australia's first woman pilots, as she landed her plane after flying into a flood area to rescue a grazier who was marooned by the rising waters. It was the first time many bush people had seen a plane, let alone a woman flying one. And she was wearing trousers, too!

Nancy had her first flight in 1928, aged 13, in a shining blue and yellow Gipsy Moth at an air pageant in country New South Wales. She paid the pilot a bit extra to loop-the-loop and from that moment Nancy was hooked. She was one of the few women game enough to fly, and she was not airsick as so many were. So began her career in flight.

Sir Charles Kingsford Smith, our most famous aviator, gave Nancy her first real flying lesson. She was so tiny (150 centimetres) that he suggested she bring a pillow so she could reach the controls. Her first test came after at least six hours of dual flying. To pass the A licence test you had to climb to 450 metres then free-fly down and land close to a fixed mark.

To gain a B, or commercial pilot's licence, you needed your record book to show you had done 100 hours of solo flying and that you had an ability to navigate and understand meteorology. As well as flying, you had to be able to do simple engine repairs.

Nancy's father and great aunt helped her buy her first plane, the same Gipsy Moth biplane that she had had her first flight in.

'Barnstorming' around the country at bush fairs gave many people their first taste of the magic of flying and soon helped to overcome the tyranny of Australia's distances. These 'joy' flights helped Nancy meet the running costs of the flimsy wood and fabric plane. Her Moth was eventually replaced by a Leopard Moth as it could carry more freight and passengers.

When Nancy met Stanley Drummond at one of these country fairs, he saw the advantage of a plane that could fly medical service into the outback. He realised Nancy and her new Leopard could reach areas not yet serviced by the Royal Flying Doctor Service that could only fly to limited areas.

So Nancy became the first owner/pilot of the Far West Children's Health Scheme and was actively involved with the New South Wales Air Ambulance. She flew the Baby Health Clinic sister on regular trips to and from Bourke in far western New South Wales.

Nancy has always said that flying is risky and lonely. The fear of being lost and never found

Nancy Bird Walton was the first woman pilot in the Commonwealth to obtain a certification to carry passengers on commercial flights. She founded the Australian Women Pilots' Association and opened up the sky for generations of women pilots.

is always present, especially in those early years when pilots navigated only by their watch and a compass. During all her years of flying, Nancy had many hair-raising experiences but she never crashed a plane.

During World War II Nancy was the Commandant of the Women's Air Training Corps. Amongst the many awards she has received for her dedication to flying is the Order of the British Empire in 1966, followed by the Order of Australia in 1990. She is also a Dame of Merit, Knights of Malta. As a patron, president and adviser to many associations, Nancy has always supported and helped people in need.

twenty

Sir Hubert Opperman
The Man of Incredible Feats

In 1930 there were three famous sporting figures: Don Bradman, Walter Lindrum and Hubert Opperman. Then Phar Lap came along and outshone them all – and he was only a horse!

Oppy – the human motor – at one time held every Australian long distance road racing and track record for cycling. Four times he was the Australasian road champion. He set 57 world and 68 Australian records.

In 1928 Oppy and his bride eloped to Europe. While in France he joined the other three Australian cycling team members, taking part in one of the world's greatest races, the Tour de France – a 5280-kilometre ride held over 22 stages. The route went from Paris to the Spanish border and over the Pyrenees Mountains on rough, precipitous roads. Oppy finished 18th, gaining him the respect of the French people. Of the other team members, two finished well behind Oppy and one retired sick.

The next race was the Bol d'Or, a 24-hour non-stop endurance race in which only the world's best cyclists took part. It attracted big punters, followed by the cheats who tried to nobble Oppy by sawing through the chains of his racing bikes. Both chains broke during the race but he did not give up, riding a heavy touring roadster while his racers were repaired. By then he was 17 laps behind, and it took him 11 hours to catch up with the field and only one more hour to pass and leave them all behind. At the end of the 24 hours Oppy had broken seven world records and ridden an incredible 900 kilometres.

Bruce Small, his manager and friend, persuaded him to continue and attempt the 1000 kilometre world record. Tens of thousands of spectators had seen the courage and determination of Oppy and began shouting over and over, 'Allez Oppy'. Soon he had broken the world record and was named the most popular sportsman in Europe by a Paris newspaper. His name is still revered today by the French people.

Sir Hubert Opperman was far more than a cyclist. He served as a Liberal politician and, as the Minister for Immigration, is credited with helping to bring an end to the White Australia Policy. He received the OBE in 1952, followed by a knighthood in 1968 and many European awards.

Oppy was invited to be the first cyclist to ride over the newly opened Sydney Harbour Bridge and, 60 years later, he was the first to ride under the harbour through the

Le Journal, a newspaper in France, described Oppy as a 'marvellous dynamo of human energy'.

new Harbour Tunnel, opened in 1992. In 1988, Australia's bicentennial year, Oppy was voted one of the ten all-time leading athletes of the country.

He died in 1996 on his exercise bike, a month before his 92nd birthday. As his son said, he died 'in the saddle'.

twenty-one

Albert Namatjira
Aboriginal Painter of World Renown

Albert Namatjira's very first name was Elea, given to him on 28 July 1902 at the Lutheran Mission near Alice Springs in the Northern Territory. He was named Albert when his parents adopted Christianity. When he was 13, Albert was initiated into the Arrernte community and taught the traditional laws and customs of his people. At the early age of 17, he eloped with Ilkalita (Rubina), a Luritja girl, and they lived happily together all their lives, raising many children.

Albert spent his early years working in leather and mulga wood, using hot metal to make plaques. In 1934 the artist Rex Battarbee was invited by Pastor Friedrich Albrecht to hold an exhibition of his and John Gardner's paintings at the Mission. Rex saw Albert's work and was impressed enough to show him the Western style of painting and would continue to mentor Albert. He introduced him to watercolour landscapes and supplied him with paints. Albert was a good pupil and a fast learner. In 1935 he made his first sale, 'My First Painting', and on the back was 'The Fleeing Kangaroo'. He received five shillings (50 cents) each for his early paintings.

In 1938 Rex organised the first exhibition of Albert's work. It was held in Melbourne and was opened by Lady Huntingfield, the Governor's wife. All forty paintings were sold. This encouraged him to take his work to an Adelaide exhibition where Hans Heysen, the winner of many prizes for his watercolours, was impressed with the freshness of Albert's work. The National Gallery of South Australia purchased 'Haast's Bluff (Alumbaura)' at this exhibition. He was recognised!

Demand for Namatjira's paintings continued, with exhibitions all around Australia through the 1950s. Success brought money and 'hangers-on', and he found it hard to cope with living two ways of life – his tribal laws were so different from the European

Albert Namatjira earned $300 at his first exhibition – a large amount of money at the time. Today his paintings sell for hundreds of thousands of dollars.

way of living. In 1949 he tried a new lifestyle by leasing a cattle station but cancelled the lease when he realised the area he had chosen would not support cattle, making it an unviable project. He tried to build a house in Alice Springs, but the law at the time did not grant him a building licence.

In 1957 Namatjira was granted full Australian citizenship rights – a big step forward for an Aboriginal man at this time. This entitled him to vote and live anywhere he pleased.

As Albert was earning considerable amounts of money, he was always spending it to help and support his people, but getting more and more in debt.

The last few years of his life were spent back at Hermannsburg, where he continued to paint. When he became very ill, he was transferred to Alice Springs Hospital where he died in August 1959. Several of his children have achieved fame as artists themselves. Today, Albert Namatjira's watercolours are fetching many thousands of dollars and are owned and exhibited by many state galleries.

Albert was a pathfinder, the first of many world-renowned Aboriginal artists.

twenty-two
Melbourne Cup and Phar Lap
Horses at Their Best

THE RACE THAT STOPS A NATION

Almost 150 years ago the famous American author Mark Twain said, 'Nowhere in my travels have I encountered a festival of the people that has such a magnetic appeal to a whole Nation. The Cup astonishes me!'

The Melbourne Cup, the horserace that stops a nation on the first Tuesday of November every year, began in 1861. That Tuesday was declared a public holiday in 1865, and it is still a public holiday in Melbourne while the rest of the country stops work and watches the race on television. A lot of money changes hands in the betting ring on this day.

The cup, now a 3200-metre race, is run at Flemington Racecourse, on an area specially marked out for the occasion near Batman's Hill where, in 1835, John Batman negotiated with the Aboriginal people of the district to sign a treaty, giving him 200,000 hectares of land to establish one of our great cities, Melbourne.

The first cup was run over a distance of two miles, and it had only 17 starters, a small number compared to today's maximum

In 1922 the Melbourne Cup trophy was valued at £200, but its worth has swelled since. The 2004 Cup was valued at $80,000.

of 24. Archer won the first Melbourne Cup and is one of the five horses to win two cups. Most recently, Makybe Diva became the first three-time champion.

In 1876 a ship headed for Melbourne, carried nine of Australia's leading runners, six of whom were considered to be possible winners, all were favourites in the betting. A violent storm hit the ship and all the horses drowned when water poured into their stables. The bookmakers made a 'killing' as the favourites did not turn up. They made so much in bets already laid (at the time bets were not returned if the horse it was placed on did not run) that they gave the captain of the ship a 'purse' in thanks.

THE HORSE THAT STOPPED A NATION

Legendary galloper Phar Lap did not win a place in his first four starts – not a brilliant beginning to a career that has no equal. The Red Terror, as he became known, went on to his first win in an event for two year olds in 1929 at Rosehill, and never looked back again.

Phar Lap, a New Zealand bred gelding, sold for 160 guineas at the sales in New Zealand in 1927 and was one in a million, an extraordinary racing machine.

The only confirmed assassination attempt on the wonder horse happened in the week before the Melbourne Cup race of 1930. Phar Lap's strapper, Tommy Woodcock, was taking him back to his stable when a gun suddenly

Phar Lap's body has been split into many parts. When last recorded his stuffed hide is in Melbourne, his 6.4 kilogram heart is in Canberra and his skeleton is in New Zealand. The saddle used in his final race was sold in Melbourne in 2004 for $87,500.

appeared at the window of a slowly passing car. Tommy saw the gun and immediately moved in between Phar Lap and the car as two shots were fired, luckily going over their heads.

This was enough for his owner who took 'Big Red', as Phar Lap was sometimes called, and his attendants into hiding. The interruption to his training and the drama of being smuggled into the racecourse 45 minutes before starting his race, with no time for him to settle down, did not upset the legendary horse. He still managed to win again.

The racing officials altered the rules of the race in 1931 to try and make it more interesting as Phar Lap was winning every race. They decided to give him a monstrous handicap weight of 70 kilograms. Carrying this weight, he lost, coming eighth. This turned out to be his last race in Australia.

After the race, Phar Lap's owners decided to conquer the world and took him to North America. When the ship carrying Phar Lap to North America sailed through Sydney Heads, the cliffs were packed with large crowds who came to farewell their 'champion'. Sadly, this was the last time he was cheered by his adoring Australian public. He won the Agua Caliente Handicap in Mexico by two and a half lengths, breaking the track record and becoming the world's second largest stake winner.

Phar Lap raced 51 times for 37 wins. His placid temperament was one of his greatest assets. When Daryl Lindsay painted his portrait, Tommy held one of his hoofs in the required position for hours on end without Phar Lap getting restless – quite an endurance test.

After out-classing some of the world's best horses and winning the only race he ran in the Northern Hemisphere, Phar Lap died in the arms of Tommy Woodcock from a still unproven attack of colic.

Phar Lap and Don Bradman were inspirations for all Australians during one of the hardest periods of our history – the Great Depression. Heroes were needed to lift the spirits and Big Red and Our Don did just that.

twenty-three

Cricket
The Ashes and Bradman's Bats

THE ASHES

The Ashes, the symbol of international cricket, came into existence after the cricket match between England and Australia that was held at Kennington Oval in 1882. This was the match when Australia, batting in the first innings, was all out for 63. England answered with 101 runs. The historic second innings gave Australia a lead of 84, despite the controversial dismissal of Jones as out of his crease when England's Dr W. G. Grace hid the ball in his beard and unexpectedly took the bails off the stumps as Jones walked down the wicket to pat down some rough spots.

When England began its second innings, Australia had a lead of 84. Spofforth, the incoming bowler, was held in awe by the English people and had taken six of the seven wickets so far. Angry at the unsportsmanlike behaviour of W.G. Grace, Spofforth was determined that England would not get the few runs they needed to win the Test. An 'awful silence' fell over the spectators as they saw him take the ball (several of them are reputed to have fainted with

the tension) and as the final wicket fell to Spofforth, a spectator dropped dead!

A memorial was published in *The Sporting Times* the next morning:

In Affectionate Remembrance of
English Cricket
Which died at the Oval on 29th August, 1882,
Deeply lamented by a large circle of
Sorrowing friends and acquaintances,
R.I.P.
N.B. The body will be cremated and the ashes taken to Australia.

At that time the ashes mentioned in the memorial were only symbolic. The next year a bail was ceremoniously burnt and the remains placed in an urn that was presented to the English side.

The Ashes remain permanently at Lord's, the home of the Marylebone Cricket Club. The Ashes Test Series between England

Cricket balls are made the same way today as they were in 1700. The cork middle is surrounded by a thick layer of rubber and then covered with either two or four pieces of leather. There are approximately 250 stitches on the average ball, aligned in six rows.

and Australia, held every two years, has been for symbolic ownership of the urn ever since that fateful match.

BRADMAN'S BATS

Don Bradman, our most famous cricketer, scored his first century at the age of 12, playing for Bowral High School in New South Wales.

He went on to rewrite the record books, scoring the incredible number of 28,067 runs and making 117 centuries. He captained the Australian Test team a record number of times in a career that spanned 20 years. The 1948 tour of England, when Australia won the Ashes undefeated, is remembered as the Don's last tour.

The Bradman Museum is in Bowral, and most of his mementoes are now kept there. His many bats could be thought of as museum pieces, such as the one from 1929 when he scored 340 not out. Then there is the bat he used to score a world record 452 runs in the 1930 New South Wales versus Queensland match – an individual score a team would be ecstatic about. A bat you won't find is the one he took to the crease for his last innings in first class cricket. Our Don was out for a duck!

twenty-four

Ladies First
Our Dawn and the Golden Girl

DAWN FRASER

Australia's great Olympic swimmer Dawn Fraser was born in 1937 in Balmain, Sydney. Dawn started competitive swimming when she was 13 and within a short time became the fastest swimmer in the world. Soon after turning 19, she won the 100 metre freestyle at the Melbourne Olympics. This started Dawn on a lifetime of breaking records. She won gold in Melbourne in 1956, Rome in 1960 and Tokyo in 1964. The winning of gold medals in the same event in three consecutive Olympic Games has never been achieved by any other swimmer. She made history by being the first woman to break the 100 metre freestyle minute barrier in an international race. The 100 metre butterfly world record also fell to Dawn, plus the 400 metre freestyle in Perth.

Dawn briefly retired from competition after the Tokyo Olympics when she was suspended by the Australian Swimming

Union for so called 'offences', which included marching in the opening ceremony without permission (no competitor was to take part in ceremonies if they had a race the next day). She was also reputed to have helped take a flag from the Emperor's palace. Despite these incidents, Dawn went on to win the 100 metre freestyle!

Dawn did not achieve her swimming records easily. Her training included swimming up to 12 kilometres every day. Sometimes her legs were tied together, other times she would tow a large empty drum. These training aids gave Dawn tremendous strength and 'stickability', as the record books tell us. Dawn's ability, training and determination rewrote swimming history.

Dawn won eight Olympic medals, four gold and four silver, and held 39 world records – a part of swimming history that has not been equalled.

In 1962 Dawn Fraser was Sports Woman of the Year, and in 1964 she was Australian of the Year. She has been a member of the New

Betty Cuthbert was the first Australian to win gold on Australian soil in the 1956 Olympics in Melbourne.

South Wales Parliament and continues to work for a variety of sporting organisations, giving her time to the young. She holds an MBE and an OAM.

BETTY CUTHBERT

'I snapped the tape and realised I'd won. I closed my eyes and said a silent prayer of thanks to God. I'd just won the 400 metres at the 1964 Tokyo Olympic Games. I couldn't shift my eyes off the Australian flag as it crawled slowly up the flagpole, bumps popping out all over my body. It was the race when I ran out of athletics and into history.'

Betty Cuthbert started running at five years old. In her teen years she broke many records, winning the National 75 and 100 yard junior titles. In 1956, the year of the Melbourne Olympics, Betty did not believe she would be selected, so she bought tickets to all the track and field events. However, she was asked to train with the Olympic squad and became part of the team to run in the 100 and 200 metre sprints. Betty won both events and was one of the four girls who won the 4x100 metre relay. She was our 'Golden Girl'.

During training for the Tokyo Olympics, influenza struck Betty and she was not the favourite to win her events. On 17 August 1964 she ran the race of her life and won gold for Australia. She felt she had run the perfect race and decided to retire from competition after 13 years of running, winning a total of four gold Olympic medals and setting many records.

In 1974, after many years of health problems, Betty's doctors confirmed that she was suffering from multiple sclerosis, a chronic disease of the central nervous system that causes loss of muscle control.

At the Opening Ceremony of the Sydney 2000 Olympics, a tumultuous crowd roared with delight when our 'Golden Girl' Betty entered the stadium with the Olympic torch strapped to her wheelchair, pushed by Raelene Boyle, another of our Olympic greats.

'I wish I could have run on these tracks and worn the clothes they wear today instead of the voluminous blouses and shorts as big as sails,' she said.

twenty-five

Flavours of Australia

VEGEMITE – 'A ROSE IN EVERY CHEEK'

Vegemite's story began in 1922 when yeast spreads made from yeast extracts, a by-product of beer making, were in short supply. This led Fred Walker and Dr Cyril P. Callister to create an Australian yeast spread. The question was 'What to call it?' They ran a competition and Fred's daughter picked an entry from his hat. An Australian icon was born – Vegemite! It is still made in Melbourne and continues to 'put a rose in every cheek'. Vegemite is now available throughout the world.

Not long after this success, Fred combined with a Canadian man, James Kraft, to form the Kraft Walker Cheese Company. Together Walker and Kraft developed a way to pasteurise cheese, and the familiar blue packet appeared in pantries across Australia.

ANZAC BISCUITS

The first army biscuits started life as Ships' Biscuits or Soldiers' Biscuits and were baked by Arnott's Biscuits Ltd for troops in the trenches of World War I. They were indestructible and kept forever, though many teeth were broken! Some soldiers would dissolve them in water, add sugar and cover the soggy mess with jam.

The Anzac biscuits we know today were first made by the wives, mothers and girlfriends who sent food parcels to the soldiers, using an old Scottish recipe that made the biscuits last through the long sea voyage. They were made from flour, rolled oats, eggs and golden syrup; sometimes sultanas and coconut were added, too. They were packed in airtight tins (Billy Tea tins made good containers) and sent to the war zones.

After the landing at Gallipoli on 25 April 1915, when Australian and New Zealand soldiers shared not only the fighting but also their food, the name ANZAC came to describe many things, including their biscuits.

These biscuits became a favourite of the troops and on their return home the boys still demanded what they now referred to as Anzac biscuits.

During World War II, refrigeration enabled the troops to have reasonably fresh food, although the indestructible army biscuits were still included in emergency ration packs.

LAMINGTONS

'Lamos' are the great standby for fund-raising fetes and rallies. Named after a Governor of Queensland, Lord Lamington (1895-1901), lamingtons are simply slabs of sponge cake cut into squares, coated with chocolate icing and then rolled in desiccated coconut. Delicious!

In April 1984 Vegemite was the first product in Australia to be scanned at a supermarket checkout.

The world's largest lamington was made on Australia Day 2005 to raise money for the Boxing Day tsunami disaster victims. It weighed 925 kilograms, was the size of a small car and contained 725 kilograms of sponge batter, 100 kilograms of jam, 50 kilograms of chocolate and 50 kilograms of desiccated coconut.

DAMPER

Stockmen didn't carry much in the way of food supplies. Saddlebags were kept light, so damper was a staple food. We still cook damper when camping, often twisting the heavy dough around a green stick and pouring on golden syrup when it browns. These doughboys are just delicious and easy to make.

Mix a handful of self-raising flour and a little salt together, then add enough water to make a stiff dough. Throw in a handful or two of sultanas, dates or other tasty morsels; shape into small log; wrap in foil and bake in the coals of an open fire for 60 minutes. Cut into thick slices and spread with golden syrup, honey or jam. Enjoy hot.

UNCLE TOBY'S OATS

Uncle Toby's Oats were born when Clifford Love and Company started rolling oats in 1893. Clifford's daughter, Nellie, designed the trademark and chose the name.

The first advertising for Uncle Toby's Oats was simple – Clifford travelled in a horsedrawn buggy to call on his customers. He usually carried a supply of used or rejected Uncle Toby's packets that he would drop on the ground at strategic locations as he travelled. Although not acceptable in today's anti-litter environment, this strategy was effective and low-cost at the time.

Wholegrain oats are considered very important in keeping our hearts pumping blood day in, day out, and carrying food and waste around our bodies. Oats have a high concentration of proteins and are rich in natural soluble fibre.

Rolled oats are an important part of many of our athletes' diets and recommended by the Heart Research Institute.

PLUM PUDDING – BIG SISTER

In 1945, when he was 50 years old, Ken Higgins made a big decision to break with his past and start his own business. He called his new company Big Sister after the family nickname for his eldest daughter.

Big Sister Plum Pudding was born when Ken needed to fill a contract for 5000 cases of plum pudding to be delivered in seven weeks to the wharves for shipping to the United States Army in India.

Ken had a fantastic recipe for plum pudding, but without any means to mix and cook large quantities, he needed a miracle and found one in a clever friend who was a boilermaker. Together they scrounged all the equipment they needed, even making a steamer out of a tank that had contained cups and saucers shipped from England. They turned it upside down, connected the steam lines – hey, presto, they had cookers!

It took five weeks to get it all together, leaving only two weeks to cook and deliver 5000 cases of pudding. When the deadline for delivery came, they had the cases on the docks, ready to be shipped.

This fulfilling of a nearly impossible order firmly established Big Sister as a renowned maker of canned plum pudding and many other products from crystallised fruits to gherkins.

GRANNY FROM RYDE

A new variety of fruit – the Granny Smith apple – first appeared in the mid-1800s in the Sydney suburb of Ryde at the home of Maria Ann Smith, known by everyone as Granny Smith.

Granny always bought her supplies at the markets and carried them home in a fruit case. She would gradually fill the case with any rotten fruit and tip it into the creek at the bottom of her garden.

One day she found an apple tree growing there, bearing brilliant grass green apples that tasted good – tart but sweet! Granny must have taken some of these green apples to market as they soon became so popular that other growers replanted their orchards with Granny Smith apple trees.

The Granny Smith apple has turned out to be a great cooking and eating apple, sweet and crunchy, with a very long shelf life. It will keep in prime condition on the long voyage to overseas markets.

Experts say it was probably the seed of a French crab apple, a sort known as 'a two-year apple' as it kept well for more than two years.

twenty-six
The Big Ones

Australia is big – the biggest island in the world – and we have built the biggest models of our icons and scattered them throughout the country, with displays inside explaining the local area and products. Most have stalls as well, selling food, craftwork and cheap souvenirs.

The city of Goulburn, one of the biggest fine wool production areas in Australia, wanted to attract the dollar of tourists who were passing the town by. They hit on the idea of a BIG, BIG fibreglass sheep, and the Big Marino was built in 1985.

A steel frame was constructed and covered in a cement and fine sand mixture that was reinforced with fibreglass. The final covering was curled to look like wool.

It has three storeys of activities, stands 15.2 metres high and is 18 metres long, weighing in at 97 tonnes. You can climb to the

top and look out of its eyes (a sheep's eye view!) surveying the Southern Highlands of New South Wales.

You can buy all sorts of bric-a-brac, have lunch or a snack, inspect the 'how to farm sheep' display or just be amazed at the construction.

The Big Merino lost its place on a main highway when the authorities moved the motorway miles away. You can still visit it and take a fun break during a long drive by turning off the Sydney to Canberra highway at the signpost to Goulburn. Remember, it is three storeys high, so you can't miss it.

The pineapple is a hugely popular fruit, especially in Queensland. As a tribute, Gympie has built the largest one – 16 metres high and over 7 metres in diameter. Thousands of people visit the Big Pineapple and walk through, pineapple drink in hand, sipping while looking at its displays.

The Big Pineapple has attracted over 20 million domestic and

Alan Chapman, an engineer, designed the Big Banana according to the exact dimensions of the prize-winning banana from the 1964 Coffs Harbour Agricultural Show.

international tourists since its creation in 1971. Today, approximately 750,000 people visit the attraction every year.

Another large pineapple is in the middle of a working plantation. A small train takes tourists on a trip through the farm, while a guide talks on the growing of Queensland's produce and all its pests.

Berri in South Australia, where juices are packaged for easy drinking in waxed boxes, has a Big Orange weighing in at 125 tonnes. Then there is the Coffs Harbour Big Banana and the Big Apple at Batlow.

The Big Rocking Horse is in Victoria and was built as a restaurant. It stands high above the road attracting customers. You can have dinner and survey the world. Inside the stomach of a Big Cow standing at Yandina, with teats as long as a cricket bat, there is an 8x11-metre space, filled with food, drink and souvenirs to buy.

Griffith in New South Wales, where they grow grapes for wine and lots of other fruit, has a giant wine bottle and wine barrel.

Ned Kelly, our most infamous bushranger, is gone but not forgotten. He's larger than life as a towering, iron-clad statue at the town of Glenrowan near where he made his last stand in 1880.

The Big Gold Miner outside Bathurst will be panning his gold for a long time to come. The discovery of gold brought thousands of settlers to Australia to try their luck. Most were unsuccessful and went on to become the backbone of the country as they found other jobs.

Big Ones are part of Australia, from the Big Boot in Brisbane and the Big Shell in Queensland to the Big Walking-stick in Victoria. They may not be things of natural beauty but are good stop-overs on long trips and tell you much about the local towns.

twenty-seven

The Principality of Hutt

A 'Nation' within a Nation

Australia has more than one so called independent community. The first and most famous is the Principality of Hutt Province formed in April 1970 by Leonard George Casley.

In that year the Australian Government imposed wheat quotas that many farmers thought were unreasonable. Casley, who farmed a 7474-hectare wheat property 500 kilometres north of Perth, declared the Wheat Board an illegal body and notified the Governor General that he had left the Commonwealth and declared himself Chief Administrator of the sovereign state of Hutt. The Government ignored all this palaver, so Casley upgraded his principality, declaring that the Principality of Hutt was a state, investing himself and his wife as Prince Leonard and Princess Shirley of Hutt.

The population grew to about 30, but were mostly relatives. Prince Leonard says that no Australian taxes are paid and that the residents do not vote in any election. When questioned on this matter, he points to a dubious letter obtained from the Department of Territories acknowledging his claim that he is not subject to Australian laws. Prince Leonard also issues diplomatic passports for his subjects and has appointed ambassadors around the world;

The Principality of Hutt lies 595 kilometres north of Perth, Western Australia. It is 75 square kilometres in size, about the size of Hong Kong.

he has even had a Papal audience in Rome. He applied for membership of the United Nations and the British Commonwealth and was bitterly disappointed when he received no replies.

He keeps declaring war and then peace on Australia. This is only a 'paper war', no battles are fought, so there are no casualties. It's great publicity and the tourists love it. Over 25,000 people visit the province each year, helping to keep its coffers full, but its main income is still from wheat.

When you visit Hutt, you are granted a temporary visa for a fee. He also sells 'honours and titles', creating dukes and duchesses or lords and ladies depending on how much you pay. Distinguished visitors are sometimes just given a title. There are many dukes, duchesses, earls and knights of Hutt!

The sale of agricultural products and wildflowers earns a portion of the state's income, though a large portion comes from the stamps and currency notes sold to tourists and collectors of fantasy items.

When Prince Leonard designed the stamps and money for his Province, he used portraits of his Royal Family, dressed in the most incredible outfits. The images of the Prince show him wearing clothes ranging from a business suit with a gold mayoral chain, to a Prince Leonard Air Lines uniform decorated with the insignia of an air marshal. Images of the world-famous wildflowers of Western Australia are used extensively on his stamps.

His coat of arms features the stylised scales of

justice inside the outline of an eagle, surrounded by the words 'Hutt River Province'. This symbol is used on the only issue of printed banknotes, all the same size. They were of five denominations: 10 cents, 20 cents, 50 cents, one dollar and two dollars. The front of the notes all have the same design but are printed in different colours. They are signed by Leonard in a big scrawl right across the middle.

At Hutt River one of the few buildings in the 'Capital' is the post office where you must obtain your entry visa.

When Prince Leonard travels the world, he says he only uses his Hutt Province passport, stating that no country has ever refused him entry. When immigration officials are puzzled, he tells them that his country is on the Australian continent and is 18 times the size of Monaco. This statement is a little hard to believe. When queried on this he replies that, 'You should remember it's the second largest country in this continent.'

Prince Leonard of Hutt is Australia's first self-declared monarch. There are about 200 tiny, unrecognised countries in the world. Australia has become the centre for micronations; there are 20 or so here. When people have a disagreement with the Government, they declare that they are independent nations and build their own empire, at least for a short time. They are mostly in the monarch's imagination but some, like Hutt, survive.

twenty-eight
Flags
Rallying Symbols

Flags, sometimes called standards, are timeless. The sight of flags flying has always been a rallying symbol. The sight of a country's flag flying encourages people to perform acts of bravery in battle. They are flown to celebrate great events and can 'talk' to distant people. Flags are used to decorate streets and houses or are just flown to say you are an Australian.

They help us express joy or sadness and to advertise events. A flag flown at half-mast is a sign of respect for the recent dead. They come in all shapes, sizes and colours and can even spell out messages.

THE EUREKA FLAG

The first symbol of Australian unity, the blue flag with a central white cross, one white star at each end and one in the centre of the cross, was flown as the rallying point for the clash between the gold-diggers and the police force at Eureka on the Ballarat goldfields in 1854.

The diggers were up in arms, objecting to the licence fee of 30 shillings per month for the right to dig and the way the tax was collected. Ballarat has built a working 'township' and the remains of its very torn flag are in the Ballarat Art Gallery.

THE AUSTRALIAN FLAG

In 1903 the first Australian Commonwealth flag was approved by King Edward VII. It was changed in 1909 when a seventh point was added to the Commonwealth star to signify the Territory of Papua.

The flag has the Union Jack in the upper quarter of the hoist. Below the Jack is the Federal Star with seven points, one for each state and one for all territories. On the fly is the constellation of the Southern Cross.

The background colour is usually blue and may be flown by any citizen of Australia from 8 a.m. to sunset. It should only be flown at night if well lit. If the background is white (the White Ensign) it is the flag of the Royal Australian Navy, if red (the Red Ensign) it's the flag of merchant ships.

Australia's states all have their own flag, based on the Blue Ensign but without the Federal Star and with a state symbol on the fly.

The Union Jack on our flags commemorates our historical link with the United Kingdom. It has, superimposed on each other, the red

Vexillology is the scientific study of flags, their history and symbolism. The Latin word 'vexillum' stood for a particular type of flag attached to a spear used by the Roman legions during their marches and battles.

cross on a white background of St George of England, the white cornerwise cross on blue of St Andrew of Scotland and the red on white cross of St Patrick of Ireland.

The stars on the fly of our national flag represent the Southern Cross constellation that is seen lying in the Milky Way near Centaurus. The four brighter stars shine in the form of a cross, giving the group of stars its name – Crux Australis.

The two stars nearby, known as Alpha and Beta Centaurus, are called the Pointers. A line drawn through them hits the head of the Cross and makes it easy to find.

The Southern Cross is at its brightest during April and May, between 8 p.m. and 11 p.m. when it is almost directly overhead; Canberra has the brightest view then. At the same hours in October and November, it is low in the horizon and only barely visible in Queensland and the Northern Territory.

The five stars have been known throughout the ages; Ptolemy, a second-century astronomer, watched them in the night sky of Alexandria and included them in the constellation of Centaurus.

Andrea Corsali, one of the first Italians to sail around Africa to the Indian Ocean, recorded that he had seen a 'Cross' in the sky during his travels. In his diary he wrote, there 'had appeared a marveylous crosse in the myddest of five stares'. He later added, 'This crosse is so fayre and bewitful that none other hevenly signe may be compared to it.' The Southern Cross was on the maps.

Apart from identifying nations or groups, flags can talk. A plain, rectangular flag in primary colours has a particular meaning according to its colour. A red flag = danger, green = safety, yellow = sickness, white = peace or surrender, black = death, orange = courage.

Semaphore is a way to talk over a distance by using two flags, one in each outstretched hand, moving them to a position, each of which means a letter in the alphabet. This was how ships at sea talked to each other but has, of course, been overtaken by modern technology.

THE ABORIGINAL FLAG

The Aboriginal flag was designed in 1971 by the Indigenous artist Harold Thomas, a descendant of the Luritja clan of Central Australia. It was raised for the first time in Victoria Square, Adelaide, on National Aboriginal Day in 1971. He designed it to reflect the relationship with the land. A black rectangle above a red one represents the Aboriginal people and the spiritual connection to the earth. The yellow circle in the centre of the flag represents the sun – the source of life.

twenty-nine
The Sydney Opera House
The Glory of the Harbour

The Sydney Opera House is considered one of the most daring pieces of architecture of the twentieth century and was built on Bennelong Point (named after Bennelong, one of the first Aboriginal people to have close contact with Governor Phillip). Bennelong lived in a hut built for him on the point that formed the east bank of Sydney Cove. In later years, it became the site of the Fort Macquarie Tram Depot.

In 1954 the Premier, J.J. Cahill, held a meeting of citizens to discuss the building of an opera house. A committee was formed and it chose Bennelong Point, one of the most beautiful sites in the world. An international competition was launched for the design.

There were 233 entries from 32 countries. The $10,000 prize was won by a Dane, Joern Utzon, with a groundbreaking design of two theatres side by side, each covered by connecting 'shells' that were both the walls and the roof. His statement was that his design was 'a

The Opera House Concert Hall is home to the largest mechanical tracker action organ in the world, consisting of more than 10,000 pipes.

The organ can also be played by remote control or programmed to play pre-recorded pieces.

clear contrast to the square harbour buildings of Sydney'.

The work began on 2 March 1959, and the finishing date was then set for Australia Day 1963. But it would be another ten years of delay before opening day!

The project became the subject of huge public scandal as the cost went from the original quote of $7,000,000 to $102,000,000. It was partly financed by a lottery run by the State Lottery Office.

In 1966, after many disagreements over fee payment and lack of creative support, Utzon left the project and never returned to Australia. Despite these problems, the building gradually grew, with many experts ranging from engineers to architects working on it. The Public Works Minister, Davis Hughes, eventually took overall charge of the project.

The 'doughnuts' that hang over the stage in the Concert Hall are made of plexiglas and their job is to reflect the sound from the orchestra, sending it bouncing back to the players so they can hear how they are playing.

The acoustics had to be tested and to do this a shotgun and then a pistol were fired in the Concert Hall and Opera Theatre – only blank ammunition was used! The echoes from this showed how the sound behaved.

To check that outside sound did not invade the theatres, a helicopter hovered low overhead and an ocean liner paused close by and sounded its horn and the noise was measured.

Queen Elizabeth came to Sydney in the royal yacht to open the Opera House in 1973. Sydney had a stunning new building on a stunning old site.

The Opera House is 185 metres long and 120 metres wide and contains 1000 rooms. The roof sections are held together by 350 kilometres of tensioned steel cable and the roof is covered in over one million white granite tiles. It is supported on 580 concrete piers buried 25 metres below sea level. There are 6225 square metres of glass and 645 kilometres of electronic cable. It conducts 3000 events a year to a total audience of two million people.

Despite never having seen his masterpiece in person, Joern Utzon made peace with Opera House officials in 1999 and agreed to consult on a $70 million renovation of the interiors and outside walkways. Too old to travel by plane, Joern relied on his son Jan (also an architect) to help him in Sydney while he stayed in Majorca, a small Spanish island in the Mediterranean Sea. One of the purposes of the work was to make the interior as Utzon originally intended it before he left the project. For example, the opera theatre was originally meant to be the drama theatre. This meant that the orchestra pit was far too small for the musicians to play their instruments and needed to be redesigned and enlarged.

Utzon also designed the interior of the former Reception Hall (now called the Utzon Room) in 2004. The refurbishment cost $4.6 million and included a 14-metre-long, distinctively coloured tapestry inspired by the music of Bach.

thirty

The Black Cat Phantom of the Mountains

The Big Black Cat is on the prowl again. Sightings have occurred in Sydney's north-west mountain area between Richmond and Lithgow. Residents have been attacked and the remains of possum carcasses and other small animals have been found in inaccessible places, surrounded by droppings and footprints of large animals. Experts called in to investigate have identified the faeces as matching those of pumas!

These giant black cats have been reportedly seen in many areas of Australia for more than 100 years, mainly on the east coast and Tasmania.

The first recorded sightings of huge cats were in the 1850s during the gold rush in Victoria. Where they came from is a complete mystery. One rumour says that American fossickers brought big cats with them – they surely would have to have been pumas (*Felis concolor*), the native American panther. When the gold ran out, they just abandoned the big cats.

A later story maintains that US Marines in Australia kept pumas as their mascots and that they were released into the

The fishermen from the islands north of Australia are believed to have left behind cats, well before the first settlers. These feral cats are now one of the main predators of native fauna in the north. They are now described as 'big, vicious and mean killing machines.'

bush when the army shipped out to fight the Japanese in New Guinea during World War II.

Bushwalkers, locals and National Parks rangers have lodged many reports of seeing big, black, panther-like creatures wandering in the scrub.

A resident of an outer suburb of Sydney no longer checks his mailbox at night after he was attacked by a large cat that leapt on him out of the dark. He came back to his house covered in blood with deep scratches on his arm and chest. He says it was no dog and was far too big to be a feral cat. Was it a panther?

In Windsor, New South Wales, a dentist was driving home late one night in June when his headlights shone on a huge cat. 'It was just there, by the side of the road. It was no pussycat. It was a panther and it was huge.'

There have been so many reports of a giant cat that in 1999 the New South Wales Government asked an expert environmentalist to investigate. After looking at photos, droppings, casts of paw prints and reading many written reports, he felt that there was evidence of a large cat-like animal living in our community, feeding on rabbits, possums and stray dogs or cats.

In the summer of 2003–4, the season when these animals are most frequently reported, a documentary film crew went to the Hawkesbury region in New South Wales, to try and catch the 'panther' on film. They managed to get a shot of the shadow of a large, black, cat-like animal. The experts said it was 'possibly a panther', but nobody would make a positive statement about this spooky vision so many people have reported seeing.

The Phantom Panther may no longer be a ghost.

Is it real? Is it the offspring of those American pumas, or is it just a large cat? Is it the descendant of the prehistoric animals that lived in Gondwanaland – or maybe it's just a legend that is still living?

Anne Ingram OAM has worked in children's books all her life as a bookseller, reviewer, publisher and writer. She grew up in Brisbane and moved to Sydney where she joined William Collins to establish their first children's list. She was the first Australian to represent our children's books at the international market of the Bologna Children's Book Fair.

Peggy O'Donnell grew up in Sydney where regular visitors to her home were Dorothy Wall, Pixie O'Harris and Frank Dalby Davidson. She was a teacher before she married and moved to the country. Since returning to Sydney 33 years ago, she and Anne worked together on many children's books as writers and editors.

Gregory Rogers studied fine art at the Queensland College of Art and has illustrated a large number of educational and trade children's picture books. In 1995 he won the Kate Greenaway Medal for his illustrations in *Way Home*, a book that also won a Parent's Choice Award in the US and was shortlisted for the ABPA book design awards.

30 AMAZING AUSTRALIAN ANIMALS

CHRISTOPHER CHENG

ILLUSTRATIONS BY
GREGORY ROGERS

RANDOM HOUSE AUSTRALIA

For J.P.R. – a really amazing Australian animal.
And for B – my favourite Australian animal. C.C.

For Harry and Pudding. G.R.

Acknowledgements

Thank you to

- the folks at the NSW State Library and the Australian National Library who directed me towards the historical information sources.

- those at the Australian Museum in the many departments who answered ALL my questions – especially when I said 'Is this right?', and those who helped from the Victorian and Queensland museums.

- Healesville Sanctuary, Australian War Memorial, Sydney Olympic Authority, and NSW and Queensland National Parks and Wildlife Services.

- Special thanks to Donz for ALL your work, and to Heather, Linsay and Kimberley.

CONTENTS

Foreword: Why Amazing Creatures? vi

1 Bilby: A Long-eared Wonder 1

2 Blue-ringed Octopus: Eight-limbed Wonders 6

3 Brumby: A Poetic New Australian 11

4 Camel: The Ship of the Desert 16

5 Cane Toad: A Great Idea (Not) 21

6 Cicada: Nature's Choir 26

7 Crocodile: What a Toothy Grin 31

8 Death Adder: A Deadly Lure! 36

9 Dingo: Australia's Own Wild Dog 42

10 Dugong: Mermaid, Sea Cow or Lawnmower? 47

11 Echidna: Pincushion On Legs 51

12 Emu: A Very Big Bird 56

13 Ghost Bat: Not So Ghostly 61

14 Goanna: A.K.A. the Lace Monitor 66

15 Great White Shark: Impressive Ocean Predator 71

16 Green and Golden Bell Frog: Very Patriotic! 76

17 Koala: At Home in the Gumtrees 81

18 Koel: The Lazy Parent 86

19 Kookaburra: The Laughing Larrikin 91

20 Lake Eacham Rainbowfish:
Magnificent Little Fish 97

21 Little Penguin: Flying Torpedoes 102

22 Mountain Pygmy-possum: A Mini Marsupial 107

23 Platypus:
A Duck Designed by a Committee 112

24 Redback Spider: Not Creepy and Crawly 117

25 Red Kangaroo: Australia's Big Foot 122

26 Sulphur-crested Cockatoo:
Noisy Bird from the Land of Parrots 128

27 Tasmanian Devil: An Island's Icon 134

28 Thylacine: Gone But Not Forgotten 139

29 Weedy Seadragon: Floating Seaweed 144

30 Wombat: Bulldozer of the Bush 149

Guys, Girls, Bubs and the Whole Gang! 155

Animal Emblems of Australia 158

How to Find Out More 160

References 162

FOREWORD

Why amazing creatures?

Most countries around the world like to think that their animals are *amazing* but we Australians really do have the most amazing animals … we've got mammals that lay eggs and mammals that give birth to young that look like pink jelly beans. But it is not just our mammals that are amazing. We have birds that have wings but don't fly, frogs that can survive in the desert right through years of drought, and miniature dragons that swim in the sea. We have insects whose young grow buried under the ground, coming to the surface maybe 7 years later, and, of course, we have the eight-legged wonder with a rather toxic bite. You'll meet each of these in these pages.

And because Australia is an island continent, isolated from other land masses for such a long time, most of our animals are found naturally nowhere else. We are home to the world's largest and most diverse range of marsupials, and to the largest carnivorous marsupial and the largest macropod. It is the only place where venomous snakes outnumber the non-venomous species. There are more lizards here than known anywhere else in the world. And Australia has a wide range of environments, from alpine to desert, in which Australia's animals have evolved their own solutions for survival.

Our fragile land

These amazing creatures have been surviving in this land that we call Australia for thousands and thousands of years. Unfortunately they have one huge problem – introduced animals: cats and dogs, pigs, cane toads, fire ants, not to mention you and me.

Australia's landscape is very fragile. Many of the introduced animals cause destruction of the natural environment. Their feet are often not designed for our fragile soils, and they may even eat native animals or the food our natives rely on. And we humans have spread our footprints on the land, destroying native habitats to make way for our buildings, roads, railways and farms.

What we can do

We need to find a balance where both humans and other animals can survive. Here are some simple things we all can do:

- Keep your pets well enclosed and under control so that they do not wander and compete with native animals for the limited food resources or even eat our native animals.

- Conserve our natural resources by using as little as you can of things like water, electricity, gas and paper. And don't forget to recycle!

- Investigate ways we can help our native animals survive, such as by supporting and encouraging organisations that protect our native animals (see 'How to Find Out More' on p 160).
- Find out as much as you can about our native animals and tell others about how special they are. Be an ambassador!

If only previous generations had really considered the native animal population before hunting the Thylacine to extinction. Then maybe you could actually see a living Thylacine – instead of reading about its *amazingness* in this book.

So, turn the pages, check out our amazing animals and maybe consider what you can do to help them continue to survive and flourish in this amazing land.

Christopher Cheng
www.chrischeng.com

1 bilby

A LONG-EARED WONDER

What animal has large ears, digs a burrow, has soft, silky grey fur and can hop? It's the bilby (*Macrotis lagotis*), sometimes called the Rabbit-eared Bandicoot or Greater Bilby. It is the largest member of the bandicoot family. An adult bilby can weigh up to 2.5 kilograms and is about the size of a small cat.

Bilbies prefer to live in hot sandy desert areas in spinifex grassland. Life in the desert isn't easy and the bilby has had to make some amazing adaptations to survive. These adaptations are so good that bilbies are the only bandicoot species that still live in the arid and semi-arid areas of Australia.

BIG EARS IN THE DESERT So why have big ears in the hot desert? Though its eyesight is poor, this creature's sensitive ears are great for hearing predators, and an excellent way to keep cool. Blood flows near the surface of the bilby's big, sparsely furred ears. The air on the ears cools the blood, which cools the bilby.

WHAT'S FOR DINNER? There's not much water to be found in the desert, so this clever marsupial gets most of the water it needs from the food it eats. This includes witchetty grubs, termites (a great source of food during times of drought), spiders and insects, plus seeds, bulbs, fungi and fruit. All this food is sniffed out by its sensitive nose and often dug up using its strong front legs and claws. Bilbies often lick seeds from the ground with their long slender tongues but they also lick up sand and soil, so a bilby's faeces (poo!) can be nine-tenths sand!

TURBO TUNNELLERS Bilbies are excellent excavators and dig deep burrows where they can escape the heat of the day, coming out after dark to feed. They may have 12 or more burrows, some spiralling down nearly 2 metres, with entrances usually hidden by termite mounds or clumps of grass. This also makes them great protection against predators.

MOTHERS AND BABIES Bilbies can live up to 11 years in captivity but possibly only 2 to 3 years in the wild. They breed when weather conditions and the food supply are favourable. The young are born in an undeveloped state only a few weeks after mating but then stay in the pouch for two months. The female's pouch has eight teats but she has only one (or sometimes two) young per litter. It's just as well that the pouch faces backwards, otherwise with all the mother's digging, she would be carrying a developing bilby plus lots and lots of dirt! After a joey leaves the pouch, usually another

litter starts suckling. But the evicted joey can still suckle for a short while.

STRUGGLE FOR SURVIVAL Bilbies were once common, but when European settlers arrived so did their livestock and their farms which began to change the bilbies' habitat. Introduced foxes and cats also hunt the bilby, and rabbits compete for their food and burrows.

There used to be two species of bilby, the Greater Bilby and the Lesser Bilby. The smaller, the Lesser Bilby, was last seen alive in 1931 in South Australia. Sadly, it's now presumed to be extinct.

There are many bilby recovery projects in place to help boost the populations, which include breeding bilbies in captivity for release into fenced areas or onto predator-free islands.

RABBIT-PROOF FENCE

Rabbits were brought out on the First Fleet as a food supply and since then they have seriously damaged our landscape. The problem is hard to fix because they breed – like rabbits! Rabbit mothers can give birth to four or five young and have numerous litters each year.

In 1901, rabbits were approaching Western Australia from the east coast and South Australia, and the government decided to try to stop them. They began erecting what was then the longest fence in the world – the rabbit-proof fence. But the rabbits were too quick for the fence-builders, so a second fence was built and then a third, a total of over 3000 kilometres of fence! But even with three fences and regular inspections, nothing could keep the rabbits from getting close to the coast of Western Australia.

For more than 100 years, rabbit trappers have used poisons, gases, chemicals, traps, and even dug out holes. But nothing reduced the rabbit population. In the 1950s, scientists introduced the disease myxomatosis and the poison 1080 to reduce rabbit numbers. It wasn't until another disease, rabbit calicivirus, was released in 1996 and put together with the 1950s controls, that rabbit populations were put in check. Scientists are still looking for ways to rid Australia of rabbits.

HOW YOU CAN HELP At Easter time, we often exchange chocolate rabbits and eggs, but there is an Australian alternative. Many people give a chocolate bilby instead, with some profits from sales going towards bilby preservation. You could even get your school involved in fundraising for the bilby at Easter. For more information go to: http://www.easterbilby.com.au/save_bilby/fundraising.asp

The second Sunday in September is National Bilby Day, when we can promote awareness of the bilby and its struggle for survival. Why not join a local or national conservation group and get involved?

You can also be a responsible pet owner. Make sure your pets are desexed and aren't allowed to wander at night or get into areas where they may be a threat to native wildlife.

AMAZING BILBY FACTS

Bilbies don't lie down to sleep. They squat on their hind legs and tuck their snouts between their front legs, folding their ears down over their eyes.

Bilbies used to be a valuable food source for Aboriginal people. Bilbies are known as 'ninu', 'walpajirri' and 'dalgyte' in some of the many Aboriginal languages.

A Greater Bilby's body can grow to 55 centimetres in length, and its tail alone can be as long as 29 centimetres – that's nearly the length of a school ruler.

2 blue-ringed octopus

EIGHT-LIMBED WONDERS

In the coastal waters of Australia dwells the world's most lethal octopus species, the beautiful Blue-ringed Octopus. But the bright blue markings only appear when the creature is threatened. They are a deadly warning of this creature's powerful venom.

Blue-ringed Octopuses often live in coastal rock pools and shallow waters. They hide in crevices, under boulders, in old shells and even in empty bottles and tin cans that have been thrown away by unthinking people!

There are several species of Blue-ringed Octopus (*Hapalochlaena spp.*) found in Australian waters. All the species have the deadly blue markings, which scientists believe are used to

frighten away enemies. So how do they turn blue? They have special pigment cells in their skin called chromatophore cells that enable them to change colour rapidly. The blue, a rare colour in nature, is a warning sign to stay away! When they are not disturbed, and are going about their normal activities, their bodies are grey or brown, blending into the surrounding environment.

CATCHING PREY The main reason why the Blue-ringed Octopus has such toxic venom is to catch prey. Like all octopuses, it's a flesh eater, or carnivore, feeding on small crabs, shrimp and fish. It can jump and grab its prey with its long, sucker-covered arms. Its deadly venom is found in two salivary glands near its mouth, so it bites its victim with its parrot-like beak, piercing the body covering. The octopus then forces saliva into the victim and that's it – the prey is paralysed. When feeding on crustaceans like crabs or shrimp, the octopus uses its beak to rip off the hard parts of its prey – that way it can get to the soft juicy flesh, leaving behind only the hard outer shell (called the exoskeleton).

If they are too far away to jump and bite, blueys have been known to swim around crabs, and spray their toxic saliva into the water. The crab absorbs the saliva and is soon paralysed. Dinner is served!

A LETHAL INJECTION

In 1954 it was discovered that the Blue-ringed Octopus could actually kill humans. A man was bitten but he didn't even feel the bite. The venomous saliva in his bloodstream slowly paralysed him, and the nerves in his body stopped sending messages to the muscles that tell the body what to do. He became weak and uncoordinated and, even though he was conscious, he couldn't respond. Soon he found it hard to breathe and it wasn't long before his heart and lung muscles failed and he died. Thankfully only two people have been known to have died from a Blue-ringed Octopus bite. No antivenom has been developed.

BRAINS, BODY AND BLOOD

Blue-rings are invertebrates, which means they don't have a backbone. Just like squids, cuttlefish, nautilus and other octopuses, they are called cephalopods, a scientific word meaning 'head foot'.

The octopus's mantle and eight long arms are attached to its head. The mantle is a thick covering of skin and muscle that protects all the internal organs. It has a large brain, which is wrapped around its oesophagus (that's the tube that runs from the mouth to the stomach. You have one too!). The octopus's mouth is found where the arms join the head. It has a beak and a jagged, chainsaw-like tongue called a radula, which is perfect for sawing though hard shells.

It has two eyes on its head. The siphon, on its mantle, is the tube the octopus uses to blow out jets of water, a great way for moving quickly through the sea. Squirting water out through the siphon propels the octopus in the opposite direction. A fast squirt and the octopus moves quickly. To change direction it simply moves the siphon. An octopus will also 'walk' with its arms along the floor of the rock pools as it searches for food.

Octopuses and other cephalopods have three hearts. Two of them pump blood through each of the two gills and the other one pumps blood around the whole body. The gills get oxygen from the water, and then the water is squirted out through the siphon.

MAKING ROOM FOR THE NEXT GENERATION

In a well-chosen shelter (maybe a discarded shell, or a rock cavity), a female will lay up to 200 fertilised eggs. The small, capsule-shaped eggs are up to six millimetres long. The mother octopus carries her eggs until they are ready to hatch. This may take up to two months, and she does not eat during this time. Females reproduce only once in their life: soon after the eggs hatch, she dies. The male also dies a few weeks after he mates with the female.

The mother might squirt her eggs, to keep them clear of rubbish. If she thinks they need protection – say from humans exploring rock pools – she may squirt her toxic saliva into the water. This can be absorbed through human skin and can make the person very uncomfortable indeed. If the mother octopus is forced to move, she can use three pairs of arms to hold onto her brood and the other pair to get through the water. About four months after hatching the young octopuses are fully mature.

AMAZING OCTOPUS FACTS

Blue-rings have lost the ability to produce the dark, cloudy ink that other cephalopods squirt into the water to escape predators. Their blue rings and bites are enough!

One Blue-ringed Octopus would have enough venomous saliva to paralyse 10 adult men.

Each one of an octopus's suckers can be moved individually. The suckers are very sensitive.

The word octopus comes from the Greek 'oktopous' – 'octo' meaning eight and 'pous' meaning feet (even though we call them arms!).

Octopuses don't have tentacles. Cuttlefish and squid, also cephalopods, have eight arms and two tentacles. These are longer than the arms and used to rapidly grab prey.

3 brumby

a poetic NEW Australian

A brumby is a feral (or wild) horse that roams free in Australia, similar to the American mustang. According to Australia's great bush poet Banjo Paterson, the word 'brumby' comes from 'boorambie' meaning horse among the Aboriginal people of the Balonne, Nebine, Warrego and Bullo rivers. Banjo Paterson's poem 'The Brumby's Run' was published in *The Bulletin* in 1895, and begins like this.

> *It lies beyond the Western Pines*
> *Towards the sinking sun,*
> *And not a survey mark defines*
> *The bounds of 'Brumby's Run'.*
> *But when the dawn makes pink the sky*
> *And steals along the plain,*
> *The Brumby horses turn and fly*
> *Towards the hills again.*
> *Ah, me! Before our day is done*
> *We long with bitter pain*
> *To ride once more on Brumby's Run*
> *And yard his mob again.*

Others say the word 'brumby' is similar to the Irish word 'bromach', which means a colt, and there were many Irish settlers in Australia's colonial past. Another possibility is that the word comes from the first record of escaped or abandoned horses. These belonged to Major John Brumby, who was a sergeant in the New South Wales Corps and also bred horses. Some say that before he sailed for Van Diemen's Land (Tasmania) in 1804 to set up the Port Dalrymple settlement, he released some horses that he could not muster into the New South Wales bush. These 'wild' horses were known as Brumby's horses, later brumbies.

One famous escape was related by Banjo Paterson in his well known poem 'The Man From Snowy River', which is about a thoroughbred, a colt, that had escaped and was running with the wild bush horses.

> *There was movement at the station, for the word had passed around*
> *That the colt from old Regret had got away,*
> *And had joined the wild bush horses – he was worth a thousand pound,*
> *So all the cracks had gathered to the fray.*
> *All the tried and noted riders from the stations near and far*
> *Had mustered at the homestead overnight,*
> *For the bushmen love hard riding where the wild bush horses are,*
> *And the stock-horse snuffs the battle with delight.*

WHERE DID ALL THOSE HORSES COME FROM?

Horses (*Equus caballus*) arrived in Australia aboard the First Fleet in 1788. Along with the military, civilians, provisions and the convict cargo there was livestock that included one stallion, four mares, a filly and a colt. Twenty years later there were more than 200 horses in New South Wales. Other horses imported from England and India arrived with the following fleets. This improved the bloodline and created a very solid working horse, perfect for Australia and for farms. For the first 100 years of European settlement, horses were essential for movement around the colony and for working on large properties. And, of course, horses carried the early explorers into the bush and beyond.

But in those early years of settlement, many properties were unfenced and horses escaped. As time went on and technology became better, other horses were released into the wild as they were no longer needed.

BRUMBIES AND THE LAND

Wild horses (as well as many other wild animals) can do severe damage to the Australian landscape. They can cause erosion at river crossings; their hard hooves compact the soil and squash the natural vegetation; and they compete with native wildlife for feed. In a good year the population of these horses can increase by 20 per cent. That is why governments are investigating the best way to manage Australia's wild horse population.

THE WALERS Australians were known as excellent riders, but they really established a great reputation late in World War I. When the call for troops came, the Australian Light Horse was formed, made up of men from around the country, along with their horses. Some horses met army standards and were purchased; others were bought from graziers and breeders. These horses were called Walers, because many came from New South Wales (but Victorian and Queensland horses were also known as Walers). Just like brumbies, these horses were

well adapted to the rough Australian conditions: they were strong, fast animals with stamina and confidence. They could move over rough ground and didn't mind extreme weather. These horses were branded, numbered and sailed on a fleet of transport ships for the battlefields of the war.

At Beersheba, in Palestine, on the afternoon of 31 October 1917, the 4th and 12th regiments of the Light Horse began a mounted charge against their Turkish opponents across three kilometres of open rocky ground. Artillery and bullets whizzed by but most of the Walers successfully delivered their riders over the enemy's trenches and into the town.

More than 120,000 Australian-bred horses were sent to World War I and only one officially returned. Australia is an island, free of many diseases found in other countries, so we have strict quarantine laws. Because of this, some Walers were sold to the British Army as remounts, and the rest had to remain in the Middle East. Some cavalry men took their trusted mounts for one final ride, to return with just their saddle and bridle.

> The Przewalksi's Horse (*Equus caballus przewalskii* or *Equus ferus przewalskii*), native to Mongolia, is the last truly wild horse. Sadly it became extinct in its native home, but zoos such as Western Plains Zoo in Dubbo, New South Wales, have successfully bred Przewalski's Horse in captivity. In May 1995, zoo-bred horses were released back into the Gobi.

AMAZING BRUMBY AND OTHER HORSE FACTS

- Australia has the biggest population of feral horses in the world, some estimates say 300,000.
- A horse's height is measured in hands: 1 hand = 10.2 centimetres.
- When fully loaded with soldier and pack, a Waler could carry up to 150 kilograms. That's about 4 ½ ten-year-old boys.
- Australia supplied over 300,000 horses to the British–Indian Army in India between 1834–1937.

4 camel

THE SHIP OF THE DESERT

Camels are not native to Australia but they have played an important role in the country's development and exploration.

The first camel was brought here in 1840. Camels were stronger than horses and bullocks, and could survive for nearly three times as long as horses without water, so they became real working animals.

Camels carried explorers across the arid continent. They transported freight and supplies, including heavy building materials, to remote settlements. When the motor car arrived in the outback, thousands of domesticated camels were released into the bush, where they rapidly bred and became feral. Now Australia has the largest population of wild one-humped camels (*Camelus dromedarius*).

EXPLORING CAMELS

On 20 August 1860, the great Burke and Wills Victorian Exploring Expedition that included 27 camels embarked on an excursion to cross the continent from south to north. The expedition team had to cross deep streams so there were even air bags for the camels 'that could be lashed under their jowls, so as to keep their heads clear'. Some camels were pack animals carrying supplies; others transported the explorers; while another was an 'ambulance camel'.

In 1866, Sir Thomas Elder imported over 120 camels and their Afghan handlers from Karachi (in modern-day Pakistan). Descendants of these people are now Australians. Camel stud farms were established and operated till the early 1900s. As well as carrying explorers and their supplies, up to 30 camels could be linked together to form a camel train. These trains transported hundreds of kilograms of goods, sometimes wool bales, salt or mined ore. Camel trains also carried material required in the construction of such great projects as the Overland Telegraph Line (1870–72) between Adelaide and Darwin, or the 1750-kilometre-long Canning Stock Route (1908–10) built for transporting cattle. In 1906, Canning and eight other men, plus 22 camels, surveyed the Western Australian landscape, crossing the deserts to find suitable water supplies. Then 70 camels were used to transport material needed to build wells. Camel trains were also used in the construction of the Trans-Australian Railway (1912–17) transporting the railway sleepers and rails for the line between Port Augusta in South Australia and Kalgoorlie in Western Australia.

ABOUT CAMELS AND THE DESERT

Australian camels are found mainly in central and central west Australia and are well adapted to living in arid environments. A camel gets most of the moisture it needs from plants, sucking the moisture from leaves, almost like a vacuum cleaner sucking up dirt.

Many desert plants are thorny or prickly, but this doesn't worry the camel because its thick lips and tough mouth are designed for this. The camel's split upper lip works like fingers, helping to draw food into the mouth. Strong sun and sandstorms are common in the desert, but the camel has a double row of eyelashes for protection. It also has a clear third eyelid, called a nictitating membrane, which it can draw across the eye if needed. The camel also has hair around its ears also to keep sand out.

Camels are two-toed ungulates (an ungulate is a hoofed animal) and have broad flat feet with leathery pads. When they stand, the foot pads spread. This gives them a better grip on the ground, which is perfect for travelling and not sinking in the sand. When they kneel and rest on the hot sands they are protected by the thick calluses on their knees and chest.

Camels, like giraffes, run with both legs on one side of the body moving together. It looks a bit rocky. Maybe that is why they are called ships of the desert.

A FUEL HUMP

A camel's hump does not store water. It is mostly fat and can weigh up to 35 kilograms. This fat is saved energy. When food is scarce then energy from the hump is absorbed. There are no bones in the hump so the hump can sag if a lot of energy is used.

WATER CONSERVATION

Camels are great water conservers. They excrete mostly dry faeces as small round pellets and only a little very concentrated urine, which is a bit like syrup. They also catch any moisture running from their nostrils. It runs down a groove to the upper lip and into the mouth – mmm! Camels can also handle a large variation in body temperature, with their temperature able to get quite high before they need to sweat to cool themselves down. This means they don't sweat as much and so save water. Another clever camel trick is to face the sun, so that less of their body is exposed to the hot rays.

CAMEL HERDS

Camels live in herds ranging in size from a few animals to several hundred. During rutting season, when camels breed, a dominant male camel, the bull, leads the herd of cows and calves, and fights off any rivals. During the summer months, the herd is led by an older female. Most bulls are solitary or roam the outback in packs. About 13 months after mating, a 40-kilogram camel calf is born – that's more than 10 times the weight of a human newborn. The baby camel drinks milk from one of its mother's two teats for up to 18 months until it is weaned.

AMAZING CAMEL FACTS

🐪 Camel meat is eaten in Australia and people even drink camel milk.

🐪 Feral camels can live for up to 50 years.

🐪 Camels don't really spit – it's more like vomiting! They regurgitate their stomach contents along with lots of saliva, especially when they are threatened, annoyed or surprised.

🐪 An average camel weighs 450 kilograms. That's about the combined weight of 6 adult men.

🐪 Camels can lose up to 25 per cent of their body weight and still feel well.

🐪 A thirsty camel can drink 100 litres of water in 10 minutes.

🐪 Camels can go for 17 days without water.

🐪 Australian-bred camels are exported for breeding, eating, racing and dairy products to places that include Southeast Asia, Canada, China and the Middle East.

5 Cane Toad

A great IDEA (not)

Back in the 1930s, Queensland's sugarcane production was being badly affected by two species of cane beetle because their larvae were eating the roots of the sugarcane plant. The solution? Bring in a biological control, the Cane Toad (*Bufo marinus*), an animal that would feast on these beetles and eliminate the problem … at least that's what some scientists thought.

Nearly 100 Cane Toads were imported from Hawaii in July 1935 and from these, more than 3000 were bred and released in Queensland. But instead of being a biological control, the Cane Toad itself became a pest and is now rampaging through Australian environments, taking its toll on many native animals. So how do we get rid of it? Do we bring in another predator to control the Cane Toad? Unfortunately no solutions have yet been found. Scientists are working on creating biological controls, but are now much more cautious about the animals they introduce.

GREEDY GUTS!

Cane toads have voracious appetites. They eat almost anything that can fit into their mouths including small lizards, small marsupials, small birds, frogs, tadpoles (including their own!) and insects of all sorts. They eat dung beetles, which could mean an increase in the fly population (as dung beetles dispose of animal dung, in which flies like to breed). Cane Toads also eat large numbers of honey bees and that reduces honey production.

Some native animals have learnt to avoid eating the toxic glands of the toad, but for most animals that decide to feast on a Cane Toad, the venom oozing from the toad's glands makes them severely ill or even kills them. In other countries humans have died from eating Cane Toads. Soup boiled from Cane Toad eggs has proved fatal. Cane Toad venom can kill dogs, and precious native animals like quolls, snakes, dingoes and even crocodiles. Cane toads are toxic at every stage of their lives.

WHAT DO THEY LOOK LIKE?

This invader is not what most people call pretty! The Cane Toad is a large, solid amphibian with dry, wart-covered skin. It is yellowish-grey, olive-brown or reddish-brown on top and pale with dark spots on its belly. The average adult Cane Toad is up to 15 centimetres long but they can grow to more than 23 centimetres. The largest recorded Queensland Cane Toad was 24 centimetres long and weighed 1.3 kilograms – the heavyweight amphibian champion of Australia (even though it's a ring-in).

Adult Cane Toads have bony heads and bony ridges that run over their eyes and meet at the nose. And the obvious lump

CANE TOAD

behind the eardrum is the parotoid gland. This is where the venom comes from. This is the Cane Toad's defence against predators. The venom oozes out or can be squirted onto the victim and can be absorbed through the eyes, mouth and nose.

THE LIFE CYCLE

It's a gooey mess. Each breeding time (perhaps once or twice a year), the females lay between 8000 and 35,000 black eggs in long ropy strands. The males fertilise them as they are laid. The eggs are covered and linked together in clear jelly. Within one to three days the eggs hatch and the tadpoles emerge and then develop for the next three weeks to five months, depending on food supply and water temperature – the better the conditions, the faster they develop. At between six to 18 months the animal is sexually mature and ready to start the cycle all over again. And considering that Cane Toads can live for up to five years in the wild, that's an awful lot of eggs produced in one toadish lifetime, though less than one per cent of these eggs survive to maturity.

MISTAKEN IDENTITY

Toads, amphibians that belong to the family *Bufonidae*, are found in most parts of the world, but Australia has no native toads, although smaller Australian frogs with short legs and chunky bodies have sometimes been confused with toads. Amphibians such as the Crucifix Toad (*Notaden bennettii*) and the Desert Spadefoot Toad (*Notaden nicholsii*) are actually frogs. The Banjo Frog (*Limnodynastes interioris*) and the Giant Burrowing Frog (*Heleioporus australiacus*) are also mistaken for Cane Toads.

The tadpoles of native frogs are usually bigger than those of the Cane Toad but the toad's tadpoles group together in huge numbers, competing with the smaller number of native tadpoles for breeding areas.

In Australia, Cane Toads have extended their range from much of Queensland, into northern New South Wales and the far reaches of Kakadu. And we now know that wherever Cane Toads are breeding, numbers of native frogs (and other animals) have declined. Cane Toads compete for food, habitat, shelters, breeding sites and they can carry disease that is transmitted to native frog populations. Not good.

TOAD WARFARE

Scientists tried to use a virus from Venezuela, one of the toad's native habitats, to get rid of them. Under laboratory-controlled conditions, scientists tested the virus on the toad and also Australian frogs. Although the virus killed the Cane Toad tadpoles, it also killed the native frogs, so that wasn't the answer.

Scientists are now trying gene therapy, which means they are exploring the toad's genetic make-up. Toads, like frogs, are amphibians, which usually have two life stages – an aquatic tadpole stage and a terrestrial adult stage. If they can find a gene that stops a tadpole developing and is safe on the rest of the environment, they could release this special breed of toad into the wild. This toad would breed with wild toads, and their offspring wouldn't grow to adulthood.

Dingoes are being trained to sniff out hiding toads, just like bomb sniffer dogs. They sniff, they find, they alert humans who can get rid of the toad – but they don't touch.

Cane toads have no natural predator, so scientists have to keep working on finding a biological control. Otherwise we are going to be hopping mad for a long time to come.

BAD TIMING Had the Queensland sugarcane industry waited a few years, Australia would still be a Cane-Toad-free habitat because an insecticide was developed that controls the cane beetles. The Cane Toad had no effect on the beetles.

AMAZING CANE TOAD FACTS

- They may be repellent when alive, but Cane Toad skin has proven popular in fashion accessories, such as jewellery or bags!

- A Cane Toad can squirt its venom up to 1 metre.

- It is estimated that there are more than 200 million Cane Toads around Australia. Yikes!

- Cane toads originally come from southern North America to tropical South America.

6 cicada

nature's CHOIR

When summer comes, it's time for the Black Prince and the Forest Demon to appear alongside the first Yellow Monday. They may even argue with the Golden Knight and the Green Baron, as the Double Drummer and the Black Squeaker announce their arrivals. But never fear: the Razor Grinder and the Black Treeticker will settle any disputes. Sumptuous treats will be prepared by the Floury Baker and Chocolate Soldier and they will all join with the Green Grocer for the festival. This is not the beginning of a glorious fantasy novel. These are the names of some of Australia's most wonderful insects – cicadas.

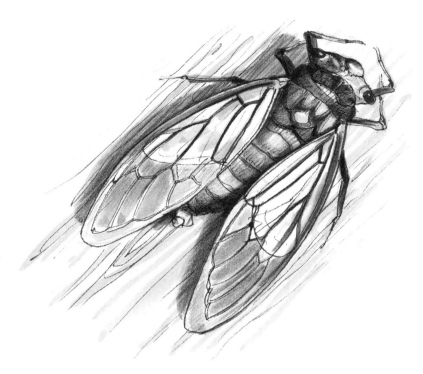

Cicadas are from the order *Hemiptera*, and most Australian cicadas come from the family *Cicadidae*.

SUMMER SONGS
Cicadas sing in summer. But it's only the males that sing – this is their mating call and each species has its own particular call. Some cicadas also have distress calls, and some have courtship calls to woo nearby females. Some songs are sung in trees in the heat of the day. Some cicadas sing at dusk, while others sing while they fly. Some cicadas, such as the Double Drummer and the Razor Grinder, gather on tree trunks and sing together so their song is intensified. This is a great protection from birds, which might otherwise feast on this delicacy as birds' ears are sensitive, so they're not likely to attack loudly calling cicadas.

A cicada's song is produced by their tymbals, ribbed membranes found on each side at the base of the abdomen. The contracting and relaxing of the muscles attached to the tymbals make them buckle or pop, like the sound when a tin can is pushed in and out. Rapid contracting and relaxing makes the song.

Some cicadas have air chambers that amplify the sound. Some can change the shape of their abdomen and others clap their wings to change sound. When a whole lot of cicadas sing together, it's very loud – too loud for many human ears! In fact, the Green Grocer is the loudest insect in the world. Its song has been measured at 120 decibels – that's as loud as a jet taking off. It's also the level when sound becomes painful to human ears. On the other hand, some smaller cicadas have such a high-pitched sound that human ears can't hear even it.

A CICADA'S LIFE

Cicadas have a hollow proboscis, a built-in sucking tube, beneath their heads to pierce plants and suck out the sap. That's cicada food. Excess liquid sap goes through their body and comes out the rear end. That's cicada rain!

Cicadas are mainly tropical insects but can be found all over Australia, from snowfields to sand dunes, mangroves to grasslands and rainforests to deserts.

Cicada life starts after mating, when the female lays several hundred eggs, depositing small batches in slits she cuts in tree twigs until all the eggs are placed. After several weeks, when eggs hatch, the nymph (the immature cicada before it becomes an adult) drops into the leaf litter and then burrows underground to look for sappy roots for food. The nymph feeds on the sap, moving to another root if the sap dries up and shedding its outer layer of skin as it grows. When it's ready to hatch into its adult form, the mature nymph burrows its way to the top, only emerging from the soil when the weather is perfect for continuing the life cycle. Then it climbs the nearest tree, attaching itself to the trunk by gripping with its legs. The outer skin splits down the back and the adult cicada emerges, shedding skin for the last time. When the body has hardened and the wings dry out, the cicada then flies away, leaving its final moult on the tree. In summer, many Aussie kids collect those brown casings.

Most Australian cicadas take six to seven years to emerge from their underground homes. That's why some years there are lots more cicadas than other years. Even eggs laid at the same time might not appear as adult cicadas in the same year. The cicada then lives for a short time, from a few days to a couple of months, depending on the species.

ART AND MEDICINE LOVE CICADAS TOO

We have evidence of cicadas from ancient times, carved on wooden boxes, on brooches worn by Roman nobility, on bronze vessels, on bone combs, on coins and on gems.

They also appear on Chinese pottery, buckles, charms and amulets. Small cicadas were carved from jade and placed on the tongues of dead people, possibly to guarantee entry into the next life. Ancient Chinese kept male cicadas in small cages to listen to their pleasant song. To the ancient Chinese, cicadas were a symbol of rebirth.

More recently, Chinese herbalists have used cicadas to 'cure' many ills and aches by boiling and eating them or drinking the broth.

AMAZING CICADA FACTS

There are about 2000 species of cicada around the world. Australia has more than 220 species, and we also have the best names for them! Other interesting names include Cherrynose or Whiskey Drinker, Hairy Cicada, Bladder Cicada and the Typewriter.

Even as recently as a few decades ago, museums advertised in newspapers for cicadas (and many other insects) as more and more study was done on the diversity of the insects. Occasionally rare specimens would be brought in. Sometimes monetary rewards were even offered. This doesn't happen any more . . . but it sure was fun! The Black Prince was highly prized by children because of this.

Cicadas vary in size from 20 millimetres to 140 millimetres.

They are sometimes incorrectly called locusts. Cicadas pierce and suck when feeding, while locusts bite and chew.

Changes in weather patterns (and global warming) have meant that some cicadas are being heard outside of their traditional summer song time.

Animals that eat cicadas include birds, wasps, ants, bats and spiders . . . and sometimes people, who pull off their wings and roast them.

7 crocodile

what a TOOTHY GRIN

All Australian crocodiles are protected... but it wasn't always so. Up until the 1970s they were hunted; the Estuarine or Saltwater Crocodile (*Crocodylus porosus*) was nearly hunted to extinction. It's frightening to think that an animal scientists believe has survived since the time of the dinosaurs can be nearly wiped out in less than 100 years. Initially the hunting was probably to protect livestock – a sheep or cow drinking at the water's edge is a big temptation for a hungry crocodile. One sheep or cow can keep it fed for weeks.

Crocodiles were also hunted for their skins, used for handbags, shoes and even jackets. Thankfully crocodile hunting was banned and now these amazing creatures are thriving again.

BEWARE AT DINNERTIME! Crocodiles wait by the edge of the water, barely moving. So when an animal arrives at the water's edge, it is unaware that its next movement could be its last. As it enters the water, suddenly the crocodile lunges. It grabs the animal with its powerful jaws. If the animal is too big to swallow completely, the crocodile drags it under the water and begins the 'death roll', rolling over and over holding its prey firmly in its jaws until it dies. It might also vigorously shake its prey with its head, breaking off body parts piece by piece. With very large prey, the crocodile usually eats some of its catch, then leaves the remains in its underwater locker, wedged under rocks or branches, for a later meal. Some adult crocs eat only once a week during summer, less during winter.

The crocodile's cone-shaped teeth are perfect for grabbing prey but not for grinding and slicing. They tear off chunks of flesh if their food is too large to swallow. And if they happen to lose a tooth, a replacement one is waiting underneath.

Crocodiles will also eat humans. You've seen the headlines – 'Woman Taken by Croc', 'Killer Croc', 'Fatal Crocodile Attack'. A person at the water's edge (or swimming) is food. If you are in crocodile territory, make sure that you don't become lunch.

Crocodiles swim by swinging their powerful tail and strong body from side to side, their legs tucked against their bodies. They can swim long distances and stay under water for up to five hours. On land they can run quickly using their short legs.

AUSTRALIA'S CROCS The Saltwater Crocodile, or 'saltie', is the world's largest living reptile. Sometimes seen in the oceans, it prefers the swamps and the estuaries where the river meets the sea. Australia is also home to the world's only freshwater crocodile, which just happens to be called the Freshwater Crocodile (*Crocodylus johnstoni*) or 'freshie'.

Like all reptiles, crocs are ectothermic. They use their

CROCODILE

environment to control their body temperature. Basking in the sun raises it. Resting in the shade with their mouths wide open, or lying in water, lowers it.

SALTIES Salties are big beasts, growing to over 6 metres long and weighing over 700 kilograms, as much as a small car. During the wet season, the female lays up to 60 eggs high on riverbanks in mounds of rotting vegetation and mud that she has scraped together. This keeps the eggs warm. For the 90 days of incubation she guards her nest. When her young begin to hatch, she gently carries them in her mouth to the water where they feed on fish, crustaceans or even small mammals. She will supervise the young until they can look after themselves. That's if they make it this far.

For many animals, crocodile eggs are a delectable feast. Other reptiles like goannas, pythons and even fellow crocs will raid an unsupervised nest. Young crocodiles are also a tempting treat, especially if they stray too far from the mother's protective reach. And every year, if the nest is not built high enough on the riverbank, flooding will destroy the incubating eggs, so usually only two or three eggs survive to maturity.

FRESHIES Freshwater Crocodiles can grow up to 3 metres long and weigh over 300 kilograms. They can be active during the daylight hours but forage mostly at night. They feed on fish, frogs, crustaceans and insects. Lizards, turtles, birds or small mammals are also fair game.

At the end of the dry season, the female lays up to 20 eggs in sandbanks, which hatch within 95 days. The mother croc does not guard the nest, so these eggs are also preyed upon by other animals, especially big lizards. When she returns at the end of the incubation period, she carries her young to the water where she remains with them for just a short while before they're left to fend for themselves.

CROCODILE TEARS 'Those are just crocodile tears,' people say, when someone is pretending to cry. So what are crocodile tears? Pretend tears, in an attempt to get some sympathy. The expression came about because people used to think that crocodiles cried as they were gobbling down their victims, as if they were pretending to be sorry for eating it!

Crocodiles do cry . . . sort of. When a crocodile has been out of the water for a long time, it produces 'tears' to lubricate, or moisten, its nictitating membrane (that's the protective third eyelid in front of the eye but behind the eyelids).

SEE YOU LATER, ALLIGATOR

Crocodiles and alligators are confused for each other. So what's the difference? The main one is the different head shapes: alligators have broad U-shaped heads while crocs have narrower V-shaped heads. The fourth tooth of a croc is visible when its mouth is shut. But don't try getting close enough to look! There are no naturally occurring alligators in Australia.

AMAZING CROCODILE FACTS

- Whether a crocodile hatchling becomes male or female depends on the temperature at which the eggs incubate.

- To break out of their egg, young crocodiles have a caruncle (a bit like a tooth) on the tip of their snout. A few days after hatching, the caruncle is lost.

- It is thought that female crocs can hear the young calling from inside the nest when they are ready to appear. Then it's excavation time.

- People are more likely to be killed by bee stings or car accidents than by hungry crocodiles.

- When the crocodile opens its mouth under water, a flap at the back of the throat stops water entering its lungs.

- Crocodile scales are like an in-built suit of armour.

8 death adder

A deadly LURE!

Common Death Adders (*Acanthophis antarcticus*) are highly venomous, nocturnal snakes with a broad triangular head and a very short, stout body that rapidly tapers to a white-tipped tail. A mature death adder only measures about 60 centimetres long.

'Lie still, wait and wriggle the tail' – that could be the death adder's motto. When it senses approaching prey, it stays very still, sometimes partly hidden in sand or leaf litter but always with its insect-like tail exposed and twitching close to its head. A curious animal moves towards the wriggling tail, then suddenly the death adder strikes, sinking its fangs into the animal's flesh, and injects small amounts of venom. The reptile then waits patiently for its latest meal to die. Sometimes, even when it can't sense a victim nearby, the death adder might wriggle its tail hoping to attract dinner. Adult death adders like to eat small mammals and birds. Young ones eat other reptiles, like lizards.

Like most snakes, death adders have strong senses of sight and smell (they flick their tongue to taste the air). And like all snakes, they cannot hear airborne sounds, such as a bird chirping or a person speaking, because they don't have external ears. But they can feel vibrations running through the ground. When it feels threatened, this secretive reptile coils and flattens its body. It only strikes as a last resort.

DEATH ADDERS AND HUMANS

Death adders can be deadly to humans, but humans are rarely bitten. At night it is easy to mistake a death adder for a lizard and, unlike many other Australian snakes, a death adder doesn't usually slither away when approached. One man who was bitten five times by a death adder made that mistake. He suffered paralysis and a heart attack, but he was given a few vials of antivenom and survived. He was very lucky!

The death adder's venom acts on the nervous system and can cause paralysis. The nerves are attacked and breathing failure can be the result. But not everyone who is bitten needs antivenom. Some people have a mild reaction to the bite, while others have no reaction at all.

MORE SNAKY SNIPPETS

Like all reptiles, snakes are ectothermic, which means they need external heat sources to warm their bodies. So when you see a snake on the footpath or a rock or the bitumen in the middle of the day, it's because the surface is hot enough to warm its body.

Lots of people think that snakes squeeze and crush other animals. This isn't true of all snakes, although pythons do squeeze to kill. These constrictors are not squeezing to break

> ## LIFESAVING HORSES
> In 1968 the CSIRO in Australia developed polyvalent, the first anti-venom that could act against the bite of most venomous Australian snakes. Lifesaving snake antivenom is produced from injecting small but increasing amounts of venom into large Percheron horses. The horses produce antibodies to fight the venom. After about a year, blood is extracted from the horses and then the plasma, filled with antibodies, is separated from the blood. This is the antivenom. When injected into a snake-bite victim, the venom is neutralised. Thank goodness for the horses.

the bones, but to suffocate their prey. Don't forget that they swallow their prey whole, and broken bones sticking out from a body would make it very hard to digest. Bulges in snakes are usually signs of recent victims.

Snakes don't have legs so they can't run, but they *can* move quickly. They tense their incredible muscles in a wave motion to move, and many have broad belly scales, which help them to grip the ground. Most sea snakes have paddle-shaped tails to help them move too.

SNAKES AND SCALES
Scales are made from keratin, just like human fingernails and hair, and are a wonderful body covering. And when their old scaly body covering is worn out, a snake sloughs off the old and reveals the new. Snakes even have a scale that covers each eye, since they have no eyelids and cannot close their eyes like we can.

And snakes aren't slimy. The scales are dry.

DEATH ADDER

SNAKES, FANGS AND VENOM Snakes aren't poisonous. Poison has to be ingested or inhaled, but some snakes are venomous. Venom is a mixture of chemicals contained in a highly developed form of saliva. Not all venoms work the same way. Some affect nerves, others muscles and others break down blood. The venom of most Australian snakes affects the nerves. When the snake bites, the victim's muscles are paralysed, it has breathing failure and other deadly problems. But not every venomous snake bite results in death.

Snake fangs can be at either the rear or front of the jaw. Front-fanged snakes, like the death adder, deliver venom through hollow syringe-like teeth. These are the most venomous snakes. Rear-fanged snakes, like the Brown Tree Snake (*Boiga irregularis*), have grooved fangs. The venom drips down the grooves into the victim. Non-venomous snakes, like pythons, don't have fangs – they have very sharp, pin-like teeth.

There has been a lot of debate about which snakes are the most venomous. The most commonly accepted measurement is not how much venom a snake has but how much venom is needed to cause death. Australia has 17 of the top 20! But don't worry – humans are more likely to be killed by cars than a snake bite.

Some snakes, like the King Brown, or Mulga (*Pseudechis australis*), bite their prey, hold on, and continuously pump venom into their victims. The Taipan, or Coastal Taipan (*Oxyuranus scutellatus*), just delivers a small jab of venom. It then lets its victim go, but the venom soon does its work. The Taipan smells its way to its prey and devours it.

SOME OTHER AUSTRALIAN SNAKES

The Fierce Snake, or Inland Taipan (*Oxyuranus microlepidotus*), is Australia's most potent land snake. One bite from this reptile and the victim is quickly defeated. No human fatalities from the bite of this plain, brown-coloured snake have been reported. The largest Australian venomous snake, the Taipan, is a close relative of the Fierce Snake. The snake with the most venom is the King Brown.

AMAZING SNAKE FACTS

- Australia has more species of venomous snakes than non-venomous species.

- Venom is extracted from a snake by a milking process quite different to milking a cow! The snake can be made to bite through a latex membrane stretched over a beaker. The venom collected is dried and sent to a laboratory. Hundreds of milkings are needed to make a single dose of antivenom.

- Most reptiles are oviparous – they lay eggs that are left to develop on their own. Some, like the death adder, are ovoviviparous – the eggs hatch internally and the young are born live. There are usually 20 young in a litter.

- Constricting snakes like pythons are usually big, but venomous snakes are usually small and fast-moving.

- The longest snake in Australia is the Amethystine, or Scrub Python (*Morelia kinghorni*). They average about 3.5 metres, but there are reports of this python growing up to 8 metres long. That's longer than two small cars end to end!

- Sea snakes breathe air just like land snakes but they can dive for up to two hours.

9 dingo

Australia's own WILD DOG

You've heard of the rabbit-proof fence (see page 12), but the longest fence in the world is the Dog Fence and it's also right here in Australia. Built to protect farm animals from dingo attacks, it winds for 5400 kilometres, from the Great Australian Bight, through New South Wales and Queensland's Bunya Mountains. Early European settlers put fences around their paddocks to protect their livestock. But as more and more sheep were attacked, larger dingo barriers were built. In 1946, after World War II, a single fence was established. Sheep were on the eastern side and dingoes on the western side. The fence is constructed from wooden and metal posts joined by strings of wire, then covered with tall wire mesh to keep the dingoes out. Some parts of the fence are over 120 years old. A government inspector riding a camel used to check the fence. Now they use a 4WD.

A NEW AUSTRALIAN

The dingo (*Canis lupus dingo*) is Australia's own wild dog, but it has only been here a few thousand years. Aborigines hunted with dingoes but fossil evidence tells us they did not bring them to Australia. The dingo originated in Asia and probably arrived with sea travellers and traders from Asia visiting northern Australia. The dingo then spread throughout Australia but not to Tasmania. When dingoes arrived, Tasmania was already separate from mainland Australia – and dingoes don't swim long distances.

ABOUT DINGOES

Dingoes live in small family groups but are often seen alone. The pack of up to 12 animals includes the dominant mating pair and possibly the offspring from the current year and the previous year. They spend their days roaming an area of the home territory, moving to another area every few days. Gradually, they cover the whole home range. Sometimes dingoes hunt in packs if large prey like a kangaroo is available. At other times they hunt alone.

Dingoes are more active at night, as is their diet of kangaroos, wallabies and even possums and wombats. But sheep and young cattle are also prey for dingoes. Early pastoralists considered dingoes a pest and this continues today. Dingoes terrorise sheep, harassing, biting and killing them without eating them. Outside our national parks, dingoes are not protected and can be hunted, killed and poisoned for attacking livestock.

JUST FOR DINGOES

The female dingo has just one litter of pups each year (domestic dogs have two). They mate from autumn to early winter (March to June). The female is

pregnant for 63 days and gives birth to between four and six pups. Two months later, the pups are weaned. The pups usually stay with the parents for up to one year, although they may be abandoned after a few months. The pups are born in a den, which can be a deserted wombat burrow, a hollow log or a cave. Because they are so closely related, domestic dogs pose a huge problem for the purity of dingoes. Through interbreeding, the dingo gene pool is being diluted with domestic dogs that have escaped into the bush. One of the few sanctuaries for pure-blood dingoes in their natural habitat is Fraser Island, off the Queensland coast, where domestic dogs are prohibited.

WHERE DO THEY FIT IN?
Scientific names tell us a lot about the relationship of one animal to another. Dingoes have had a few scientific names. They have been known as *Canis dingo* and as *Canis familiaris dingo*, because they were thought to have evolved from dogs. But now scientists believe that dingoes are a subspecies of wolf and descendants of the Pale-footed Wolf or Indian Wolf (*Canis lupus pallipes*), so they are now classified as *Canis lupus dingo*.

Scientists once classified dogs as their own separate species, *Canis familiaris*, but not any more. DNA analysis has shown that domestic dogs evolved from the Grey Wolf (*Canis lupus*). That also makes them a subspecies of wolf, and so dogs are now known as *Canis lupus familiaris*.

These scientific names are Latin. That was the language that all scholars, including scientists understood.

Domestic dogs include the tall Irish Wolfhound and the small Chihuahua and all sorts in between, but they are all related. People have bred dogs for specific characteristics, like hunting (hounds), guarding (Dalmatians), catching rats (terriers) or warming laps (Pekinese). But no matter what size or what task, they are all related back to the Grey Wolf.

EXTINCTION
Thylacines (*Thylacinus cynocephalus*) once existed on the Australian mainland, and fossils show that they were here until about 500 years after dingoes were thought to have arrived. Some people believe that the dingo contributed to the extinction of the mainland Thylacine, because dingoes competed with Thylacines for food and habitat.

Thylacines also existed in Tasmania but by the 1930s they had been hunted by people into extinction (see also chapter 28, Thylacines).

COATS OF MANY COLOURS

Over 80 per cent of pure dingoes are yellow-ginger in colour. They can also range from near black and tan to a light sand colour. Black and tan dingoes live in the forests, while the lighter sand-coloured dingoes live near sandy areas, making it easier to blend in with their surroundings when hunting.

AMAZING DINGO FACTS

- Dingoes are not only found in Australia. They also live in Thailand and other parts of Southeast Asia.

- Dingoes mark their territory by scratching at the ground and urinating.

- Domestic dogs bark. Dingoes howl. They howl to communicate, keep a group together and warn of intruders.

- Dingoes live for about 10–12 years in the wild.

- Like all members of the dog family, dingoes have a scent gland on their tail.

10 dugong

Mermaid, sea cow OR lawn-mower?

Early traditional legends describe mermaids – supernatural beings that lived in the sea – as a combination of human and fish. As time went on, they were described as having a human body and a fish's tail. But where did the mermaid legend come from?

For centuries, sailors travelled the oceans and returned to their homelands with tales of exotic creatures from distant shores, one of which was the mermaid. And no wonder. These sailors had been on the high seas for months. They may have been dehydrated, suffering from sunstroke, ill or simply lonely, when in the distance they saw creatures with smooth bodies and long flowing hair swimming through the water. Mermaids!

Of course to our eyes a dugong (*Dugong dugon*) does not look much like a mermaid. But to a lonely sailor with the sun in his eyes, these graceful aquatic human-like creatures could have captured the imagination. The long flowing hair was possibly sea grasses, which the dugong feeds on.

AN EARLY RECORD

In his book, *A Voyage to New Holland*, the explorer Captain William Dampier wrote in 1699 about a shark that his men had caught, slaughtered and ate 'very savourily'. He describes that in the mouth of one:

> . . . *we found the head and bones of a hippopotamus; the hairy lips of which were still sound and not putrefied, and the jaw was also firm, out of which we plucked a great many teeth, 2 of them 8 inches long and as big as a man's thumb, small at one end, and a little crooked . . .*

Dampier was describing a dugong. In an earlier book from 1688, *A New Voyage Around the World*, he writes of the dugong's close cousin, the manatee:

> *This creature is about the bigness of a horse, and 10 or 12 foot long. The mouth of it is much like the mouth of a cow, having great thick lips. The eyes are no bigger than a small pea; the ears are only two small holes on each side of the head. The neck is short and thick, bigger than the head. The biggest part of this creature is at the shoulders where it has two large fins, one on each side of its belly.*

In Dampier's time, there were many natural discoveries being made in yet undescribed lands like New Holland (Australia). Even though there are no hippopotamuses in Shark Bay, Western Australia, Dampier can perhaps be forgiven for thinking there were. Dugongs are more closely related to hippos and elephants than they are to marine mammals like whales and dolphins.

SIRENS OR SEA COWS? Dugongs, manatees (*Trichechus spp.*) and the extinct Steller's Sea Cow (*Hydrodamalis gigas*), are in the animal order *Sirenia*, named for the beautiful sea sirens of classical mythology – a sea nymph, part woman and part bird. Legends tell of sea nymphs bewitching sailors with their siren song, luring ships to a shattering end on rocky seabeds. Maybe the bewitching sound that entranced the lonely sailors was the whistling sound made by the large, strong male dugongs to keep their herds together.

Dugongs are large creatures, up to 3 metres long and weighing 400 kilograms. Even though they have small ears and eyes, their hearing and eyesight are excellent. Their heads are round and the mouth on their large fleshy snout faces down towards the seabed, which makes it easy for dugongs to feed on their favourite food – the young shoots of sea grasses. These grow in the muddy beds of shallow waters in northern Australia. Because they graze on sea grasses, dugongs are commonly called sea cows. Dugongs also have moustaches – heavy bristles that are excellent for helping find the sea grasses in the murky water stirred up when they tear out the whole plant, roots and all. They manoeuvre the sea grasses into their mouths with their sensitive upper lip.

SLOW AND STEADY Dugongs are slow and graceful. They steer and balance with their front flippers using them to 'walk' as they graze. They have a fluked or 'wing-shaped' tail which beats slowly up and down moving them through the water. Adult males and some elderly females have tusks. These are useful weapons for males during breeding season, when they need to fight off competing males.

Dugongs are slow breeders, giving birth under the water to only one pup about every three years. The calf often rides on the mother's back or swims nearby, never straying far. They suckle for up to 18 months from the teats close to the base of the flippers. The calf begins feeding on sea grass within a few weeks of birth and remains with the mother until it is nearly the same size as her and is fully weaned. Its place will then be taken by another pup.

AMAZING DUGONG FACTS

- Dugongs can live up to 70 years.

- These mammals are found in the tropical waters of over 40 countries in the western Pacific and Indian oceans.

- Dugongs breathe through the nostrils on top of their heads but, unlike other sea mammals, they can't hold their breath for long underwater.

- Tiger sharks are the dugong's main predators in Australian waters. They immobilise the dugong by biting off the tail.

11 echidna

PIN-CUSHION on legs

Only one native mammal is found right across Australia, from the wet and dry forests, and the snow-covered Alps to the deserts – not to mention most of the land in between. It is the Short-beaked Echidna (*Tachyglossus aculeatus*).

Spiny anteater, porcupine, hedgehog. Confused? Imagine how the poor echidna feels. It has a much larger nose than any of these creatures and it isn't a rodent, although some people do call it a porcupine, which *is* a rodent. (Rodents have sharp teeth like rats for gnawing, unlike the echidna.) Even though it eats ants, has a long nose and no teeth, it isn't an anteater. And even though it has prickly spines like a hedgehog, which make a wonderful defence mechanism, it isn't a hedgehog. And even though it is a mammal, like the hedgehog, the porcupine and the anteater, it doesn't live in any of the countries they live in. It lives only in Australia. These other animals are placental mammals, but the echidna is a monotreme (a mammal that lays eggs, just like the platypus).

A SPIKY LINE OF DEFENCE

The spikes or stiffened hairs covering the echidna are not simply for good looks. When the echidna senses a threat and it's on hard ground it can roll into a ball of spines. If it is on soft ground, within about 30 seconds it can use all four feet to burrow straight down, flick some dirt or leaves onto its back and disappear from sight. Hollow logs and rock crevices make great defensive shelters as the echidna extends its spines and wedges itself firmly inside. No animal wants a mouthful of spines!

THE LURVE TRAIN

Echidnas are solitary animals, except during breeding time. Their spines look like they might be a bit of a problem in the mating season, but echidnas seem to have it all worked out. Around July and August each year, the courting begins. At this time the waddling female echidna leaves a scent trail that the male echidnas find very attractive. It's not unusual to find four or five (or maybe ten) attentive male echidnas following a female. They form a line, biggest to smallest, head to tail processing behind the large female. These trains stay together for six weeks!

The male has worked out a clever way to mate with the female and not have his belly pierced by all those spines. Once the female echidna agrees to mate with a male, he digs a trench next to her. He waddles in alongside the female, lifts her tail with his feet and then he pushes his tail underneath while lying

on his side in his trench to mate. If there are two males they might dig trenches on either side of the female. And if there are more males then they all start digging but it is the first one in who is successful. Simple.

It is very difficult to tell the difference between a male and a female echidna. This can only be done by close observation because an echidna's sexual organs are all within the body. Male echidnas have the muscles to form a pouch just like a female but they probably can't lactate (produce milk) like a female. And male echidnas have spurs like the male platypus, although their spurs are not venomous.

ECHIDNA BREEDING

An echidna's offspring is hatched from a single, sticky, grape-sized, soft-shelled egg. The tiny hairless baby uses the tiny claws on its front legs to latch onto the hairs in the mother's pouch. Like female platypuses, echidnas do not have nipples. The youngster laps up milk that oozes from the mother's milk patches. At first the young echidna does not have any spines—they start to develop at

> ## THEY'VE GOT IT LICKED!
> An adult echidna tongue can be up to 17 centimetres long, great for poking into termite mounds and licking up termites. The echidna's scientific family name is *Tachyglossidae*, which comes from the Greek, 'tachys' meaning 'swift' and 'glossa' meaning 'tongue'.

about seven weeks. This is very uncomfortable for the mother who pushes the prickly youngster away. But she still looks after the young echidna while the spines continue to develop, placing it in a temporary burrow while she forages for ants and termites, sometimes only returning every five days to feed her young. It takes six to seven months to wean them. A mother's milk is always best for young growing mammals, especially for echidnas. The milk is filled with iron-laden proteins – that can make it look pink! So next time you see a procession of spiky balls waddling along, stay quiet and do not disturb. Baby echidnas are being made.

AMAZING ECHIDNA FACTS

- Echidnas have no teeth.
- Echidnas have very strong forelimbs and claws, great for digging and busting open termite mounds.
- The echidna is a close relative of the platypus and the Long-beaked Echidna from the New Guinea highlands.
- Echidnas have fur between their spines.

- Check out your 5c coins – there is an echidna proudly on display.
- Echidnas can live in the wild for about 50 years.
- There is a lot of dirt in the echidna's diet. It comes out in its poo.
- George Shaw published the first account of the echidna in the 1790s. He thought that it was related to the South American Ant Bear.
- Echidnas are good swimmers. Their long snouts make great snorkels.
- The common name 'echidna' comes from an early scientific name that included the word echidna, named after the Greek goddess 'Ekhidna'. She was half reptile, half woman!
- Sometimes young echidnas still in the pouch are called puggles.

12 emu

A very BIG bird

Early European settlers were amazed by the emu (*Dromaius novaehollandiae*). Governor Lachlan Macquarie was so impressed that, in 1822, he sent two emus as gifts to the Governor-General of India, the Marquis of Hastings. When Macquarie set sail from Australia back to England on the *Surry*, he wrote that voyaging with the passengers were pets that included kangaroos, swans and six emus, travelling in roomy, well-aired pens. The 'pets' were to be given as gifts to friends and patrons of Governor Macquarie back in England. Unfortunately, many of the 'pets', including one of the largest emus, died on the trip.

In 1791, John Harris, who arrived in the new colony as a surgeon, wrote that emus were swifter than the fleetest of their greyhounds. Emu eggs were described as:

> . . . a Dark Green Colour with little black specks about the Size of Pin points all over it and is Very Beautiful its about a degree larger than that of a Gooses.

ABOUT EMUS

The emu is Australia's largest bird, standing up to 2 metres high. It has wings but it can't fly. It can run really quickly – up to around 50 kilometres per hour. The legs are also very powerful fighting tools, especially if males are fighting over females.

Emus are common throughout mainland Australia but not in dense rainforest and urbanised areas. They are highly nomadic, which means they move as they need to in search of food, water and shelter.

FATHER KNOWS BEST!

An emu's courtship is a boisterous affair. There's lots of bobbing up and down, weaving and dipping, throat drumming, grunting and fluffing of feathers.

Mating begins late in December and into January. The female flattens a platform of grass into a large nest and lays her clutch of between 7 and 11 dark green eggs (although she might lay up to 20). If it is a good season and there is plenty of rain she might lay one or two more clutches with different males. Then she leaves. He has the sole responsibility for parenting.

When the eggs are laid, the male gets broody and begins incubation before the clutch is completed. She stops mating with the male but might continue to lay eggs in the nest, which are fertilised by other males. It takes 56 days of incubation before the eggs hatch and the striped chicks appear, usually in early spring. During this time the male emu sits on the eggs, rarely leaving the nest and only standing to turn the eggs every

few hours. He doesn't eat or drink at all, drawing on his fat reserves instead. While incubating the eggs, he may lose up to eight kilograms.

Once hatched, the chicks follow the male during the day and shelter beneath his feathers at night. Chicks stay with the father for up to 18 months before venturing alone. At one year old they are at full height and at two years old they are fully mature. The father emu, having missed a breeding season, will mate again.

EGGS-CELLENT MEAL

Emu eggs make a very satisfactory meal. Early settlers could create large omelettes from one emu egg. One egg can weigh up to one kilogram – that's 16 big chicken eggs! The emu egg was cracked into a bowl and allowed to separate overnight. Then the cook would skim off the oil and get cooking.

In his 1906 verse 'Santa Claus in the Bush', Banjo Paterson writes:

And there he has gathered the new-laid egg —
  'Twould feed three men or four —
And the emus came for the half-inch nails
  Right up to the settler's door.
. . .
Sit doon, sit doon, my bonny wee man,
  To the best that the hoose can do
An omelette made of the emu egg
  And a paddy-melon stew.

Emu meat was enjoyed by Aborigines. Because emus are naturally inquisitive, they were easily lured, with a twirling ball of feather and rags, to a tree. Then, from up in the tree, the emu was speared.

EMU PLUME

Emu feathers were first worn in the bands of the slouch hats by the colonial troops of the Queensland Light Horsemen in the late 1890s. In 1923, a military order stated that all Light Horsemen could officially wear the emu plume . . . as long as the military (and so the taxpayers) did not have to pay for the feathers. Today the armoured units of the Australian Army still wear the emu plume.

DOWN ON THE FARM

People have tried farming emus for Australian and international markets over the last few decades — with varying degrees of success. They are farmed for feathers, skin (leather), oil, meat and even the eggs for carving on the shells.

AMAZING EMU FACTS

- Emus are good swimmers.

- In good years, females can lay several clutches of eggs so they can quickly replenish the population after a drought.

- Emus travel in flocks of up to 20 unless they hit fences or other barriers, then the merging flocks become a very large flock.

- Emus are well adapted for wandering and feeding during the heat of the day when other animals are resting. This is because their feathers are a great protection from the sun as the black tips absorb large amounts of heat.

- Emus conserve water by condensing it in their nasal passages as they breathe out.

- A 1100-kilometre emu-proof fence was constructed from Esperance to Geraldton in Western Australia to keep emus out of the wheat farms. They love to eat the green shoots and later the ripe wheat, which is easily trampled by emus.

- The word emu comes from the Portuguese word 'ema' which means 'crane'.

- You'll find the emu on the Australian coat of arms, along with the kangaroo.

13 ghost BAT

not so GHOSTLY

If there is one animal in the animal kingdom that is grossly misunderstood then it would have to be the bat. Blind as a bat, bats in the belfry, gone batty – bats are none of these things! And the Ghost Bat (*Macroderma gigas*) is not a ghost! Let's look at some batty facts before we read about the Ghost Bat.

BLIND AS A BAT? There is no such thing. All bats have eyes and can see, although some bats have better eyesight than others. There are two types of bats. The large bats are the megabats (*Megachiroptera*) – the flying foxes and fruit bats. The smaller bats are the microbats (*Microchiroptera*). They feed on insects, although some eat small birds and mammals.

So what about that expression 'blind as a bat'? It probably came about because bats can locate their prey even on the darkest night. Microbats do this by using echolocation. They emit a high frequency sound as they fly. The sound hits the objects and bounces back to the bat, helping it locate exactly where the prey is. It's like radar used in submarines, but bats had it first.

BATS IN THE BELFRY

If someone says that you have 'bats in your belfry' then you are supposed to be crazy. They might even say you are 'batty'. This is unfair to bats, because bats are neither crazy nor unpredictable. A belfry, usually a tall building, was where bells were stored and bats often roosted there, flying out at dusk. But bats have a definite purpose. The seemingly strange flight path that a bat might take is often in response to the pulses from their echolocation.

HANGING OUT WITH GHOST BATS

In Australia we don't have any true vampire bats but we do have a member of the false vampire bat family. Only found naturally in Australia, the Ghost Bat is the largest microbat in the world and is Australia's only meat-eating (carnivorous) bat.

Ghost Bats usually roost in colonies. At night they leave their roosting sites in caves, mines or deep cracks in rocks to hunt for their next meal, which might be large insects, lizards, frogs, birds and small mammals – even other bats like the Horseshoe and Bent-wing bats.

As well as using echolocation, which we cannot hear, the Ghost Bat uses its eyes to scan the surroundings for its prey. Once located, the bat silently swoops from above, wraps its wings around the prey and then delivers a fierce bite. It then takes the prey back to the feeding site, usually an overhanging rock or a cave to eat.

GHOST BAT

Beneath the feeding site lie the remains of its meals, even body parts, in an ever-growing pile.

BABY GHOST BATS Young Ghost Bats are hairless at birth. They feed on milk from the mother's nipples, which are under her armpits. They roost in nursery colonies and also feed on prey that the mother brings back to the roost. Soon they hunt with the mother until they become independent.

CHECKING OUT OTHER BATS Not all bats are blood-sucking carnivores. Some are sap-sucking, nectar-licking, pollen lappers, like Australia's megabats, the fruit bats and flying foxes. The Grey-headed Flying Fox (*Pteropus poliocephalus*) is the largest megabat in Australia. They roost in trees in camps that can contain thousands of bats. Like all the larger bats they have big eyes, simple ears, long noses and fox-like heads. A screeching black cloud flying above at sunset could be a flying fox colony beginning their nocturnal adventures. Flying fox mothers carry their young for the first month while they are developing their fur. Then, when furred, she leaves them in the camp at night while she feeds, before returning to suckle her young.

Of Australia's megabats the funkiest-looking bat is the Eastern Tube-nosed Bat (*Nyctimene robinsoni*), especially with its large protruding nostrils and the light-green to yellow polka dots on its wings, back and ears. When it wraps its wings around its body as it roosts in the thick vegetation, these dots give it the perfect camouflage.

'I VANT TO SUCK YOUR BLOOD'

Bela Lugosi, the actor who played Count Dracula in the original 1931 movie, never said, 'I vant to suck your blood'. (Count Dracula, based on the Transylvanian warlord Vlad the Impaler, is the literary creation of Bram Stoker.) But there are bloodsucking bats!

Vampire bats don't suck the blood from their prey. Their sharp triangular front teeth make a small cut in the skin of their victim. Then they lap up the blood with their tongue. Bat saliva has an anticoagulant that stops the blood clotting so that the bat can feast until it is full. They prey on sleeping mammals, usually pigs, cows, horses and even humans. If they can't dine for a few nights, then vampire bats will probably die.

BAT'S GOOD LUCK

In Chinese the word for bats is 'fu'. It is also the written Chinese character for luck and good fortune so bats symbolise luck, long life and happiness. An image of a bat hanging upside down means that good fortune has arrived.

AMAZING BAT FACTS

- Bats are the only flying mammals.

- Most bats fold their wings on the side of their bodies when resting but flying foxes wrap themselves in their wings. If they are hot they use their wings as fans.

- Fruit bats are excellent flyers but do not land very neatly at all. They might crash into bushes or trees to stop or grab with their claws. Their noisy landings sometimes even start squabbles.

- Fruit bats have a really important role. They disperse seeds and pollinate flowers.

- Bats are found on every continent except Antarctica.

- About a quarter of all mammal species are bats.

- The world's smallest bat (and the smallest mammal) is Kitti's Hog-nosed Bat or the Bumblebee Bat (*Craseonycteris thonglongyai*). It was discovered in Thailand in 1973 and weighs less than 2 grams (that's about the weight of a 5 cent coin) with a head and body length of about 3 centimetres and a wingspan of less than 15.2 centimetres (half a school ruler).

- The smallest Australian bat is the Timor Pipistrelle (*Pipistrellus tenuis*), which normally weighs 3.5 grams.

14 goanna

a.k.a. THE lace MONITOR

One of the biggest Australian lizards is the Lace Monitor (*Varanus varius*), sometimes known as the Tree Goanna, or simply the Goanna. It is one of more than 50 species of goannas, which are also known as monitor lizards in other countries. Half of these are found in Australia.

This large arboreal (tree-living) lizard is found in the forests of eastern Australia from Cape York Peninsula through to the Flinders Ranges in South Australia. When the weather is cool and during winter, it spends its time resting in tree hollows or other sheltered areas, under fallen trees or large rocks in burrows. In the warmer weather it actively forages for food, mainly in the afternoon.

A Lace Monitor can cover large distances in its quest for food. It has a very distinctive walk, head low to the ground moving from side to side with its long forked tongue flicking in and out, sensing the air for food. Much of its food is found on the ground and includes insects, reptiles and small mammals, but it also likes possums and nestling birds.

Trees aren't only for finding food or for shelter. They are also a means of escape. When a Lace Monitor is disturbed it spirals up a tall tree trunk on the opposite side of its pursuer, grasping with its strong claws. These claws are also very useful for excavating burrows.

GOANNA FEEDING When a Lace Monitor catches its prey, it clamps its powerful jaws on the victim, which is eaten whole. For large prey, the monitor rips and tears its victim into bite-sized pieces. It is also an opportunistic feeder. This means that if it smells out carrion (dead meat) with its forked tongue then it will soon be eating the carcass. If it's a big carcass, other goannas will join the feast.

Human picnic areas are often good feeding grounds for Lace Monitors. Frightened humans often offer food, hoping for the goanna's hasty exit.

EASY INCUBATION Lace Monitors are egg-laying reptiles, but rather than laying the eggs and incubating them with their bodies or using the earth like some other reptiles, they use active termite mounds, which can be up to eight degrees warmer than the soil, to do the incubation. The female monitor digs a hole in a termite nest – this might be on the ground or in a tree. Then she usually lays between 6 and 12 eggs in the hole. The termites seal up the hole in their nest and for the next six to eight weeks the eggs are incubated at just the right temperature and humidity, and are protected from

predators. Sometimes the female monitor returns to the nest and excavates her hatchlings but usually they burrow out of the incubation chamber themselves.

For males, breeding time is a contest to see who will mate with the female. They chase and battle for breeding privileges.

MISUNDERSTOOD BY MANY
Early settlers mistakenly identified this monitor as a herbivorous, or plant-eating, iguana. And early naturalists had a rather unkind view of the Lace Monitor. In the *Prodromus of Zoology of Victoria* (1878 and 1890) the Lace Lizard (which it was called then) was described as having a 'fierce and bloodthirsty disposition' and was an 'unwelcome visitor in the poultry yards'.

GOANNA OIL
Early Australian bushmen noticed Aborigines using Lace Monitor fat to dress wounds and to

soothe aches and pains, and soon they developed their own bush remedies, extracting the same fat. Goanna oil had many medicinal properties and it was claimed to be the cure for anything that ached. It was also claimed to be excellent for oiling guns!

In Queensland, the production of goanna oil, liniments and salves was soon a highly successful business. Made from purified goanna oils with herbal additives, it was marketed under the Iguana brand (possibly a link with the belief of early settlers that the goanna was in fact an iguana) and identified as an Australian bush remedy. Not even the declaration by the Queensland Government that goannas were a protected species could stop goanna oil production. Goannas were caught in New South Wales and kept in a 'goannery' opposite the factory and goanna oil was eventually trumpeted around the world.

Thankfully no goannas are harmed in the production of today's goanna oil. The 'Goanna' range of products is still sold today but doesn't contain goanna fat. Goanna oil liniment is now made of eucalyptus oil, pine oil, mint and menthol as a remedy for aches and pains.

LIVING ON IN VERSE

Joseph Marconi, maker of 'Iguana' goanna salve, was remembered by Queensland schoolchildren in their chant:

Old Marconi's dead,
Knocked on the head.
Goannas are glad,
Children are sad.
Old Marconi's dead.

AMAZING GOANNA FACTS

- All Lace Monitors are carnivores, or meat-eaters.

- The Lace Monitor is the totem of the Bunjalung people of northern New South Wales.

- Adult male Lace Monitors are usually about 1.5 metres long, although large ones can reach 2 metres, the height of a very tall person.

- Frightened Lace Monitors can run very fast. They may even run on their hind legs.

- Australian monitor lizards occupy most parts of Australia, living in habitats as diverse as sandy deserts, arid rocky outcrops, or around rivers and lagoons.

- Gould's Goanna (or Sand Monitor) (*Varanus gouldii*) is Australia's most widespread monitor lizard.

15 great white SHARK

impressive ocean PREDATOR

Jaws, the man-eater, white death, the most feared shark in the world – it's the Great White Shark (*Carcharodon carcharias*). We might panic at the thought of them, but humans aren't normally part of their diet. Sometimes, even with their well-developed sense of smell and hearing, a shark mistakes a human surfer or swimmer for a seal, and attacks.

Great White Sharks are found in waters around most of the world, from the sub-Antarctic to the equator, inshore and offshore. They are the world's most aggressive meat-eating fish, dining on sea lions, seals, dead whales and dolphins as well as large fish, turtles and sea birds. After a large meal, the Great White Shark might not need to eat again for many weeks.

> **LONG-DISTANCE CHAMPION**
> Nicole is a tagged Great White Shark. She has swum from the coast of South Africa near Cape Town, 11,000 kilometres to the Australian coast near Exmouth Gulf in 99 days. And then she turned round and swam back!

Great White Sharks or White Sharks live for about 25 years. They weigh over 3000 kilograms (the same as about 40 adult humans) and can grow up to six metres long. They are certainly the most fearsome of sea creatures.

GREAT WHITE TEETH
Great White Sharks have a lot of teeth – an awful lot of teeth – and they are constantly being replaced. Behind each row are more rows of teeth and when a front tooth is lost, the tooth behind moves forward. Thankfully Great White Sharks don't have tooth fairies. They don't have chewing teeth either. The teeth, which can be over 5.5 centimetres long, are razor sharp, triangular and serrated, perfect for biting and tearing.

GREAT WHITE CAMOUFLAGE
Great whites are wonderfully camouflaged. They have a white belly and a grey back. From beneath, the white belly blends in with the surface of the water. From above the grey back blends in with the ocean. This is perfect for hunting prey, which usually never knows that the killer is there until it is too late. These sharks can also leap out of the water to grab their surprised victims. And when they are hunting they can reach swimming speeds of up to 40 kilometres per hour. Female great whites are usually larger than males.

GREAT WHITE SHARK

WHAT'S FOR LUNCH? About one per cent of all species of living fishes are sharks. There are over 370 species of sharks and 166 of these swim in Australia's waters. Sharks can be as small as 25 centimetres long. Deepwater dwellers can reach 12 metres. Some sharks swim along the bottom of the ocean eating clams and crabs. A Port Jackson Shark grabs its prey with its front pointed teeth and then crushes it with the back flat molar-like teeth. Others swim the open oceans and feast on large fish and sea mammals, often waiting for weak or older animals to stray behind the rest. Some sharks are filter feeders, taking in large quantities of water and eating the tiny animals that they strain from the water. Whale Sharks use spongy tissue to strain their plankton. Plankton is made up sea animals and plants that float in the water. The word plankton comes from the Greek word 'planktos', meaning 'wandering' or 'drifting'. Plankton is one of the most plentiful life forms on earth and is a vital part of the marine food chain.

HATCHED FROM A MERMAID'S PURSE Some sharks are oviparous. This means they lay eggs that hatch on the ocean floor. A mermaid's purse is an empty egg case. The Port Jackson Shark (*Heterodontus portusjacksoni*) lays spiral-shaped egg cases that she pushes into rock crevices. While in the egg case the baby feeds on the yolk but when that is finished the young shark, called a pup, escapes through a slit in one end of the egg case.

Other sharks are viviparous. These sharks are nourished inside their mother, attached to a placenta (similar to mammals) before they are born, the mother providing the nourishment. An example is the Blue Shark (*Prionace glauca*).

And other sharks, like the Great White, are ovoviviparous. These sharks hatch from eggs inside the mother but are nourished from the egg yolk sac. A pregnant female Great White Shark may carry up to 14 babies. When the pups are born they are about 1.5 metres long and weigh up to 22 kilograms. Immediately they swim away from the mother – they don't want to be her next meal! Many will not survive their first year, because they will be eaten by other ravenous sharks.

AMAZING SHARK FACTS

The Great White is the only shark that can hold its head out of the water.

Many sharks hunt during the night but the Great White Shark is active during the day.

Bottles, tin cans and even hats have been found in the stomachs of Great White Sharks.

- Sharks are cartilaginous fishes – their skeletons are made of cartilage, a firm, elastic and flexible substance, not bone.

- Shark skin is covered by tiny, sharp tooth-like structures called dermal denticles. The skin is so rough that it was once used for sandpaper.

- A shark's liver is fat and oily. It helps it float in the water.

- All sharks use gills (between five and seven of them) to extract oxygen from the water.

- Sharks can detect the weak electrical fields produced by all live animals.

- The Whale Shark (*Rhincodon typus*) is the largest shark and so the largest fish swimming the oceans (remember, real whales are mammals). The Whale Shark has been measured at 12.65 metres long and weighs 21.5 tonnes.

- The Megamouth Shark (*Megachasma pelagios*) could be described as the most unusual shark. It is not often seen and lives in the deep ocean – possibly at depths of 1000 metres. It has small hook-like teeth in its huge mouth and is a filter feeder, straining small food from the water such as plankton, shrimp and jellyfish.

16 green and golden BELL FROG

VERY patriotic!

Green and gold are true Australian colours and in 1994 a green and gold problem of Olympic-sized proportions was uncovered at an old brick pit during building preparations for the Sydney 2000 Olympic Games. This was the site planned for the Olympic tennis centre. It was also home to one of the few remaining populations of the Green and Golden Bell Frog (*Litoria aurea*). When the frogs were discovered, building work stopped. But Australia was committed to the construction. What could be done? Keep building and destroy the frog population? No way! They relocated the tennis centre and now the site is an aquatic haven for these frogs.

But how can an area that had once produced three billion bricks over 100 years become a sanctuary for an endangered animal?

SHRINKING HABITAT

It all comes back to humans. Green and Golden Bell Frogs once ranged up and down the east coast of New South Wales (especially the Southern Highlands) and into Victoria. They were so common in their natural habitat that they were the specimens students dissected in biology classes. Even in the 1960s they were common in suburban Sydney, but with the spread of urban development, more than 90 per cent of this glorious frog's natural habitat has disappeared.

But it wasn't the people sprawl alone. Scientists think that one reason the frog survived in the brick pits was that the area is free of predatory fish. Some fish love eating frog eggs and tadpoles, none more so that the introduced Mosquito fish (*Gambusia affinis*), which irresponsible pet owners have allowed to escape into the natural environment. When the tennis centre was moved, the brick pit habitat was enhanced and more frog-friendly environments were constructed in surrounding areas with freshwater ponds, boulders and suitable vegetation. Now this frog is surviving very nicely.

TADPOLES GALORE!

Green and Golden Bell Frogs lay between 3000 and 10,000 eggs each time they spawn. This egg mat floats for up to 12 hours, sometimes clinging to the plants, and then sinks. Usually two days later tadpoles appear. The tadpoles feed mainly on algae and other plant material. About two months later immature frogs 'hop' out of the water.

DID YOU KNOW . . .

This frog has a very distinctive croak, consisting of a four-part call. It sounds just like a motorbike changing gears. The male frogs call to attract the female frogs during the warmer months of the year.

The toes of the Green and Golden Bell Frog are almost fully webbed to their tips, while the fingers are unwebbed. They are skilful climbers, and able to hang onto reeds. Their colourful body patterns camouflage them well in this vegetation. Although they are part of the tree frog family, they also like the water and are strong swimmers. These frogs can be found basking in the sun in the reeds and grasses near or at the edge of streams, swamps, lagoons or even garden ponds.

Adult bell frogs are carnivorous. They feed on insects like crickets, grasshoppers and cockroaches, but will also eat any moving animal they can capture and fit into their mouth, such as small lizards. They even feed on other Green and Golden Bell Frogs. Birds, lizards, snakes and other frogs like to eat this frog too. That's the way the food chain works.

MORE AWESOME FROGS TO CROAK ABOUT

Giant Burrowing Frog (*Heleioporus australiacus*)

This frog has a great defense mechanism. It inflates its body then stands side-on, on the tips of its toes and shows the attacker how big it is, hoping that the attacker will leave it alone thinking it is too big to eat. They also ooze a creamy sticky liquid from the skin glands. Giant Burrowing Frogs are rarely in the water. They burrow straight down into the loose soil with their hind feet, corkscrew-like, until they are just below the soil surface.

Hip Pocket Frog (*Assa darlingtoni*)

This tiny frog (up to three centimetres long) has pockets on its hip. Really! When the male has fertilised the eggs (up to 18 of them) and they are ready to hatch, he places his body in the middle of the clump. The hatching tadpoles (up to five millimetres long) enter his pouches, and he carries them until the tiny frogs leave. They can even be seen growing inside the pouch! No wonder this animal is also called a Pouched or Marsupial Frog.

Turtle Frog (*Myobatrachus gouldii*)

All tadpoles swim in water, right? Wrong. This bizarre-looking frog from Western Australia lays large yolky eggs in nesting chambers up two metres deep. The soil is sandy and when it rains in their semi-arid homes, the pools of water soak into the soil or evaporate. They have short stumpy limbs to burrow through the sand. There is no aquatic tadpole stage for the turtle frog. After the egg is laid in the burrow the embryo goes through its complete development inside the egg capsule. It looks like a baby turtle without a shell.

FROG OR TOAD?

Frogs and toads are amphibians. The word 'amphibian' means 'double life'. In the early stage most young amphibians breathe through gills and live in the water.

At the adult stage they breathe with lungs, live on land and most need water to breed.

Generally frogs have smooth moist skin. They move by jumping or climbing. Generally toads have rough warty skin and they move by walking.

AMAZING FROG FACTS

A frog's tongue is attached to the front of its mouth, not at the back like our tongues.

Frogs are excellent swimmers but if they don't have access to land they can drown.

Frogs do not give warts.

Only males croak . . . to alert females to their presence for breeding.

Frogs absorb oxygen through their moist skin. This makes them very susceptible to any change in their environment.

17 koala

AT home IN THE gumtrees

The name koala probably came from an Aboriginal word meaning 'no drink'. They nearly had it right. Koalas obtain most of the moisture they require from the leaves they eat and the rain, but if they need water, they will drink water.

When it came to allocating a name for this wonderful animal the scientists got it wrong. In 1817 the koala was named *Phascolarctos cinereus*. *Cinereus* means ash-coloured or grey, the colour of koala fur, so that works, but the name *Phascolarctos* comes from the Greek words 'phaskolos' meaning 'pouch' and 'arktos' meaning 'bear'. Koalas do have the pouch but they are not bears – they are marsupials and like all marsupials their babies are very undeveloped at birth. Baby bears, on the other hand, are well developed when they are born.

European scientists gave the koala its scientific name but at that time they knew very little about marsupials, so when they looked at koalas, they thought that of all the mammals they knew, koalas were most like bears.

In 1798 John Price was the first European to record observing a koala, which the local Aboriginals called a 'cullawine'. In 1811 George Perry published his description of what he called a 'koalo', or the New Holland Sloth:

> *. . . we are at a loss to imagine for what particular scale of usefullness or happiness such an animal could by the great Author of Nature possibly be destined . . .*

Aboriginal tribes spoke many different languages with different names for the koala, but one tribe had a word close to Perry's – 'kaola'. Other names include 'koolah', 'boorabee' and 'colo'.

FASTIDIOUS FEEDERS AND GREAT SLEEPERS!

Koalas spend at least 18 hours a day sleeping and when they wake up they eat eucalyptus leaves. They may move between trees to eat, and then it is back to sleep again. Before selecting which leaves to eat, the koala moves to the tree, sniffs the trunk with its extremely sensitive nose and then decides whether the leaves are the right ones to eat. If they are the preferred leaves the koala climbs the tree using its strong limbs, hugging the tree as it climbs and gripping the branches with its non-slip paws. A koala has two 'thumbs', three 'fingers' and non-slip pads on its palms, which makes the climb easier. There are over 500 species of eucalypts but only about 50 of these are on the koala's menu. That's why they need such a good nose to sniff out the different trees. An adult koala can eat 500 grams to

KOALA

one kilogram of leaves every day, but there is not much energy in all those leaves, so they might also get a few extra nutrients from eating some soil. To conserve energy, a koala sleeps.

THE FIRST YEAR
Thirty-two days after mating (a rough and speedy act), a koala baby is born. It looks like a pink jelly bean. It makes its way from the birth canal to the mother's backward facing pouch using its partly developed front legs

> **STRESSED OUT?**
> Chlamydia is a disease that impacts on some koala populations. It is sexually transmitted and can cause a koala to become sterile, blind or suffer other illnesses. It might be stress related, occurring when koalas are attacked, are overcrowded or lose their habitat.

and claws. Then it finds a nipple and grabs on. For about seven months a joey spends all its time in the mother's pouch. For the first 13 weeks it is attached to the swollen nipple – sleeping, growing and drinking milk. At 22 weeks the eyes are open and the head pops out of the pouch. Now it is time to learn about its very special eucalyptus diet. But the joey doesn't start eating leaves just yet. Something important enters the joey's diet first – pap. This runny liquid is licked from its mother's anus. This doesn't sound very hygienic to us, but for koalas it is essential. The pap provides the bacteria that a koala needs to safely eat eucalyptus leaves – because eucalyptus leaves are toxic.

Two weeks later, from the safety of the pouch, the joey takes its first nibble of a eucalyptus leaf followed soon after by short trips out of the pouch. By about 36 weeks the joey is too big for the pouch. Instead it rides high on its mother's back eating leaves but sometimes sneaking some milk. The joey will make short trips away from Mum, but never more than a metre. Finally, at about 12 months, the joey is weaned and if another joey arrives, it is on its own. The cycle begins again.

AMAZING KOALA FACTS

🐨 Koalas were once hunted for their fur. It wasn't until the late 1920s that the fur trade ceased and legislation was introduced to protect it because of the severe decline in koala populations.

🐨 Male koalas have a scent gland on their chest which they rub on the trees to mark their territory.

🐨 Males bellow to warn off other males – a call that has been described as a cross between a donkey and a pig!

🐨 Female koalas have two nipples in their backward-opening pouch and occasionally twins are born.

🐨 Bush fires, droughts, domestic dogs, fast cars, disease and habitat destruction are all threats to the survival of this national treasure.

🐨 PS: Koalas are not bears!

18 koel

THE LAZY parent

Not all Australian birds spend their whole lives in one place. Some birds, like the Common Koel (*Eudynamys scolopacea*), are winged travellers. This bird flies to Australia and lives in the tall forests, woodlands and the suburbs of northern and eastern Australia. Koels arrive here for breeding during the spring and summer months and then fly back to their northern winter homes in New Guinea and Indonesia around March. Some koels may spend their lives in Australia.

The male koel is easily recognised by his glossy black feathers, with blue and green tinges, and his stunning red eyes – if he can be seen. Even though he is often heard, he usually remains hidden in the tree canopy. The smaller secretive female koel is not as glamorous as the male. She still has some glossy black feathers and red eyes, but also brown and white spotted feathers on her back and wings.

Often koels are perched alone in trees, or in small groups – especially if the female is being wooed by noisy male koel suitors. These suitors sometimes chase each other in flight, to demonstrate their mating suitability. At feeding times koel groups can be quite large. Occasionally they might be in mixed flocks with other birds.

From the tree canopy, where they spend most of their time, adult koels eat native and introduced fruits including figs and berries, as well as the occasional insect.

WHAT'S THAT NOISE?

Males are often the first to arrive at the breeding grounds where they begin their singing. Have you heard that repetitive 'cooee' from the male koel early in the morning, late in the afternoon or sometimes all through the night? Koels make some other noises including chuckles and gurgles, but the most recognised call, at least by humans, is that whistling crescendo-ing 'coo-ee' (or ko-el) that goes on and on and on! It's persistent and loud and annoys many people because it keeps them awake at night.

For early European settlers, birds like the koel were great weather predictors. When they heard the call of the koel, to them this call signalled that a storm was brewing and rain was coming. That's why they were also known as the Rainbird or the Cooee Bird.

NESTING

Koels are members of the cuckoo family and like many cuckoos parenting is a job that they totally avoid. Koels are parasites, at least for egg hatching. They do not build a nest. Instead, after mating, the female koel lays her egg

in the nest of another bird that has just laid her own (often similar-looking) eggs. The male koel provides a distraction and the female host leaves the nest to chase it away. This gives the female koel the chance to secretly deposit her egg. Honeyeaters, orioles and magpie-larks make wonderful koel host parents!

Unfortunately, the foster mother's eggs are unlikely to survive. Two or three days after hatching, the young koel evicts all other eggs and any other hatchlings. This youngster does not want any competitors. That way the foster parents, which

> ## COOEE MATE!
> So recognised is the cooee that it has become a sign of being Australian. Men used to cooee to each other in the bush, and as a welcome or greeting. Possibly the most famous cooee greetings were in 1915. During World War I, a small band of men began a march from Gilgandra to Sydney to enlist and in every town they came to they called cooee to announce their arrival. By the end of the march six weeks later more than 260 men had left their homes and were ready to volunteer to fight in the war to end all wars. This march became known as the great 'Cooee Recruitment March'. Soon many recruitment posters were emblazoned with the call 'cooee'.

look nothing like the koel chick, can devote all their time to feeding the ravenous hatchling. The koel chick will eat any food that arrives, even though it may not be part of a koel's normal diet. If there happens to be another hatchling in the nest, it will probably starve because the koel chick is more aggressive with its feeding.

Even when the hatchling has left the nest, the foster parents' job is not complete. The young koel perches on branches nearby and continues to cheep, incessantly demanding food, which the host parents continue to supply. Over the next four to six weeks the young koel doubles in size. Eventually it realises that it is not related to the host parent and leaves, following other koels to the northern wintering grounds. Next spring it will return, this time to breed.

AMAZING KOEL FACTS

- Koels are migratory cuckoos.

- Along with blowflies buzzing, cicadas chorusing and frogs croaking, the call of the koel is a sign that spring has sprung.

- In many parts of Australia the arrival of koels means the rainy season is near.

- The call of the female koel is a repetitive 'wook-wook-wook'.

- They are between 39 to 46 centimetres long.

- Other koel names include the Black Cuckoo, Cooee Bird and Rainbird. John Gould in his famous book, *Birds of Australia*, called it the Flinders Cuckoo.

19 kookaburra

THE laughing LARRIKIN

*Kookaburra sits in the old gum tree
Merry merry king of the bush is he,
Laugh, kookaburra! Laugh, kookaburra!
Gay your life must be.*

This is a round many Australian children sing in their early school years, but is the kookaburra really laughing? And what is the bird laughing about?

KOOKABURRA CALLING

Kookaburras have a range of calls but the one most people recognise is the call used to identify that an area belongs to them. One kookaburra (usually the dominant male) will begin calling and then the rest of the family joins in, raising the intensity.

And what are they doing? The kookaburras are identifying the boundaries of their territories. Soon neighbouring families begin registering their calls. A careful listener can even identify the boundaries of each family. Another call, a 'kooaa' is used when they are hanging out together.

THE FAMILY LIFE Unusually, kookaburras don't flee the nest like most birds. Kookaburras can live for 20 years and young ones stay with the adults for four or five years. They help the family look after the following broods; incubating eggs, protecting offspring, teaching the kookaburra calls and finding up to 60 per cent of the food for the new hatchlings.

There is a very strong social order in the kookaburra world. The parents, the dominant male and female, stay together for life and they are the only ones in that family that breed. This occurs in the spring and summer months from September to January.

The eggs (usually two but up to four) are laid over a few days in an unlined hollow of a tree, branch or a termite mound. As soon as the first egg is laid, incubation begins – so the eggs hatch at different times. They incubate for 24 days and take 36 days to fledge (be able to fly). For the next 8 to 13 weeks they are fed by the parents or older siblings until they have developed their own hunting skills.

INSTANT DEATH It's no laughing matter – a kookaburra nest can be a risky place for a chick. Like most birds, kookaburras are born as blind, tiny, flightless, pink blobs. But in some kookaburra nests the staggered hatching of the eggs poses a deadly problem for the later arrivals. Even though they are nearly helpless, that doesn't stop the chicks flopping around the nest attempting to bite with their beaks. If these blind chicks happen to latch onto another hatchling, especially around the neck, then death is the likely outcome. And the firstborn is often the victor.

KOOKABURRA

A VARIED DIET Kookaburras are often seen perching on branches, waiting to pounce on the next meal passing by. They have a reputation as snake killers, but snakes are a very small part of their diet. They also feed on frogs, small mammals, birds and reptiles. Insects and other invertebrates (animals that don't have a backbone) are also a major source of food, especially during insect plagues. If necessary, kookaburras kill their prey, by smashing it against a tree branch or on the ground before swallowing it.

KOOKABURRA IMAGES Probably Australia's most recognised bird image is the Laughing Kookaburra (*Dacelo novaeguineae*), perched on a branch with its head thrown back, beak open, emitting its acclaimed koo-hoo-hoo-hoo-haa-haa-haa-haa. The kookaburra has been used many times as a symbol of Australia (see facts, pages 95–96).

NAME CALLING Before it was known as the Laughing Kookaburra, early European settlers called this bird other less flattering names. They noticed that at daybreak it cackled loudly, so it was called Bushman's Clock or Breakfast Bird. The settlers were also unimpressed by the strange calls. They thought that the kookaburras were laughing and mocking their attempts at farming so another name also became common – the Laughing Jackass. This name has appeared in many poems, stories and reports from the 1800s.

In 1862, W.A. Cawthorne wrote *Who Killed Cockatoo?* This is probably the first picture book published in Australia. Here's a sample:

> *Then flying very fast,*
> *Came Laughing Jackass.*
> *Hoo hoo hoo! Ha ha ha!*
> *While he gobbled a snail*
> *And wagged his big tail,*
> *Hoo hoo hoo! Ha ha ha!*

And this verse appeared in the 1871 *Young Australian's Alphabet*:

> *J is for jackass*
> *A very strange bird*
> *Whose Laugh in the forest*
> *Is very absurd.*

Australian poets also acclaimed the Laughing Jackass. Banjo Paterson wrote a poem called 'Why the Jackass Laughs' in his book *The Animals Noah Forgot*. In his poem 'Morning in the Bush', Henry Kendall uses a very different word for the kookaburra, a word he heard from the Wiradhuri Aboriginal language:

> *And wild goburras laughed aloud*
> *Their merry morning songs . . .*

Other Aboriginal tribes had different names, such as 'cocopura', 'cucuburra' and 'kukuburra' for the bird we call the kookaburra.

FAMOUS KOOKAS

Many companies have used a kookaburra logo.

The Widows Guild New South Wales have used a kookaburra; Olly the kookaburra was a mascot for 2000 Olympics, and the kookaburra is even on the crest of some councils. And of course May Gibbs included a kookaburra in her *Complete Adventures of Snugglepot and Cuddlepie*.

AMAZING KOOKABURRA FACTS

- The Laughing Kookaburra, naturally occurring in eastern Australia, was introduced to Western Australia in 1897 and also to Tasmania.

- Australia's first miniature postage stamp sheet was issued in 1928 and featured a kookaburra on a gum tree.

- Kookaburras are the world's largest kingfisher, all of which have large heads, long, sharp, pointed bills, short legs and stubby tails.

- Old enamel cooking stoves called 'Early Kooka' had a picture of a kookaburra with a worm in its beak on the oven door.

The logo and opening images on the *Fox Movietone News – Australian Edition* was a kookaburra, accompanied by the cackling call. The weekly newsreel began in the 1931 and lasted for forty years. Newsreels were shown at the theatres when people went to see the movies – before news on television!

The Kookaburra company, established in Australia in 1890, are renowned makers of fine cricket balls and other cricket and hockey equipment, all stamped with their brand logo of a kookaburra. The Kookaburra cricket ball is used in all one-day international cricket and 85 per cent of Test cricket matches.

In 1919–21, a square kookaburra coin was made, although it was never circulated.

Australia's men's hockey team is known as the Kookaburras.

The kookaburra is the bird emblem of New South Wales.

20 Lake Eacham rainbowfish

magnificent LITTLE FISH

This small silvery-blue fish with orange and black stripes is Australia's most well known rainbowfish.

EXTINCTION IS FOREVER

In 1982, at Lake Eacham in Queensland, naturalists came across a freshwater fish that was similar to other fish found in surrounding lakes but not as brightly coloured as other members of the rainbowfish family. The differences were great enough for it to be named a new species – the Lake Eacham Rainbowfish (*Melanotaenia eachamensis*). At the time naturalists thought that Lake Eacham was the only place where this fish was found.

Sadly, it was not a long time from description to extinction. In a survey of the lake less than five years later, naturalists discovered that this rainbowfish had completely disappeared, presumed extinct in the wild . . . at least that was what the biologists thought.

WHEN BAD TURNS GOOD

For generations, Australians have been keeping fish in aquariums and Australia's rainbowfish, including the Lake Eacham species, have always been popular pets. Lake Eacham is within the Lake Eacham National Park and so the animals were protected. During the 1970s, Lake Eacham Rainbowfish were illegally collected from the lake and kept in household aquariums. When it was found that the fish was extinct in the wild, hobbyists, who had been successfully breeding and trading the fish, bred more and more. In 1989 enough had been collected to reintroduce this rainbowfish back into the lake. Now, that's a positive outcome for an illegal activity!

Unfortunately, restocking the lake with the thousands of captive bred rainbowfish was not successful. Its predators were still swimming in the lake and were probably thrilled to have a whole new supply of the Lake Eacham Rainbowfish to eat. Within six months the captive-bred fish had disappeared.

MORE LAKE EACHAMS FOUND!

Naturalists and scientists are always checking things. When they were checking the lakes and streams near Lake Eacham on a later survey, they found that there were more rainbowfish. Some were genetically the same as the Lake Eacham species (although some of them were coloured a little differently), some were of another species, the Eastern Rainbowfish (*Melanotaenia splendida splendida*), and some were hybrids, a mixture of the two. It was good news, but the mystery remained – how did the same species exist in two separate locations of unconnected waters?

HOW DID IT GET THERE?

Naturalists aren't really sure. Lake Eacham is located in Queensland's Atherton

LAKE EACHAM RAINBOWFISH

Tablelands. It is a small volcanic lake and the water that fills this lake comes not from rivers and streams that flow into the lake, but rather from the surrounding catchment area. Somehow, at some point, this rainbowfish appeared in the lake.

SOLVING THE MYSTERY The disappearance of this rainbowfish would still be a mystery if it weren't for the naturalists' surveys. When they surveyed the lake and found the rainbowfish missing, they discovered that four other Australian fish had appeared and were also swimming in the lake. These four larger fish with exotic common names, the Mouth Almighty (*Glossamia aprion*), Barred Grunter (*Amniataba percoides*), Sevenspot Archerfish (*Toxotes chatareus*) and the Bony Bream (*Nematalosa erebi*) were native to other waters in Australia. Their arrival is no mystery: they were introduced to the lake after the 1982 survey when the rainbowfish was first discovered. As a result they competed with the rainbowfish for the food supplied by the lake as well as becoming predators of the rainbowfish and their eggs, wiping them out of this lake in just a few years.

Even though this rainbowfish, or its very close relatives have been found in other lakes, it is not possible to restock Lake Eacham with its native fish until the exotic predators have been completely removed.

LAKE EACHAM LIVING

Like other similar species of rainbowfish, the Lake Eacham species feeds on algae, aquatic invertebrates and insects. The males grow to about 6.5 centimetres, with the females slightly smaller. Over several days, a pregnant female deposits her clear eggs. They are stuck to the aquatic plants by thin, sticky strings. Between seven and ten days later the eggs hatch and the young begin their life in the water.

WHAT A BLAST!

A maar is a volcanic crater. When molten hot magma and groundwater meet, steam is produced. It explodes through the surface and a crater is eventually formed. Lake Eacham was created this way.

The lake is 65 metres deep and is fed by underground springs, so it has a fairly constant water level, unaffected by drought.

AMAZING RAINBOW FISH FACTS

- The Lake Eacham Rainbowfish is now listed as vulnerable rather than extinct in the wild because of populations found in nearby rivers and streams.

- Males are slightly more colourful than the females.

- Rainbowfish are unique to Australia, New Guinea and nearby islands.

- The first rainbowfish was described in the 1800s.

- Blue-eyes, the tiny fish of the genus Pseudomugil, are closely related to rainbowfish. They are found only in the waters of Australia and New Guinea.

- One of the smallest rainbowfish is the Threadfin Rainbowfish (*Iriatherina werneri*) from New Guinea and Northern Australia. It averages about three centimetres in length. This fish has a fan-shaped dorsal fin while the second is very long and thin. The anal fin is also long and flowing.

21 little penguin

flying TORPEDOES

With their streamlined shape and their ability to 'fly' through the water, Little Penguins (*Eudyptula minor*) are nature's mini torpedoes. Like all penguins, Little Penguins cannot fly, but their small flippers, which are modified wings, propel them through the water at up to 8 kilometres per hour. Their short legs provide direction through water, and on land give the penguin its distinctive waddle.

CLEVER CAMOUFLAGE

The Little Penguin's feathers provide a camouflage called countershading. From the water below, the penguin's white belly feathers blend in with the light from above. The dark blue feathers on its back make it blend in with the surface colour of the water.

Penguin feathers are short, stiff and much denser than those of flying birds. Beneath them are the down feathers that trap air and insulate the bird against the cold. An added protection is the oily liquid the penguin produces, which it rubs all over its feathers to help repel the water. Preening feathers is also hugely important – feathers need to be clean to work properly.

PENGUINS ON PARADE

At sunset, a faint 'yap-yap' can be heard out to sea. Soon it is joined by another and then another, until a chorus of yappers announce their arrival, gathering beyond the waves. Now the world-famous penguin parade begins.

In the dark the Little Penguins return to their colonies on land. They arrive on shore and waddle to their burrows over sand and rocks. This is when they are most vulnerable. Their sleek bodies allow them exquisite manoeuvrability in water but on land they have to dodge feral animals: cats, dogs and foxes. Once safely in their nests they shelter for the night, resting or feeding their young.

At sunrise the parade resumes. They emerge from their burrows, head for the paths and scurry awkwardly back to the water. Some penguins come ashore every night; others remain at sea, sometimes for months.

A Little Penguin's nest can be a bowl shape at the end of a long tunnel. Other nests are beneath tussocks of grass, or under rocks and rock ledges. There may even be connecting tunnels. Little Penguins and their nests were once a common sight along the coastlines of south-east and south-west Australia. But now feral animals and the demand for waterfront housing have scattered them. Today penguins are still found in select coastal habitats of south-eastern and south-western Australia, on Tasmania and coastal islands, and also in New Zealand. They dine mainly on small school fish, squid and krill that they gather in short shallow dives.

PENGUINS ASHORE During the breeding season males return to shore ahead of females. Their task is to renovate old burrows, or dig new ones. Noisy male courtship greets arriving females.

After penguins mate, two eggs are laid. Sometimes only one egg survives. The penguins take turns incubating the eggs for up to 35 days. After the eggs hatch, parents work in shifts to care for the hatchlings. For the first two weeks one parent remains with the hatchlings, while the other gathers food and returns to regurgitate it for the young penguins. The next day they swap roles. For the next five weeks both parents find food because the young penguins are ravenous eaters. From five weeks of age, the young penguins wait outside the burrow for the returning parents and then at about eight weeks venture into the water. During their first year, when they spend most of their time at sea, young penguins may travel up to 1000 kilometres to find a suitable colony and nesting site. If the parents have bred early in the season they may breed again.

Little Penguins moult annually. This shedding of feathers takes up to 20 days and because they can't go into the water while moulting they don't eat. So, before they moult, they build up extra body fat, sometimes doubling their weight. During moulting the penguins remain on land living off their body supplies. This is a dangerous time – if they are forced into the water they may die, because the new feathers are not waterproof.

PENGUIN JUMPERS

Little Penguins are not always formally attired in their deep dark blue and white waterproof suits. Some might be seen in black and gold or red and white, or any colour of the rainbow. Some have coloured neckbands and waistbands and stripes in all directions. These are the ones that have been rescued from oil spills.

When a penguin gets caught in an oil spill, it tries to swim to shore to preen its feathers to remove the oil. As it is preening it swallows some of the poisonous liquid. The detergents used by rescuers to clean the oil can also be deadly to penguins. So rescuers dress the penguins in these fashionable woollen jumpers. It absorbs some of the oil, stops them preening and also keeps them warm while they wait for their turn in the bathtub. They are surely the best dressed birds on parade!

AMAZING PENGUIN FACTS

🐧 Little Penguins are also known as Fairy Penguins or Blue Penguins.

🐧 There are 17 species of penguin in the Southern Hemisphere but Little Penguins are the only penguins resident in Australia.

🐧 The scientific name for the Little Penguin, *Eudyptula minor*, comes from the Greek 'eudyptula', meaning 'good little diver'.

🐧 Penguin chicks have a chipping or egg 'tooth' they use to hatch out of their egg. It's not a real tooth but a sharp bump on the top of the bill.

🐧 The Emperor Penguin (*Aptenodytes forsteri*) is the largest penguin in the world, weighing about 40 kilograms and standing just over 1 metre tall (about three school rulers end-to-end).

🐧 A penguin's beak has a hook on the end and sharp cutting edges to grasp food, which they swallow whole on the water's surface.

22 mountain pygmy-possum

a mini MARSUPIAL

Humans can be such a problem for native wildlife. We build roads over the wildlife trails so we can zoom down to the ski fields, not worrying about the native casualties that get squashed along the way. But humans can also be the solution . . . as we have been with the endangered Mountain Pygmy-possum (*Burramys parvus*). There are possibly only a few thousand of these *amazing* animals left in the wild. They live in the snow-covered alpine and subalpine regions of New South Wales and Victoria, above 1400 metres. They are the only Australian mammals found nowhere else but here.

LOVE TUNNELS For most of the year male and female possums live separate lives scurrying among rock crevices, boulder fields and alpine shrubs. Adult females live in the best locations on the rocky slopes. Males live further down the hill. Come breeding time, these males make the hazardous trek across the roadways, attempting to avoid all the human-made obstacles in their way. For some of the possums this is the end of their migratory journey. Only when they have made it to the other side of the roadway can they consider scurrying up the hills to find the waiting females. It's a wonder they have any energy to mate at all!

When the ski runs are covered in snow they are compacted by all the skiing – not good for possum movement. Luckily humans have realised the problem. They haven't diverted the roadways or ski runs but they have done the next best thing. They have constructed rocky tunnels – 'love tunnels' – under the roadway and under some of the ski runs, so love-struck male possums can migrate between residences with relative safety.

Once breeding season is over and the young are weaned, it is back down the hill for the males, battling with mechanical contraptions again, to the safety of their home range.

TAILS AND TEETH, NESTING AND FOOD

In ski lodges, a Mountain Pygmy-possum is often mistaken for a mouse. You don't want to kill a native animal, so how do you tell the difference? The possum's second and third toes are joined, unlike a mouse's, but the most obvious difference is its curly tail. This tail has an essential task. It is prehensile, which means it can grasp things, like the thin-stemmed grasses that the possum uses for nest building. The possum's sharp premolar teeth on the side of the mouth are large and grooved, just right for cutting these grasses. They are also great for eating hard-shelled seeds and insects.

MOUNTAIN PYGMY-POSSUM

More than half of the possum's diet is invertebrates such as beetles and caterpillars. It especially likes the energy-rich Bogong Moth (*Agrotis infusa*), which is the main part of its diet during spring and summer. It also eats fruits and seeds, especially from the Mountain Plum Pine. This plant is very sensitive to fire and can take decades to recover from a bushfire. In 2003 a large bushfire in Kosciuszko National Park caused problems for the possum's diet and also affected much of the plant cover that it uses to hide from predators.

FAT POSSUMS Being a fat Mountain Pygmy-possum is very important. A fat possum has lots of stored energy, which will sustain them through the winter food shortage. In springtime, after hibernation, the possum might weigh about 40 grams but by wintertime they might weigh more than 80 grams. This possum is also a great hoarder. During winter it uses not only the energy stored in its body, but it can also eat from its hidden store of seeds and nuts. It is the only known Australian marsupial to do this.

BALLS OF FUR During winter the possum hibernates, going into a state of inactivity or torpor. It slows down its breathing and heartbeat, and reduces its body temperature to 2 degrees Celsius. That's how it saves energy. This requires a good cover of insulating snow, at least 1 metre. The possum is torpid for up to 20 days when it is very cold. Then it wakes for less than a day, maybe eating from its storage supplies, before once again resuming its 'sleep'. This cycle goes on for up to seven months. The Mountain Pygmy-possum is the only marsupial that hibernates.

THE POSSUM'S FAVOURITE FOOD

The Bogong Moth is a sweet morsel for the possum. In spring, this small brown moth migrates annually from its breeding grounds on the western slopes and plains and spends summer dormant (or resting) among rocks and boulders of the alpine peaks. Most moths are found on the mountain peaks and this is where the possums must travel to get their food.

AMAZING PYGMY-POSSUM FACTS

- The Mountain Pygmy-possum was thought to be extinct until one was discovered in a ski chalet at Victoria's Mount Hotham in 1966.

- Its tail is about 14 centimetres long, longer than its head and body length of 12 centimetres.

- Females have one litter of four young each year. The young spend 30 days in the pouch and 35 days in the nest before weaning.

- Females are known to have lived for 12 years, the longest age for any small terrestrial mammal.

- Global warming is increasingly a threat. Less snow means less habitat (and many other consequences).

23 platypus

a duck DESIGNED BY a COMMITTEE

In 1798, George Shaw, a scientist at the British Museum, received a parcel containing a strange creature from the newly established colony of New Holland (Australia). It was not unusual for him to receive new animal specimens. Much of the world was unknown to Europeans, and exciting new species were being discovered everywhere, but this animal was quite extraordinary and perhaps a bit suspicious. It had the beak of a duck attached to the body of a four-legged creature covered with fur. Could this be a hoax?

Scientists had been fooled before so they had to be cautious. They had received specimens of mermaids from Asia which had turned out to be the heads and bodies of monkeys with tails of fish, expertly stitched together by Chinese taxidermists. (A taxidermist is someone who stuffs animal skins and mounts them to look as real as possible.)

But once George Shaw and other scientists closely examined their new specimen they agreed it was real. The British Museum still has the original pelt with Shaw's scissor marks where he tried to remove what he thought was the stitched-on bill. Even in his published description, he wondered if his eyes were playing tricks on him.

> *Of all the Mammalia yet known it seems the most extraordinary in its conformation; exhibiting the perfect resemblance of the beak of a Duck engrafted on the head of a quadruped.*

WHAT'S IN A NAME?

Scientists had trouble naming this exciting new discovery. It had flat, webbed feet and was duck-like, so, at first, Shaw gave it the scientific name *Platypus anatinus* ('platypus' means flat-footed, and 'anatinus' means duck-like). But a beetle had already been named *Platypus*. So Shaw's new specimen with its duck-like snout and webbed feet was named *Ornithorhynchus anatinus* ('bird-snout' and 'duck-like'), but its common name stayed as the platypus.

Of course, Australian Aborigines had known of this creature for thousands of years with names like 'mallangong' and 'tambreet'. Early British settlers called it after animals from home: 'the water mole', 'duckbill' and 'duckmole'.

A MAMMAL THAT LAYS EGGS!

There were more amazing things to be discovered about the platypus. It took almost another hundred years before scientist William Caldwell confirmed that the platypus actually lays eggs, just like another unique Australian animal, the echidna. These animals were given their own 'order' (or group) called monotremes, meaning 'one hole'. This is because of another unique feature: unlike

other mammals, they have a single body opening used for both reproduction and getting rid of body wastes.

The female platypus lays two or three leathery, soft-shelled eggs (like reptile eggs) in her nesting burrow, which is up to 10 metres long. The eggs are the size of grapes and often stick together. The mother incubates the eggs by holding them against the lower part of her stomach with her curled up tail. Ten days later the eggs hatch and the young start to suckle like all mammals – though not *exactly* like them. The female platypus doesn't have nipples. She has patches on her belly where the rich milk oozes out for her young to lick. After three or four months the babies are weaned and emerge from the burrow.

Platypuses are very secretive and very difficult to breed

in captivity. Corrie, the first captive-born platypus, made its appearance at Healesville Sanctuary in Victoria in February 1944. It then took another 55 years for another successful birth – twins – again at Healesville in 1999, then another in 2001. The first platypus births at Taronga Zoo in Sydney were twins in 2003. Another set of twins (2005) and a single young (2006) have also been born there.

AN ELECTRIFYING DISCOVERY

The platypus is an excellent swimmer. It spends much of its time in water and keeps its eyes, ears and nostrils tightly shut when swimming. So how does it find its food? This puzzled scientists for years. Then in 1985 scientists tried an experiment where they imitated the platypus's prey (or food) using shrimp tails attached to both live and dead batteries. The platypus went to the live ones. Scientists found that the platypus has special sensory organs in its bill that can pick up tiny amounts of electrical energy made by the muscles of its prey. The platypus sweeps its bill from side to side and when it 'feels' the energy of its prey, the platypus hones in, grabs it in its bill and stores the food in special pouches in its cheeks. Later it grinds the food with the horny grinding plates and ridges on its jaws.

OUCH!

Anyone who studies the platypus knows to be very careful when picking up the male – he has a spiky defence; a spur connected to a venom gland which he uses for fighting other males during breeding season. The venom is extremely painful for humans but not deadly. The female platypus is born with the spur but she sheds hers during the first year.

CONSERVATION

The platypus is found in rivers, lakes and streams in eastern Australia. There is an introduced colony on Kangaroo Island, South Australia. In the early 1900s the platypus was hunted for its fur but they are now protected. They are common but this could change if the water in their habitats is polluted or destroyed further by humans. If you see a platypus in the wild, watch from a distance but try not to disturb it.

A RAT WOOS A DUCK

Aboriginal legend tells that the first platypus was born after a young female duck mated with a very persuasive water rat. The baby had the mother's bill and webbed feet, and the father's legs and fur.

AMAZING PLATYPUS FACTS

- The platypus can stay underwater for up to 10 minutes.
- A chubby platypus tail is a good sign – it's where they store fat.
- Platypuses growl when they're disturbed.
- The first live platypus was displayed at New York Zoo in 1922 – the only one of five to survive the trip to America.
- In 1933, 'Splash' was the first platypus kept in captivity in Australia. A permit was issued for his capture.
- Fossils show that platypus ancestors lived in South America millions of years ago.
- Look at a 20 cent coin – you'll see a platypus!

24 redback spider

NOT creepy AND crawly

One of Australia's best-known spiders is the Redback Spider (*Latrodectus hasselti*), a close relative of America's Black Widow Spider (also of the genus *Latrodectus*). A Redback Spider is easily identified by the wonderfully striking orange or red slash on its glossy black (sometimes brown) body.

WATCH THAT TOILET SEAT!

The Redback Spider was immortalised in Slim Newton's 1972 hit song, 'Redback on the Toilet Seat':

> *There was a Redback on the toilet seat when I was there last night,*
> *I didn't see him in the dark but boy*
> *I felt his bite.*

It probably wasn't a male spider that bit the man in the toilet. Mostly it's only the female that bites. Male redbacks are only about a tenth of her size. He has fangs but they usually can't penetrate human skin.

REDBACK BREEDING

The male redback is probably unique in its mating process. He spins a special web and deposits sperm on it, which he then sucks into two palps (like hollow legs) found between the jaw and first leg. Once he's on the female's back, he stands on his head and somersaults, landing with his abdomen on the female's jaws. This is a dangerous and usually deadly activity. If the female is not ready to mate, or mistakes him for food, then this could be the end of his short life as she bites him, injecting her digestive juices into his abdomen. If she is ready to mate the male will transfer his sperm from one palp. At the same time the female might also have pierced him with her fangs. If he is strong enough he will pull away and then insert his second palp. Either way, his job is done as the female continues to eat him. She might not have to mate again for another two years.

Redback breeding time is between September and May. The female produces a small cotton-like sac, which she hangs in the web. This holds up to 300 eggs and within three weeks she is ready to place another sac. She can lay about eight sacs each season. That's a lot of redback hatchlings, but most of the spiderlings do not survive as they make wonderful food for the other young.

FEEDING HABITS

Insects trapped in their sticky webs are a major component of a redback's diet, but it will also eat other spiders and even lizards. Large female redbacks will also steal food stored in another spider's web. Only the female, which lives up to three years, spins a food-gathering web. During the summer months, males, which live for just six or seven months, might be seen lurking at the edge of the female's web in anticipation of an exciting mating time.

REDBACK SPIDER

SILKY SPIDER HOMES
Redbacks spin their webs in dry sheltered areas under rocks or logs. They also love our human places – under eaves, floorboards, garden sheds, in junk piles, gardens and the outdoor dunny!

Their webs are spun from spider silk, which is amazing stuff. It comes from glands in the spider's abdomen. Different glands create different silks. Silk can be used for building a web, delivering sperm, holding eggs in a sac, lining burrows and catching prey in sticky nets or single threads. You can recognise a redback's web because it is tangled and messy, not a beautiful work of art like the orb-weaver's.

SPIDER BITES
Hundreds of redback bites are reported each year. Thankfully, today there is antivenom that can be injected into the victim to treat the bite.

To make spider antivenom, first you need to get venom from the spider. For redbacks this means dissecting (cutting open) the glands and tissues of the spider. The purified venom is then injected into horses, in small but gradually increasing doses. The horse produces antibodies to fight the venom. These are taken from the horse using a needle so the life-saving antivenom can be made.

A Redback Spider bite can be very painful and the person bitten may also sweat, become weak, feel sick and vomit. The best thing to do is put an icepack on the bitten area and get the person to hospital for treatment. An adult should try to collect the spider to be sure of its type.

There have been no deaths from Redback Spider bites since the antivenom has been available.

THE MYSTERIOUS MISS MUFFET

Little Miss Muffet sat on a tuffet,
Eating her curds and whey,
Along came a spider and sat down beside her,
And frightened Miss Muffet away.

Just who was Little Miss Muffet? There are a few possibilities, one being Patience, the stepdaughter of Dr Thomas Muffet, an English entomologist who wrote *The Theatre of Insects*, the first scientific catalogue of British native species. Another theory is that Little Miss Muffet symbolises Mary Queen of Scots and that the spider is John Knox, a church minister who did not agree with her religious ideas and wanted to scare her off the throne.

AMAZING SPIDER FACTS

🕷 Spiders are arthropods. They have an exoskeleton, a hard outer skeleton (rather than having bones inside, like we do).

🕷 Spiders moult – they shed their outer skeleton as they grow, replacing it with a new, larger exoskeleton.

🕷 Spiders are not insects. They have eight legs (insects have six), two main body parts (insects have three), piercing jaws (insects have chewing jaws) plus silk spinnerets (silk spinning organs).

🕷 Most spiders are nocturnal, meaning they are active at night.

🕷 A spider's silk line can be as thin as 0.004 millimetres. Some spiders create silk to cast lures, others use silk to help build a cover for their home's entrance, and others use silk to travel on the wind.

🕷 Net-casting spiders make a small web, a net, which they can stretch out to catch their prey. Jumping spiders may stalk and then jump on their prey.

🕷 Bird-dropping spiders have a wonderful method of camouflage to protect them from being eaten. They look like bird droppings!

25 RED kangaroo

AUSTRALIA'S BIG FOOT

Of all of Australia's amazing animals the most widely known is probably the kangaroo. From the old one-penny coin, the boxing kangaroo to the flying kangaroo (the Qantas logo), the kangaroo has come to signify anything Australian.

BIG RED! Kangaroos are the largest marsupials. And the largest kangaroo is the Red Kangaroo (*Macropus rufus*). Males can weigh up to 90 kilograms and stand nearly 2 metres tall. Males are usually a reddish-brown colour and females are often a bluish-grey – that's why they are sometimes called 'blue fliers'.

Red kangaroos live over most parts of central Australia and in all sorts of terrain, including scrub, grasslands and deserts. If conditions are right, the Red Kangaroo can breed all year round. Thirty-three days after mating, a hairless baby is born, looking like a pink jellybean and weighing less than 1 gram. It crawls to its mother's pouch and spends the next 235 days growing. When it leaves the pouch it continues to suckle for up to four months. By this time another young Red Kangaroo is developing on a different teat. Amazingly, the teats have different types of milk, one for the young in the pouch and fattier milk for the older joey out of the pouch.

If a female has a suckling baby, she can also have another fertilised egg waiting to develop. She delays the birth of the new offspring until the joey has left the pouch. This is called embryonic diapause.

The Red Kangaroo can survive with very little water, getting most of its moisture from the grasses and plants that it eats, but like all animals it still suffers during drought.

Kangaroos are sometimes seen as pests by farmers because they compete for food with livestock and can destroy fences when trying to jump through them.

HOP, HOP, HOP! Kangaroos belong to a group of animals called macropods, which means 'big foot'. Other macropods include wallabies, wallaroos, potoroos, pademelons, tree kangaroos, rat kangaroos and bettongs. Kangaroos have a distinctive feature – their hop. Their powerful hind legs, long feet and tail allow them to hop. In fact, the kangaroo is the only large animal that moves with a hopping motion. When it has to move slowly, for example when grazing, it uses all five limbs – two short forelimbs, two hind limbs and its tail for additional support. Amazingly, as the animal hops faster it uses less energy. Other animals use more energy to go faster. A Red Kangaroo can reach a hopping speed of over 60 kilometres per hour, and can leap as far as 8 metres and as high as 3 metres.

When they are hopping around, female kangaroos keep their joeys snug in their pouches by tightening their muscles. The muscles are loosened to let the joey out.

Kangaroos keep cool by resting in the hottest part of the day, sometimes lying under shady trees or in cool sand. Another great way that kangaroos keep cool is to lick their arms and let the moving air cool them.

EUROPEAN EXPLORERS AND KANGURUS

When Europeans first arrived in Australia they were amazed by these hopping animals. 'Kangurus' featured in many journals, reports and paintings. When reporting on how few species of land animals they had seen in Australia, Captain James Cook wrote: 'The sort which is in the greatest Plenty is the Kangooroo or Kanguru, so called by the Natives; we saw a good many of them about Endeavour River . . .' Cook and his men also discovered what the Aborigines had known for ages – that kangaroo meat is 'very good eating'.

In his journal (1768–1771), botanist Sir Joseph Banks wrote:

> *Quadrupeds we saw but few . . . The largest was calld by the natives Kangooroo. It is different from any European and indeed any animal I have heard or read of except the Gerbua of Egypt, which is not larger than a rat when this is as large as a midling Lamb; the largest we shot weighd 84 lb. It may however be easily known from all other animals by the singular property of running or rather hopping upon only its hinder legs carrying its fore bent close to its breast; in this manner however it hops so fast that in the rocky bad ground where it is commonly found it easily beat my grey hound . . .*

The English word 'kangaroo' originated in northern Queensland. When Cook's ship *Endeavour* was being repaired, the men ventured ashore, meeting local Aborigines, the Guugu Yimidhirr people, who called the Grey Kangaroo (*Macropus giganteus*) 'kanguru'. The sailors interpreted 'kanguru' as the word for all kangaroos and wallabies, and both Cook and Joseph Banks used the word in their records. The word 'kangaroo' made its way to England and soon became part of the English language.

THE BOXING KANGAROO

In 1983 when Australia battled the United States of America for the America's Cup – the prized yachting trophy – a new 'sporting' Australian flag was unfurled. It was the boxing kangaroo. Since that time, this flag has decorated many sporting arenas where Aussies are competing. But it was not the first time that the boxing kangaroo was seen. During World War II, planes and other vehicles of the Royal Australian Air Force used a boxing kangaroo as their insignia. This image may have come about because when male kangaroos fight each other they can look like they're boxing.

In the 1800s one of the attractions at travelling sideshows around Australia was the 'sport' of boxing – between men and kangaroos. This could be dangerous, as kangaroos can kick out with their strong back legs, using their tails to support their weight. Thankfully, boxing matches between humans and kangaroos no longer occur in Australia.

AMAZING KANGAROO FACTS

- A male Red Kangaroo is sometimes known as a 'boomer' – now made famous by the Australian Christmas carol 'Six White Boomers'.

- Red Kangaroos are nocturnal (active at night) and crepuscular (active at dawn and dusk). They spend most of the daylight hours sleeping or resting.

- Kangaroos live just about everywhere in Australia, from the rainforests all the way to arid deserts – even into the tropical areas. Red Kangaroos are generally found in arid and semi-arid areas.

- *Macropus rufus* is from the Latin for 'big foot' and 'red'.

- The kangaroo and the emu appear on our national coat of arms. They were chosen because they are always moving forwards (they can't walk backwards!).

Unlike wombats and koalas, macropods like kangaroos have a forward-opening pouch with four teats, but they usually have only one young in the pouch at a time.

Kangaroos can only move their hind feet together, except tree kangaroos, which can move each leg independently as they travel through the trees.

26 Sulphur-crested Cockatoo

noisy BIRD from the LAND of PARROTS

Australia is home to over one-sixth of the world's 340 species of parrots and they cover every habitat across this vast continent. Gerard Mercator, a Belgian mapmaker who lived almost 500 years ago included in his world map a land (located near present-day Australia) called *Terra psittacorum* – the land of parrots.

We have some amazing parrots – cockatoos, parrots, lorikeets and rosellas – including the Galah (*Cacatua roseicapilla*), Gang-gang Cockatoo (*Callocephalon fimbriatum*), Glossy Black Cockatoo (*Calyptorhynchus lathami*), Little Corella (*Cacatua sanguinea*), Eclectus Parrot (*Eclectus roratus*) and the Rainbow Lorikeet (*Trichoglossus haematodus*). But one of the best known parrots is the Sulphur-crested Cockatoo (*Cacatua galerita*).

Its white-feathered body and impressive yellow crest are magnificent, but many would agree that this bird's most striking feature is its scratchy, squawky call. Its ear-piercing screech, often heard at sunrise or in the early evening, announces the cockatoo's arrival or departure from its roosting tree.

Sulphur-crested cockatoos naturally occur in the timbered forests of northern and eastern Australia and into Tasmania, as well as a colony now established around Perth. They are found in a variety of timbered environments, building nests in tree hollows. They are also popular pets, although it is sad that they are kept in cages. They can live for more than 65 years, so a cockatoo is a life-long pet and may even outlive its human.

COCKATOOS AND EARLY SETTLERS

Early European settlers in Australia referred to New Holland as Parrot Land. When Governor Lachlan Macquarie returned to England from Australia on board the *Surry* in 1822, he took a menagerie of 'pets' that included two white cockatoos 'and also several Parrots and Lowries'. These 'souvenirs' were often given as gifts. Today it is illegal to take parrots out of Australia without a permit. Sadly, because of the demand for them as pets, parrots like the Sulphur-crested Cockatoo are still found in the luggage of smugglers trying to take them out illegally. Many of these parrots die in transit.

A COLONIAL DELICACY

Early settlers had to get used to new tastes in the colony. Native wildlife provided a new dining experience, which was not always appealing to their taste buds. Newton Fowell, a midshipman on the First Fleet, wrote to his father from Sydney Cove in Port Jackson on 12 July 1788:

> *I forgot to mention among the birds the Cockatoo they are about the size of a large owl quite as white as Milk all over except a few yellow feathers on the top of their head which have a pretty effect they*

are very indifferent food, & make a disagreeable Noise so the only handsome thing belonging to them is their Plumage.

Parrot pie was a regular dining experience for the early settlers in 'the land of parrots'. Letters home to England, journal records and memoirs identify parrot pies as being 'very good, very like pigeon'. Peter Cunningham, a convict ship surgeon wrote that parrot pies were even 'selling at a shilling a dozen'. When mapping the New South Wales coast, Lieutenant John Grant wrote that an Australian King Parrot was 'far preferable for flavour' than pigeon. For Christmas dinner in 1844, explorer Ludwig Leichhardt and his companions feasted on 'suet pudding and stewed cockatoo'. Parrot recipes in colonial cookbooks directed that the parrots be plucked and rubbed with butter, cooked alone or sometimes with other tasty treats. Parrots were a very pleasant change to the usual beef and mutton meals. How tastes change – thank goodness!

AN ARTIST'S DREAM

The vivid colours and unusual variety of Australia's wildlife provided early settlers with wonderful subjects for their art, and cockatoos were popular with painters.

There were no professional painters on board the First Fleet who arrived in Australia in 1788. The task of recording the animals and plants was taken up by those convicts and naval men who were trained in drawing and painting – skills mostly meant for drawing charts and mapping coastlines. One of the most talented of these was George Raper, midshipman on the *Sirius*. While the ship was being repaired, he did the first known painting by a European artist of the Port Jackson area. He also created a series of paintings that included his famous Glossy Black Cockatoo.

John Gould's landmark seven volume work, *The Birds of Australia* (published 1840–48), contained illustrations of all 681 of the then known species of Australian birds. One of these was the Sulphur-crested Cockatoo. Gould says:

> ... As may be readily imagined, this bird is not on favourable terms with the agriculturist, upon whose fields of newly-sewn grain and ripening maize, it commits the greatest devastation.

WHAT TREE IS THAT?

Today it is not the farmers who are crying the loudest, but people in urban areas. Instead of feasting on its native diet of berries, seeds, nuts and roots, the cockie's powerful bill destroys timber decking and woodwork on houses. In the wild when they are not feeding, cockies will often be seen perched in trees biting off small branches and leaves, even shredding the bark. This keeps their beaks in good shape and helps the trees flourish. For cockies, wooden features on houses are simply different trees.

HANGING ABOUT Cockatoos have zygodactyl feet (two toes forward and two toes pointing backward), which are perfectly adapted for climbing and holding, and for gripping branches to eat seeds while hanging upside down in trees. Sometimes cockatoos spin around on branches simply to have fun. They are nature's acrobats.

> ## BLOWING THE WHISTLE
> A flock of cockatoos feeding on the ground often have one or two others on lookout in a tree surveying the area. This is a great warning system – the cockies screech loudly if there is an intruder. Humans, too, have used this warning system. During illegal activities, such as a two-up game, someone would be hired as the 'cockatoo'. It was his job to be on the lookout for police. If they arrived, the cockie 'blew the whistle' and everyone disappeared.

AMAZING COCKATOO FACTS

🦜 The oldest authenticated Sulphur-crested Cockatoo died in London Zoo in 1982. The cocky was over 80 years old.

🦜 Sulphur-crested cockatoos originally congregated west of the Great Dividing Range but have now moved eastwards where there is more water. And pet cockatoos that have been released or escaped are now resident in the cities.

🦜 Large old trees with hollowed trunks make perfect nests for some cockatoos. If those trees are removed, the birds are likely to disappear.

🦜 Sulphur-crested Cockatoos lay up to three eggs. Both parents incubate the eggs for about 30 days before hatching.

🦜 Cockatoos are large parrots with crests. All species are found only in Australasia.

🦜 Each flock of cockatoos has its own roosting site. They fly long distances in search of food.

27 Tasmanian Devil

an island's ICON

The Tasmanian Devil *(Sarcophilus harrisii)* may be the largest living carnivorous marsupial scavenging on the carcasses of dead animals; it may have the most spine-chilling, blood-curdling screech of any Australian animal; it may be able to snap bones apart with its vicious teeth and monstrously powerful jaws . . . but this majestic marsupial is not the devil its common name implies.

In fact people who have spent time with devils are more likely to describe them as shy and timid. Devils might look aggressive to intruders but it is more bluff than action. A devil is more likely to escape than fight – unless there's food involved!

Early Tasmanian farmers quickly grew to dislike the devil, which devoured their chickens at night. As with the Thylacine (see next chapter), a bounty, or paid reward, was introduced by the Van Diemen's Land Co., to rid farming lands of the creature. Females were worth three shillings and sixpence (35 cents), a decent sum of money in those days, while males were worth two shillings and sixpence (25 cents). Thankfully, the devils survived the trappings and poison, and in 1941 became a protected species.

A DEVIL OF A FEAST

Tasmanian Devils are more scavengers than hunters. They eat any dead or sick animal they can find. These nocturnal hunters might eat as much as 40 per cent of their body weight in one night if they are really hungry.

They are known to feast on wallabies, pademelons and, possibly their favourites, fatty wombats! Devils also like sheep and cattle as well as smaller mammals like possums. Other meals include echidnas, platypuses, frogs, fish and birds (especially chickens, if they can get into their pen). As well as eating flesh, devils also eat fur and the smelly guts and bones of their meal. They've been known to feast on the animal from the inside out – nothing is wasted, except maybe the skulls of some of the larger animals like wombats. They will have a go at anything that has a meaty smell to it – including people's clothes and shoes!

Tasmanian Devils usually hunt and scavenge alone. But many devils could be at the table if carcasses of large animals like cows or wallabies are on offer. This can become a very noisy event as they fight for the best feeding position. They push, shove, growl, yowl, scream, and even bite each other to get the best spot. Fighting is especially vicious if there is a ravenous female who has left her young in the den. Younger devils must wait until other devils have finished before they can start. At the end of a feast, a devil may curl up inside the remains of the animal for a rest. Feasting is a tiring business.

A DEVIL OF A LIFE Usually the female devil is dominant but once a year during mating season (usually March) the male is in charge. Mating lasts for up to five days.

Three weeks later a young devil emerges, just 10 millimetres long (about the size of your smallest fingernail). A mother devil can give birth to between 20–40 immature young but she has just four nipples so only the toughest four (usually less) will survive the first journey from the birth canal to the backward opening pouch and attach onto the milk supply. Devils' pouches are not large so it is not uncommon to see females ambling through the bush with the back legs of a young devil or two hanging from the pouch and dragging on the ground – a rough ride for both mother and young.

For four months the young develop in the pouch. Then for the next five months they live in a simple den, sometimes a hollow log, a small abandoned burrow or a cave. Their mother returns frequently to feed them milk (until they are five or six months old) and then to begin teaching them how to scavenge and feast out in the bush. At this stage, the young ones either ride on the mother's back or scamper by her side. Finally, ten months after mating, the young devils are sent off to start their own lives.

A DEVIL OF A DISEASE

In the early 1900s there was a dramatic decline in the number of devils, possibly as a result of disease. It also happened again in the 1950s. The devils are now in trouble again. They are developing facial tumours and dying a horrendous death. Scientists think this cancer could be transferred when devils bite each other. Devil's Facial Tumour Disease begins at the mouth but soon the devil has lumps or lesions on its face, neck and other parts of its body, and sometimes the eyes. The devil then has trouble eating and dies within about six months. A decrease in devil populations from this disease could mean an increase in the recently introduced fox, or the feral cat populations, which in turn would have a devastating impact on native animals.

AMAZING DEVIL FACTS

- The Tasmanian Devil's scientific name is *Sarcophilus harrisii*. *Sarcophilus* means flesh lover, and *harrisii* is after the deputy surveyor-general who first described the devil, George Harris.

- The inside of a devil's ear is nearly hairless. When they get excited or distressed their ears 'glow' in the sun as they are flushed with extra blood.

- Devils were once found on mainland Australia.

- Devils can travel up to 20 kilometres each night searching for food.

- Devil's scats (that's poo) often contain large amounts of fur and bones. Other contents can include feathers, claws, teeth, and even boots and shoes!

- Devils can run at about 13 kilometres per hour. Devils can also swim and young devils can climb well.

- Males are heavier than females and weigh six to eight kilograms.

28 thylacine

Gone but NOT FORGOTTEN

On Monday 7 September 1936, the last captive Thylacine (*Thylacinus cynocephalus*) died, and with him the likelihood of anyone seeing a living Thylacine again. All that remains of this once magnificent animal, also known as the Tasmanian Tiger, is some grainy movie footage taken at Hobart Zoo of the animal listlessly roaming in a chicken-wire cage, as well as some skins, a few stuffed specimens, or photos of hunters with their dead prize. There are no known photographs of a Thylacine alive in the wild. Isn't it a pity that people won't again see the Tasmanian Tiger's amazing jaw, which could open to a width of 120 degrees, the wolf-like head, its stiff heavy kangaroo-like tail, or its black tiger-like stripes?

How did we get to this point where a remarkable marsupial, once common in Tasmania, is now no longer with us? For that explanation we have to look into our history. When Europeans settled in Tasmania in 1803 the Thylacine was common. This nocturnal hunter was frequently sighted. It was the largest living carnivorous (meat-eating) marsupial and should have been worthy of excitement not extermination. But it wasn't.

A DEATH SENTENCE Sheep farming was introduced into Tasmania early in the 1800s. Sheep were a tempting treat for Thylacines, and they were possibly easier to kill than their usual meal of wallabies or other small animals. Now they had mutton to feast on. More and more sheep were slaughtered, although not necessarily by Thylacines. The growing population of wild dogs were predators too. More and more farmers pressed to get rid of Thylacines. So in 1830 the Van Diemen's Land Co. put a bounty (a paid reward) on the head of the Thylacine.

A dramatic reduction in the number of Thylacines must have been already obvious by the middle 1850s. Even the famous naturalist John Gould, in his book *The Mammals of Australia, 1845–1863*, predicted the end of the Thylacine when he wrote:

> *When the comparatively small island of Tasmania becomes more densely populated, and its primitive forests are intersected with roads from the eastern to the western coast, the numbers of this singular animal will speedily diminish, extermination will have its full sway, and it will then, like the Wolf in England and Scotland, be recorded as an animal of the past.*

In 1888 the Tasmanian parliament placed an additional bounty of £1 on an adult and ten shillings on each pup. The combined bounties were devastatingly effective because by the early 1900s few bounties were being paid. By the time the bounty was removed in 1909 over 2000 bounties had been

THYLACINE

paid. Many more Thylacines were killed and many of the skins went to tanneries and were exported. By that time, sighting the Thylacine was uncommon. But worse was to come.

Already greatly reduced in number by the slaughter, the remaining Thylacines were probably hit with a fatal disease, so seeing a Thylacine now became extremely rare. Even so, urgent action wasn't taken to reduce the possibility of extinction. The last wild Thylacine was probably shot in 1930.

TIGER ON DISPLAY By then zoos around the world wanted to display this tiger-like marsupial. Thylacines were on display in London's Regent Park Zoo (the last one purchased for £150 in 1926). In 1933 Hobart Zoo purchased its last Thylacine, caught in the Florentine Valley. Sydney's Taronga Zoo and the Bronx Zoo, New York, also displayed the Thylacine.

But eventually the last captive Thylacine died, possibly of exposure as the day shift keeper might have forgotten to lock it up in its hut the night before. It is a sad irony that the Thylacine was only added to the endangered wildlife list *after* the death of this last captive specimen. It was too little too late. This marsupial was probably already extinct.

Since 1936 there have been hundreds of claimed sightings of the Thylacine in Tasmania and as far away as the Northern Territory but searches have been unsuccessful. No concrete evidence, such as footprints, scats, or specimens have been found. And it is amazing that there are no authenticated photographs of the animals that are sighted.

CAN THYLACINES BE CLONED?

Cloning is the process of making an identical copy of something. In living things, cloning involves creating a copy using special material called DNA from the original animal. DNA is like building blocks with an instruction booklet of how that living thing goes together.

So could a Thylacine be cloned? This is a question that has caused much discussion in recent years. Dolly the sheep was cloned, and also many other animals, so why not a Thylacine? Scientists still hold Thylacine DNA material. Many scientists agree that cloning is possible, but is it worthwhile? A successful cloning would be great but there would only be one. And the components of the DNA from which the cloned specimen would be created are very old. The specimen, a young Thylacine pup, has been preserved in alcohol since 1866. This makes the process even more difficult. The issue of cloning creates a lot of discussion and argument!

AMAZING THYLACINE FACTS

🐾 Thylacines weren't *officially* classified as extinct until 1986, 50 years after the last captive Thylacine died.

🐾 Aboriginal rock paintings and fossil remains show that the Thylacine was once on mainland Australia. Competition with the dingo (which never made it to Tasmania) might have caused its mainland extinction.

🐾 The Tasmanian coat of arms has a shield supported by two Tasmanian Tigers.

🐾 Thylacines lived in zoos for up to nine years. No Thylacine was ever bred in captivity.

🐾 The Tasmanian Tiger's fur was sandy brown, coarse with 15 to 20 black stripes.

🐾 The scientific name (*Thylacinus cynocephalus*) means dog-headed pouched dog or is sometimes translated as 'pouched dog with wolf's head'.

29 WEEDY SEADRAGON

floating SEAWEED

Named after the dragons of Chinese legends, these amazing creatures are dragons in miniature, growing to about 46cm, and are only found in ocean waters of southern Australia. Adult Weedy Seadragons (*Phyllopteryx taeniolatus*) are usually reddish with yellow spots and purple-blue stripes, and have pipe-shaped snouts. But their main costume is their leaf-like appendages which make Weedy Seadragons look like swaying seaweed, keeping them hidden among the seaweed-covered rocky reefs where it is found.

THE DAD GIVES BIRTH! It's a wonderful life being a male seadragon, swimming around in the temperate water, sucking up plankton, larval fish or mysid (small shrimp-like crustaceans), fertilising eggs and watching your young swim away after birth. But male seadragons do more than watch. Unlike most other animals, it is the male seadragon that carries and incubates the eggs. The male seadragon becomes pregnant and the male dragon 'gives birth' to the baby seadragons.

With the approach of spring, male and female seadragons pair off and begin their courtship. During mating, the female seadragon places 100–250 bright pink eggs on the underside of the male seadragon's tail, into the brood patch. Once her job is done, she swims away and the rest is up to the male.

The brood patch contains small pits or egg-cup suction caps, each holding an egg. The male fertilises and then nourishes the eggs for up to eight weeks while they develop. Then hatching takes a while. Over a number of days, fully formed young seadragons emerge from the eggs, one or two at a time. They hang their tails out of the eggs, for up to six hours, eventually wriggling to freedom. The male seadragon spreads his offspring as he swims through the waters. For the first two days the baby seadragon obtains nourishment from the yolk sac but then it must find its own food. The young dragons are fast-growing, reaching full size after two years.

Once free of his parental responsibilities, the male seadragon has time for a second incubation in the one breeding season.

TUBE-SNOUTED COUSINS
Weedies belong to the family of Syngnthids (Latin for tube-snouted) that includes seahorses, pipehorses and pipefish. Syngnathids are long, slender fish with bony plates around their bodies. The family name describes their tube-shaped mouth. Seadragons don't have teeth so they suck in their food, along with some water. They do this by expanding a joint on the lower part of their snout, which makes a suction force that pulls in the food.

Seadragons and seahorses may look quite similar but there

30 AMAZING AUSTRALIAN ANIMALS

are some important differences. Unlike seahorses, seadragons don't have a pouch for rearing their young but carry the eggs on their tails until they hatch. Also seadragons can't curl their tails, but seahorses have prehensile tails, which means they can curl their tail to hold onto objects such as blades of seagrass.

The Weedy Seadragon is closely related to the Leafy Seadragon (*Phycodurus eques*) which has even more leaf-like appendages but is usually smaller than its weedy cousin.

CRAFTY AT CAMOUFLAGE
Mimicry is a wonderful form of camouflage and there is none better at this than the seadragon. Like all fish, seadragons have gills and fins. The fins

of seadragons are so fine that they are almost transparent. This makes them look leafy, which is the perfect camouflage for a life among the sea grasses. They even rock back and forth imitating the movement of the grasses by the ocean currents.

Like many species of seahorse, seadragons can change colour depending on their age, what they eat or even how stressed they are!

Many fish have scales, but not seadragons. They have a series of bony plates that cover their body. This 'armour' is great for protection but not good for easy movement which is why they rely mostly on their camouflage for their survival. They are slow swimmers, drifting and swimming in shallow waters, although they have been seen at depths of up to 50 metres.

AMAZING SEADRAGON FACTS

- The Weedy Seadragon and the Leafy Seadragon are unique to Australia.

- Seadragons are protected by law – it's illegal to take or export them without a permit.

- Seadragons are under threat from their habitat being destroyed or polluted, and from those illegally collecting them for sale.

- Sometimes seadragons can be found washed up on the beach, because their bony plates help to preserve them after death. Look closely in the clumps of weed because they may be camouflaged.

SEARCHING FOR DRAGONS

We don't know how long wild seadragons live, though it's thought they can live for five to seven years in captivity. As with all other fish, seadragons have ear bones that show growth rings. New growth rings appear throughout its life. So dead seadragons washed up on the beach can be very useful to researchers to perhaps be able to tell the age of the seadragon and so learn more about these fantastic Australian fish.

There is a seadragon monitoring program called Dragon Search which encourages members of the community to provide information on seadragon sightings. (www.dragonsearch.asn.au) The information is used to help find out more about where seadragons are found, the sort of habitat they need, and the kinds of things we might be able to do to help protect them. Anyone who visits the beach in Australia can get involved.

It is thought that seadragons may be sensitive to changes in water quality. So if the water quality becomes worse, the effect on populations of seadragons may be a warning signal that quick action needs to be taken. Frogs are used as a similar warning signal in freshwater environments.

30 wombat

bulldozer of the BUSH

They may look sleepy, docile and dozy but looks can be deceiving. Resting on the pathway or in the bush, the Common Wombat (*Vombatus ursinus*) looks as though it is dozing in the sunshine and it probably is, but disturb a wombat and it can run at an amazing speed – up to 40 kilometres per hour. That will only last for about 150 metres, then it will need a rest. Their doziness is one way of conserving energy by dropping their body temperature when they doze.

Another wonderful conservation method used by the wombat is to get almost all the moisture it needs from what it eats. So when it goes to the toilet its scats (that's poos!) are really dry. A wombat's droppings are easy to spot. They are usually a cube shape, about 2 centimetres long, dropped in a bundle of four to eight and lying out in the open. And the smudge on the rock nearby? That's where the wombat wiped its bottom! Wombats eat lots of grass, and when the grass supply is scarce, they dig for tubers and roots.

There are three species of wombat found in Australia, the Common Wombat, the Southern Hairy-nosed Wombat (*Lasiorhinus latifrons*) and the Northern Hairy-nosed Wombat (*Lasiorhinus krefftii*). As the name suggests, the nose or muzzle of a hairy-nosed wombat is covered with short brown hairs. Hairy-nosed wombats also have a wider face and longer, more pointed ears than a Common Wombat.

A QUADRUPED CALLED WOMBAT

When early Europeans began exploring New Holland (Australia) they were intrigued and amazed by all the unique wildlife they were finding. Records were taken in the field and specimens were sent back to England for further study. These animals were unknown to science at the time.

One of the earliest descriptions of a wombat comes from George Bass (the man who circumnavigated Tasmania and the man after whom Bass Strait is named). His notes, written over 200 years ago, were titled 'Some Account of the Quadruped Called Wombat, in New South Wales' and his descriptions are wonderful. This is some of what he wrote from his observations of wombats at Furneaux Islands and from his discussions with a 'mountain native' about the 'wombat' living in the Blue Mountains behind the Sydney settlement:

> *The wombat ... is a squat, thick, shortlegged, and rather inactive quadruped with an appearance of great stumpy strength. Its figure and movements, if they do not resemble those of the bear, at least remind one of that animal ...*

> *The head is large and flattish and, when looking the animal full in the face, seems, independent of the ears, to form nearly an equilateral triangle ... The hair upon the face lies in regular order, as if combed with its ends pointed upwards in a kind of radii from the nose, their point of supposed junction.*

Bass describes the mouth as small and the front of each jaw having two grass cutting teeth 'like those of the kangaroo'. The neck was thick and short, not allowing much movement and, according to Bass, 'looks rather as if it was stuck upon the shoulders'. The 'size of the two sexes are nearly the same' with the female being a little heavier. Bass described the wombat's movement as 'hobbling or shuffling, like the awkward gait of the bear', and said that most men could outrun a wombat.

He described the voice of a wombat as 'a low cry between a hissing and a whizzing' that was only ever uttered in anger and could only be heard for 25 or 35 metres. For Bass the wombat appeared mild and gentle. He was even able to carry the wombat for a mile in his arms and on his shoulders just like humans carry their babies. Bass also tied a wombat's legs together so that it wouldn't shuffle away. Today we consider this inappropriate, but back then it was part of the process of observing the animal. He soon found out that the gentle wombat can become very annoyed when provoked as it 'whizzed with all his might, kicked and scratched most furiously and snapped off a piece from the elbow of my jacket with his long grass cutters'.

EXPERT EXCAVATORS

In Bass's time no one had yet opened a burrow to look inside. Today people have even crawled inside a wombat's burrow and we know much more. Wombats don't just have one burrow, they have many burrows and some may reach up to 20 metres or more underground and two metres below the surface. There will be nesting chambers

and connecting tunnels. And there is usually more than one entrance to the burrow system. A wombat's hard bony bottom is great protection in a burrow. They can block the entrance or crush a predator against the burrow walls. Wombat burrows also offer fantastic protection from weather extremes and bushfires.

Wombats are mainly solitary and nocturnal, coming up when the air is cool to graze on their favourite foods – native grasses. On summer days they will usually stay in their burrows to escape the heat but in winter they will often come out to bask in sun.

Wombats have feet wonderfully adapted for digging. They also have a backward opening pouch (just like its koala relative), which stops it getting full of dirt when the wombat digs. In the pouch there are two teats but usually only one young is born. The joey will live in the pouch for 6 months and then stay with the mother until it is 18 months old. If there is plenty of food, wombats can breed throughout the year.

For wombats their biggest threat lies with humans – our destruction of their habitat, introduction of animals that compete for food, and our cars!

RARER THAN THE GIANT PANDA!

The Northern Hairy-nosed Wombat is one of the rarest animals in the world and is classified as critically endangered. There is only one small group left in the Epping Forest National Park in central Queensland. They were once found as far south as the Victorian border but their numbers became drastically reduced due to drought, clearing of land for farming, and competition for food from introduced rabbits, sheep and cattle. The Epping Forest population got down to as few as 35 animals but once the park was fenced from cattle and sheep, and later from dingos, numbers built up to over 100 – still a very fragile situation. Researchers are trying to find out as much as they can about this hairy-nosed hermit so that they can help the present population to increase and hopefully establish new populations elsewhere.

AMAZING WOMBAT FACTS

🐻 The Common Wombat's scientific name is *Vombatus ursinus*. *Vombatus* is possibly derived from the aboriginal names for wombat: 'wambad', 'wambaj' or 'wambag'. *Ursinus* is latin for 'bear-like'.

🐻 Wombats have long front teeth for chewing – a bit like a rodent's. The tough grasses they eat wear their teeth down, but luckily a wombat's teeth never stop growing so it can still grind its food even when it's old.

🐻 Wombats are the largest burrowing herbivorous marsupial.

🐻 It is for good reason that the wombat is called the bulldozer of the bush. Most fences are no trouble for a wombat on a mission. They simply will bulldoze straight through the fence and leave another hole to be repaired.

🐻 The wombat's nearest living relative is the koala.

🐻 Wombats can live to 15 years in the wild, and up to 20 years in captivity.

guys, girls, bubs and the whole gang!

Here are some great names used to describe the males, females, young and groups of some of our amazing Australian animals.

ANIMAL	MALE	FEMALE	YOUNG	COLLECTIVE NOUN
Bird (general)	Cock	Hen	Hatchling, chick	Dissimulation (small birds only), fleet, flight, flock, parcel, pod, volery
Brumby/horse	Stallion	Mare	Foal, colt or filly	Stud, team, herd
Camel	Bull	Cow	Calf	Herd
Cane Toad/ toad (general)				Knot (for toads)
Cicada			Nymph	
Crocodile			Hatchling	
Death Adder/ Snake (general)			Snakelets, neonate (newly born) hatchling (newly hatched)	Lair, den, slither, nest, pit
Dingo/dog	Dog	Bitch	Pup, whelp	Litter (pups from one mother), pack (hunting), kennel, colony
Dugong	Bull	Cow	Pup, calf	Herd, pod, school
Echidna	Male	Female	Puggle	Train (in mating season)

Emu	Cock	Hen	Chick	Flock, mob
Fish (general)	Male	Female	Fingerling, fry	School, shoal, draft, run
Ghost Bat	Male	Female	Pup	Colony
Great White Shark/shark (general)	Male	Female	Cub	School, shiver
Green and Golden Bell Frog/frog (general)	Male	Female	Tadpole, polliwog	Army, knot, croak
Kangaroo	Jack, buck, boomer	Jill, doe, flyer	Joey	Mob, troop, herd
Koala	Boar	Sow	Cub	Group, colony, sleep
Kookaburra				Watch (for kingfishers)
Lake Eacham Rainbowfish/ rainbowfish (general)			Fingerling, fry	School, shoal, party
Little Penguin			Chick	Colony, rookery
Rabbit	Buck	Doe	Kit, kitten	Colony, nest
Redback Spider			Spiderling	
Sulphur-crested Cockatoo				Flock, company (for parrots)
Weedy Seadragon				Herd (seahorses)
Wombat	Jack	Jill	Joey	

Not all animals have been assigned particular names for the sex of the animal; many are simply male or female. Some animals do have a collective name for a group while others that are not usually found in groups don't.

Here are some other really awesome collective nouns for animals:

PARLIAMENT of owls
EXULTATION of larks
MUSTERING of storks
UNKINDNESS of ravens
MURDER of crows
RAFTER of turkeys
EXULTATION of larks
CHATTERING of starlings
PADDLING of ducks
HOST of angelfish
FLOTILLA of swordfish
SMACK of jellyfish
CRASH of rhinos
SHREWDNESS of apes
SLEUTH of bears
LEAP of leopards
AMBUSH of tigers
PACE of donkeys
HUDDLE of hippopotamus

Animal Emblems of Australia

Aust. Capital Territory

Mammal: No official emblem
Bird: Gang-gang Cockatoo (*Callocephalon fimbriatum*)
Marine: No official emblem

New South Wales

Mammal: Platypus (*Ornithorhynchus anatinus*)
Bird: Kookaburra (*Dacelo novaeguineae*)
Marine: Eastern Blue Groper (*Achoerodus viridis*)

Northern Territory

Mammal: Red Kangaroo (*Macropus rufus*)
Bird: Wedge-tailed Eagle (*Aquila audax*)
Marine: No official emblem

Queensland

Mammal: Koala (*Phascolarctos cinereus*)
Bird: Brolga (*Grus rubicundus*)
Marine: Barrier Reef Anemonefish (*Amphiprion akindynos*)

ANIMAL EMBLEMS OF AUSTRALIA

South Australia

Mammal: Southern Hairy-nosed Wombat (*Lasiorhinus latifrons*)
Bird: Piping Shrike, also known as White-backed Magpie (*Gymnorhina tibicen leuconota*) (unofficial). Appears on state badge.
Marine: Leafy Seadragon (*Phycodurus eques*)

Tasmania

Mammal: Tasmanian Devil (*Sarcophilus harrisii*) (unofficial)
Bird: No bird emblem, but the Yellow Wattlebird (*Anthochaera paradoxa*) is generally acknowledged to be their most identifiable bird.
Marine: No official emblem

Victoria

Mammal: Leadbeater's Possum (*Gymnobelideus leadbeateri*)
Bird: Helmeted Honeyeater (*Lichenostomus melanops cassidix*)
Marine: Weedy Seadragon (*Phyllopteryx taeniolatus*)

Western Australia

Mammal: Numbat (*Myrmecobius fasciatus*)
Bird: Black Swan (*Cygnus atratus*)
Marine: No official emblem

How to find out more

Thankfully we have many organisations in Australia that promote our amazing animals.

Check out your local state or territory museum, government environment and parks and wildlife organisations, and don't forget that our zoos are a fantastic source of information about our native animals – they display many of the smaller species (including the nocturnal ones) that you will rarely see in the wild. You might even want to become an official friend of your zoo!

SOME ORGANISATIONS AND WEBSITES ARE:

Australian Faunal Directory: http://www.environment.gov.au/biodiversity/abrs/ online-resources/fauna/afd

Australian Museum: http://www.amonline.net.au

Australian Regional Association of Zoological Parks and Aquaria: http://www.arazpa.org.au

Cephalopod Page: http://www.thecephalopodpage.org

CSIRO and especially the biodiversity and ecology link: http://www.csiro.au/csiro/channel/ich2u.html

Department of Environment and Water Resources: http://www.environment.gov.au/biodiversity/index.html

Frog and Tadpole Study Group: http://www.fats.org.au

Frog Watch: http://www.frogwatch.org.au

Museum of Victoria: http://www.museum.vic.gov.au

Science in the News NOVA: http://www.science.org.au/nova/index.htm

References

Australian Regional Association of Zoological Parks and Aquaria Animal Fact Sheets: http://www.arazpa.org.au/default.aspx?ArticleID =66

Australian State of the Environment 2006 (SoE2006) report: http://www.deh.gov.au/soe/2006

Cogger, Harold; *Reptiles and Amphibians of Australia*; Reed Books; 1992

Fleay, David; *We Breed the Platypus*; Robertson and Mullens, 1944

Museum of Victoria: 'Caught & Coloured: Zoological Illustrations from Colonial Victoria', collection of Frederick McCoy's *Prodromus of the Zoology of Victoria*: http://www.museum.vic.gov.au/caughtandcoloured/Zoology.aspx

National Library of Australia and their collections including: 'The World Upside Down', National Library of Australia: http://www.nla.gov.au/exhibitions/upsidedown/index.html Perry, George; *Arcana; or the Museum of Natural History*, London, 1811

Reader's Digest Complete Book of Australian Birds; Reader's Digest; first ed (2nd revised); 1983

State Library of NSW and their collections including: the papers of Sir Joseph Banks: http://www.sl.nsw.gov.au/banks/series_35/35_43.cfm
and the papers of John Harris, 1791–1837: http://image.sl.nsw.gov.au/Ebind/cy157/a1369/a1369000.html

Strahan, Ronald (ed); *The Australian Museum Complete Book of Australian Mammals*; Angus and Robertson, 1983

Christopher Cheng worked as a teacher in city and country schools before moving to Taronga Zoo as an education officer for 8 years, establishing Australia's first Zoomobile. He has been National Children's Development Manager at Dymocks, and Education Advisor for the BioScope Initiative, a science based CDROM project at Purdue University, USA.

He is an accomplished children's author, now writing full time, conducting workshops and visiting schools. He has also presented to students at schools and universities in the USA. Chris writes both fiction and non fiction. His picture book *One Child* (illustrated by Steven Woolman) won the Wilderness Society Environment Award for Picture Books (Australia) and the 2000 Skipping Stones Honour Book (USA).

Chris has a Master of Arts in Children's Literature and is also the Literacy Ambassador for the Federal Government's Literacy and Numeracy Week Initiative.

Chris lives in Sydney, Australia, near wonderful coffee shops and restaurants in a very old (newly renovated) terrace with his wife.

Find out more about Chris at: www.chrischeng.com

Gregory Rogers studied fine art at the Queensland College of Art and has illustrated a large number of educational and trade children's picture books including four books in the Random House *30 Australian* . . . series. In 1995 he won the Kate Greenaway Medal for his illustrations in *Way Home*, a book that also won a Parent's Choice Award in the US and was shortlisted for the ABPA book design awards.

His first wordless picture book *The Boy, the Bear, the Baron, the Bard* was selected as one of the Ten Best Illustrated Picture Books of 2004 by the *New York Times* and short-listed for the CBCA Awards, Younger Readers, 2005 and the APA Best Designed Children's Picture Book, 2004. It also received a 2004 Australian and New Zealand Illustration Award from Illustrators Australia and was a Notable Children's Book of the Year for the American Library Association. His second wordless picture book, *Midsummer Knight*, was published in 2006. It is the companion to *The Boy, The Bear, The Baron, The Bard* and is also published in the USA, France and Germany.

Gregory lives in Brisbane, Australia.

30 Australian SPORTS Legends

Loretta Barnard

Illustrations by
Gregory Rogers

RANDOM HOUSE AUSTRALIA

To my favourite sportsmen,
John, Beau and Casey.
LB

For Rex Rogers,
a cricket legend and my Dad.
GR

Contents

Introduction		viii
1	Australian Rules: Swans take flight	1
2	Basketball: Lauren Jackson, gem of a player	7
3	Boxing: Lionel Rose, king of the ring	12
4	Canoeing: The Murray Marathon	18
5	Cricket: The bodyline series	23
6	Cricket: Border patrol	29
7	Cycling: The phenomenon of Opperman	35
8	Golf: Karrie Webb, champion golfer	40
9	Hockey: Hockeyroo heroines	45
10	Horseracing: The race that stops Australia	50
11	Marathon: Going the distance	57
12	Marathon Swimming: Susie Maroney, a fish in water	63
13	Motorcycling: Casey Stoner, speed demon	69
14	Motor Racing: Brocky, all about speed	74
15	Novelty Sports: The dry regatta and other unusual sports	79
16	Paralympic Perfection: Louise Sauvage, against the odds	85
17	Rowing: The Oarsome Foursome	91

18	Rugby League: Dragon power	96
19	Rugby Union: Mark Ella, making a difference	101
20	Running: John Landy, one cool character	107
21	Running: Cathy Freeman, the real Australian idol	113
22	Sailing: The Sydney to Hobart	118
23	Sailing: Kay Cottee and Jesse Martin, solo sailors	123
24	Soccer: Heads up for the Socceroos!	129
25	Speed Skating: Steven Bradbury stands tall	135
26	Sporting Animals: Best hoof forward	140
27	Surfing: Midget Farrelly, first-ever surfing champ	146
28	Swimming: Dawn Fraser, athlete of the century	152
29	Swimming: Ian Thorpe, our greatest Olympian	158
30	Tennis: Evonne Goolagong Cawley, tennis ace	164
Training and diet		170
Olympic sports		176
Some interesting sporting websites		178
Index to people, teams and animals		183

Introduction

We have so many truly remarkable sportsmen and women in Australia that it's just about impossible to name them all. Even from early colonial times, we loved to play sport. In those early days, our sports were British – cricket, boxing and horseracing. In fact, horseracing was one of our first major sports; races were being held in the early years of the 1800s, and the Sydney Turf Club was established in 1825, just 37 years after Captain Philip arrived on our shores with boats filled with convicts.

The Australian Cricket Club began in 1826 in Sydney and what is possibly our most famous sports club, the Melbourne Cricket Club, began in 1838. By the 1850s, Australians were wrestling, swimming and rowing as well. By 1900, we also played football, croquet and athletics.

Today, sport is one of Australia's favourite pastimes. Just think about how many people you know who play a sport, and then think about all the people you know who love to watch sport, either live or on television. And even if a game is being played in another part of the world, that doesn't mean we will miss it. Your parents have probably sat up half the night to watch Wimbledon or the Rugby World Cup televised live from

Introduction

halfway across the world. Even if we walk around half-asleep the next day, many of us wouldn't miss watching the finals as they actually happen.

***

We don't just love the sports themselves. The athletes — the people who play the sports — are just as important to us, and this book tells the stories of many of our favourites. The athletes who are featured in this book are just some of the amazing people, living or dead, who have made enormous contributions to sport both in Australia and across the world. We chose these particular athletes for two reasons: first, we want to show the enormous range of sports that we play here and second, these athletes are genuine sporting legends. There might be many books about Don Bradman, but he's here because he's probably the most famous Aussie sportsman of all. And Dawn Fraser, also included in this book, is an official legend, having been named Best Female Swimmer of the Twentieth Century in the World Sports Awards.

There are so many great sports stars who are not even mentioned in this small book. But they're out there, making news and breaking records. Australia has Olympic medal winners in a range of sports, including diving, shooting and baseball. There are Australian champions in squash, netball, water polo, softball, billiards and waterskiing. We have world class equestrians, beach volleyballers, hurdlers and weightlifters.

The people in this book are all incredible sports stars. Some of them had pretty tough childhoods or suffered major health problems or disabilities, and they still became champions because they love their sport. Staying focused on their goals, they have not only fulfilled their own dreams, they have inspired others to dream.

We really do love our sport. According to the Australian Bureau of Statistics, two-thirds of Australians of all ages participate in sport and physical activity each week. Our favourite activities include aerobics classes, yoga, walking, swimming, cycling, golf, tennis, soccer and running. People also play Aussie Rules, cricket (both indoor and outdoor) and netball.

Playing sport is not only enormous fun, it's also good for us. We should all do some exercise every single day, even if it is just walking to and from school. The good thing about sport is that there's something for everyone. You can do individual sports like running or swimming, or play team sports like cricket or basketball. Some of the best friends you'll ever make will be people you've met while playing sport. And it's terrific fun to cheer on your friends when they play, or to support your favourite footy team.

Perhaps the stories of the athletes in this book will inspire you to be as good as you can be. Of course, the most important thing to remember is to enjoy yourself. Whatever sport you play, make sure that you're having a great time.

1. Australian Rules

SWANS TAKE FLIGHT

Every team has a story to tell, but this story is a little bit special. It's about one particular game – the grand final between the West Coast Eagles and the Sydney Swans in 2005 at the Melbourne Cricket Ground. The Swans used to be based in South Melbourne; they moved to Sydney in 1982. They had not won a premiership for 72 years. Seventy-two years – that's how old your grandpa might be.

In 2005, the Swans had a great team, and it was felt that they had a good chance of taking the premiership, even though the last time they had won a grand final (as South Melbourne) was way back in 1933! The Swans were up against the West Coast Eagles – and West Coast had some of the best players in the league, including Chris Judd, David Wirrpanda and Ben Cousins. There was no doubt it was going to be a fight to the finish.

TERRIFIC TEAMWORK Training in AFL, like all elite sports, is hard work. Players jog, do weight training and run on a treadmill so that they are in peak physical condition. Once their fitness levels are at their highest, they begin footy training, which includes running, kicking and learning game plans. The Swans trained for long hours leading up to the grand final match. It was do or die!

It was an exciting match. Although they were leading by 20 points at half-time, by the last quarter, the Swans were behind by 10 points. The strain was enormous, as the game could go either way. Captain Barry Hall scored a goal from the 50-metre mark, and then midfielder Amon Buchanan kicked a fantastic goal.

AUSTRALIAN RULES: Swans take flight

Next, West Coast's Dean Cox kicked into the goal square and the players frantically tried to get into position. As the final few moments of the game ticked on, defender Leo Barry made the most brilliant mark of his career, winning the match for the Swans. The crowd of almost 92,000 roared with excitement. The drought was broken!

The final score was Swans 8.10.58, West Coast 7.12.54, the lowest scoring grand final for nearly 30 years. The Swans won by just four points.

The Norm Smith Medal is given to the best player in the grand final. Although West Coat lost the game, Chris Judd was awarded the Medal, only the fourth time that a player from the losing side has won it.

AFL Lingo

▶ There are four posts at either end of an Aussie Rules football field. The two taller ones in the centre are the goal posts. Six points are awarded for each goal. The two shorter posts are called the behind posts. If the ball goes between the goal post and the behind post it is called a 'behind' and one point is scored.

▶ A handball is another way, apart from kicking, that the ball is passed to other players. The player cannot throw the ball, but must punch it towards a team mate.

▶ When a player catches the ball on the full after it has been in the air for 15 metres, it is called a mark. The player is then allowed to have a free kick without being tackled by the other team's players.

▶ Have you ever wondered why three numbers are given for each team at the end of a match? If one team scores 10 goals and seven behinds, this is written on the scoreboard as 10.7.67. The last number is reached by adding up all the points. It doesn't matter if one team scores more goals, it's the point tally that's important.

Oops!

In the 1920 grand final, Richmond defeated Collingwood in front of 54,000 fans. Bill James was playing his first game for Richmond, and kicked the last goal in the match. Unfortunately, not long after the grand final he went out rabbit hunting and accidentally shot himself in the foot. He never played again. This makes Bill the only player ever to have played just one game and won the premiership.

AUSTRALIAN RULES: Swans take flight

FABULOUS FOOTY FACTS

- Australian Rules footy had its beginnings in the 1850s in Melbourne when the game was developed by Tom Wills and some friends. By the late 1890s, the Victorian Football League was established, and VFL became Victoria's favourite sport. In the 1990s, the game became national when the VFL became the AFL (Australian Football League).

- The Brownlow Medal is awarded each year for best and fairest player, as chosen by the umpires. The first Brownlow Medal was awarded to Geelong player Edward 'Carji' Greeves in 1924.

- Four players have won the Brownlow Medal three times: Fitzroy's Haydn Bunton, Essendon's Dick Reynolds, South Melbourne's Bob Skilton and Ian Stewart who played for both St Kilda and Richmond.

- Roy Cazaly is an AFL hero. During his long career, he played for St Kilda, South Melbourne (now the Sydney Swans) and New Town, Tasmania. Even though he wasn't as tall as many of the other players, he seemed to be able to leap higher than anyone else, and before long the expression 'up there Cazaly' meant that Roy was going for one of his famous marks.

- John Curtin, who was Australia's Prime Minister from 1941–1945, played for Brunswick in the Victorian Football League from 1905–09.

- Players often pick up peculiar nicknames. Forward Tony Lockett, who played with St Kilda and later the

Sydney Swans, was known as Plugger; Gary Ablett, who was voted Geelong's greatest ever player, was called God! Melbourne's Brock McLean is known as Chooka.

- The biggest number of people to go to an Aussie Rules match was 121,700 at the 1970 grand final between Collingwood and Carlton at the Melbourne Cricket Ground (MCG). Carlton won the game with a 10-point lead.

- Chris Judd, the former captain of the West Coast Eagles and now playing for Carlton, is one of Australia's greatest ever footballers. Among his many awards are the 2004 Brownlow Medal, the 2005 AFL Goal of the Year and the 2006 Leigh Matthews Trophy for Most Valuable Player.

- Each year, the best 22 players from across the league are selected to be part of the All-Australian team. AFL is not played internationally, so being selected to this team is a way of recognising the top players in the game, even though no games are played. The All-Australian team is sort of like naming a 'dream team'.

2. Basketball

The year 2007 was a very memorable one for Lauren Jackson. The WNBA (the United States Women's National Basketball Association) named her their Most Valuable Player (MVP) for the second time, and she was also named 2007's WNBA Defensive Player of the Year and Peak Performer of the Year, having led her team, the Seattle Storm, to the finals.

Her average for the year was 23.8 points per game, the highest average she'd achieved in her career. She also became the youngest ever player to score 4000 points in the WNBA. And for the sixth time, she was chosen as part of the All-Star team. Lauren was also named the Women's Korean Basketball League's

LAUREN JACKSON, GEM OF A PLAYER

MVP in 2007, having also played a season for South Korea. What a busy year!

So how did a girl from Albury, New South Wales, reach the top of the international women's basketball scene?

BRED FOR SUCCESS Lauren began playing basketball when she was four years old, learning from her parents, who were fantastic basketballers. Her mother, Maree Bennie, had played for the Australian national women's team, the Opals.

Lauren attended the Australian Institute of Sport in her early teens, where she led the women's team to victory in the

BASKETBALL: Lauren Jackson, gem of a player

National Basketball League finals. By the time she was 16 years old, Lauren was almost 2 metres tall, and such a good player that she joined the Opals. She was the youngest member of the team.

At 18, Lauren joined the Canberra Capitals, winning four finals between 1999 and 2006. So it wasn't surprising when she was chosen as Australia's captain at the 2000 Olympic Games, where she was the top scorer and rebounder on the team and helped the Opals win the silver medal. She also captained the 2004 Olympic side, again taking silver. In 2006, with Lauren as captain once again, the Opals won gold at the Commonwealth Games, and at the International Basketball Federation (FIBA) Women's World Championships.

By this time, Lauren Jackson was our most famous basketball player. Her fantastic shooting ability and all-round skills had won her Australia's Most Valuable Player three times, as well as MVP for the 2006 grand final.

STORMING THE WORLD

Basketball selectors outside of Australia had been impressed by Lauren as well. She was recruited to play in the American league, the WNBA, and joined the Seattle Storm in 2001. In her first game with the Storm, she scored 21 points. All through that first season, she scored so well that she was runner-up as Rookie of the Year. (A rookie is a first-year player, and this was Lauren's first year with Seattle.) When you think about all the unbelievably great players in America, you have to admit that even being runner-up was a brilliant achievement.

By 2003, Lauren had dazzled fans across the world. That year, she became the youngest player to score 1000 points in the WNBA. The all-rounder finished the season in the top five in rebounds and blocks and was voted the year's MVP. She even played a season with a Russian team in 2005, and in 2006 the Australian Institute of Sport included her in their '25 Best of the Best'. Lauren Jackson is easily the best female basketball player in Australia's history and she is certainly one of the top women players in the world.

Slam Dunkin' Basketball Words

- When a player close to the basket jumps up and shoves the ball through the hoop, it is known as a slam dunk, or just a dunk. Sometimes, the player grasps the rim while forcing the ball in. It's a pretty spectacular sight.

- When a goal is attempted, but the ball bounces off the rim or the backboard, it is known as a rebound. A player who then catches the ball is a rebounder.

- A block is when a player touches the ball as it is going into the basket, stopping a goal from being scored.

- When basketballers dribble, they're not actually slobbering all over the ball. Dribbling is when a player bounces the ball repeatedly as they move across the court.

- The game starts (or continues) when an official tosses the ball into the air between the two opponents. The players jump up and try to tap the ball towards their team mates. That move is called jump ball.

- There are two types of foul. If a player elbows, trips or pushes another player, or does anything that might cause injury, that's a personal foul. If players are being unsportsmanlike, such as saying mean things to the opposing team, a technical foul can be called. The other team then gets a free throw. It's called a free throw because the player gets to shoot the goal without an opponent standing in the way.

BASKETBALL: Lauren Jackson, gem of a player

SHOOTING STARS

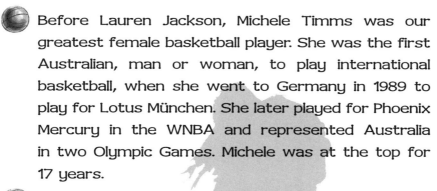

- Before Lauren Jackson, Michele Timms was our greatest female basketball player. She was the first Australian, man or woman, to play international basketball, when she went to Germany in 1989 to play for Lotus München. She later played for Phoenix Mercury in the WNBA and represented Australia in two Olympic Games. Michele was at the top for 17 years.

- Andrew Gaze is probably Australia's best known male basketball player. The National Basketball League's Rookie of the Year in 1984, Andrew represented Australia in five Olympic Games between 1984 and 2000. He was named Most Valuable Player a record seven times, and was a member of the All-NBL All-Star team for 12 years. Andrew had great training – his dad, Lindsay Gaze, also played for Australia in three Olympic Games.

- Luc Longley is possibly our most successful player. He was the first Australian ever to play in the US National Basketball Association, when he joined the Minnesota Timberwolves in 1991. He's played with the Chicago Bulls, who won three NBA titles, the Phoenix Suns and the New York Knicks. He also played for Australia at the 1988 and 1992 Olympics. Luc is 2.18 metres tall – that's about the height of two seven-year-olds, one standing on the other's shoulders!

3. Boxing

LIONEL ROSE, KING OF THE RING

It was a tough match. Nineteen-year-old Lionel Rose was in Tokyo, Japan – a long way from the Victorian country town of Jackson's Track where he grew up. He was boxing for the 1968 world bantamweight championship. The judges were Japanese, his Japanese opponent was the current world champ and the favourite to win, and Lionel was definitely the underdog. It was a demanding 15-round competition and no one seriously thought the young Australian had a chance.

FIGHTING HARADA Masahiko Harada, the great Japanese boxer known as Fighting Harada, was the World

BOXING: Lionel Rose, king of the ring

Boxing Association's bantamweight champ. He is still the only man ever to have won both the flyweight and bantamweight titles. In 1968, he was in peak condition and had held the bantamweight title four times.

On that February evening at Budokan Hall in Tokyo, Lionel Rose entered the ring ready to fight his hardest fight. Jack Rennie, Lionel's coach, told him to hold back a little, which took Fighting Harada by surprise. Lionel ducked some of the champ's punches and threw a couple of good ones himself. By the eighth round, Harada's eye was injured and when he took a right cross in the fourteenth round, it looked as if Lionel had won. The judges were impressed with Lionel's technique and his staying power. At the end of the fifteenth round, he was declared the winner. Not only was Lionel Rose the new World Bantamweight Champion, he was also the first Indigenous Australian in boxing history to win a world title!

AIMING FOR THE TOP Lionel Rose had been working up to this match for a few years. The oldest of nine children from a poor family, Lionel used to watch his father, Roy, box in tent-shows. (These were shows that travelled around country towns. They were sort of like the circus, but instead of clowns and acrobats, they held boxing matches.) Lionel showed some talent for boxing and he was determined to make something of his life.

At 15 he became the Australian Amateur Flyweight champion and this spurred him on to bigger things. He trained hard and fought his first professional match when he was 16 years old, beating his opponent in just eight rounds. He then went on to win more and more matches and, although he had suffered a couple of losses, he never lost heart. In 1966, Lionel defeated Noel Kunde and won the Australian bantamweight title. There was nowhere to go but up.

AFTER THE WORLD TITLE Nineteen sixty-eight was a big year for Lionel. He'd beaten Fighting Harada in February, then in July he successfully defended his world title against another Japanese boxer, Takao Sakurai. In December, he went to California to fight Mexican boxer Chucho Castillo and won again. But Chucho's fans were angry with the judges' decision and starting objecting violently – throwing bottles, chairs and whatever else they could find. About 12 people had to go to hospital.

Later in 1968, Lionel Rose was named Australian of the Year, the first time that an Indigenous Australian had ever won that honour.

In 1969, Lionel kept his championship title when he defeated Britain's Alan Rudkin, but later that year, he lost against Mexican boxer Rubin Olivares.

BOXING: Lionel Rose, king of the ring

During his career, Lionel fought 53 professional bouts, winning 42 of them. He retired from the ring in 1976.

The Deadly Awards are the Aboriginal and Torres Strait Islander awards for achievement in sport, music and community work. In 2005, Lionel was awarded a Lifetime Achievement in Sports Award at the Deadlys. Also that year, Australia Post issued a postage stamp carrying a picture of Lionel's boxing gloves to celebrate his sporting achievements.

WHICH WEIGHT? SOME BOXING FACTS

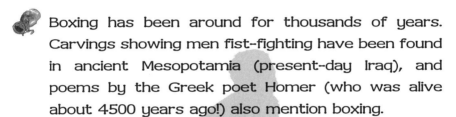

- Boxing has been around for thousands of years. Carvings showing men fist-fighting have been found in ancient Mesopotamia (present-day Iraq), and poems by the Greek poet Homer (who was alive about 4500 years ago!) also mention boxing.

- A boxing ring is not a circle, but a square. The name 'ring' comes from the early days of the sport when people used to gather in a circle to watch the fighters.

- Boxing has a number of classes for competition. To make sure that the matches are fair, the classes are based on the weight of the competitors. For example, flyweight contenders must weigh between 48 and 51 kilograms. Bantamweight contenders (like Lionel Rose) must not be heavier than 54 kilograms. Heavyweights must weigh more than 90 kilograms. There are also featherweights, middleweights, welterweights and super heavyweights.

LES DARCY: AUSSIE HERO

Les Darcy is an Australian boxing legend. In his short life, he fought 50 professional matches, losing only four. In 1916, it was the middle of World War I and young men across the country were expected to become soldiers. Instead of joining the army immediately, Les accepted an offer to box in the United States. This was not a popular decision, and people called him a coward, saying he should have gone to war instead. But Les wanted to earn some money for his family first, and so he sailed to America.

Unfortunately, when he got there, boxing managers cancelled his fights. Les gave a few exhibitions, but one day he suddenly collapsed and was rushed to hospital, where he died from an infection. He was only 21 years old. After his death, he became popular again. People remembered that he had been a loving son and a great boxer. Les Darcy is now one of Australia's favourite heroes.

Some Other Aussie Boxing Greats

- Jeff Fenech won the world title in three different boxing divisions: bantamweight, super bantamweight and featherweight. His nickname was 'The Marrickville Mauler'.

- Before he began boxing, world super middleweight champion Anthony Mundine was a great rugby league player. Anthony was trained as a boxer by his father, legendary boxer Tony Mundine, who, during the 1970s, was Australian boxing champion in four different weight divisions as well as Commonwealth middleweight champ!

Oops!

The Australian welterweight championships in April 1900 in Sydney ended not with one knock-out, but two! Australian Frank 'Snowy' Sturgeon was fighting New Zealander Otto Cribb for the title. At the very same instant that Otto landed a powerful blow on Frank's jaw, Frank hit Otto right on the chest and both men fell to the floor, ending the fight.

4. Canoeing

The Murray is 2575 kilometres long. It is Australia's second longest river after the Darling, and flows through three states – New South Wales, Victoria and South Australia. Every year on 27 December, thousands of people gather on the banks of the Murray at Yarrawonga, Victoria, ready to begin the world's longest annual canoe race, the Murray Marathon. The race lasts for five days, and ends at Swan Hill in northwest Victoria, 404 kilometres from the starting point! That's a huge distance, almost ten times as long as a typical running marathon. It's certainly a challenging race. Even better, each year contestants in the Murray Marathon raise money for the Red Cross to continue its good works in the community. They come from all over Australia and also from overseas.

THE MURRAY MARATHON

The first Murray Marathon was held in 1969 for about 10 paddlers. These days, the race attracts more than 800 paddlers every year.

SOMETHING FOR EVERYONE What makes the Murray Marathon so popular and so successful is that you don't have to be an Olympic champion to enter it – although that would probably help you to win it! There are a few different categories. Experienced paddlers enter the original marathon, either as individuals or as part of a relay team. In the relay, four or more people take turns paddling – when one person reaches the checkpoint and gets out of the canoe, the next team member gets in and continues down the river. There's also a secondary school relay event and some junior events for teenagers aged between 13 and 18 years.

Paddlers can use a canoe, a kayak or a surf ski, depending on which event they enter, and each paddler needs a support team.

GOTTA BE TOUGH! It's tough going. You need to be pretty fit to paddle for five straight days down the mighty Murray, and there are a lot of things that competitors need to think about before they start. Apart from sunscreen and a hat, they need plenty of water, and even though the marathon is held in December, it can get cold out on the water, so they have to take something warm. Another thing to worry about is blisters! All that paddling is hard on hands.

And then there is the river itself. Even though this is a flatwater race (that means that the river is usually slow-moving), the most experienced paddlers know that the river has its moods. Currents can change and sometimes the water can get a bit rough. Branches and other obstacles can also find their way into the river, so you always have to keep your eyes open.

Oops!

At the 1988 Olympic Games in Seoul, kayaker Grant Davies finished his 1000-metre singles race and saw his name up on the scoreboard as winner! He was thrilled because it had been a neck-and-neck race against the American Greg Barton. Unfortunately, only 11 minutes after declaring Grant the gold medallist, Olympic officials realised that they'd made a mistake, and that Barton had in fact won. Grant was disappointed, but he is such a great sportsman that he accepted the judges' decision and congratulated his opponent.

CANOEING: The Murray Marathon

MOVING ALONG On each day of the Marathon, there are about four checkpoints where the paddlers' progress is noted. As the paddlers move down the river, their friends and supporters follow them on shore, bringing with them tents and supplies for the end of each day.

On the first day competitors have to paddle 92 kilometres to Tocumwal before they get to rest. Over the next four days, they paddle the remaining 312 kilometres. It's exhausting work – just as well the Red Cross is on hand to help with first aid, sore muscles and blistered hands. On New Year's Eve, paddlers arrive at Swan Hill, happy but tired. They can feel proud of themselves for going the distance.

THE HAWKESBURY CANOE CLASSIC

In 1977 a group of students organised a 111-kilometre canoe race along the Hawkesbury River, northwest of Sydney, to raise money for medical research. Like the Murray Marathon, the race soon became a big event. That first year, 250 paddlers entered the race. Over the last few years, about 650 people have entered the race each year.

The Hawkesbury Canoe Classic is held in October and is considered one of the world's toughest canoe marathons. Beginning in Windsor and ending at Brooklyn, paddlers use either canoes or kayaks and set off in the evening, paddling overnight to reach the finish line. The race is timed so that paddlers work their way up the river by the light of the full moon.

AMAZING CANOEING FACTS

 A canoe is a long narrow boat with pointy ends and is completely open. A kayak is similar, but it usually has a waterproof covering so the paddler is enclosed. Both are very light and can only be moved by using paddles.

 The first time an Australian flatwater canoe/kayak team competed in the Olympic Games was in Melbourne in 1956. In the 1992 Barcelona Olympics, our kayakers won 14 medals!

 Dennis Green competed in the 1000-metres canoeing event in five different Olympic Games – Melbourne in 1956, Rome in 1960, Tokyo in 1964, Mexico City in 1968 and Munich in 1972. Adrian Powell also represented Australia in five Olympics, from 1960 to 1976. What champions!

 'Gunwale' (pronounced gunnel) is the upper edge of the side of a canoe or boat.

 Whitewater canoeing is held in river rapids. Rapids are fast-flowing, choppy sections of a river, and sometimes it's tricky just staying inside the canoe!

 When a canoe or kayak capsizes and then rolls back to its proper position, it is known as an Eskimo roll.

5. Cricket

THE BODYLINE SERIES

You've heard of Donald Bradman, right? He might just be the most famous sportsman in Australian history. Back in 1930, in the Test match between England and Australia, there was no doubt that the English side felt that Bradman was the one man who stood in the way of an English victory. So they came up with a plan to defeat him in the next Ashes tour. It was called bodyline.

Bodyline is a method of bowling where the bowler aims the ball at the batsman's body. This forces the batsman to protect himself by pulling the bat across his body, which limits where the ball can travel off the bat as he hits it. Fielders then place themselves where there is a bigger chance of catching the ball and so stop the batsman from scoring runs.

Bradman

The English captain, Douglas Jardine, and his team, including fast bowlers Harold Larwood and Bill Voce, worked on the method for the next year or so, so that it would be perfect when England met Australia again in 1932–33.

Why were the English so frightened of Bradman? Well, in the Test series played two years earlier, 22-year-old Don Bradman, already being called Australia's greatest ever batsman, had scored 974 runs, at an average of 139.14. It was an astonishing score, and Australia won the series 2–1. (Working out an average is easy – if the batsman bats 10 times during a Test series, you add up all the runs he scored in those innings and divide it by 10.)

WAR WITH ENGLAND! In the 1932–33 Test series the bodyline tactic took the Australian team by surprise and it was difficult for them to score many runs. They suffered a few injuries – Larwood bowled a ball that hit Australian captain

CRICKET: The bodyline series

Bill Woodfull just above his heart. The crowd was horrified but Jardine thought it was an excellent bowl. Wicket-keeper Bert Oldfield was hit on the head and batsman Bill Ponsford was covered in bruises from bodyline bowls. Not even the amazing skills of Don Bradman, who averaged 56 in the series, could get the better of bodyline and England won the series 4–1.

Australians were furious at the unsportsmanlike behaviour of the English side, and many of the English cricketers were not happy using the bodyline tactic either. People were so angry that the Australian Cricket Board of Control sent a message to the Marylebone Cricket Club (MCC), the organisation in charge of English cricket, to complain about it. Even politicians became involved, and there was a lot of bad feeling between the two countries. By the time the series had reached Adelaide, the police were there to make sure the crowd didn't run on to the field and attack the English team!

One thing you might not realise is that in the early 1930s times were difficult for many people – there weren't many jobs and there was a lot of poverty (this time is referred to as 'The Depression'). But Australia's sporting success, particularly at cricket, was something everyone could enjoy and take pride in. Australia had always had a friendly rivalry with England, ever since the early days of the colony, but the bodyline series angered people. Australians thought the English were bad sports.

Jardine

After this Test series, bodyline bowling was banned. Douglas Jardine never played against Australia again.

There are two teams out there. One is trying to play cricket and the other is not.

— Bill Woodfull

Cricket Lingo

Like all sports, cricket has its own language. Some of the words used are a bit peculiar!

- 'Off side' relates to the batsman. If the batsman is right-handed, then the area of the field to his right is the off side. If he's left-handed, then off side is to his left. The area behind him is the leg side.
- In cricket, 'silly' doesn't mean scatterbrained. If a fielder is very close to the batsman, it is called silly. For example, the silly mid-off is next to the bowler on the batsman's off side.
- A googly has nothing to do with the internet. It is a bowl that looks like it's going to spin in one direction, but ends up spinning in another.
- If a batsman gets a score of zero, he's 'out for a duck'.
- An over is six balls bowled in a row. If no runs are scored, then it's called a maiden over.
- For more cricket lingo, see pages 32–33.

CRICKET: The bodyline series

Oops!

When Australia played England in the 1890 Test match, Tasmanian batsman Ken Burn was a member of the side, scoring a low 41 runs in four innings. But the extraordinary thing about Ken's inclusion on the side was that he was chosen as second wicket-keeper. Naturally he was thrilled to be part of the team, so he waited until the ship had already set sail for England before telling them that he had never kept wickets in his life! (By the way, England won that Test series 2–0.)

MORE ABOUT THE DON

- In Don Bradman's remarkable cricket career, he scored a total of 29 centuries. (A century is 100 runs.) He played the first of his 52 Test matches in 1928 and for the next 20 years he was an important member of the Australian team.

- Bradman is remembered as the ultimate cricketer, but even he had his bad days. As he walked onto the pitch at his very last Test match in England in 1948, the crowd went wild, cheering on the famous batsman. Then English bowler Eric Hollies bowled Bradman a googly. Bradman miscalculated the spin on the ball and was out for a duck!

- In spite of this, Bradman had a Test total of 6996 Test runs, only four short of 7000 and his batting average was 99.94, which is pretty amazing.

- In 1949, Donald Bradman was knighted, the first Australian cricketer to receive this honour. In 1979 he was awarded an Order of Australia and in 1985 he became the very first person to be inducted into Sport Australia's Hall of Fame. In 2000, *Wisden Cricket Almanack*, the most famous cricket reference book, voted Bradman the greatest cricketer of the twentieth century. Every single one of the 100 judges chose Bradman for this honour.

- If you're ever in Bowral, New South Wales, you can visit the Bradman Museum. It has plenty of fascinating information and exhibits about Australian cricket and 'The Don', as he was known. The legend of The Don lives on.

6. Cricket

BORDER PATROL

Who played in 156 Test matches, captained Australia 93 times, scored more Test 50s than any other cricketer in history, and scored over 11,000 runs? If you said Allan Border, you'd be right on the nose! Allan Border, or AB as everyone calls him, is one of Australia's most impressive cricketers ever.

In late 1984, Allan, nicknamed Captain Courageous, was chosen as captain of the Australian team. The Australians had not done well in the last few Tests, but AB changed all that. Under Allan's leadership, the Aussies became almost unbeatable.

RUNNING HIGH The first year of AB's captaincy was difficult. In the 1985–86 season, Australia lost to New Zealand and India, but Allan worked hard with his team, building up their confidence and skills. He was a pretty strict captain and

sometimes he was called 'Captain Grumpy', but his hard work really paid off.

The first Cricket World Cup was held in 1975. In 1987, Australia won the World Cup for the first time, beating England by seven runs. Allan, holding the trophy high in the air, was carried off the pitch on the shoulders of his team mates.

CRICKET: Border patrol

Their success continued. In a Test match against New Zealand in 1987–88, Allan scored a massive 205 runs, making him Australia's highest Test scorer. It was his 22nd Test century.

Although there were a few losses after that, by the time the 1989 Ashes rolled around, the Aussies were in top form.

THE 1989 ASHES

The Ashes is the long-running competition between England and Australia. The first match was played over 125 years ago. It has always been a hotly contested series, with each side desperate to win the trophy.

When the Australians arrived in England for the 1989 Ashes series, no one seriously thought they had a chance. But they were wrong! In the first Test, the Australians were on fire. Mark Taylor scored 136 and Steve Waugh scored 177 not out, while Dean Jones, Merv Hughes and AB made half-centuries. They won that match by 210 runs.

They won the second Test as well, but drew in the third. They then went on to win the fourth Test by nine wickets (they still had nine wickets standing when they passed the number of runs scored by England); and the fifth Test by an innings and 180 runs (that is, they had so many runs on the board that they didn't have to bat a second time and were still 180 runs in front when they dismissed all the English batters). The last Test was a draw, making the series score 4–0. Australia had won the Ashes for the first time in 55 years.

MORE ABOUT AB

After their spectacular Ashes win, Australia remained at the top of the cricket world for the next 15 years, thanks largely to Allan's leadership. Allan Border retired from Test cricket in 1994 and was replaced by Mark Taylor. AB then played for Queensland in the Sheffield Shield (now called the Pura Cup). This was an exciting time, because that year, 1994, Queensland won the trophy for the very first time in the Shield's history.

Later Allan became a cricket selector — that's one of the people who choose players for the Australian international team.

Allan's record of 11,174 runs held until 2005, when West Indian cricketer Brian Lara beat it. Allan still holds the record for the most Test matches played in a row (153). And how about this? In Test cricket AB caught 156 balls, the exact same number as the Test matches he played.

Allan was named 1982's Wisden's Cricketer of the Year. In 1990, he was inducted into Sport Australia's Hall of Fame; in 1994 he was awarded an Order of Australia; and in 2000, he entered the Australian Cricket Hall of Fame. Now that's fame!

Stumped for Words

▶ Stumps can mean a few things. A 'stump' means one of the three posts that make up the wicket; stumps can also mean the end of play for the day; and it is also used when talking about dismissing a batsman. Being dismissed means the batsman is out.

▶ It's a big deal to score a century in a Test match because only the best players compete in them. Scoring a Test 50 (a half-century) is an achievement to be proud of.

▶ LBW! If a ball that would have hit the stumps hits the batsman's body before hitting the bat, it's called leg before wicket and the batsman is out.

CRICKET: Border patrol

- There are a few other ways to be out in cricket. For example, you can be bowled, caught, stumped, run out or timed out (this one's very rare). You're also out if you hit the ball twice or if you hit the wicket.

- Ever heard the expression 'sticky wicket'? It comes from cricket and refers to a field that is drying out after heavy rain, which makes it tricky for the batsman because the ball may bounce in an unexpected way.

Oops!

It was the last ball of the 1981 one-day final between Australia and New Zealand in Melbourne, and New Zealand needed six runs to tie up the match. Captain Greg Chappell told his brother Trevor to bowl underarm to New Zealand batsman Brian McKechnie. The idea was that it would be impossible for the batsman to score a six. Trevor rolled the ball along the pitch and Australia won the match, but the team was booed by the crowd.

Although the underarm bowl was not really against the rules, it was not very sportsmanlike and cricket lovers all over the world thought that Trevor and Greg had done the wrong thing. The New Zealand Prime Minister, Robert Muldoon, called the Australians cowards! Since that game, underarm bowling has no longer been allowed.

HOWZAT!

- Since 1960, three cricketers have been named Australian of the Year — Allan Border in 1989, Mark Taylor in 1999 and Shane Warne in 2004.

- One of our best wicket-keepers ever is Adam Gilchrist. He is the only Australian wicket-keeper to have captained the Australian Test and One Day international sides.

- The Allan Border Medal has been awarded to one great player each year since 2000. Australia's current captain, Ricky Ponting, has won it four times. The other winners are Glenn McGrath, Steve Waugh, Matthew Hayden, Adam Gilchrist, Michael Clarke and Brett Lee.

- In 2000, super bowler Shane Warne was named one of the five Wisden Cricketers of the Century.

7. Cycling

Hubert Opperman, or Oppy as he was known, was a 24-year-old cyclist when he entered the famous 24-hour Bol d'Or cycling classic in 1928.

Oppy was born in Rochester, Victoria, in 1904, and worked as a telegram delivery boy when he was in his teens. (Telegrams were important messages sent across a telegraph line to the post office and then typed out and delivered in person.) When he was about 17 he entered a race and won himself a beautiful new Malvern Star bicycle. From then on, he always used a Malvern Star.

THE PHENOMENON OF OPPERMAN

Before he went to Paris, Oppy was already a champion, having won the Australian Road Cycling titles in 1924, and then again in 1926 and 1927. He'd also

won the Warrnambool to Melbourne Classic and the Goulburn to Sydney Classic. But it was the race in Paris that ensured his place in sporting history.

THE BOL D'OR The Bol d'Or was held in a velodrome, a cycle-racing stadium with high curved sides. It was a real endurance test; it lasted 24 hours and the competitors cycled over 900 kilometres. That's like going from Alice Springs to Uluru and all the way back again!

Oppy was in fine form for the race, and everything seemed to start off well. However someone had tampered with his two racing bicycles: the chains had been filed down and it was not safe for him to ride. He had to wait for about an hour while another bike was found for him. The one he ended up with was not a racing bike and the handlebars were turned the wrong way. So as well as missing the first hour of the race, Oppy had no choice but to ride an inferior bike.

But he was determined to compete, and off he sped, trying to make up for lost time. He sat on that old bike for a mind-boggling 17 hours without getting off once. Just imagine it – going round and round the velodrome nonstop, his whole mind and body focused on his goal. Even though he began at a disadvantage, Oppy worked hard and kept his eye firmly on his target.

Despite the terrible thing that had happened to his bikes, Oppy won that race, beating his opponents by 30 minutes. The crowds loved him; they cheered his victory with cries of 'Allez Oppy!', which means 'Go Oppy!' in French. When the news reached Australia, people went wild with excitement and Oppy's name became very well known, especially in Victoria. Later that year, a French sporting magazine did a survey and Hubert Opperman was voted France's favourite sporting star!

OTHER VICTORIES

Oppy returned to Melbourne to a hero's welcome in 1928, but he didn't sit back and relax. He won the Australian Road Cycling race again in 1929. In 1931, he again won the world's admiration when, in just 49 hours and 23 minutes, he won the 1116-kilometre Paris–Brest–Paris non-stop endurance race.

In 1937, when he was 33 years old, he cycled from Perth to Sydney. You only have to look at a map of Australia to see how far *that* is. He did it in 13 days and 10 hours, and this record stood for some 30 years!

LIFE AFTER CYCLING

In 1940, Hubert Opperman quit professional cycling and joined the Royal Australian Air Force, serving as a flight lieutenant. After the war, he became a politician. He was the federal Liberal member for Corio in Victoria for 17 years. He held some important positions in the government, including a period as the Minister for Immigration.

When he left politics in 1967, Oppy became Australia's first High Commissioner in Malta. He wrote all about his life in a book called *Pedals, Politics and People* in 1977.

His death at the age of 91 in 1996 brought to an end the life of a truly great Australian.

More About Oppy

- In 1952, Oppy was awarded an OBE (Order of the British Empire) and in 1968 he became Sir Hubert Opperman when he was knighted for his services to the nation.

- In 1984, Oppy was inducted into Sport Australia's Hall of Fame.

- In Oppy's home town of Rochester, Victoria, you can visit the Hubert Opperman Museum and you can also have your photo taken as you stand beside his statue.

Oops!

At the 1996 Atlanta Olympic Games, Victorian-born world sprint cycling champion Shane Kelly was the hot favourite to win the gold medal in the men's 1000-metres time trial. As he readied himself for the race, his foot slipped out of the pedal, and he lost his chance at Olympic gold.

MORE ABOUT CYCLING

 At the 2004 Athens Olympics, Australian cyclists took home nine medals, six of them gold. Sara Carrigan won gold in the women's road race and sprinter Ryan Bayley won two gold medals. The men's team won the 4000-metres men's pursuit, beating their own record in the process!

 Cyclist Cadel Evans won the 2006 Sir Hubert Opperman Medal and was named Cyclist of the Year. He took second place in the 2007 Tour de France, the best ever result by an Australian.

 According to the Australian Bureau of Statistics, cycling is becoming more popular, both as a way of keeping fit and also for transport. A 2006 Australian Sports Commission survey found that cycling is now the fourth most popular form of physical exercise. And with all the talk about global warming, riding your bike is not only good for you, it's good for the planet.

 Traffic planners are now including cycling paths on major roads in towns and cities all over Australia.

 There are various different kinds of cycling events, such as track, road cycling, mountain bike and BMX. There are also plenty of events for people with disabilities.

8. Golf

KARRIE WEBB, CHAMPION GOLFER

In November 2005, having played professional golf for 10 years, Aussie golfer Karrie Webb was inducted into the World Golf Hall of Fame. She was the youngest person ever to receive this honour. And it's no wonder. With eight major championship titles, including four Women's Australian Open titles, and a big bundle of awards, Karrie Webb is probably the best female golfer Australia has ever had. In 2007, she was ranked second-best female golfer in the world (after Mexico's Lorena Ochoa).

Only four other Australians have been inducted into the World Golf Hall of Fame: Walter Travis, Peter Thomson, Greg Norman and Kel Nagle. Karrie is the only Australian woman.

GOLF: Karrie Webb, champion golfer

TEEING OFF Karrie grew up in Ayr in Queensland and began playing golf with her family when she was about eight years old. By the age of 18, she was representing Australia in international amateur competitions. In 1994, she joined the professional golfing circuit and came second in the Australian Ladies Open. She also won Rookie of the Year. (A rookie is a player who is in her first full season in a professional sport.) Over the next few years, she really cleaned up on the golf course. For example, in 1995 when she was 20 years old, she won the British Women's Open and in 1999, she set a record for the Ladies Professional Golf Association (LPGA) Tour by finishing in the top 10 players 22 times.

In 2001, aged 26, Karrie was the only player at the US Women's Open to finish the course under par. She became the youngest ever winner of the LPGA Career Grand Slam.

The year 2002 was a real corker for Karrie. The year before, the LPGA decided to make the Women's British Open a major tournament. So when Karrie won the tournament, she clinched the Super Career Grand Slam – that's when you win all the major tournaments available across your career (there were five that year, but there are now only four major tournaments). Achieving a Super Career Grand Slam had never been done before and Karrie Webb made golfing history.

MORE ABOUT KARRIE Also in 2007, Karrie and Golf Australia set up a scholarship to help young female golfers. Karrie will train young players and help them to travel to overseas tournaments. She is keen to see more Australian female golfers get ahead in the sport. In 2008, Karrie won her fourth Women's Australian Open tournament. Now in her thirties, Karrie is playing as well as ever.

Gabbing About Golf

▶ There are two meanings for 'hole' in golf. One means the hole in the ground where the ball is supposed to go. Hole also means the area from where golfers tee off, all the way to the putting green. A standard golf course has 18 holes, although small clubs may only have nine holes.

▶ To win at golf, you must get the ball into the hole in the least number of hits, or strokes.

GOLF: Karrie Webb, champion golfer

- Par is the number of strokes that a top golfer needs to finish a particular hole. If the hole is par-four, then the golfer should be able to complete the hole in four strokes. A golf course is also given a total par rating – an easy nine-hole course might have a par of 36.

- Like other sports, golf uses a handicap system to make the competition fairer. An average golfer might have a handicap of 20. That means that at the end of the game, the player can take 20 points off the final score. Top golfers have no handicap – they are called scratch golfers.

- If the ball goes into the hole one stroke over par, it is called a bogey. If it goes in one stroke under par, it is called a birdie. A score of two strokes under par is called an eagle. Three strokes under par is an albatross. Golfers really like their birds!

- Of course, every golfer dreams about getting a hole in one. It's pretty rare. The ball must go straight into the hole on the first shot, which is hard when you can't even see the hole from way back at the tee. Some par-three holes can be up to 250 metres long – five times the length of an Olympic swimming pool.

- Have you ever wondered what the difference is between amateur and professional golf, or any sport for that matter? Amateur sportspeople play the game for enjoyment and there's usually no money involved. Professional sportspeople are paid to compete, because the sport is now their job. Professionals try to keep at the top of their game because the better they are, the more money they earn.

Oops!

For 331 weeks during the late 1980s and early 1990s, Greg Norman was ranked the world's top golfer, and there's no doubt that he's a golfing legend. A multi-award winner, British Open champ and Sport Australia Hall of Fame Legend, Greg's nickname is 'The Great White Shark'. Sometimes, however, Greg had a bit of bad luck and he often found it tricky to play his best in major competitions. In the first round of the 1996 US Masters tournament, Greg shot 63. By the final round, he was leading his nearest opponent, English golfer Nick Faldo, by six strokes. But Greg hit a few bogeys during the game and two double bogeys, one on the 12th hole and one on the 16th hole, where his ball landed in the water. Although Greg had the largest ever lead in a major tournament, Faldo went on to win the title five shots ahead of Greg.

9. Hockey

Now, how's this for success? The Hockeyroos, Australia's national women's hockey team, have won three Olympic gold medals, two World Cups, two Commonwealth Games gold medals and six World Championships. They were also voted the Best Australian Team at the 2000 Olympics by members of the Australian Olympic squad. That's a real honour. And they were named Australia's Team of the Year five years in a row from 1994 to 1998. The Hockeyroos are certainly something special.

OLYMPIC VICTORIES

Women's hockey became an Olympic sport in 1980 at the Moscow Games, but the Hockeyroos' first Olympics was the 1984 Los Angeles Games. They didn't win a medal then, so for the next four years,

they trained hard, kept fit, and honed their skills. Like all athletes, they ate a balanced diet, making sure to eat plenty of protein (which is great for muscles and bones) and carbohydrates (for energy). There's more about what athletes eat on page 173.

Then in the semi-finals of the women's hockey at the 1988 Seoul Olympics, the Hockeyroos defeated the Netherlands 3–2. In the finals, they were up against South Korea, the home team, and they won the game 2–0. That's a pretty good achievement for only their second Olympic Games.

In 1996 at Atlanta, the Hockeyroos won every one of 38 games they played before the finals. Once again in the finals they met the South Koreans, this time beating them 3–1.

Then, in the 2000 Sydney Games, when the Hockeyroos defeated Argentina 3–1 in the final, they became the first team in the history of the Olympic Games to retain the women's hockey title. The goals in that heart-stopping final were scored by Alyson Annan, Juliet Haslam and Jenny Morris.

It was the third Olympic gold medal for the Hockeyroos and one player, captain Rechelle Hawkes was especially thrilled. She was captain of the team for eight years, and represented Australia 279 times! One of the world's greatest hockey players, she was in the team that had also won at Seoul and at Atlanta. With this third gold medal, Rechelle became the third Australian to win a gold medal at the same event in three different Olympics. The others are swimmer Dawn Fraser and equestrian Andrew Hoy. Rechelle was inducted into Sport Australia's Hall of Fame in 2002.

HEROIC HOCKEYROOS Among some of the Hockeyroo champions is striker Alyson Annan, whose goal-scoring is legendary. In 228 international games, Alyson has scored a total of 166 goals. In 1999, she was voted the Best Female Hockey Player in the World by the International Hockey Federation. You can't get any better than that!

Other well-known players include Lianne Tooth, who has competed in four Olympic Games, and Jackie Pereira, Juliet Haslam, Kate Starre and Lisa Carruthers, who have competed in three. And history was made in 1996 when Hockeyroo Nova Peris became the first Aboriginal Australian to win Olympic gold. In the 2000 Olympics, Nova also competed in athletics, in the 400-metre track and field event.

The team's current captain, Nikki Hudson, has played 250 international games and is often called hockey's 'golden girl'.

Coming to Terms with Hockey

- Hockey is played on grass or a synthetic surface. It is sometimes called field hockey so that it's not confused with ice hockey.

- The team that has possession of the ball is called the attacking team and their players are called attackers. The team not in possession of the ball is called the defending team and so their players are called defenders. There are 11 players per side.

- When the ball is pushed and then raised off the ground with the J-shaped hockey stick, it is called a flick. When a player puts the stick underneath the ball and lifts it off the ground, it is called a scoop.

- To score a goal, the attacking player must be inside the goal circle. That's the area near the goal post in the shape of a semi-circle or the letter D.

- The only player on the field who is allowed to use their feet to control the ball is the goalkeeper. Goalkeepers usually wear a helmet and some protective gear. Sometimes they also wear a different coloured shirt from the rest of the team.

- If the umpire gives someone a yellow card, that player has to leave the field for at least five minutes. A yellow card is given when a player does something that's against the rules, for example playing roughly, or anything else that could be dangerous to the other players.

HOCKEY: Hockeyroo heroines

HOORAY FOR HOCKEY

Hockey is one of only a few sports that can be played by people of all ages. There are players who are six years old, and players who are older than 60. (You don't see too many 60-year-olds playing rugby league!) Another good thing about hockey is that it can be played indoors or outdoors, so you can play it all year round. According to Hockey Australia, there are more than 800 hockey clubs across Australia, with a total of about 138,000 registered hockey players.

MEN IN CHARGE

- The Australian men's hockey team is called the Kookaburras. They won gold at the 2004 Athens Olympics, bronze at both Sydney and Atlanta, and silver at Barcelona. That makes them the only Australian team to have won a medal in four Olympics in a row. They also have seven World Cup medals, three Commonwealth Games gold medals and a swag of championship medals. The Kookaburras are one of Australia's most successful teams in any sport.

- In his long hockey career, midfielder Jay Stacy has played 319 games for Australia, scoring a total of 160 goals. The International Hockey Federation (FIH) named him Most Valuable Hockey Player of the Year in 1999.

10. Horseracing

THE RACE THAT STOPS AUSTRALIA

Every year at about 3 pm on the first Tuesday in November, all Australians stop what they're doing and turn on the television or radio. Why? They're waiting for the country's most famous horserace, the Melbourne Cup. At the first Melbourne Cup back in 1861, 17 horses competed in front of a crowd of about 4000 for the grand total of £170 prize money and a gold watch!

These days, 24 of the world's best horses run the 3200-metre race, competing for some of the biggest prize money in the business – about $5 million. And not only are the crowds huge at Flemington Racecourse, but more than 700 million people around the world also watch the race on television.

TRAINING RACEHORSES

Training begins each morning before dawn and trainers work very long hours with their horses. Before a big race like the Melbourne Cup, a horse trains solidly for months. It will run the same distance as the race many times, so that it gets used to running that distance and so that its speed improves.

Training needs time and lots of patience and horses soon learn to trust their trainers. Not only do trainers run the horses, they must check for injuries, check that the hooves are not cracked and make sure the horse is eating properly.

Diet is very important for racehorses. Each day, they must eat a balanced diet of grains (like oats and corn), chaff (like hay), proteins and vitamins. Trainers often feed horses specially prepared dosages of these essential foods, especially proteins, so that they can be sure the horse is getting all the nutrition it needs. Racehorses need more protein than other horses because of all the energy they use.

WHAT'S A HANDICAP? Horses racing in the Melbourne Cup are 'handicapped'. This is to make the race fairer. Handicapping is done by giving the better horses more weight to carry. The weight of the jockey plus weights added to the saddles make up the total weight. For example, if a horse is given a handicap of 60 kilograms, and the jockey weighs 53 kilograms, then an extra 7 kilograms is added to the saddle to make the weight equal to the handicap.

A racing official decides what handicap each horse will have. Handicaps are worked out based on each horse's record of wins and how much prize money the horse has won.

MORE THAN JUST A HORSERACE Many people bet on which horse will win the Cup. This is often called 'having a flutter'. A lot of people only ever bet once a year – on the Melbourne Cup.

Melbourne Cup Day is like a party. It doesn't matter if you are not at Flemington to see the race yourself. People all over the country, and many in other countries too, hold Melbourne Cup parties, where they dress up, catch up with friends, and, of course, watch the race!

Dressing up is a regular part of Melbourne Cup Day. Each year there are competitions to find the best dressed man and woman at the racing carnival.

Oops!

The winner of the 1902 Melbourne Cup was The Victory, ridden by champion jockey Bobby Lewis. The Victory's owner, Lionel Robinson, spent part of Cup Day mowing his lawn and missed watching his horse win. He found out the results when the paperboy told him the next day.

HORSERACING: The race that stops Australia

MAGNIFICENT MELBOURNE CUP FACTS

 Lots of horseraces have certain conditions. To run in the Melbourne Cup, horses have to be three or more years old.

 The first Melbourne Cup was won by Archer in 3 minutes and 52 seconds.

 The fastest time ever recorded in the Cup was in 1990, when Kingston Rule ran the race in 3 minutes, 16.3 seconds.

 Four horses have won the Cup twice: Archer (1861, 1862), Peter Pan (1932, 1934), Rain Lover (1968, 1969) and Think Big (1974, 1975).

 Makybe Diva is the first horse in history to win the Melbourne Cup three times and she did it three years in a row (2003, 2004 and 2005). Each time, her jockey was Glen Boss.

 Among his many racing victories, trainer Bart Cummings has won a record 12 Melbourne Cups, the first with Light Fingers in 1965, the latest with Viewed in 2008.

Oops!

It didn't happen at the Melbourne Cup! In August 1984, a horse called Fine Cotton was racing at Eagle Farm in Brisbane. Lots of people bet a lot of money that the horse would win. But it wasn't really Fine Cotton racing that day. Another horse called Bold Personality had been made up to look like Fine Cotton. It had even been painted with some dye to hide its own colouring. As Bold Personality disguised as Fine Cotton made its way to the finish line, the dye wore off and the horse was disqualified. People who had bet that Fine Cotton would win lost their money, and the people involved in the fraud got into big trouble!

HORSERACING: The race that stops Australia

THE MYSTERY OF PHAR LAP

Australia's best known race horse, Phar Lap, is still the only horse to have been the favourite at three Melbourne Cups in a row. Although he only won the race once, in 1930, he won many other important races and he soon became the people's favourite. In his 51 races, he won 37 times.

In March 1932, Phar Lap was to compete in a race called the Agua Caliente Handicap. He travelled by ship to San Francisco, then was driven about 800 kilometres to Mexico (that's the same as going from Albany to Geraldton in Western Australia). The long trip exhausted him, and then he injured his heel, so his chances of winning weren't good. But Phar Lap surprised everyone and won the race. A few weeks later, something terrible happened. His trainer found the champion horse in pain, and Phar Lap died soon afterwards. Many believe that he was poisoned, so that he couldn't win any more races in North America. However, nothing was ever proved, and Phar Lap's death is still a mystery.

You can see Phar Lap's heart, which weighs over 6 kilograms, if you visit the National Museum in Canberra. (The heart of a normal horse weighs about 4 kilograms.)

Racing Words

- The favourite is the horse that the betting agencies think has the best chance of winning.
- A slow track is one that is a bit wet, and the horses usually run slower because it's more difficult. A fast track is a track that's dry and even, giving horses a better grip on the ground.
- Sometimes you hear that a horse has won by a length. A length in racing means the length of a horse, which is now a standard 3 metres.
- 'Colours' is the word used to mean the racing outfits worn by jockeys. The colours of a jockey's jacket and cap are chosen by the horse's owners and approved by racing authorities.
- Stewards are the people who make sure that the racing rules are obeyed and that no one is cheating.
- A strapper is a person who looks after the horse, grooming it before and after the race, and taking care of it in the stables.

11. Marathon

GOING THE DISTANCE

Who would have thought that an ancient battle would give rise to the endurance race, the marathon? It's true. Way back in 490 BC, Greece was being invaded by the mighty Persian army. The Athenians rallied their troops and even though they were outnumbered, they defeated the Persians at the Battle of Marathon. A runner called Pheidippides was ordered to run from Marathon all the way back to Athens to announce the Greek victory. It was a distance of 42 kilometres.

Things didn't work out for poor old Pheidippides. The stories say that he died from exhaustion after the run, but when the modern Olympic Games began in 1896, organisers decided to hold a 42-kilometre race in memory of Pheidippides' historic run. The marathon has been a part of the Olympic Games ever since.

PREPARING FOR A MARATHON

Apart from the Olympic Games, there are major marathons all around the world. In Australia, we have the Gold Coast, Melbourne and Toowoomba marathons, and the Sydney Marathon.

Training for a marathon is hard work. Just the thought of running 42 kilometres sends some people running for cover! But serious runners train very sensibly and carefully, otherwise they could do themselves some damage, like straining muscles, getting a stitch, or ending up with a footful of blisters.

Runners also ensure they eat nutritious food and avoid fatty or fried foods. Most trainers recommend a very high intake of carbohydrates, like bread, potatoes, fruit and vegetables, because these foods give you energy. Carbohydrates make up over two-thirds of the diet of most marathon runners.

Long distance runners train for months before the event, each day running just a bit further than they have run before. It's important to run at a steady pace – if you sprint at the beginning, you'll soon be puffed out, and the marathon is a test of endurance, not a sprint.

Another thing to think about is dehydration. This can happen when the body sweats so much it loses water. Dehydration is dangerous, so runners are careful to take regular small drinks along the way.

MARATHON: Going the distance

There are many things to think about before running in a long distance event, even the type of running shoes to wear. The best shoes are light, can absorb the bumpiness of your feet pounding on the ground, and must fit properly.

DASHING DEEK . . . Before Robert de Castella, or Deek as he is also known, won a gold medal at the 1982 Commonwealth Games in Brisbane, marathon running wasn't a very well known sport in Australia. Deek changed that, impressing everyone with his easy running style.

At the 1983 World Athletics Championships, Deek won his second gold medal. His third came at the Edinburgh Commonwealth Games, the same year he won the Boston Marathon. It's not surprising that he was 1983's Australian of the Year. In 1986 he was inducted into the Sport Australia Hall of Fame.

Robert de Castella has run more than 20 marathons around the world, winning nine of them, a record to be proud of.

. . . AND SUPER STEVE
Steve Moneghetti has represented Australia in four Commonwealth Games, four Olympic Games, six World Athletics Championships and numerous international marathon events. Born in Ballarat in 1962, Steve began

de Castella

running seriously in 10,000-metre events before he decided to tackle the mighty marathon. Now he is known as one of our greatest runners ever.

In 1990, Steve took the silver medal at that year's Commonwealth Games and then went on to win the Berlin Marathon, where he clocked his personal best time of 2 hours 8 minutes and 16 seconds. That's covering five and a half metres every single second!

He won the gold medal in 1994 at the Commonwealth Games in Canada, and the same year he won the Tokyo Marathon in 2 hours 8 minutes 55 seconds. He has three world-best times for the half marathon, and has won many shorter events. Steve retired from marathon running in 2001.

Moneghetti

Running well is a matter of having the patience to persevere when you are tired and not expecting instant results. The only secret is that it is consistent, often monotonous, boring, hard work. And it's tiring.

— ROBERT DE CASTELLA

MARATHON: Going the distance

AMAZING LISA ONDIEKI
When a 400-metre hurdler decided to try her hand at marathon running, she wasn't sure how it would all pan out. In 1983, Lisa Ondieki (then known as Lisa Martin) switched from one sport to another and within a few years she became Australia's best ever female long distance runner.

At the 1986 Edinburgh Commonwealth Games, the women's marathon event was held for the first time. Lisa streaked ahead of her opponents and won the gold medal. She won another gold medal at the 1990 Auckland Commonwealth Games and took the silver medal in the 1988 Seoul Olympic Games. Just before the 1988 Olympics, Lisa raced in Osaka, Japan where she set an Australian record, finishing in 2 hours 23 minutes and 52 seconds. She has been ranked in the world's top 10 female marathon runners six times. Now that's amazing.

Ondieki

CHASING SHEEP PAYS OFF

The first Sydney to Melbourne Ultra Marathon, a distance of 875 kilometres, was held in May 1983. Plenty of hopefuls entered the race including some top athletes, but the runner people remember is Cliff Young, the 61-year-old farmer who won it. No one could have imagined that Cliff would win. His age was against him, and he seemed to shuffle along the route rather than run. But he had the last laugh when, after 5 days 15 hours and 4 minutes, he was the first to cross the finish line.

How did he do it? Cliff used to chase his sheep across his farm, rounding them up whenever the weather looked bad. This made him pretty fit. And his other secret weapon? Well, everyone knew the race would take at least five days, most of it running, with about five or six hours put aside for sleep. But Cliff only took short naps and just kept running all the way to the end. He won $10,000 and a place in Ultra Marathon history.

MORE MARATHON MATTERS

- A half marathon is, just as you'd think, half the distance. It's 21.0975 kilometres long to be exact.
- Most marathons are also open to wheelchair athletes and others with disabilities.
- There are plenty of family fun runs held across the country. These are usually only about 4 kilometres long.

12. Marathon Swimming

Marathon or long distance swimming is swimming in open waters such as the ocean, a river or a lake. Although there are long distance swimming competitions, most often, swimmers swim on their own. Can you imagine swimming the 34 kilometres from England to France? That's the sort of distance that marathon swimmers cover. The swimmer is alone in the water and is not allowed to wear a wetsuit. Even though the swimmer is covered in grease to protect them against the cold, it still gets incredibly chilly in the water. And it might be hard to believe, what with being surrounded by all that water, but swimming long distances really makes you thirsty!

SUSIE MARONEY, A FISH IN WATER

A team of people, including the coach, travels near the swimmer in a boat. They are there in case the swimmer gets into trouble, such as getting a cramp, and they make sure the swimmer gets food and a little rest along the way.

SENSATIONAL SUSIE Australia's best known marathon swimmer is Susie Maroney. She began swimming when she was four to help her cope with asthma, and within a few years she was swimming competitively. She began long distance swimming at 11, and at just 15 years of age she became the first Australian woman and the youngest person ever to swim across the English Channel, completing the swim in 8 hours and 29 minutes.

Susie then set herself another challenge, this time to swim both ways across the Channel! She was 17 when she became the youngest person to make the double crossing.

SWIMMING THE WORLD Susie won the 46-kilometre Manhattan Island Marathon three times (1991, 1992 and 1994). Then she made world headlines again when at the age of 22, she swam 180 kilometres from Cuba to Florida in the United States. She did this in a little less than 25 hours. Think about it – in 25 hours, most of us have slept, eaten, gone to school or work, played some sport or read a book, watched television, done homework, washed the dishes, sent a few text messages, had a bath, brushed our teeth and gone to sleep again. Susie spent all this time swimming!

The next year, 1998, she spent 38 hours and 33 minutes swimming through jellyfish-infested waters from Mexico to Cuba, a distance of almost 200 kilometres. It was the longest distance ever swum in the open sea without flippers and Susie was seasick for much of the swim because it was impossible not to swallow salt water. To protect herself from sharks, she swam

MARATHON SWIMMING: Susie Maroney, a fish in water

in a specially designed cage. The seas were rough and Susie was exhausted by the time she walked ashore. She was bruised from bumping against the cage and the jellyfish had covered her in bites.

FISH OUT OF WATER After these swims, Susie Maroney kept on breaking records. In 1999, she swam from Jamaica to Cuba and made *The Guinness Book of Records* for non-stop swimming. Susie was awarded an Order of Australia in 1993.

These days Susie is a great ambassador for people suffering from asthma and other disabilities. She still swims, but now she also wants to help others to achieve their goals.

DES RENFORD: A LATE STARTER

At the age of 39, Des Renford decided to take up marathon swimming. This was considered a little old to be starting such a demanding sport, but Des had been around the water all his life, and he was determined to succeed. He trained on winter mornings in the chilly waters of Sydney's Clovelly Beach and his first competition was the 38-kilometre race across Melbourne's Port Phillip Bay, where he came third.

When he was 43, he swam the English Channel for the first time. Over the next decade, Des crossed the Channel 19 times, becoming known as 'king of the Channel'.

Des broke the record in Queensland's Moreton Bay Marathon swim in 1973. In 1974 he swam the 79 kilometres from Sydney to Wollongong and in 1975 he was named Australian Marathon Swimming Champion. Des even swam in the frosty waters of Loch Ness in Scotland, although he didn't finish that race.

Des Renford later went on to coach long distance swimmers, including the great Susie Maroney.

MARATHON SWIMMING: Susie Maroney, a fish in water

Darlings of the Distance

● Perth girl Shelley Taylor-Smith was born with a condition called scoliosis, which leaves the spine with an abnormal curve. To keep fit, she began swimming and was doing very well when she became partially paralysed. While many people would have given up, Shelley began long distance swimming. Among her many achievements, Shelley won the Manhattan Island Marathon five times, and is a three-time winner of the Australian Swimming Championships. She retired from the sport in 1998.

● Victorian-born Tammy van Wisse has more records than you can poke a stick at! Amazingly, she has swum more than 60,000 kilometres! She has swum across the English Channel, New Zealand's Cook Strait, Scotland's Loch Ness and across the dangerous waters of Bass Strait. Tammy has even swum the entire length of the Murray River, the first person ever to do this! It took her 106 days.

MORE ABOUT MARATHON SWIMMING

 Marathon swimmers are not allowed to wear wetsuits because they are thought to give swimmers extra buoyancy and speed. They can, however, wear goggles and earplugs.

 Some of the things that the support crew must carry on the boat are blankets (to wrap the swimmer in when they leave the water), a torch, a compass and a flare (in case of emergencies).

 Support crew members must have first aid training and be able to recognise when a swimmer may need to come out of the water. This could happen if the swimmer gets cramps, or gets hypothermia, which is when the body temperature becomes too low.

 Long distance swimming is controlled by the Fédération Internationale de Natation (FINA).

 Marathon swimmers must swim only freestyle.

13. Motorcycling

Imagine entering a world-wide competition made up of 18 motorcycle races held in 16 different countries. In each race you score a certain number of points depending on how well you did, so if you win a race you get 25 points, and if you come last you only score one point. The person with the most points after all 18 races wins the world championship.

Now, picture yourself riding a motorcycle that weighs about 150 kilograms – roughly the same as four 10-year-old boys. That's a big bike and it has a very powerful engine, so you have to be totally in control. You have to have nerves of steel and never, not even for a nanosecond, can you take your eye off the road. You are racing against the very best riders

CASEY STONER, SPEED DEMON

69

in the world, and one of them has been the world champion seven times.

Now imagine you have come sixth in the 15th race of 18, but you have already won the world championship. Incredible! This is what happened to 21-year-old Gold Coast sports star Casey Stoner, the 2007 MotoGP World Champion.

A BORN CHAMPION

It's not often that someone shows an outstanding talent at a very young age. Mozart did – he was writing all sorts of wonderful music at the age of four. When Casey Stoner was four, he wasn't composing music, but he *was* riding motorbikes. Casey's parents knew a lot about motorcycles and had allowed to him to start riding dirt bikes when he was still a toddler – after taking lots of precautions to ensure he couldn't get hurt.

MOTORCYCLING: Casey Stoner, speed demon

RIDING THROUGH LIFE One weekend when he was 12, Casey competed in 35 races at the Australian Long Track Titles and won 32 of them! By the time he was 14, Casey had competed in races all over Australia and had won more than 100 races.

Because he was too young to be in road races in Australia (you need to be 16), the Stoner family moved to England for a few years so that Casey could compete there. He raced in Spain and Britain and won the English 125cc Aprilia Championship in 2000 when he was only 15 years old. He raced in both 125cc and 250cc Grand Prix categories and by the time he was 20, he was ready for the MotoGP, the most important of the Grand Prix races.

TAKING THE TITLE Casey's first MotoGP was in 2006, when he was part of the Honda team, finishing eighth in the season. Not bad for his first time in the motorcycle world's premier race.

The 2007 MotoGP was the first 800cc grand prix. Up until then, it had been a 500cc race. Riding for Ducati in 2007, Casey won the race, in Qatar. He then went on to win another seven grand prix races. In five of those races, he started in pole position (that's on the inside lane, a great place to start). You need to qualify for pole position, so having it five times is pretty amazing.

At the Japanese Grand Prix in September 2007, the rain caused a few problems – some parts of the track were damp, some parts were dry. This makes it harder for the riders because it's tricky working out which parts of the track might be slippery, but Casey was undaunted. Although he came sixth in the 24-lap race, he was 83 points ahead of his nearest rival, Italian rider Valentino Rossi, and there was no way anyone could possibly catch up. And even though there were still three races to run, Casey Stoner had already won the world championship. He is the second youngest person, and the third Australian, ever to win the MotoGP. In 2008, Casey was named Young Australian of the Year.

> Towards the end, everything was creeping into my head, so I just tried to stay focused on the job in hand. I wanted to bring it home for my team.
>
> – CASEY STONER

Oops!

Australian motorcycling legend Harry Hinton was racing in the 1951 Isle of Man Tourist Trophy (TT). When the British motorcyclist Maurice Cann was unable to race due to injury, he offered his bike to Harry, who, during a practice round, went on to beat the existing lap record by 60 seconds. Harry was favourite to win the Junior TT (for 350cc bikes). Unfortunately, he crashed, breaking his hand and he never competed internationally again. But it wasn't all bad for Harry – he was the Australian motorcycle champ five times.

MOTORCYCLING: Casey Stoner, speed demon

MOTORCYCLE HEROES

In 1987, Wayne Gardner won the 500cc World Championship, the first Australian to win it. He won the first Australian Grand Prix, held on Phillip Island in 1989, and when he stopped racing motorcycles, he became a touring car champion, even competing in the Bathurst 1000.

When Michael Doohan entered his first race in 1984, he had no idea that he would later win an unbelievable five consecutive 500cc world titles. From 1994 to 1998, he was unbeatable. In his racing career, Michael had a total of 54 Grand Prix wins.

THE MotoGP

In Grand Prix motorcycle racing, there are three separate events, each based on the size of the engine: 125cc, 250cc and MotoGP, where the motorcycles can be up to 800cc. The size of the engine is measured in cubic centimetres (cc). The more ccs, the more powerful the bike's engine. These bikes are very different from regular motorcycles, because they are specially designed for racing and can reach speeds of over 330 kilometres per hour. That's fast!

14. Motor Racing

BROCKY, ALL ABOUT SPEED

On most days of the year, the Mount Panorama racetrack in rural New South Wales is just another mountain road, and although it's very winding and there are lots of sharp bends, people drive on it on their way to work or school. But on one Sunday every October, Mount Panorama is the site of the Bathurst 1000, one of the most challenging motor races around. When the Bathurst motor car race began, it was called the Bathurst 500 because the distance was 500 miles (800 kilometres), but in 1973, the race distance was changed to 1000 kilometres.

Today, the track is 6.213 kilometres long, so drivers must drive around the track 161 times to make up the total distance of 1000 kilometres. It takes enormous concentration to keep up the speed needed to finish the course.

MOTOR RACING: Brocky, all about speed

The racetrack has three main sections – a short straight leads to the steep straight which is about 175 metres up the mountain, then there's a section that crosses the mountain, and finally there's the downhill section, where racing cars travel at up to 300 kilometres per hour. When you think that the average street speed is 60 kilometres per hour, you start to realise just how fast these drivers are going.

KING OF THE MOUNTAIN There have been some incredible drivers at Bathurst, but one name stands above the rest – Peter Brock. He won the Bathurst 1000 a record nine times. No one has ever beaten this record and Peter became known as the 'king of the mountain'. His other nickname was Peter Perfect.

So just what was so perfect about Peter Brock? In his nine wins at Bathurst, Peter won the respect and admiration of many people. His first win was in 1972 driving a Holden Torana XU-1. He won again in 1975, 1978, 1979, 1980, 1982, 1983, 1984, and his last win was in 1987, driving a Holden Commodore VL.

Peter's win in 1975, with co-driver, Brian Sampson, was considered a big win, because he won by two laps: that's 12 kilometres ahead of his nearest rival. But it was his performance in the 1979 race that has become legendary.

In that race, he beat his nearest opponent by a whopping six laps, and in the last lap he set the record for the fastest ever lap at Mount Panorama, taking nearly five minutes off the race record. His co-driver was Jim Richards and they drove a Holden Torana A9X. Peter said the car had lots of power and excellent brakes, something you'd need coming down that steep mountain! Although it happened almost 30 years ago, Brocky's 1979 race is still talked about in Bathurst.

In his 32 Bathurst 1000 races, Peter had pole position six times. Just as with motorcycling, pole position is given to the driver who is fastest in the qualifying rounds. It means that the driver gets to start in the inside lane, closest to the fence. This is *the* best place to start.

MORE ABOUT PETER PERFECT

As well as taking the Bathurst 1000 by storm, Peter Brock also won the Repco Round Australia in 1979. He made a big impression at the Sandown 500, the 500-kilometre, two-driver race held just near Melbourne, winning it nine times, the first time in 1973. Then from 1975 until 1981 he was undefeated, winning the race seven times in a row. That's really something. In 1997, when Peter retired from racing, the front straight of the Sandown track was renamed Brock Straight to recognise his amazing talent.

Brocky also raced in the Australian Touring Car/V8 Championships, winning it three times. One of the amazing things about this championship is that Peter won 37 of the preliminary races, and this was a record in the Australian Touring Car/V8 Championships until 2007 when Mark Skaife finally beat it with 38 wins.

REMEMBERING BROCKY

When Peter Brock died in an accident in September 2006, the motor racing world lost one of its great achievers. Soon after, the Peter Brock Trophy was introduced to reward the winner of the Bathurst 1000/V8 Supercar race. The first person to win the trophy was Craig Lowndes (and his co-driver, Jamie Whincup), just one month after Brocky's death.

In memory of Brocky, a section of the Mount Panorama circuit, right at the point where drivers begin to go down the mountainside, was renamed Brock Skyline.

SUPERCARS

The Bathurst 1000 is a touring car race. Touring cars, also called V8 supercars, are obviously very different from grand prix Formula 1 racing cars. They are normal four-door sedans that have been adjusted for race conditions. So a regular family car might be fitted with a new engine and racing wheels and tyres, giving it the power and safety features that are needed in these long endurance races. Peter Brock mostly drove Holden cars, especially Toranas and Commodores.

Raving About Motor Racing

- Because of the long distances in endurance races like the Bathurst 1000, there must be two drivers. At Bathurst, drivers are not allowed to drive more than 106 laps altogether.

- If a driver is on the throttle, that means his or her foot is pressing the accelerator to the floor.

- A pit stop is where drivers stop for a short time so that the racing crew can change the tyres, put more petrol in the car and check that everything else is okay.

- We all know what a blister is, but in motor racing, a blister is what happens to a tyre when it's getting worn out through heat and speed. When a tyre is blistered, it can be dangerous for the driver. Because the tyre has less grip on the road it can be harder to control the car, and the driver usually takes a pit stop to fix it.

15. Novelty Sports

THE DRY REGATTA AND OTHER UNUSUAL SPORTS

Each spring, not far from the main shopping area of Alice Springs, a rather curious race takes place. It's called the Henley-on-Todd Regatta. Now, as you might know, a regatta is a series of rowing and sailing races held on a river or the ocean. What makes this boat race so unusual is that it is held in a dry sandy river bed, and the contestants cut the bottoms out of their boats and run to the finish line holding their boats around their waists. It's a crazy sight!

THE FIRST HENLEY-ON-TODD REGATTA

In 1962, a couple of Alice Springs weather forecasters came up with a wild idea. They thought it would be fun to copy the famous Henley-on-Thames regatta held between Cambridge and Oxford universities in England, where teams row down the Thames River. They named it after the famous regatta, even though Alice Springs is in the middle of Australia, and nowhere near a river big enough to hold a regatta.

But that's what made the idea so attractive. The Todd River runs through Alice Springs and is mostly dry. So immediately,

NOVELTY SPORTS: The dry regatta and other sports

everyone knew that this race was going to be a lot of fun. In fact, they had so much fun that the Henley-on-Todd Regatta is now an important part of life in the Northern Territory.

Each year, the regatta attracts about 4500 people, of whom more than 400 are competitors. They come from around Australia and overseas to take part in this unique event.

BRILLIANT BOATS

The first competitors had to come up with very inventive boats. After all, there was no water in the river. Some people simply cut the bottom out of their wooden boats and they were ready to go. As time went on, other clever 'rowers' used the metal frame of boats, attached straps to the boat's sides, then looped the straps over their shoulders. Some wacky boats were made using recycled drink cans.

Every year competitors race in yachts, kayaks and other boats. The boats are clever and very funny.

REGATTA RACE EVENTS

There are all sorts of events in the Henley-on-Todd. The Oxford Tubs is a two-person event where the boat, usually an old petrol drum, is rowed or more precisely, shovelled, along the riverbed. In the Surf Rescue event, the 'lifesaver' must paddle a surf ski along rails and rescue a damsel in distress (that's an old-fashioned way of saying a girl in trouble). The two contestants are then reeled back to the 'shore' by their two team mates.

The Bath Tub Derby is one of the most popular Regatta events. Four people must carry a girl in a bath tub to a particular spot in the river. Then they must fill the tub with some water and carry it as fast as they can to the finish line. Just imagine how awkward that would be.

There are also triathlons, boogie board events and iron man competitions. You can see why the Regatta is such a popular day with both adults and kids alike.

GRAND FINALE The final event in the Regatta is the Battle Boat Spectacular. Three trucks are decorated to look like battleships. They race through the sandy river bed firing flour bombs and water cannons at their opponents and at the crowd. There are often many messy spectators standing on the riverbank!

At the end of the day, everyone's had the best time, and sponsors have raised money for the three Alice Springs Rotary Clubs to continue their many good works in the community.

Oops!

The Henley-on-Todd has been a major event in Alice Springs every year since 1962. Or has it? In 1993, plans had been made and the competitors were ready for the race, but that year there was a lot of rain and there was too much water in the Todd River. Organisers had to cancel the event due to flooding!

MORE MADCAP RACES

 Another Northern Territory novelty race that attracts a lot of attention is the Beer Can Regatta, a charity event held at Darwin's Mindil Beach each July. It began in 1974 as a fun way to recycle beer cans, but these days any kind of soft drink can is permitted. Boats are made from cans and rowed out to a buoy, then back again.

 In the Milk Carton Regatta, yes, you guessed it, the boats are made entirely from milk cartons. This race is held in Hillary's Boat Harbour in Perth each year.

 Tasmania hosts the Great Huon Apple Race every October. Competitors float an apple down the Huon River for about 300 metres. The owner of the first apple over the finish line is, of course, the winner.

THE DUNNY DERBY

The Winton Outback Festival in central western Queensland is held every two years in September. There are plenty of fun events for everyone, but the most interesting event is the Dunny Derby. Imagine it – teams of four take their places at the starting line. One person sits on the dunny and the others pull it along the 250-metre racetrack. Luckily, the outback racing toilet has wheels!

You may not have heard of Winton, but it has a pretty important place in Australian history. Banjo Paterson is said to have written the words to 'Waltzing Matilda' in Winton, and Winton is also the birthplace of Qantas. (Qantas moved to Longreach soon after it was founded.)

16. Paralympic Perfection

If you were to ask sports reporters, sports managers and fans which Australian sportsperson most inspires them, many would probably have the same answer: Louise Sauvage. Louise is a world champion athlete. She's won a load of sporting titles and medals since her first major competition in 1990, and has dominated her sport since 1992. And she does all this from her wheelchair.

Louise was born with a condition called myelodysplasia which affects the spine, so she has only limited movement from her waist down. She has been in a wheelchair since she was eight years old. But Louise has a natural talent for sport and even when she was little,

LOUISE SAUVAGE, AGAINST THE ODDS

85

she was as active as she could be. She swam, threw discuses and played basketball, and by the age of 10 she became the youngest athlete to compete in the National Paraplegic and Quadriplegic Games.

OPERATION LOUISE Louise has had many operations since she was a small girl, but in her early teens, metal rods were put into her back to stop her spine from curving any

PARALYMPIC PERFECTION: Louise Sauvage

further than it had. She had to go through three long and painful operations and the doctors told her that she wouldn't be able to swim competitively again. Louise worried that maybe she'd never be able to play any sport again.

Yet slowly, very slowly, Louise recovered and she went back to her training on the track. Only a couple of years later, at the age of 16, she represented Australia at the International Paralympic Committee's World Championships, winning gold in the 100 metres. It was clear that Louise was going places.

PARALYMPIC GOLDEN GIRL Louise is a four-time Paralympian and has won nine gold medals. Her first Paralympics in Barcelona in 1992 made her a household name. She won gold in the 100, 200 and 400 metres, and a silver medal for the 800 metres.

In 1996 at Atlanta, she won four gold medals. In 2000, Louise lit the Paralympic cauldron to mark the start of the Sydney Paralympics, where she also won two more gold medals. Her fourth Paralympics was in Athens in 2004, where she won two silver medals. To be in one Paralympics is wonderful, but to be in four is amazing!

During these years, Louise also started training for road races, which are over longer distances.

MARATHON EFFORTS Between Paralympic Games, Louise competed in many of the world's most famous marathon events, including Boston, Berlin, Honolulu, Sydney and Los Angeles. The paralympic marathon is the same distance as for able-bodied athletes: 42 kilometres. Louise has won at least 18 of these, among them four Boston Marathons! In 1997, she won four marathons, and then won another four the following year.

Training for these events is hard work. Louise trained every day in her wheelchair, pushing herself at least 25 kilometres every single day. To keep fit and prepared for competitive events, she also did some weight training, a little boxing and she also made sure to swim a few times a week. She ate the right foods too – that's important for any sportsperson.

Louise's talents have been recognised with many awards, including Australian Paralympian of the Year four times (1994, 1996, 1997, 1998) and she received an Order of Australia in 1992. In 1995 she was inducted into the New South Wales Sports Hall of Champions. The International Association of Athletics Federation (IAAF) named Louise the World Athletics Champion five times between 1993 and 2003. Her hard work and dedication make Louise a great role model.

FIGHTING UNFAIRNESS

It's hard to believe, but for years, many people thought that disabled athletes were not as talented as able-bodied athletes. It is certainly true that for a long time, they didn't receive as much praise as other great sportspeople. And although the Australian Institute of Sport has been providing training programs for elite disabled athletes since 1989, it's taken able-bodied people quite a while to recognise the talents of those with disabilities.

Louise Sauvage is helping to change the way people think about disabled athletes. First, her incredible sporting talent has shown that being disabled doesn't mean you can't be a champion, and people are now much more supportive of disability sporting events. Louise now visits schools and sporting clubs to encourage disabled people to become more active and to believe in themselves.

Nowadays, disabled athletes compete in all sorts of sports, including archery, basketball, table tennis, swimming, canoeing, tennis and rugby. In almost any sport you can name, you're sure to find some awesome disabled athletes.

PARALYMPIC PERFECTION: Louise Sauvage

I never thought of myself as being different, or disadvantaged. I'm just me, the way I am. The circumstances of my life put me in a wheelchair, but it has been my own efforts that have taken me around the world, and to the successes I have had.

– LOUISE SAUVAGE

WHEELCHAIR RACING

 Wheelchair racing has been an official Paralympic sport since 1960 when the first Paralympic Games were held in Rome. It is also an important part of the Commonwealth Games and the IAAF World Championships, and it is a demonstration sport at the Olympic Games. Competitions range from sprints of 100 metres right through to 10,000 metres (that's 10 kilometres!).

 Wheelchair athletes must use special racing chairs, usually with a single front wheel and two rear wheels. The chairs are very expensive, and athletes can often wear one out in just a year.

 The rules forbid any mechanical steering levers because these would make the chair go faster. It's okay to have a hand-operated lever. When racing, it's compulsory for competitors to wear a helmet.

MARVELLOUS MICHAEL MILTON

Champion skier Michael Milton lost a leg to bone cancer when he was only nine years old, but like many fantastic disabled athletes, he has never let his disability stop him from achieving his goals. He loved skiing, so he taught himself to ski on one leg. He was so good that when he was 14, he competed at the 1988 Winter Paralympic Games. Michael has 10 Paralympic medals, six of them gold. In 2006, he became the fastest Australian speed skier, either able-bodied or disabled. Michael is one of our most accomplished sportsmen!

Ahead of the Rest

- Perth-born Priya Cooper is a champion swimmer with nine gold Paralympic medals.
- Grant Boxall was left almost quadriplegic after a surfing accident. Now he is a champion wheelchair rugby player.
- Paralympic swimmer Siobhan Paton holds world records in the 100 metres freestyle. She was honoured in 2000, when Australia Post issued a stamp with her picture on it.

17. Rowing

In 1990, a group of first-rate rowers entered the World Rowing Championships, the most important international rowing competition in the world. Nick Green, Mike McKay, James Tomkins and Sam Patten easily won the coxless fours and that's when they earned their nickname, the Oarsome Foursome. The following year, they won the coxless fours again. The next big international sporting challenge was the 1992 Barcelona Olympic Games. By the time they set off for Spain, Sam had been replaced by Andrew Cooper.

Australian rowers got off to a great start at the 1992 Olympics. First, Peter Antonie and Stephen Hawkins won the gold medal for the double sculls. Then it was time for the coxless fours event. It turned out to be a very close contest

between Australia, the United States and Slovenia, but the Oarsome Foursome pipped their opposition at the post when they completed the race in 5 minutes and 55.04 seconds.

When they won the coxless fours, it was Australia's first gold medal for rowing since Mervyn Wood won the single scull back in 1948.

In 1995, Andrew Cooper left the team and Drew Ginn became the fourth awesome crew member. They then began training for the 1996 Atlanta Olympics. Again, they dazzled everyone with their long easy strokes and they rowed straight for the gold medal position, claiming it for Australia.

Australia won another Olympic gold medal for rowing in 1996, when Megan Still and Kate Slatter won the women's coxless pair.

TAKING ON THE WORLD In 1998, the Oarsome Foursome won yet another gold medal at the World Championships when they won the coxed four. They were now the world leaders in their sport. It was thanks to them that the sport of rowing became better known across Australia.

A Little About Rowing

- Like all championship sports, rowing requires enormous concentration and absolute fitness. Rowing is a speed race, but one thing that makes it unusual is that the rowers face backwards from the finish line.

- There are two main types of rowing: sweep rowing, in which each rower uses one oar, and sculling, in which each rower uses two oars. In double sculls, one rower sits behind the other and they each pull two oars.

- The Oarsome Foursome were sweep rowers. We all know what 'sweep' usually means, but in rowing, it has nothing to do with cleaning the floor. A sweep is someone who rows with a sweep oar: a long heavy oar that 'sweeps' through the water.

- In coxless teams, each of the rowers is a 'sweep', because they each use one oar. It's called coxless because the team doesn't have a coxswain. A coxswain faces forward and steers the boat while telling the rowers what to do. In coxless fours, one of the rowers steers the boat by controlling the rudder with a foot pedal.

- A bowman doesn't use a bow and arrow. The bowman is the rower who sits closest to the front, or bow, of the boat.

- When rowers talk about the 'catch', they mean the spot where the oar goes into the water.

- If the oar goes into the water at the wrong angle it can be hard to pull it out, and it really slows down the boat. Rowers call this a crab.

- There are 14 different rowing events in the Olympic Games, each over a distance of 2000 metres. Try taking one big step – that's about 1 metre. If you took 2000 big steps, you'd know how far rowers have to row!

Oops!

In the 2004 Athens Olympic Games, the Australian women's eight rowing team had a very good chance of winning the bronze medal. Instead they came last. About 600 metres from the finish line, spectators were amazed to see that one of the rowers was not rowing. In fact, she was lying down! Sally Robbins had lain back onto Julia Wilson's lap. She said she was so tired that she just couldn't move.

Her team mates were furious. They accused her of quitting, saying that as part of a team, she should have pushed herself harder. Sally said that she was feeling so much pressure that she couldn't cope and that's why she collapsed. Even today, many people are still upset by what happened that day.

ROWING: The Oarsome Foursome

MORE OARSOME FACTS

 James Tomkins has competed in five Olympics, from 1988 through to 2004, and has three Olympic gold medals. He also has nine World Championship gold medals and one Commonwealth Games gold medal. James has more rowing medals than any other Australian rower. And he is the only rower in history to have won world titles in every sweep-oared race. How amazing is that!

 Mike McKay has also competed at five Olympic Games. In the closing ceremony of the Atlanta Games, he was chosen to carry the Australian flag.

 Andrew Cooper and Nick Green have been inducted into the Sport Australia Hall of Fame, Andrew in 1999 and Nick in 2001.

 Drew Ginn and James Tomkins won gold at the 2004 Athens Olympics in the coxless pair. Drew has also won four coxless pairs World Championships, the most recent one in 2006 with Duncan Free.

 The Oarsome Foursome appeared on a series of television commercials advertising a popular brand of canned fruit. They even sang the jingle themselves!

18. Rugby League

The 1956 New South Wales rugby league grand final between St George and Balmain was played in front of a crowd of more than 60,000 people at the Sydney Cricket Ground. For the first half of the game, the Dragons and the Tigers were pretty evenly matched, but when the final siren rang, St George had won the game 18–12. This was the start of an extraordinary run of success. For the next ten years, St George won every rugby league grand final. That's 11 years in a row at the top, something that had never happened before in the game's history. And that record has never been beaten!

The Dragons had been around for a long time, playing their first big match in 1921 against Glebe at the Sydney Sports Ground. Based in Kogarah in Sydney's southern suburbs, their first premiership was in 1941 when they defeated Eastern Suburbs. By the mid-1950s, St George had some of

DRAGON POWER

RUGBY LEAGUE: Dragon power

the finest players in the league, and once they won the 1956 premiership, they weren't going to let it go without a fight.

MUDDY GLADIATORS One of rugby league's most memorable grand final matches was on 24 August 1963 between St George and the Western Suburbs Magpies. The venue, the Sydney Cricket Ground, was soaking wet. It was the third time that the Dragons had met Wests in a grand final, and Wests were determined to win.

As the game progressed, the players were covered from head to toe in mud. Sometimes, the spectators couldn't quite tell who was who! Imagine how hard it was to hold the slippery ball or how easy it was to lose your balance on that boggy ground. Mud flew into the players' eyes and up their noses. It was a very difficult and dirty match. St George scored two tries (one each from George Evans and Johnny King) and one goal (from Reg Gasnier) to win the match 8–3.

At the very end of the match, Dragons captain Norm Provan and Magpies captain Arthur Summons gave each other a muddy hug. A photographer called John O'Gready took a picture of the hug and called it 'The Gladiators'. The photograph became a symbol of mateship and good sportsmanship. The image now appears on the National Rugby League trophy.

A TEAM OF CHAMPIONS

What a year 1963 was for the Dragons. They were premiers in all three grades, and later that year they played New Zealand in an international match, winning 22–7. As well as Norm Provan, Reg Gasnier and Johnny King, other members of the champion team were Kevin Ryan, Graeme Langlands, Billy Smith and Johnny Raper, all of whom also played for Australia.

DRAGON DEEDS

- In the 1957 grand final against Manly-Warringah, St George's Harry Bath scored eight goals, the most goals ever scored by one player in a premiership match.

- In 1959, St George won every single game they played. Only four other clubs have gone right through a season without losing a match – Balmain in 1915, North Sydney in 1921, South Sydney in 1925 and Eastern Suburbs in 1936 and again in 1937.

- In the 1962 grand final against Wests, only one try was scored in the entire game, by St George's Johnny King.

- St George was the favourite to win the 1967 grand final against Canterbury-Bankstown. Although they led in the first part of the match, the Dragons were finally defeated 12–11. After 11 incredible years, the Dragons were no longer the reigning premiers of rugby league.

- In 1998, St George combined with Illawarra and together they became the St George Illawarra Dragons.

RUGBY LEAGUE: Dragon power

A LEAGUE OF THEIR OWN

Rugby league developed in England during the 1890s. It has been played in Australia since the early years of the twentieth century. In fact, in 2008 we celebrated the centenary of rugby league. League is very similar to rugby union, although there are a few main differences. For example, in union, there are 15 players per side. In league there are only 13, and scrums are more important in union than they are in league.

Rugby league quickly became the most popular winter sport in New South Wales and Queensland, with other states preferring Australian Rules. The first club, Newtown, was founded in 1908 and before too long, there were a number of clubs playing and promoting league. St George entered the third grade league in 1910. In 1920, the New South Wales Rugby League gave permission for St George to set up a first grade team. They played their first game on 23 April 1921 – St George's Day. That's the real St George, the patron saint of England and the man famous for killing a dragon.

League Language

- When a player places the ball on the ground in the opposition's goal area, it is called a try. A try is now worth four points. (In the 11 years that St George were the premiers, tries were worth three points.)

- After a try is scored, the scoring team attempts a conversion. This means that a player can kick for goal and score two extra points if successful.

- A field goal scores only one point. The ball must be drop-kicked and go above the bar that crosses the goal posts.
- After a tackle, the play-the-ball gets the game moving again. To play-the-ball, the tackled player rolls the ball back to a team mate with his foot.
- If a player passes the ball to a team mate who is in front of him when facing the opposing team's goal post, it is called a forward pass. This is a real no-no, and the referee usually awards the other team a penalty (which means they take possession of the ball).

Oops!

In early 2007, Queensland forward Ben Czislowski was playing for Wynnum Manly against Tweed Heads when he and his opponent Matt Austin crashed head first into one another. Ben was cut above the eye and needed stitches. For weeks afterwards, Ben's eye was swollen and he suffered terrible headaches. He was very sick, his eye became infected, and he lost all his energy.

After about 15 weeks, he went back to see his doctor, who discovered that one of Matt Austin's teeth had been pushed deep into Ben's forehead! It had been there all that time. It was removed and Ben recovered, but Matt didn't get his tooth back. Ben keeps it in a jar at his home.

19. Rugby Union

MARK ELLA, MAKING A DIFFERENCE

One of the greatest rugby union players of all time has to be Mark Ella. An all-rounder, he had a short but outstanding career, representing Australia in 25 international matches, 10 of them as captain. Mark was the first Indigenous Australian ever to captain an Australian international sporting team. And he is still the only Australian to score a try in each of four Test matches played against Great Britain. He did this in 1984.

Growing up in a working class area of Sydney, Mark Ella was always playing cricket and rugby league with his 11 brothers and sisters. In his teens, he discovered rugby union. He played in the 1977 Australian rugby schoolboy team, which travelled to Britain, the Netherlands, France and Japan. They didn't lose a single game. In 1978 Mark started playing for

Randwick Rugby Club. His easy style and incredible ability were quickly spotted and in 1980 he was selected to join the Wallabies, Australia's national rugby team.

PLAYING FOR AUSTRALIA Mark made his international debut against New Zealand in 1980 when he was 21 years old. Australia won that game 13–9. Mark's position was five-eight (also known as fly-half in some countries), the player who helps to lead the backline by calling out what moves to make. Because he was a great kicker, a fast runner and was able to keep an eye on the whole field, he was perfect in this position.

RUGBY UNION: Mark Ella, making a difference

He also represented Australia at the Hong Kong Sevens (a rugby competition that has only seven players per side, instead of the usual 15) from 1979 until 1984, and in 1981 was named Player of the Tournament.

Mark played his last game for the Wallabies in December 1984 against Scotland, when the Wallabies won the Grand Slam tour of Britain and Ireland, 37–12. When he decided to retire at the age of 25, he was at the top of his form. Many people were shocked and disappointed that he was giving up professional rugby, but Mark wanted to do other things in his life. He is still involved in Australian sport.

Mark was named 1982 Young Australian of the Year. The following year he received an Order of Australia. His enormous talents were further recognised in 1987 when he entered Sport Australia's Hall of Fame, and again in 1995 when he was inducted into the International Rugby Hall of Fame. Mark is both a great rugby player and a great Aussie hero!

The Ella family produced other amazing athletes. Mark's twin brother Glen and his younger brother Gary also played international rugby. In 1981, the three brothers were selected in the same Wallabies team, the first time three brothers had ever been chosen. Their sister Marcia was the first Indigenous woman to represent Australia in netball (1983–85).

FABULOUS FOOTBALLERS

- Ken Catchpole is possibly Australia's best ever scrum half. In 1961 he made his test debut as captain. He went on to play 27 tests with the Wallabies.

- Zambian-born Aussie boy George Gregan has made 131 appearances with the Wallabies. This is more than any other player in the game's history.

- Michael Lynagh holds the record for the most points scored. Over 72 games for Australia, Michael scored a massive 911 points!

- David Campese, another awesome player, represented Australia 101 times. Many people think he's the best fullback Australia's ever had.

- A few great players have represented Australia in both rugby union and rugby league, including Ray Price, Wendell Sailor, Mat Rogers and Lote Tuqiri.

- The Wallaroos is the name of the Australian national women's rugby union team. They have competed in three Women's Rugby World Cups, the most recent in 2006.

- Stirling Mortlock is the current Wallabies captain and one of the all-time best Test scorers. He also plays with the ACT Brumbies.

- Apart from Mark Ella, there are six other Wallabies in the International Rugby Hall of Fame – Ken Catchpole, David Campese, John Eales, Nick Farr-Jones, Michael Lynagh and Tim Horan.

RUGBY UNION: Mark Ella, making a difference

OTHER RUGBY TOURNAMENTS

The Bledisloe Cup is an annual tournament between the Wallabies and New Zealand's All Blacks. It's been a fierce competition ever since the first match was played in 1931 in Auckland. New Zealand won that first match 20–13. Australia's first win was in 1934. In the history of the Cup, Australia has won just 12 times. Since 1995, the Bledisloe Cup has been part of the Tri-Nations Tournament, a series between Australia, New Zealand and South Africa's Springboks.

The most important international rugby trophy is the Rugby World Cup, which began in 1987 and is held every four years. Twenty teams compete in the finals and the winner is awarded the William Webb Ellis Cup. The Wallabies have competed at every single World Cup, and they hold a very special record. The Wallabies are the only team ever to have won two Rugby World Cups, the first time in 1991 and the second in 1999, both times under the leadership of John Eales. (Eales is one of the most respected captains ever. He also led Australia to victory in the Bledisloe Cup six times.)

In the 2007 World Cup, hosted by France, the Wallabies qualified for the semi-final, but were beaten 12–10 by England.

Union Usage

- When the ball goes out of the touch lines (the two lines running down the sides of the field), a line-out is called. In a line-out, between three and seven forwards line up parallel to each other, while a player from the team in possession of the ball throws it in. The players then jump as high as they can to catch it. Often, team members will lift one of their players so that he can reach the ball.

- In a rugby union scrum, eight forwards from each team pack together in three rows and push against each other. The ball goes into the gap and each team tries to get possession of it by moving it backwards with their feet, while also trying to push the other team.

Oops!

During the 1966 tour of Great Britain, Wallaby Ross Cullen bit the ear of British player Ollie Waldron. Cullen said that it wasn't his fault because Waldron had purposely put his ear into Cullen's mouth! After he made this announcement, he was sent home in disgrace.

20. Running

Even though John Landy never won an Olympic gold medal, he is still one of Australia's favourite sporting heroes. Not only was he a fantastic runner, he was also a great sport.

In 1954, John Landy became the second ever person to run 1 mile (1600 metres) in less than four minutes. Unfortunately for John, Englishman Roger Bannister had broken the four-minute mile only a few weeks before. The two men – at that time the only men in the world to have run the mile in less than four minutes – competed in the British Empire Games in Canada later that year. The race was being called 'The Miracle Mile' and millions of people sat by their radios to listen to this match between these two great runners.

John was doing very well until on the

> JOHN LANDY, ONE COOL CHARACTER

last lap he turned back to see where Bannister was. This tiny action made a huge difference – Bannister overtook him. John took second place in that race, and immediately congratulated Bannister on his win.

AN ACCIDENTAL HERO

There's an even more famous story about John Landy. The 1500 metres final on 11 March 1956 at the Australian national titles, just before the Melbourne Olympic Games, is now a part of Australian history. (The 1500 metres had replaced the 1 mile race.)

In the third lap of the race, the junior 1500 metres champ,

Ron Clarke, tripped on another runner's heel, lost his balance and fell. John was running close behind and to avoid falling over Ron, he jumped over the top of him. As he jumped, the spike in his running shoe cut Ron's arm. By now, other runners were running around him or leaping over him.

A moment later, John turned around and went back to see if Ron was all right and to say sorry for hurting him. Imagine that – he was competing in the national titles and instead of heading straight for the finish line, he turned back to make sure the runner he had accidentally injured was okay. Ron thanked him, picked himself up and told John to keep running.

Now, you'll never believe it, but in those last two laps, John Landy ran so fast that he actually made up for the time he'd lost by checking on Ron. Incredibly, John won that race in 4 minutes and 4.2 seconds. It's one of the most impressive wins of all times.

John proved he was both a champion and a true sportsman. John Landy and Ron Clarke were inducted into Sport Australia's Hall of Fame in 1985. In 1999, 43 years after this remarkable race, the Hall of Fame named it Australia's finest sporting moment of the twentieth century.

Almost every part of the mile is tactically important: you can never let down, never stop thinking, and you can be beaten at almost any point. I suppose you could say it is like life.

– JOHN LANDY

RUNNING WITH RON After that historic race in 1956, Ron Clarke went on to become one of Australia's best runners. He set 18 world records, six of them over 5000 metres and 10,000 metres. In just one year, 1965, Ron raced 18 times in eight countries in 44 days, setting 12 records! One of these records, the 10,000 metres, wasn't broken for 30 years! And

Clarke

between 1965 and 1972, Ron held every single record from the 2 miles to 20 kilometres. This amazing achievement has never been beaten. Although Ron is rightly considered one of our most talented runners, he only ever won one Olympic medal: bronze at the 1964 Tokyo Games. He hoped to do better at the 1968 Games in Mexico City. That city is 2300 metres above sea level. Being so high means there is less oxygen in the air and it takes a couple of days to get used to it. Many people find it hard to breathe, so imagine how hard it was for all the athletes competing there.

Ron held the world record for this distance, so he should have won a medal. But he became breathless during the race and fell behind, eventually finishing in sixth place. At the end of the race, Ron fainted from lack of oxygen. Many people complained that it was unfair to hold an Olympic Games at such a high altitude because many athletes suffered from the shortage of oxygen.

Ron's world records and great sportsmanship just go to show you that you do not have to win Olympic gold to be a champion.

RUNNING SHEET

 Ron Clarke carried the Olympic torch at the opening ceremony of the 1956 Olympic Games. Sparks from the flame singed his arms!

 John Landy read out the Athletes' Oath at the 1956 Olympics.

 From 2001 till 2006, John Landy was the Governor of Victoria.

 In 2004, Ron Clarke was elected Mayor of the Gold Coast in Queensland.

 In March 2006, during the Commonwealth Games opening ceremony, both Ron Clarke and John Landy carried the Queen's Baton around the Melbourne Cricket Ground. John passed the baton directly to Queen Elizabeth II.

 In Geelong, Victoria, at the Ron Clarke Classic, runners race at Landy Field.

 The current record for the 1500 metres is 3 minutes, 26 seconds, run by Morocco's Hicham el Guerrouj in 1998.

 The Empire Games became the Commonwealth Games in the 1950s.

30 AUSTRALIAN SPORTS LEGENDS

Running Rules

- There are many different running events, from relay races to sprints, to middle and long distance races.

- Many runners do sprint training as well as running over longer distances. Training also usually involves doing squats, stretches, weights and even yoga.

- Runners also work on their technique. This means that they think about how they stand, how they stretch their legs and how they place their feet on the ground. This helps to improve speed and lessens aches and pains.

Elliot

HERB ELLIOT

Between 1956 and 1962, Herb Elliott was the master of the 1500 metres. During that time, he ran 44 races, winning every single one. At the 1960 Olympic Games in Rome, Herb dazzled spectators in the 1500 metres when he led the field, being some 20 metres in front of his opponents. He took home Australia's only gold medal for athletics at the 1960 Games.

21. Running

Picture yourself in the starting position on the Olympic athletics track. There are thousands of people in the stands watching you. Cameras are flashing and reporters have been writing endless stories about you. Olympic officials are walking around the arena. There are millions of people sitting in front of their televisions waiting for the 400-metre race to begin, cheering you on from their lounge rooms. Picture yourself beside the fastest runners in the world. Every single person in Australia wants you to win this race. How does that make you feel?

> CATHY FREEMAN, THE REAL AUSTRALIAN IDOL

Nervous? A bit sick in the tummy? Absolutely terrified?

Cathy Freeman went through all of this. The 400 metres sprint at the 2000 Sydney Olympic Games was possibly the toughest race of her career because the whole of Australia wanted her to win and she didn't want to let them down.

REACHING FOR THE STARS
In 2000, Cathy was already a champion. She grew up in Mackay, Queensland, where her stepfather was her first trainer. Later she won a scholarship to a boarding school in Toowoomba, where she was one of only three Indigenous Australian children in the whole school. A natural athlete, she was soon competing in the national school championships, and was asked to try out for the Commonwealth Games team.

As a member of the relay team, she won gold at the 1990 Commonwealth Games in Auckland, aged only 16. At the 1992 Barcelona Olympics, she became the first Indigenous Australian to represent Australia in athletics, and she won two gold medals at the 1994 Commonwealth Games. She also won gold at two World Championships. Cathy was the Young Australian of the Year in 1990 and in 1998 was named Australian of the Year, making her the first person ever to have been awarded both honours.

At the 1996 Atlanta Olympics, Cathy faced one of her toughest opponents, French runner Maria-José Perec, who beat her by only a couple of metres. Cathy took the silver medal. That race was Cathy's personal best – she ran the 400 metres in 48.63 seconds. At another race in Europe later that year, Cathy beat Perec in the 400 metres. The two runners were to meet again at Sydney and sports lovers were looking forward to an exciting race.

THE RUN OF HER LIFE

At the opening ceremony of the 2000 Sydney Games, with all eyes on her, Cathy lit the Olympic cauldron. She was thrilled to do this, but she knew it placed even more pressure on her.

Then a few days before the track events began, Maria-José Perec, Cathy's fiercest rival, suddenly left Sydney without ever saying why. Now Cathy was the hot favourite to win.

On the day of the 400 metres final, Cathy came on to the track wearing a green and gold bodysuit, complete with hood, and warmed up as usual. She looked calm, but everyone could feel the tension in the air.

All eyes were on her. She and her opponents took their places, Cathy in lane six, and when the starting pistol fired, they were off. The noise of the crowd was deafening. With the entire country barracking for her, Cathy ran like she had never run before. She was way ahead of her opponents, and ran the 400 metres in 49.11 seconds to win the prized gold medal. The crowd roared with delight at her win. Cathy's dream of Olympic gold had come true.

In her victory lap, Cathy carried both the Australian and Aboriginal flags. She was Australia's pride and joy.

> I think the greatest amount of pressure is the pressure I place on myself.
>
> – CATHY FREEMAN

FANTASTIC FREEMAN FACTS

- Cathy's Olympic gold medal was the 100th gold medal for Australia in the history of the modern Olympics.
- On the list of all-time champions in the 400 metres, Cathy is rated in sixth place.
- Among her many awards are the international 2000 Laureus Female Athlete of the Year and the Order of Australia (2001).
- In July 2003, she retired from professional running.
- In 2005 Cathy was inducted into Sport Australia's Hall of Fame.
- Cathy knows how hard it is for people, especially those from disadvantaged families and communities, to find chances to get ahead. She set up the Catherine Freeman Foundation to help and encourage people to fulfil their dreams.

Oops!

Raelene Boyle is one of Australia's greatest ever sprinters, having represented Australia in every Olympic and Commonwealth Games between 1968 and 1982. In her fabulous career, she won 12 medals, seven of them Commonwealth gold medals and three of them Olympic silver medals.

At the 1976 Montreal Olympics, she was the first woman to be given the honour of carrying the Australian flag at the opening ceremony. Things were looking good for her.

But in the semi-finals of the 200 metres, Raelene was disqualified for breaking twice. Breaking is leaving the starting block before the starting pistol has been fired. Raelene objected to the decision, saying that she had not made a false start and she certainly hadn't done it twice! Games officials took no notice of her and Raelene had to watch the race from the sidelines. She missed out on her chance to win an Olympic gold medal.

Later, film of the race showed that Raelene was telling the truth. She had not made a false start. The race starter on that day had made a terrible mistake.

22. Sailing

At 1 pm each Boxing Day, crowds mill around Sydney Harbour to watch the beginning of the annual Sydney to Hobart yacht race, one of the most famous – and toughest – yacht races in the world. Competitors must sail 628 nautical miles through the mouth of Sydney Harbour, down the east coast of New South Wales and Victoria, through Bass Strait, south down the Tasmanian coast, up the Derwent River and into Hobart's Constitution Dock.

Even though the race is held in summer, it can get very cold on the open ocean and Bass Strait has dangerous wild winds and churning seas, so it can get pretty scary out there. Only experienced sailors can enter this race, and sometimes even they get scared.

Sailors come from around the world to compete in this blue-water race

THE SYDNEY TO HOBART

SAILING: The Sydney to Hobart

(a race on the open ocean). All kinds and sizes of yachts enter the event, ranging from ultra-modern sloops with all the latest technology and equipment, to maxi-yachts, to old and rather battered yachts.

On average, each boat has around 11 crew members. There is usually a roster system in place, so that there is always someone awake, making sure that everything is running smoothly.

THE FIRST RACE

The Sydney to Hobart began in 1945 when members of the Cruising Yacht Club of Australia in Sydney decided to sail down to Hobart the day after Christmas. An Englishman called John Illingworth was in Sydney with the British Navy and he suggested making it a race, rather than just a leisurely sail. And so the race was born! Nine yachts entered the first race, which was won by Captain Illingworth's yacht *Rani* in 6 days 14 hours and 22 minutes.

Since that first race, the Sydney to Hobart has become one of Australia's most popular summertime events.

Over the years, race officials decided that two prizes would be at stake – line honours and a handicap section. Line honours go to the first boat across the finish line. The handicap section is awarded to the boat estimated to be the fastest overall.

ABOUT HANDICAPPING

Handicapping is used in many sports to make the competition fairer. In yacht racing, there are a few things that the judges look at, such as the size and shape of the boat, and the size of the sails. If someone has a bigger boat with bigger sails then they have a better chance of winning, so the time they take to run the race is adjusted by racing officials. They call this 'correcting' the time. This gives smaller boats a chance of winning on equal terms.

MORE ABOUT THE SYDNEY TO HOBART

 The fastest recorded time in the Sydney to Hobart was in 2005, when *Wild Oats XI* completed the course in 1 day 18 hours 40 minutes and 10 seconds.

 The slowest race was run in 1945 when *Wayfarer* took over 11 days to reach Hobart.

 Both line honours and handicap honours have been won by the same yacht only six times: *Rani* (1945), the US yachts *American Eagle* (1972) and *Kialoa II* (1977), *New Zealand* (1980), and two New South Wales sloops, *Sovereign* (1987) and *Wild Oats XI* (2005).

 Nine yachts took part in the first race in 1945. In 1994, 371 yachts entered the race – a record number. In 2006, there were 78 entrants, although nine of them didn't finish.

SAILING: The Sydney to Hobart

THE SEA STRIKES BACK

In the 1998 Sydney to Hobart, there was a raging storm in Bass Strait and more than 50 sailors had to be rescued by helicopter; six men drowned. It was a sad reminder of the dangers of the sea. From then on, there were stricter rules about competing. These rules were written by the race's organisers – the Cruising Yacht Club of Australia and the Royal Yacht Club of Tasmania.

Sailing Speak

- A nautical mile is used to measure distances at sea. A nautical mile is approximately 1.8 kilometres.

- The keel is the timber structure that runs along the centre of the boat's bottom; the boat's framework is attached to the keel.

- A sloop is a yacht with a single mast and a mainsail that is parallel to the keel. Most of the yachts that enter the Sydney to Hobart are sloops.

- A ketch is a two-masted sailing boat, with one mast shorter than the other.

- The main mast is the tallest mast on the boat. The mizzenmast is a shorter mast and is the one closest to the back of a ketch.

- A maxi-yacht is a racing yacht that is usually at least 21 metres long. That's about as long as 16 eight-year-olds lying end to end!

- For more sailing lingo, see page 128, 'More Sailing Speak'

THE AMERICA'S CUP

The America's Cup is one of the longest running sailing races in the world. It began in 1851 when a British yacht raced an American yacht around the Isle of Wight. The trophy was won by the Americans who held it until 1983, when for the first time in 132 years, they lost to a challenger! *Australia II*, captained by John Bertrand, won the Cup. Can you imagine how upset the Americans must have been to lose their trophy after all that time?

Australia II was designed by Ben Lexcen. He came up with a specially designed 'winged' keel, which helped to make the yacht go faster. For a while it looked like the new keel might not fit in with the race's rules, but the officials finally approved it. The Australian yacht and its experienced crew certainly made a huge impression on yacht racing when they beat the American champion *Liberty*.

It was a big day in Australia when people heard the news. The Prime Minister, Bob Hawke, was so happy he thought that everyone should have the day off!

Australia held that precious trophy for only three years before an American team won it back in 1987. In that race, *Kookaburra III* was defeated by *Stars and Stripes*.

23. Sailing

KAY COTTEE AND JESSE MARTIN, SOLO SAILORS

On 5 June 1988, Kay Cottee sailed into Sydney Harbour in her 11-metre yacht *First Lady*. She had just completed a 189-day solo, non-stop sailing voyage around the world. She also sailed into the history books because she was the first woman to do this.

Can you just imagine being on your own for 189 days on the open ocean? That's more than six months. Think what you would face – rough seas and stormy weather could blow you off course; icebergs and rocks could damage your boat; your only contact with the rest of the world would be by radio. Not to mention that you'd have no fresh fruit, vegetables, meat or milk. You wouldn't be able to get much sleep either, because you'd always need to keep an eye on things.

Luckily Kay Cottee was more than able to look after herself. She had been sailing her whole life and had even built her own yacht, the *Joy Too*, when she was still a girl. When she came up with the idea of sailing solo and without any help around the world, she began building *First Lady*. With the help of some sponsors, Kay set off in November 1987, sailing east from Sydney.

WOMAN OVERBOARD! Kay had a particularly scary experience off the coast of southern Africa. Strong winds and rolling waves knocked her into the water and it was only because she was wearing safety lines attached to the boat that she was able to get aboard again. She faced many perils on the ocean, but that incident was the most dramatic. However, it was all worthwhile when she sailed triumphantly into Sydney Harbour. Kay had sailed 22,000 nautical miles!

Among Kay's many awards are Australian of the Year and an Order of Australia. Ten years after her epic voyage, Kay Cottee donated *First Lady* to the National Maritime Museum in Sydney. If you ever have a chance to visit the Maritime Museum, you'll be astonished at the size of it. At little more than 11 metres, it's roughly the size of a bus. And to think that Kay sailed all the way round the world in it is just amazing. She is a sailing superstar.

JESSE THE LIONHEART In December 1998, when he was just 17 years old, Jesse Martin sailed out of Melbourne's Port Phillip Bay in his 10-metre yacht *Lionheart*. His plan was to sail solo and unassisted around the world. He set off, sailing

SAILING: Kay Cottee and Jesse Martin, solo sailors

south of New Zealand, through the Pacific, around South America, across the Atlantic towards Africa, then across the Indian Ocean back to his starting point. A born adventurer, Jesse had kayaked in New Guinea rivers and had also sailed extensively with his father, but this solo expedition was a real challenge.

Jesse had been inspired by the solo round-the-world voyage of Western Australian David Dicks, who set off from Fremantle at the age of 17 in February 1996 on his boat *Seaflight*. David returned 264 days later, having celebrated his 18th birthday in October. He was, at the time, the youngest person to have circumnavigated the globe alone.

Jesse was hoping to break David's record. It took him 328 days and he sailed 27,000 nautical miles, taking a different route from Kay Cottee. When he arrived back in Melbourne in October 1999, he was the youngest person to have circumnavigated the globe alone, non-stop and unaided.

ALONE ON THE OCEAN One of the hardest things about being a solo sailor is that you have to rely on yourself for absolutely everything, and apart from some radio contact, there's no one to talk to. Picture yourself in a boat with no friends, no parents, no brothers or sisters, no teachers, not even any strangers . . . and then think what it would be like for almost a whole year. How lonely would it be! That's just one of the many things Jesse had to put up with.

Like Kay Cottee, he also had to battle gale-force winds and stormy seas. One time he almost crashed into an oil tanker; another time he bumped into a whale. It was a nerve-racking time for him. Sometimes, though, the days were fine, the waves were calm and he sailed alongside cheerful dolphins.

Many of Jesse's meals were freeze-dried – as soon as the food was cooked, it was frozen and sealed in an airtight parcel so it

SAILING: Kay Cottee and Jesse Martin, solo sailors

would last longer. Other food was covered in special wrapping to keep it as fresh as possible. He also took flour with him so he could make damper.

Jesse carefully recorded his trip and when he returned – to a hero's welcome – he wrote a book and produced a documentary called *Lionheart: a journey of the human spirit*. His solo trip was a dream come true for Jesse and an inspiration for all sailors young and old.

More Sailing Speak

- The front part of the boat is the bow. Aft means towards the rear or 'stern' of a boat. Astern means behind the boat.
- The right side of the boat is the starboard side. The left side is the port side.
- There are a few types of sails. A jib is a triangular shaped sail that is forward of the mast. A spinnaker is a light triangular sail used when sailing before the wind (that's when the wind comes from behind you).
- Lee means sheltered from the wind.
- The helm is the wheel or tiller of the boat.
- If a boat is listing, it means it is leaning to one side, often because there is too much weight on that side.
- Circumnavigation means to sail around the whole world.

24. Soccer

HEADS UP FOR THE SOCCEROOS!

Here in Australia, it's commonly called soccer, but in most other parts of the world, it's called football. Soccer is the fastest growing sport in Australia and more children now play soccer than rugby league or Australian Rules. Altogether, there are now over one million Australians who play soccer. And because soccer is played around the world, the really top players in any country have a chance of playing internationally at the highest levels. Among the biggest soccer-playing nations are Brazil, Germany, Italy, Argentina, Uruguay and France.

The national Australian men's team is the Socceroos; the national women's team is the Matildas. Since the Socceroos and the Matildas have been gaining ground in international competition, soccer is becoming even more popular, both as a sport to play and a sport to watch.

WORKING TOWARDS THE WORLD CUP

Since 1930, the international football federation, FIFA, has held the soccer World Cup every four years. Qualifying matches are played for the three years before the finals. Qualifying is certainly not easy – 198 countries tried to make the finals of the 2006 World Cup, and only 32 teams succeeded.

The Socceroos first made the finals (held in West Germany) in 1974, where they played three games, losing twice to Germany and drawing with Chile. It was a fabulous achievement to get that far, and it was a long time before Australia made the finals again. In 2005, Australia met Uruguay in the play-off, winning the game 4–2 to qualify for the finals of the 2006 World Cup in Germany. What a thrill to make it through!

In the four games they played in the 2006 World Cup, the Socceroos beat Japan, drew with Croatia and were defeated by Brazil and Italy. They played well before being eliminated in the sixteenth round. Now they are in training for the next World Cup to be played in 2010 in South Africa.

ASIAN CUP 2007

In 2007, the Socceroos entered the Asian Cup for the first time. Their first match was against Oman and the Socceroos were the favourites, but they were losing for most of the game. It wasn't until Tim Cahill managed to score late in the second half that they drew the game 1–1. They lost the next game to Iraq 1–3, and then trounced Thailand 4–0. Of those four goals, two were scored by Mark

SOCCER: Heads up for the Socceroos!

Viduka. The Socceroos' final match was against Japan, and this was also a draw. The Socceroos' run was over, but Australian soccer fans were very proud of what they had achieved.

THE MIGHTY MATILDAS

The national women's team has been around since 1978, and there have been some really amazing players, like current Matildas captain, Cheryl Salisbury. She has played more international games than any other Australian player, male or female!

The Matildas qualified for the 2000 and 2004 Olympic Games and in 2007 they also qualified for the Women's World Cup in China, winning against Ghana 4–1, which was their very first win at a Women's World Cup. They then drew with Norway 1–1 and in a nail-biting game against Canada, which

also ended in a draw, they qualified for the quarter-finals, the first time an Australian team has made it this far. Although they lost their next match 3–2 against Brazil, it was a fantastic feat. The Matildas had made Australian sporting history.

PLAYING AWAY Some of Australia's best players also play for other countries. As well as playing for Australia, Harry Kewell has played for English teams Leeds United and Liverpool. Mark Viduka has played for Croatia and for English teams Middlesborough, Leeds United and Newcastle United. Michael Beauchamp plays for the German team FC Nürnberg, Jason Culina plays for the Dutch team PSV Eindhoven, and Marco Bresciano plays for the Italian team Palermo. These are just a few, so you can see just how international soccer is, and how good our Aussie players are.

Soccer Stoppers

- Tackling in soccer is a little different from tackling in other football codes. In soccer, tackling is when a player takes the ball away from another player by kicking it or stopping it with his or her feet. This means that it is the ball itself that is tackled, not the opposing player.

- The penalty area is the big rectangular box in front of the goal. Any foul committed inside this area is awarded a penalty kick. The goalkeeper is the only player who can use his hands to stop the ball.

- If a player runs into an opponent, it is called a charge. It's not really okay to charge, although if two players are going for the ball, then they are allowed to use their shoulders to push against one another. It's against the rules to charge at someone from behind, or at someone who isn't holding the ball.

- If a player does something wrong on the field, such as being unsportsmanlike or delaying the start of play, the referee gives him or her a yellow card. This is a warning – the player is cautioned not to do it again.

- A red card is given to any player who seriously breaks the rules, such as being violent. When a player receives a red card, they must leave the game immediately and the team is not allowed to have a substitute, so the side is a player short!

GETTING YOUR KICKS

Penalty kicks are awarded when a foul is committed inside the penalty area. Only the person kicking and the goalkeeper are involved. A penalty kick almost always results in a goal.

Free kicks can be direct or indirect. A direct free kick is played at the spot on the field where a serious foul, such as pushing or using your hands, took place. It scores when the ball goes straight into the goal.

An indirect free kick is played where a less serious foul happened, such as being offside. The ball must touch another player – it doesn't matter from which team – before a goal can be scored. Sometimes it's a bit tricky trying to figure out whether a kick should be direct or indirect. An easy way to remember is that most of the time a direct kick comes from a foul involving body contact or a handball. Pretty much everything else is indirect.

Oops!

In June 2006, Australia met Italy in the FIFA World Cup in Germany. In the final moments of the game, defender Lucas Neill tried to tackle Italy's Fabio Grosso, who fell over him. A penalty was awarded against Lucas Neill and Italy went on to win the game 1–0. There were quite a few protests about the penalty, many saying that it was unfair and that the game should have been a 0–0 draw. With that one penalty, Australia was knocked out of World Cup competition.

25. Speed Skating

No one was more surprised to win the gold medal for the 1000-metre short track speed skating race at the 2002 Winter Olympics at Salt Lake City than the man who won it! Steven Bradbury made history that day, becoming the first Australian to win gold at the Winter Olympics.

Steven was not even sure that he was going to make the finals at his fourth Winter Olympics. In the semi-final, he was at the back of the pack and only gained ground when some of his opponents crashed into one another. Then came the final race.

It was a most extraordinary event. Steven was keeping up a good pace but he was nowhere near his rivals, American Apolo Anton Ohno,

STEVEN BRADBURY STANDS TALL

South Korea's Ahn Hyun-Soo, China's Li Jiajun and Canadian Mathieu Turcotte. Apolo Ohno was the race favourite and was in front for much of the race. But as the skaters came to the final lap, with Steven half a lap behind, Li Jiajun lost his footing and as he fell over, he took the three other skaters down with him. It was a big mess of arms and legs.

Steven was the only man left standing and he skated past his opponents to claim the gold medal. He'd done it in 1 minute and 29.10 seconds. Ohno managed to get himself out of the muddle of fallen skaters to take the silver medal in 1 minute and 30.16 seconds.

From coming last, Steven had suddenly won the race. He was flabbergasted! He knew he'd been lucky to win, but he had worked hard for this moment for many years.

BEFORE GOLD Steven Bradbury has been skating all his life and he had competed in some of the toughest competitions in the world, including the World Championships in the first half of the 1990s. He competed in three earlier Winter Olympics – Albertville in 1992, Lillehammer in 1994, where he was a member of the Australian short track relay team that won the bronze medal, and Nagano in 1998.

In 1994, he had a terrible accident and almost died. During a championship race in Montreal, another skater's razor-sharp blade cut right through Steven's leg. He lost an enormous amount of blood and needed 111 stitches. He was in hospital for more than two weeks and it was many months before he could resume his training. Then in 2000, he broke his neck while training and had to wear a special neck brace for over six weeks. For a while Steven wondered whether he'd ever be able to skate again.

Little by little, Steven started training again. And he was more than ready for the 2002 Games. He was not the favourite

SPEED SKATING: Steven Bradbury stands tall

by any means; that place was filled by the American, Ohno. Yet by keeping up a steady pace and staying evenly balanced while those around him tumbled to the icy ground, Steven became a champion.

DOING A BRADBURY

Have you ever heard someone say 'he's doing a Bradbury'? Ever since Steven's unforgettable win, people use these words to mean that someone has succeeded when no one expected it. It means having good luck in an unusual situation. It doesn't just apply to sport. If you think you are not very good at art and then the best artist in the school breaks her wrist and you win the art competition, then you're doing a Bradbury.

More About Steven

▶ Steven Bradbury was awarded an Order of Australia in 2007.

▶ Steven is now a public speaker, helping people to achieve their own goals. He is also involved with the Australian Olympic Committee. He wrote a book about his life in sport, called *Last Man Standing* – a perfect title!

▶ At the 2002 Winter Olympics, Australia won a second gold medal when Alisa Camplin won the women's aerial skiing race. Their wins were marked by Australia Post, which issued special postage stamps, one featuring Steven and another featuring Alisa.

A BIT ABOUT SPEED SKATING

- Short track speed skating first became an Olympic sport in 1992, at the Albertville Winter Olympics.

- There are eight short track events. Both men and women skate in 500-metre, 1000-metre and 1500-metre events. The men's relay is 5000 metres, and the women's relay is 3000 metres. The racetrack is not very wide, which is why competitors sometimes crash into each other.

- Long track speed skating for men has been an official Olympic sport since 1924, when the first Winter Olympics were held in Chamonix, France. The women's event began in 1960. The longest distance for long track races is 10,000 metres.

SPEED SKATING: Steven Bradbury stands tall

- Ice skates have a sharp blade attached to the bottom of the boot. This is what you wear at the icerink. Speed skaters wear special skates called clap skates, where the blade is attached to the boot by a hinge at the front. Clap skates are faster because when the skater lifts his heel, he can still have the whole blade on the ice.

- Figure skating is also an Olympic sport. There are singles and paired events as well as ice dancing, which is what it sounds like — dancing on ice. In all figure skating events, the skaters must first show the judges their technique, that is, that they can do everything that the rules say they should. The next event is called a 'free skate', where skaters can bend the rules a little and show how artistic they can be.

- Training for any speed skating, indeed for any sport, involves warming up properly with a little gentle exercise, followed by sprint training on the ice. Athletes tend to train at least six days a week. They also get plenty of sleep and eat nutritious, high energy foods. No junk food allowed!

26. Sporting Animals

BEST HOOF FORWARD

It's not just horses and greyhounds that compete in organised races. Lots of animals can run fast, and when animals run, there are often competitive people who have fun by betting on which animal is the fastest. You might have raced animals yourself – perhaps your dog, or pet mice, or even flies crawling up a window. It's fun to watch and be part of animal races, but it's also very important to make sure that the animals are not hurt.

In parts of Australia that are a long way from the big cities, people have come up with some great racing ideas. Some of these started as local events, but are now famous tourist attractions.

THE EULO LIZARD RACES

Every August in the tiny outback town of Eulo, almost 890 kilometres west of Brisbane, the world championship lizard races are held. You might not have realised that there even *were* world racing championships for lizards, but it's a very important event! Since 1967, lizard collectors have gathered at the Paroo Track ready for the biggest contest of the year.

The competitors are mainly shingleback lizards and bearded dragons, but western blue-tongue lizards also make an appearance. Many people have a bet on which lizard will win, but it's pretty hard to pick the winner because it usually takes a while for the lizards to start moving. Often they just sit in the middle of the track and have to be gently prodded to move at all!

FINDING A CHAMPION

The lizards are collected from the local bush, and there are strict rules about catching them. The Queensland government has laws to make sure that not too many lizards are taken from the bush and that they are not hurt. When a lizard is taken from the wild, the collector must put a tag on it, saying exactly where the lizard came from. A marker must also be placed in the ground where the lizard was taken. That way, collectors can make sure they return the lizard to its proper home after the race.

Collectors are careful to look after their lizards so that they are healthy and happy. And, of course, each collector wants his or her lizard to win first prize.

ACROSS THE SPECIES

One of the best known stories about the Eulo lizard races is the time in 1980 when a cockroach called Destructo entered the race against the champion lizard, Wooden Head. Destructo ran towards the finish line and easily won the race against Wooden Head.

Unfortunately, soon after the race, someone accidentally stepped on him. There is now a memorial plaque to the plucky cockroach at the track.

THE CAMEL CUP: A BUMPY RIDE

Races are usually highly organised and predictable events. Just look at the Melbourne Cup, or any other sporting event you can think of. The Camel Cup, held each July in Blatherskite Park in Alice Springs, is also a very organised event. But . . . and this is a big but . . . camels are not at all predictable. Just when everyone thinks that things are running smoothly and that the day is going to plan, a camel might have a tantrum and run in the opposite direction. Or a camel may decide that it's not going to race at all. Or it may take off before the official start.

Not knowing exactly what's going to happen makes the Camel Cup one of the Northern Territory's most enjoyable sporting contests. Camels are very big animals. They can weigh more than 500 kilograms (that's as much as six and a half medium-sized adult men), and can be over 2 metres tall.

That's a lot for one jockey to handle, and although camels and their jockeys train for the race, that's no guarantee that a camel will behave on the day.

It might be hard for the rider but it's great fun to watch, especially when these mighty beasts take off. They can run very fast when they want to. Some racing camels have been clocked at 35 kilometres an hour! Like the Eulo lizard races, it's almost impossible to pick the winner.

The racetrack is 450 metres long and it is the only purpose-built camel racing track in the country.

RACING HIGHLIGHTS
The Camel Cup began in 1970, when two friends raced camels along the dry bed of the Todd River. Today, there are nine races on Camel Cup day. As well as the actual Camel Cup, there are novelty races and there is even a special trophy for the prettiest camel. You can see that it's a fun day, and all money raised is donated to local charities.

THE GREAT GOAT RACE

Lightning Ridge, 765 kilometres northwest of Sydney and very close to the Queensland border, is famous for its black opals. It's the only place in Australia where these precious stones are found. But Lightning Ridge is also famous for its annual Great Goat Race, which has been held in the town's main street every Easter for the last 30 years.

Jockeys dress in racing silks, just like horse jockeys, and sit in racing carts that are pulled along by wild goats. When the race begins, the handlers let go of the goats and while everyone hopes they'll run to the finish line, no one really knows which direction they'll take. But there is also a serious race using trained goats and people place bets on which goat will take first prize.

SPORTING ANIMALS: Best hoof forward

CAMEL CHATS AND GOBBLING GOATS

- Camels have been in Central Australia for over 160 years. They were brought here to carry heavy loads across the long distances covered by early explorers, miners and settlers. The use of cars and trucks in the twentieth century meant that camels were no longer needed for transportation and many were released into the wild. Australia now has the biggest wild camel population in the world.

- A camel's hump stores fat, so it can go without food for a week or more. Camels store water in their bloodstream and they can go for days before they need another drink.

- Goats first arrived in Australia with the First Fleet. They were used to provide the early settlers with milk and meat. They were easy to care for because they eat just about any type of plant.

- Wild or feral goats can cause lots of environmental problems in Australia, because they compete with native animals for food and water, especially in times of drought.

27. Surfing

MIDGET FARRELLY, FIRST-EVER SURFING CHAMP

On a clear May day in 1964, a 19-year-old Australian surfed into history when he won the very first World Surfing Championships at Sydney's Manly Beach. Everyone had expected the trophy would go to either Joey Cabell or Mike Doyle, young American surfers who were at the top of their form. Imagine their surprise when Midget Farrelly out-surfed everyone else.

MIDGET MAKES HIS MARK Like many Australian boys and girls who live near a beach,

SURFING: Midget Farrelly, first-ever surfing champ

Sydney-born Bernard Farrelly used to race home from school, grab his board, run to the beach and paddle out to catch some waves. Nicknamed 'Midget' because he was a little shorter than his friends, he spent hours practising, always trying bigger waves and improving his technique. He had a natural style and he wasn't afraid to try new things.

In the 1950s and 1960s many Australians thought that surfing was not a real sport. They thought that it was only about having fun mucking about in the surf. Midget Farrelly changed all that. By 1961, when he still only 16 years old, the surfing fraternity considered him Australia's best surfer. The following year, Midget bought himself a ticket to Hawaii, where he entered and won the Makaha International surfing competition.

SURFING BIG TIME! People surfed for the love of it in the 1960s. No one had a sponsor or got free surfboards or clothing, like the top surfers get today. Winners received a trophy, but no prize money. And surfing competitions were not as formally organised as they are today. A few competitions were held in different parts of the world, such as Peru, Hawaii and California, but these were local events and often surfers in one country had never even heard of surfers from other countries. (Remember, there was no internet in those days.) There was no major international competitive surfing event – that is, until 1964.

That year, the newly formed International Surfing Federation decided that it was time for a world championship competition. They invited top surfers from 10 countries, including Australia, New Zealand, South Africa, Peru, France and the United States, to come to Sydney to compete in the first World Surfing Championships.

MAKING HISTORY AT MANLY Manly Beach was chosen as the venue for the new competition. Thousands of people made their way to Manly to sit in the autumn sunshine and watch this historic event. All the competitors were gifted surfers, and it was difficult to say who would win. But Midget glided through the surf, his last wave an especially impressive ride, and it soon became clear that he would win the Men's Open title.

The Women's Open at that first World Surfing Championships was also won by an Australian, Phyllis O'Donnell. This was a great thing for 27-year-old Phyllis, because in the 1960s, the male surfers gave her a hard time for surfing. They didn't think girls should be surfing at all – but she showed 'em!

Thanks to Midget and Phyllis, the first World Surfing

SURFING: Midget Farrelly, first-ever surfing champ

Championships put Australia on the surfing map. Midget became the face of surfing and, from that time on, surfing gained recognition as a competitive sport. Held in different locations around the world, the World Surfing Championship is now the surfing community's most important competition.

Surf Speak

- A grommet is a young surfie who shows a bit of talent.
- A bombora is an Aussie surfing word that means a wave that breaks over an underwater rock or reef.
- A Malibu is a long, light board with a rounded end. It was named after the beach in California.
- All surfers use wax on their boards so that they don't slip, but 'wax bum' is surf speak for a person who just sits on the beach, constantly waxing their board, but never actually goes into the water!
- 'Dropping in' is catching a wave that is already being surfed on. It's not polite, because the first surfer has the right of way.

LAYNE'S WAVES

Sydney woman Layne Beachley is undoubtedly the best female surfer ever. She has been the Women's World Surfing Champion a record seven times! She was named the 2003 Australian Athlete of the Year. Layne grew up in Manly, where she took to the water like the natural she is. Hard work, loads of practice and sheer determination have put Layne at the very top of women's surfing. She is a true legend!

You've always got to be aware of why you don't win, otherwise you'll keep losing. Every mistake is a learning experience and, hopefully, you won't make the same mistake again.

– Layne Beachley

AMAZING SURFING FACTS

The first famous surfer was a Hawaiian man called Duke Kahanamoku. He won an Olympic gold medal for swimming way back in 1912, but his favourite hobby was surfing – not surprising considering he grew up in Hawaii, where surfing had its beginnings. He was so good at it that word of the new sport began to

SURFING: Midget Farrelly, first-ever surfing champ

spread around the world, but surfing didn't take off in a big way until the late 1950s and early 1960s.

- When Duke Kahanamoku visited Australia in the summer of 1914–15 to show people how to surf, he gave a demonstration at Sydney's Freshwater Beach. When he asked for a volunteer from the crowd to help in a surfing display, 15-year-old Isabel Letham stepped forward and became the first Australian to ride a surfboard.

- The Association of Surfing Professionals (ASP) was set up in 1976 and since then has held a world championship competition every year. Australian Mark Richards won the men's title four consecutive times: 1979, 1980, 1981 and 1982.

- Wendy Botha won the 1987 Association of Surfing Professionals title for South Africa. She became an Australian citizen in 1989 and won the women's title three more times: in 1989, 1991 and 1992.

- Nat Young won the world championships in 1966. He had a long surfing career, and is a four-time winner of the ASP Longboard Championships.

- Australians dominate the world surfing scene. Among the top male surfers are Aussie boys Mick Fanning and Taj Burrow. Among the the top women surfers in the world are Aussie girls Chelsea Hedges and Stephanie Gilmore.

- Surfing has been responsible for some major fashions. Boardshorts are now worn even by non-surfers and some surfing clothing labels are big business all over the world.

28. Swimming

DAWN FRASER, ATHLETE OF THE CENTURY

In 1999, swimmer Dawn Fraser was not only named Female Athlete of the Century by Sport Australia's Hall of Fame, she was also awarded the title Best Female Swimmer of the Century at the World Sports Awards in Vienna, Austria. Just think about how many outstanding swimmers there have been from all over the world over the 100 years of the twentieth century – out of all these marvellous athletes, Dawn Fraser was chosen as the best. So, just what did Dawn do to win such awesome honours?

SWIMMING: Dawn Fraser, athlete of the century

QUEEN OF THE POOL

Dawn started swimming to help her asthma, but she was very good and began training properly when she was 14 years old with coach Harry Gallagher. In 1964, Dawn Fraser was the first woman to swim the 100 metres freestyle in less than a minute, a record that wasn't broken for another eight years. Dawn was also the first swimmer to win gold for the same event (100 metres freestyle) in three Olympics in a row – 1956, 1960 and 1964. If that isn't amazing enough, in her 15-year swimming career, she broke 41 world records. She has eight Olympic medals, four of them gold, six Commonwealth Games medals and more Australian Championship titles than you have fingers and toes.

BANNED!

After the 1960 Rome Olympics, Australian swimming officials argued with Dawn over what she had been wearing while representing Australia and they banned her from competing in international events for 18 months. Dawn kept training in preparation for national competitions. After the ban was lifted, she did very well in the 1962 Commonwealth Games in Perth, winning four gold medals.

In 1964, Dawn was involved in a serious car accident. Sadly, her mother was killed and Dawn was very badly injured, so much so that she didn't know whether she would go to the Tokyo Olympic Games later that year. But she did, and it was there that she won her third 100-metres gold medal. She also got into big trouble.

Dawn had always loved a little bit of mischief, but this time it backfired. She marched in the opening ceremony even though she wasn't supposed to. Then, instead of wearing the regulation swimsuit, she wore her favourite pair of bathers. Finally, one night, Dawn and a couple of friends tried to steal the Japanese flag from a flagpole outside the emperor's palace.

The police arrived and took them to the police station, but luckily, when they discovered that they'd arrested the famous medal-winning swimmer, they let her go.

Unfortunately, this event led to Dawn being banned from competition swimming for 10 years! This was a devastating judgment because she was already 27 years old, and the ban meant that she'd never be able to swim competitively again. (Most champion swimmers retire in their twenties.) Her high

SWIMMING: Dawn Fraser, athlete of the century

jinks didn't stop people admiring Dawn and even though she'd been in trouble, she was still named Australian of the Year in 1964. Dawn appealed to swimming officials and the ban was lifted after four years, but by then she had decided to retire from the pool.

I've always been known to be outspoken and to speak my mind and I think that's what Australian people like.

– DAWN FRASER

AFTER SWIMMING Dawn returned to her home in Balmain, Sydney, where she began coaching other swimmers. For a while she also owned a hotel in Balmain. In 1988 she entered state politics when she was elected as the independent Member for Balmain. She left the New South Wales parliament in 1991.

Dawn is still involved in sports and she loves helping people, especially those with disabilities. She is patron of the Wheelchair Sports Association of Victoria and a member of the Cerebral Palsy Sports Association. Dawn Fraser has received many honours and awards, including an Order of Australia. She is Australia's most loved athlete, and many people refer to her as 'Our Dawn'.

Swimming Superstars

There are many Australian women who have achieved great things in swimming. Here are just a few:

- Aussie girl Fanny Durack was the first female swimmer in the world to win an Olympic gold medal. She did this at the 1912 Stockholm Games, beating fellow Australian Mina Wylie in the 100 metres freestyle.

- In Shane Gould's short swimming career, she broke 11 world records and 21 Australian records. At the 1972 Munich Olympics, Shane won three gold, one silver and one bronze medal. She is the only swimmer to have held all the freestyle world records at the same time – the 100, 200, 400, 800 and 1500 metres, as well as the 200 metres individual medley. That's incredible.

- Susie O'Neill (or 'Madame Butterfly' as she is known for her skill at the butterfly stroke), won a medal at every single international swimming competition she was in. She has eight Olympic medals.

- Petria Thomas has won eight Olympic medals, equalling Susie O'Neill and the great Dawn Fraser. Petria has also won 13 Australian championships, nine Commonwealth Games gold medals and three World Championships.

- Leisel Jones is a fantastic swimmer whose best stroke is breaststroke. Since 2000, she has won five Olympic medals, seven gold Commonwealth Games medals and 12 World Championships medals.

- Libby Lenton (now known as Libby Trickett) won a gold and a bronze medal at the 2004 Athens Olympic Games, her first Olympics. At the 2006 Commonwealth Games, she won five gold and two silver medals. She also holds the world record for the 100 metres freestyle.

- Jodie Henry won three gold medals at the Athens Olympics. When she won the 100 metres, it was the first time since Dawn Fraser's win in 1964 that an Australian woman had won gold in this event.

SWIMMING: Dawn Fraser, athlete of the century

SWIMMING RULES

The four main swimming strokes are freestyle, breaststroke, backstroke and butterfly. In Olympic competitions, there are also medley events, where all four strokes are swum — for example in the 200 metres individual medley, competitors swim 50 metres of each stroke.

In backstroke and freestyle, swimmers tumble-turn at the end of a lap — they somersault in front of the wall, then push off with their feet.

Breaststroke and butterfly swimmers do not tumble-turn because at the end of each lap they must touch the end of the pool with both hands.

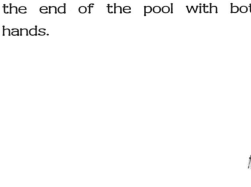

157

29. Swimming

IAN THORPE, OUR GREATEST OLYMPIAN

Just about everyone knows about Ian Thorpe, nicknamed 'Thorpedo' for his amazing speed in the water. He is the sensational swimmer who dominated men's swimming from 1998 to 2004. Ian has won nine Olympic medals, five of them gold. He has more Olympic medals than any other Australian athlete.

STARTING OUT

Ian began swimming when he was a small boy. When he was 13, he entered the national junior championships and won just about every event he entered. At 14, he was the youngest ever male swimmer to represent Australia when he competed

SWIMMING: Ian Thorpe, our greatest Olympian

at the 1997 Pan Pacific Championships in Japan. Then at the 1998 World Championships in Perth, Ian won two gold medals, one in the 400 metres freestyle. This event quickly became his preferred race. He was 15 – the youngest world champion swimmer ever!

At Ian's first Commonwealth Games, also in 1998, he went home with four gold medals. By the time the 2000 Olympic Games came around, Ian was already famous around Australia. He cleaned up at the Sydney Games, winning three gold and two silver medals. And at the closing ceremony, Ian was given the honour of carrying the Australian flag.

Between the 2000 and 2004 Olympics, Ian continued to excel in the pool, and in fact, in everything he did.

OFF HIS BLOCK An amazing thing happened in the lead up to the Athens Olympic Games in 2004. During the qualifying round for the 400 metres freestyle, Ian Thorpe slipped on the starting blocks and fell into the pool. He was instantly disqualified from competing at the Olympics in his favourite race. Craig Stevens automatically became the second member of the 400-metres team, joining Grant Hackett.

Ian was disappointed but, being the sportsman that he is, he accepted the decision. Many people felt that the decision was unfair, because they knew that Ian would have been in the running for a gold medal in this event.

Before long, Olympic officials joined in the debate. They said that if Craig gave up his spot in the 400 metres, then Ian could swim instead. What a tough decision for Craig! Swimming in the 400 metres was a big chance for him, although his best race was the 1500 metres. A month after Ian's disqualification, Craig Stevens announced that he would give up his place so that Ian could swim the 400 metres in Athens.

CREATING THE LEGEND On the first night of the swimming at the Athens Games, Ian Thorpe won the 400 metres freestyle, becoming the second man to win this event at two consecutive Olympics (the first was Australian Murray Rose in 1956 and 1960). Australia did very well in the 400 metres, with Grant Hackett taking the silver medal. (Craig Stevens also won a silver medal, as part of the 200-metres relay team.)

Ian then went on to win another gold medal in the 200 metres and a silver medal in the 200 metres relay. When he came third in the 100 metres, winning his ninth Olympic medal, he became our greatest ever Olympian.

When he retired from professional swimming in November 2006, he was only 24 years old.

I wouldn't have swum this race if I wasn't satisfied about the decision Craig had made and how he made the decision.

— IAN THORPE

MORE ABOUT IAN

When Ian first started swimming as an eight-year-old, the chlorine in swimming pools made him sick, so he used to swim with his head above the water. Luckily, he managed to get used to chlorine!

When Ian won $25,000 in 1999 at the Pan Pacific Championships for breaking four world records, he gave all the money away to Lifeline and the Children's Cancer Institute of Australia.

Ian has really big feet — he takes a size 17 shoe!

In 2000, Ian was named Young Australian of the Year. He also set up Ian Thorpe's Foundation for Youth, which helps children in need.

After the 2004 Olympics, Australia Post issued two stamps to celebrate Ian's Olympic wins. They showed Ian with his gold medal for the 200 metres and 400 metres freestyle.

In his career, Ian has broken 22 world records and won 10 Commonwealth Games gold medals and 11 World Championships.

Favourite Fellas

Australian swimmers are among the best in the world and we have many champions. Here are just a few of our best male swimmers:

- Jon Konrads won three medals at the 1960 Olympics. He set 26 world records during his swimming career. His sister Ilsa was also a well-known swimmer during the 1960s.

- Grant Hackett won the 1500 metres at both the 2000 and 2004 Olympic Games. He has a total of five Olympic medals and has won 18 World Championship medals, more than anyone else.

- Kieren Perkins is a great long-distance swimmer – he's won two Olympic gold medals for the 1500 metres. In 1994, he set the world record for the 1500 metres. This record wasn't broken until Grant Hackett beat it in 2001.

MIRACULOUS MURRAY ROSE

Long before Ian Thorpe, one of our swimming heroes was Murray Rose. He was born in Scotland, but came to Australia when he was a toddler. He loved the water and by the age of 17, he was an Olympic champion, having won three gold medals at the 1956 Melbourne Olympics. He was the youngest person to win three gold medals in one Olympics. Murray won three more medals, one gold, one silver and one bronze at the 1960 Rome Olympics.

In his swimming career, Murray set 15 world records and in 1983 (when Ian Thorpe was only one year old), he was voted Australia's best male Olympian.

SWIMMING: Ian Thorpe, our greatest Olympian

Oops!

Long distance swimmer Glen Housman broke the world record for the 1500 metres during the swimming trials for the 1990 Commonwealth Games in Auckland. He finished the race well and truly ahead of the others, but the electronic timing device wasn't working properly and Glen's record-breaking swim was not recognised! (Fortunately for Glen, he went on to win the 1500 metres at those Games.)

30. Tennis

EVONNE GOOLAGONG CAWLEY, TENNIS ACE

In 1971, a shy 19-year-old girl from country New South Wales won both the French Open and the Women's Singles title at Wimbledon, the first Indigenous Australian woman to do so. Before she knew it, she was a celebrity, both in Australia and overseas.

Evonne Goolagong was born in 1951 in Barellan, about 580 kilometres west of Sydney. One of eight children, she loved sport and showed a real talent for tennis. She was so good for her age that she was allowed to join the local tennis club

TENNIS: Evonne Goolagong Cawley, tennis ace

when she was just seven years old. A few years later, while she was practising, a tennis coach from Sydney called Vic Edwards visited Barellan to watch her play. He was so impressed with Evonne's grace and style that he asked her parents if he could take her to Sydney so he could coach her.

When she was 13 Evonne moved to Sydney, where she lived with the Edwards family. When she was not at school, she was training.

WINNING WIMBLEDON In 1970, Evonne was ready to compete at Wimbledon, but she lost in the second round. The following year, she beat fellow Australian Helen Gourlay in the French Open. Then it was time for Wimbledon again.

This time she was playing against the great Margaret Court, one of Australia's finest ever tennis players. Court was not only Wimbledon champion, she was also Evonne's favourite player. And it was the first time in Wimbledon history that two Australian women were competing in the finals. Just think how nervous Evonne must have been. But on court she showed great confidence and played beautifully, beating Margaret Court 6–4, 6–1. The crowd went wild and suddenly Evonne was famous.

MORE VICTORIES Evonne's Wimbledon win was just the beginning. She was a member of the Federation Cup team from 1971–76, and during the 1970s, she won the Australian Open four times, as well as the French Open and the Italian Open.

In 1975 Evonne married Roger Cawley; two years later she had a daughter, and took a break from tennis. In 1980, she competed at Wimbledon once more, beating the up-and-coming American tennis star, Chris Evert. This was the first

time since 1914 that a mother had taken the singles title. Evonne was now a legend!

By the time Evonne retired from professional tennis in 1983, she had won 92 tournaments. She was heaped with honours and awards, including the 1971 Australian of the Year. She was named a Member of the British Empire (MBE) in 1972 and received an Order of Australia in 1982. In 1985, she joined the Sport Australia Hall of Fame, and the International Tennis Hall of Fame made her a member in 1988.

TENNIS: Evonne Goolagong Cawley, tennis ace

ABORIGINAL HERITAGE
Evonne was often referred to as an 'Aboriginal tennis player', but she was living in a white world and never knew much about her history. When she retired from tennis, she decided to find out about her ancestors and she also encouraged Indigenous children to become active in sports. She was involved with the Australian Sports Commission during the 1990s and is now a 'sports ambassador' for Indigenous Australians.

Tennis Talk

- When a player serves a ball that doesn't touch the opponent's racquet, that serve is called an ace.

- A Grand Slam tournament is one of four tournaments that are played once a year – the Australian Open, the French Open, Wimbledon (in the UK) and the US Open. To win the Grand Slam, a player must win each tournament in the same year. There are Grand Slam titles for singles, doubles and mixed doubles.

- Deuce means the game is tied at 40–40. Whoever wins the next serve has the 'advantage', because if that player wins the point after that, then he or she has won the game!

- When a serve goes outside the permitted area or into the net, it's called a fault. Two faults in a row is called a double fault, and the server loses a point.

- Love – that's a nice way of saying zero! A love game is one where one of the players has not scored a single point and loses 0–40 or vice versa.

- If a player hits the ball before it bounces on the court, it's a volley shot.

MORE AUSSIE TENNIS GREATS

There are so many wonderful Australian tennis players, it's impossible to include them all. Here are just a few:

- Margaret Court won her first Australian Open title at 17. She won seven straight titles and was the first Australian woman to win Wimbledon. In her amazing career, she won more than 20 Grand Slam singles titles.

- Rod Laver won 11 Grand Slam singles championships and was a four-time Wimbledon winner. He is still the only player ever to have twice won all four Grand Slam titles in one year, first in 1962 and again in 1969. The Rod Laver Arena in Melbourne, the venue for the Australian Open, was named for this great sportsman.

- John Newcombe won Wimbledon three times (1967, 1970 and 1971). He won the Australian Open and the US Open twice, and was a member of four winning teams in the Davis Cup. (The Davis Cup is considered the most important men's tennis event.)

- In 2001, 20-year-old Lleyton Hewitt became the youngest man ever to be ranked the world's number one male tennis player. This fantastic player has won the US Open and Wimbledon and was a member of the winning Davis Cup team in 1999 and 2003.

TENNIS: Evonne Goolagong Cawley, tennis ace

Oops!

At the final of the 2003 Davis Cup match between Australia's Lleyton Hewitt and Spain's Juan Carlos Ferrero, a very embarrassing thing happened. Before the game began, trumpet player James Morrison played what he thought was the Spanish national anthem — but it was the wrong anthem. Spanish officials were furious, refusing to allow the game to start and demanding an apology. To make up for the mistake, the correct Spanish anthem was played later in the day and also on the next day. (By the way, Hewitt won the match against Ferrero.)

Training and diet

A little about how athletes train

All athletes train long and hard – they stretch, jog, run, lift weights, punch boxing bags, jump rope, do sit-ups, walk on a treadmill, as well as train for their particular sports. A swimmer might work out at the gym and go for a run before swimming any laps. Likewise, footballers run and do weight training, and even do yoga and pilates, before they begin to focus on football training.

It's not enough simply to train for your particular sport. Athletes work on strength, balance, agility, flexibility and endurance. Whether they're bowling or batting, cricketers need strength and balance. Being agile, which means being able to move quickly, is vital for boxers if they are to get out of the way of a strong right hook. Endurance is pretty important in constantly moving sports such as basketball, marathon running or rowing.

One of the most important things about any form of training is to start gradually. Athletes always make sure to warm up first by stretching, and this is good advice for anyone playing any

Training and diet

sport. They usually begin a training program slowly, that is, they don't just leap in and run a marathon on the first day. If you think about it, you'll know it's right – try jumping in the pool and swimming 1500 metres without stopping. Chances are you'll be pooped. You might not be able to swim the whole way. You might even pull a muscle. But if you start out swimming short distances, you will build up your strength and ability, and your technique will also improve. As you swim more you'll get better and better and be able to swim longer distances, until you reach a point when 1500 metres is a piece of cake.

So athletes work at building up their fitness levels and skills by working on their strength, balance, agility, flexibility and endurance. With lots of training, they can become champions.

Working out at the gym helps athletes keep up their fitness levels. Weight training is especially useful, because it tones and builds muscles and increases strength. Being toned means that you have more control over your muscles, so throwing a ball or swimming that 1500 metres becomes a whole lot easier than if you'd done no weight training at all. Most athletes do at least some weight training. Tennis players find that it helps them to avoid tennis elbow. This is what it's called when the tendons get really sore and the elbow gets tender because the muscles have been working overtime. (A tendon is a body tissue that attaches muscle to bone.) Because tennis players use one arm more than the other, tennis elbow is common. Weight training strengthens their muscles and makes it less likely that they'll suffer tennis elbow. (By the way, it's not just tennis players who suffer from this – anyone who lifts a lot repeatedly or who throws with one arm can get it. Baseball pitchers and lawn bowlers can suffer from tennis elbow, as can carpenters and gardeners!)

One other training tip that many coaches use is to tell athletes to imagine that they are playing their sport and performing at their best. This builds up a positive mind picture and it makes athletes feel good about themselves. And psychologists tell us that when we feel good about ourselves, we perform better. This isn't just true of playing sport – it also applies to other activities like telling a story, doing homework or making a cake.

Getting down to particular sports

Training for your own particular sport is also tough. Athletes who play seasonal games, such as soccer and other forms of football, still train year-round. Training is not as intense in the off-season, but they must keep fit, so footy players participate in other sports such as swimming, golf, softball or tennis. They also run or jog all year, concentrating on speed closer to the start of the season. That way, they minimise the chance of injury.

The pre-season training program gets more football-specific. For example, training includes running backwards, jumping, catching balls while running, passing and receiving the ball and so on, because these are things that happen in the game.

Before the cricket season begins, cricketers cycle and run to keep their fitness levels high. Cricketers are on the field for a long time, sometimes six hours at a go. Fielders stand in their positions and must be fit enough to go from being still to running or jumping to catch a ball. Bowlers must have strong muscles to bowl well without injuring themselves. Another thing they do is to practise throwing and catching. Their eyes are always on the ball!

Golfer Greg Norman is said to hit 600 golf balls every single day! It's no wonder he's such a great player. Other sportsmen and women also focus on their own sports – swimmers get to the pool early in the morning and swim laps for hours on end, basketball players shoot countless goals, surfers catch wave after wave, and tennis players practise their serves over and over again.

What do athletes eat?

We are always told we should eat the right foods and do plenty of exercise to keep us fit and healthy. It's also good for our brains. Athletes know this and they make sure to eat properly so they'll have the energy to train hard. So what do athletes eat?

Naturally they don't eat too many hamburgers or chocolates! They might be able to burn off the fat through exercise, but eating fatty or fried foods makes it hard to build up strength and endurance.

Carbohydrates are an important part of an athlete's diet. When we eat carbohydrates, the liver breaks them down into glucose, or blood sugar, and this gives us lots of energy. There are simple and complex carbohydrates. Sugar is a simple carbohydrate. Complex carbohydrates are better for us because they take longer to break down in the stomach so our energy levels don't go up and down like a yoyo. Some foods that contain complex carbohydrates include potatoes, wholemeal bread, pasta, fruit and vegetables, cereals, brown rice and milk.

Sportsmen and women eat more carbohydrates than non-athletes because they need more physical energy, both when training and competing. Non-active people who eat too many carbohydrates tend to get a little fat, but athletes use up all the energy provided by the carbs and they don't put on any weight.

The average person's diet should contain about 50 per cent carbohydrates, but an athlete's diet is usually made up of 65–70 per cent carbohydrates. This is because they need far more energy than the rest of us.

Protein is another essential food we must all eat, because it helps to build up muscles, blood, skin, bones and our organs (like the liver). We get most of our protein from lean red meat, chicken, fish, shellfish, lentils, soya beans, dairy foods, nuts and eggs. It's recommended that an adult woman weighing about 58 kilograms should eat about 45 to 50 grams of protein a day, but athletes need more than other adults. This is because they put much more strain on their bodies, and proteins help to repair any damage to tissues and muscles. So a 58-kilogram athlete might eat about 90 grams of protein a day – that's twice as much as the rest of us.

How much water do athletes drink?

Without water, there would be no life on our planet. Water is necessary for life and in fact more than half our body weight is water. When we sweat, we get thirsty. Thirst is the body's way of telling us to drink water. In really bad cases, say if someone was stranded in the desert, dehydration can be dangerous, even life-threatening.

Every day we lose water from our bodies: from sweat, from breathing, and when we go to the toilet. So we must keep topping up our water supplies. You can drink water a number of ways, including in a cup of tea, in a glass of cordial, in

Training and diet

orange juice, or straight from the tap. There's also lots of water in certain foods, like watermelon and cucumbers, and even milk contains some water.

There are different opinions on how much water we need. Some experts say that adult men need about 3 litres of fluids every day – that's about 13 cups; others say that 2 litres is enough. For a 58-kilogram person, 2 litres a day is about right. Active children should have a big glass of water before going out to play – especially in summer – as well as frequent smaller drinks during play. It's a good idea to drink water even when you're not thirsty. The average eight-year-old should have about one and a half litres of fluids each day.

Athletes exercise a lot more than other people, so they perspire a lot more. And that means that they lose more water through sweating than the rest of us, so they drink more to put fluids back into their bodies. The more you exercise, the more fluid you need to replace. As well as their regular daily intake of fluids, marathon runners often drink two or three cups of water or sports drinks every hour while training and competing. Sports drinks contain sodium, which is great for athletes because they also lose sodium (salt) through perspiration.

Athletes generally drink before, during and after training even if they are not thirsty because they know that we lose water without even knowing it. Water is essential for athletes because as well as keeping them hydrated (that means there's enough water in their bodies), it also avoid tiredness and sore muscles, and they certainly don't want to be tired and sore in the middle of a big match.

So you see, eating right, drinking enough water and having plenty of exercise is important for all of us. Athletes set a good example because they look after themselves by eating properly, drinking lots of fluids and training regularly.

OLYMPIC SPORTS

There are now 35 Olympic sports. The Summer Olympics has 28 sports, and the Winter Olympics has seven sports.

The Summer Olympics sports are:

- aquatics
- archery
- athletics
- badminton
- baseball
- basketball
- boxing
- canoeing/kayaking
- cycling
- equestrian (they're the events involving horses)
- fencing
- football
- gymnastics
- handball
- hockey
- judo
- modern pentathlon (that's where competitors compete in five separate events: running, swimming, horseback riding, fencing – with swords! – and target shooting)

- rowing
- sailing
- shooting
- softball
- table tennis
- taekwondo (this is a Korean martial art, similar to karate)
- tennis
- triathlon (competitors run, swim and cycle)
- volleyball
- weightlifting
- wrestling

The Winter Olympic sports are:

- biathlon (that's competing in cross-country skiing and rifle-shooting)
- bobsled
- curling (this is an unusual sport: four team members slide a heavy round stone down the ice towards a goal)
- ice hockey
- luge (competitors lie down on a sled, their feet facing forward, and race down icy chutes)
- skating
- skiing

Some interesting sporting websites

There are loads of fascinating websites where you can find out more about your favourite sporting heroes.

There's also a great book you can flip through to find out a little about a lot! Check out *Australian Sport Through Time*, 2007 edition, published by Random House Australia, Sydney.

General information

Australian Bureau of Statistics (2007): Participation in Sports and Physical Recreation, Australia 2005–06. www.census.abs.gov.au/ausstats (search for 'participation in sports')

Australian Dictionary of Biography online: www.adb.online.anu.edu.au

Australian Institute of Sport: www.ais.org.au

Australian women in sport: www.womenaustralia.info/exhib/sg/sport-home.html

Australian of the Year: www.australianoftheyear.gov.au

Photographic Encyclopaedia of Sports: www.sporting-heroes.net

Sport Australia Hall of Fame: www.sahof.org.au

Some interesting sporting websites

Australian Rules
Australian Football League: www.afl.com.au
Sydney Swans: www.sydneyswans.com.au

Basketball
Basketball Australia: www.basketball.net.au
Women's National Basketball Association (USA):
   www.wnba.com

Boxing
Australian National Boxing Federation: www.anbf.org
World Boxing Association: www.wbaonline.com

Canoeing
Australian Canoeing Online: www.canoe.org.au
Murray Marathon:
   www.redcross.org.au/vic/murraymarathon.htm
Hawkesbury Canoe Classic: www.canoeclassic.asn.au

Cycling
Australian Cycling Federation: www.cycling.org.au
Australian Bicycle History Centre:
   www.bicyclehistory.com.au

Cricket
Bodyline: www.334notout.com/bodyline
Bradman Foundation: www.bradman.org.au
Cricket Australia: www.cricket.com.au
Melbourne Cricket Ground: www.mcg.org.au

Golf
Golf: www.pgaprofessional.com

Ladies Professional Golf Association: www.lpga.com
World Golf Hall of Fame: worldgolfhalloffame.com

Hockey
Hockey Australia: www.hockey.org.au

Horseracing
Melbourne Cup: www.melbournecup.com

Marathon
Gold Coast Marathon: www.goldcoastmarathon.com.au
Sydney Marathon: www.sydneymarathon.org

Marathon swimming
Susie Maroney:
  www.womenaustralia.info/biogs/AWE2266b.htm

Motor cycling
Casey Stoner: www.caseystoner.com.au
Official MotoGP website: www.motogp.com

Motor racing
Confederation of Australian Motor Sport: www.cams.com.au
Peter Brock:
  www.brock05.com; www.peterbrockfoundation.com.au
Mount Panorama: www.bathurst-nsw.com/MtPanorama.html

Novelty sports
Henley-on-Todd Regatta: www.henleyontodd.com.au

Paralympic perfection
Wheelchair sports: www.wheelchairsportswa.org.au
Louise Sauvage: www.e-bility.com/speakers/sauvage.php

Some interesting sporting websites

Rowing
Australian Institute of Sport:
   www.ais.org.au/ais/sports/rowing/home

Rugby League
National Rugby League: www.nrl.com
St George Illawarra Dragons: www.dragons.com.au
World of Rugby League:
   www.rleague.com/db/index.php?id=4546

Rugby Union
Wallabies: www.rugby.com.au
International Rugby Board: www.rugbyworldcup.com

Running
Cool Running Australia www.coolrunning.com.au
Cathy Freeman: www.catherinefreemanfoundation.com
John Landy: www.geocities.com/geetee/bios/landy.html
Ron Clarke:
   www.goldcoast.qld.gov.au/t_standard2.aspx?PID=346

Sailing
America's Cup official website: www.americascup.com
Cruising Yacht Club of Australia: www.cyca.com.au
Jesse Martin: www.jessemartin.net
Sydney to Hobart: http://rolexsydneyhobart.com
Australian National Maritime Museum: www.anmm.gov.au

Soccer
Australian Football Federation: www.footballaustralia.com.au
Asian Cup: www.afcasiancup.com/en/

Speed skating

Steven Bradbury: www.stevenbradbury.com/index.asp

Sporting animals

Camel Cup: www.camelcup.com.au

Eulo Lizard Races: http://www.legislation.qld.gov.au/LEGISLTN/REPEALED/N/NatureConEuCP95_001.pdf

Great Goat Race: www.australianexplorer.com/events/lightning_ridge.htm

Surfing

Association of Surfing Professionals: www.aspworldtour.com

Legendary surfers: www.legendarysurfers.com

Swimming

International Swimming Hall of Fame: www.ishof.org

Swimming Australia: www.swimming.org.au

Dawn Fraser: www.dawnfraser.com.au; ABC Sunday Profile, Dawn Fraser speaks to Monica Attard, 15 April 2007, http://www.abc.net.au/sundayprofile/stories/s1897086.htm

Ian Thorpe: www.grandslamint.com (and go to athletes/ianthorpe)

Tennis

International Tennis Hall of Fame: www.tennisfame.com

Evonne Goolagong Cawley: http://sports.jrank.org (and search for Evonne Goolagong)

Index to people, teams and animals

Ablett, Gary 6
Ahn Hyun-Soo 136
America's Cup 122
Annan, Alyson 46
Antonie, Peter 91
Archer (horse) 53
Austin, Matt 100

Balmain Tigers 96
Bannister, Roger 107
Barry, Leo 3
Barton, Greg 20
Bath, Harry 98
Bayley, Ryan 39
Beachley, Layne 150
Beauchamp, Michael 132
Beer Can Regatta 83
Bertrand, John 122
Bol d'Or 35–36
Bold Personality (horse) 54
Border, Allan 29–34
Boss, Glen 53
Botha, Wendy 151
Boxall, Grant 90
Boyle, Raelene 117
Bradbury, Steven 135–139

Bradman, Donald ix, 23–28
Bresciano, Marco 132
Brock, Peter 74–77
Buchanan, Amon 2
Bunton, Haydn 5
Burn, Ken 27
Burrow, Taj 151

Cabell, Joey 146
Cahill, Tim 130
Camel Cup 142–145
Campese, David 104
Camplin, Alisa 138
Carlton Blues 6
Carrigan, Sara 39
Carruthers, Lisa 47
Castillo, Chucho 14
Catchpole, Ken 104
Cawley, Evonne Goolagong 164–167
Cazaly, Roy 5
Chappell, Greg 33
Chappell, Trevor 33
Clarke, Michael 34
Clarke, Ron 109–111
Collingwood Magpies 4, 6

183

Cooper, Andrew 91–95
Cooper, Priya 90
Cottee, Kay 123–126
Court, Margaret 165, 167
Cousins, Ben 1
Cox, Dean 3
Cribb, Otto 17
Culina, Jason 132
Cullen, Ross 106
Cummings, Bart 53
Curtin, John 5
Czislowski, Ben 100

Darcy, Les 16
Davies, Grant 20
de Castella, Robert 58–60
Dicks, David 126
Doohan, Michael 73
Doyle, Mike 146
Dunny Derby 84
Durack, Fanny 155

Eales, John 104–105
Eastern Suburbs Roosters 96, 98
Edwards, Vic 164–165
Ella, Gary 103
Ella, Glen 103
Ella, Marcia 103
Ella, Mark 101–104
Elliott, Herb 112
Eulo Lizard Races 141

Evans, Cadel 39
Evans, George 97
Evert, Chris 165

Faldo, Nick 44
Fanning, Mick 151
Farrelly, Midget 146–149
Farr-Jones, Nick 104
Fenech, Jeff 17
Ferrero, Juan Carlos 169
Fine Cotton (horse) 54
Fraser, Dawn ix, 47, 152–156
Freeman, Cathy 113–116

Gallagher, Harry 153
Gardner, Wayne 73
Gasnier, Reg 97, 98
Gaze, Andrew 11
Gilchrist, Adam 34
Gilmore, Stephanie 151
Ginn, Drew 92, 95
Goolagong, Evonne *see* Cawley, Evonne Goolagong
Gould, Shane 156
Gourlay, Helen 165
Great Goat Race 144, 145
Great Huon Apple Race 83
Green, Dennis 22
Green, Nick 91–95
Greeves, Edward 5
Gregan, George 104
Grosso, Fabio 134

Index to people, teams and animals

el Guerrouj, Hicham 111

Hackett, Grant 159, 160, 162
Hall, Barry 2
Harada, Masahiko 12–14
Haslam, Juliet 46, 47
Hawkes, Rechelle 47
Hawkesbury Canoe Classic 21
Hawkins, Stephen 91
Hayden, Matthew 34
Hedges, Chelsea 151
Henley-on-Todd Regatta 78–82
Henry, Jodie 156
Hewitt, Lleyton 167, 169
Hinton, Harry 72
Hockeyroos 45–47
Hollies, Eric 27
Horan, Tim 104
Housman, Glen 163
Hoy, Andrew 47
Hudson, Nikki 47
Hughes, Merv 31

Illingworth, John 119

Jackson, Lauren 7–11
James, Bill 4
Jardine, Douglas 24–26
Jones, Dean 31
Jones, Leisel 156
Judd, Chris 1, 3

Kahanamoku, Duke 150–151
Kelly, Shane 38
Kewell, Harry 132
King, Johnny 97, 98
Kingston Rule (horse) 53
Konrads, Jon 162
Kookaburras 49

Landy, John 107–111
Langlands, Graeme 98
Lara, Brian 32
Larwood, Harold 24
Laver, Rod 167
Lee, Brett 34
Lenton, Libby 156
Letham, Isabel 151
Lewis, Bobby 53
Lexcen, Ben 122
Li Jiajun 136
Light Fingers (horse) 53
Longley, Luc 11
Lowndes, Craig 77
Lynagh, Michael 104

McGrath, Glenn 34
McKay, Mike 91–95
McLean, Brock 6
Makybe Diva (horse) 53
Maroney, Susie 63–66
Martin, Jesse 124–127
Martin, Lisa *see* Ondieki, Lisa
Matildas 129–132

Melbourne Cup 50–55
Milk Carton Regatta 83
Milton, Michael 90
Moneghetti, Steve 59–60
Morris, Jenny 46
Mortlock, Stirling 104
Mundine, Anthony 17
Mundine, Tony 17
Murray Marathon 18–21

Nagle, Kel 40
Neill, Lucas 134
Newcombe, John 167
Norman, Greg 40, 44, 172

O'Donnell, Phyllis 148
O'Gready, John 97
O'Neill, Susie 156
Oarsome Foursome 91–95
Ochoa, Lorena 40
Ohno, Apolo Anton 135–137
Oldfield, Bert 25
Olivares, Rubin 14
Ondieki, Lisa 61
Opperman, Hubert 35–39

Paton, Siobhan 90
Patten, Sam 91
Perec, Maria-José 115
Pereira, Jackie 47
Peris, Nova 47
Perkins, Kieren 162

Peter Pan (horse) 53
Phar Lap (horse) 55
Pheidippides 57
Ponsford, Bill 25
Ponting, Ricky 34
Powell, Adrian 22
Price, Ray 104
Provan, Norm 97, 98

Rain Lover (horse) 53
Raper, Johnny 98
Renford, Des 66
Rennie, Jack 13
Reynolds, Dick 5
Richards, Jim 76
Richards, Mark 151
Richmond Tigers 4, 5
Robbins, Sally 94
Robinson, Lionel 52
Rogan Josh (horse) 53
Rogers, Matt 105
Rose, Lionel 12–15
Rose, Murray 160, 162
Rossi, Valentino 71
Rudkin, Alan 14
Ryan, Kevin 98

Sailor, Wendell 104
Sakurai, Takao 14
Sampson, Brian 76
Sauvage, Louise 85–89
Skaife, Mark 77

Index to people, teams and animals

Skilton, Bob 5
Slatter, Kate 93
Smith, Billy 98
Socceroos 129–132
St George Dragons 96–99
Stacy, Jay 49
Starre, Kate 47
Stevens, Craig 159–160
Stewart, Ian 5
Still, Megan 93
Stoner, Casey 69–73
Sturgeon, Frank 17
Summons, Arthur 97
Sydney Swans 1–6
Sydney to Hobart yacht race 118–121

Taylor, Mark 31, 34
Taylor-Smith, Shelley 67
The Victory (horse) 52
Think Big (horse) 53
Thomas, Petria 156
Thomson, Peter 40
Thorpe, Ian 158–162
Timms, Michele 11
Tomkins, James 91–95
Tooth, Lianne 47
Travis, Walter 40
Tuqiri, Lote 104
Turcotte, Mathieu 136

van Wisse, Tammy 67
Viduka, Mark 131, 132
Voce, Bill 24

Waldron, Ollie 106
Wallaroos 104
Warne, Shane 34
Waugh, Steve 30, 34
Webb, Karrie 40–44
West Coast Eagles 1, 3, 6
Western Suburbs Magpies 97
Whincup, Jamie 77
Wills, Tom 5
Wilson, Julia 94
Wirrpanda, David 1
Wood, Mervyn 92
Woodfull, Bill 25, 26
Wylie, Mina 155

Young, Cliff 62
Young, Nat 151

ABOUT THE AUTHOR

Loretta Barnard is a freelance writer and editor who has worked in the publishing industry for a Very Long Time. She has a Master of Arts in English Literature from the University of New South Wales, and she gives occasional seminars on the writing process. She has been involved with a wide range of publications in a huge variety of fields, including science, history, biography, archaeology, law, business, botany, film and fiction – both for adults and children. Loretta wrote for *Historica* (ABC Books, 2006) and *Historica's Women* (Millennium House, 2007) and has done some ghost writing for people who will remain nameless.

Her interests include music, reading and the theatre. Loretta loves walking and her favourite sport is tennis.

ABOUT THE ILLUSTRATOR

Gregory Rogers studied fine art at the Queensland College of Art and has illustrated a large number of educational and trade children's picture books including five books in the Random House *30 Australian . . .* series. In 1995, Gregory won the Kate Greenaway Medal for his illustrations in *Way Home*. His first wordless picture book, *The Boy, The Bear, The Baron, The Bard* was selected as one of the Ten Best Illustrated Picture Books of 2004 by the *New York Times* and received numerous other awards and nominations. Gregory is also the illustrator of the Roland Wright series of medieval adventures for young readers.

Gregory lives in Brisbane, Australia. He shares a cluttered old house with his partner and two cats.

AUTHOR ACKNOWLEDGEMENTS

Thank you to Linsay Knight who gave me the opportunity to write this book and to Kimberley Bennett for her careful reading and constructive criticism of the manuscript.

A big thank you to my mother, Patricia Barnard, who offered many helpful suggestions along the way.

And the biggest thank you of all goes to my husband, John Golden, without whom, as the saying goes, this book could not have been written.

30 australian stories for children

EDITED BY
LINSAY KNIGHT

PICTURES BY
GREGORY ROGERS

30 Australian Stories for Children

30 AUSTRALIAN STORIES FOR CHILDREN samples some of the best stories for children that Australia has to offer. From May Gibbs to Elizabeth Honey, from Colin Thiele to Tim Winton, this collection of Australian treasures showcases the depth and scope of our Australian storytelling heritage. With a lively, up-beat tone that will have both children and adults chuckling, here is an anthology to inspire the imaginations of Australian children and reflect what is special about growing up in Australia.

30 australian ghost stories for children

EDITED BY LINSAY KNIGHT
ILLUSTRATED BY GREGORY ROGERS

30 Australian Ghost Stories for Children

A gaggle of googly ghosts, ghouls, spectres and spirits . . . a ragbag of unruly presences trying to find new homes in other people's bodies . . . a series of spooky happenings and bewitching spells that no one can explain . . . these are just some of the things sent to haunt you in 30 AUSTRALIAN GHOST STORIES FOR CHILDREN.

This collection is sure to have readers on the edge of their seats or shivering under the sheets! A combination of old favourites and contemporary classics in one collection, designed to inspire children of all ages.

Edited by
Clare
Scott-Mitchell
& Kathlyn
Griffith

Illustrated
by Gregory
Rogers

100 australian poems for children

100 Australian Poems for Children

From emus to magic puddings, this feast of Australian poems for children is both fresh and familiar. With beautiful illustrations from award-winning Gregory Rogers, this collection of favourite classics and contemporary gems shows us what is special about growing up in Australia.

Most Importantly
No REAL AUSSIE
DRINKS FOSTERS
As a matter of fact

YANKS DRINK BUDS
AUSSIES HAVE MATES
and most importantly
I drink CORONAS

?